ASCENDANT

BOOK 3 THE MADE ONES SAGA

VICKI STIEFEL

To Sheila Ryan~
a deep and wise woman who has inspired me throughout our lives
For your incredible love and enduring friendship

Never underestimate the power of dreams and the influence of the human spirit. We are all the same in this notion: The potential for greatness lives within each of us. —Wilma Rudolph

PRAISE FOR VICKI STIEFEL

CHANGED, THE MADE ONES SAGA

"This was a fantastic second book. The world is now more familiar which helped but, for me, the best part was Bree's attitude. She is attacked how many times, by people she thought were friends, and she still manages to come out of it with a smile on her face. Audi and Fortis are just sublime and I really hope to see more of them in the last book. A fantastic addition to the series and now I will (im)patiently wait for Awakened. Absolutely recommended by me!" —Archaeolibrarian

"*Changed* is complex, captivating, dangerous and heartwarming. So if you are looking for fantasy, scifi, and/or romance you might want to check this one out."—Whiskey with My Book

ALTERED, THE MADE ONES SAGA

"*Altered* contains romance, humor, flying horses, and a playfulness that any lover of fantasy or romance will want to spend their entire weekend devouring. This superbly written and well-edited book necessitates a rating of 4 out of 4 stars." —OnlineBookClub

"*Altered* is a delightfully different book. I loved the characters and the world the author created. The whole subject of parallel universes is fascinating. It's a simple story but tugs at your heartstrings. Makes one wonder, how would I react if this happened to me?" —Cranky The Book Curmudgeon

"First things first...this was such a unique storyline and I found myself totally involved with Kit and especially Rafe." —StarAngel's Reviews

The Afterworld Chronicles

"This third book in the Afterworld Chronicles, *Chest of Time*, sets quite the fast pace putting them all including Larrimer and their band of followers in even more dangerous, complex, and challenging situations...enjoy this wild and intense ride. — Lynn Latimer, reviewer

"*Chest of Stone* is a fast-paced urban fantasy with plenty of action and eclectic, vibrant world-building. Ms Stiefel's... writing is very original, it just flows, always in the moment, always unconstrained. There was nothing formulaic about *Chest of Stone*, and I thoroughly enjoyed that. — Nocturnal Book Reviews

"*Chest of Bone's* writing style is innovative, the world is very interesting and provocative. It's a great story! I's a bunch of crazy, but it's GOOD crazy, with some super vivid scenes and fascinating characters." —Nocturnal Book Reviews

The Tally Whyte series

"This is an amazing thriller with action on almost every page. The heroine is strong, independent and sees things nobody else does... Vicki Stiefel writes a brilliant psychological thriller." —Book Review.com

"Tally is a compelling protagonist—edgy, compassionate and vulnerable—with a clipped narrating style that keeps the tricky plot in focus. She can hold her own against genre heavyweights like John Sanford and Patricia Cornwell." —Publishers Weekly

"Compelling, touching, and a pleasure to read." —Robert Parker

"Three words describe the Tally Whyte series: Intense. Addictive. Chilling. Tally's personality will draw you in as surely as the mystery does in this series." —Fresh Fiction

A Woman Ascendant

What if you could be young again? Would it be a dream come true or truly a nightmare?

For Sybelle, the youngest of the Balazova sisters, awakening on the parallel world of Eleutia is no delight. From experiencing near suffocation to changes in her flesh, Eleutia seems a strange and hostile place, though the world itself feels oddly familiar. Her resonance with The Kestrel, the mysterious leader of the CastOuts, only increases her bewilderment, as does the appearance of Mother Tree.

As Mother pulls Sybi into her orbit, the controlling Alchemics tighten their noose on Eleutia. War is brewing— no longer will Eleutia's symbiotic animal clans tolerate the Alchemic strictures.

Could Sybelle be the fulcrum fated to avoid destruction and save this strange world? Or is she merely a pawn to be used by the Alchemics in their battle for supremacy? Worse, will Sybi's tug-of-war ultimately destroy her, the sisters she adores, and the man who has come to mean the world to her.. Or will she ascend, triumphant, and save all she holds dear?

ASCENDANT follows CHANGED and is the third book in the Made Ones Saga.

CHAPTER

ONE

akeup...wakeup...wakeup

Stop it!

The voice in her head was relentless, driving her near mad, insisting she wake up over and over...

She wanted to sleep.

Where had the voice come from? It was a woman's voice, low and deep and weighted with age.

Like mist on a sunny morning, the voice dissipated to silence.

She slept.

Wakeup...wakeup...wakeup

Not *yet*. She was so comfy, dream clouds luring her to faraway places. She was of the ether, dancing and twirling like the Firebird in Stravinsky's magical ballet. The lotus eaters welcoming Odysseus and his men. Daphne pursued by Apollo, while the laurel tree's bark rose to encompass her.

Wakeup...wakeup...wakeup

Shouting!

Her eyes flew open, dry and crusty. She blinked rapidly, still tired, the kind of tired where you wanted to sleep forever. Her nose was stuffy, her muscles achy. She blinked again. Blue wisps of fog surrounded her, and high above their swirls, a faint sun. She lay on her back—why?—she never slept that way. She raised her arms to stretch.

Ow.

Her hands had hit something. Odd. Sybi squinted, seeing a clear arched lid above her. She pushed. The cover didn't budge, and she smoothed her palms up and down the clear, curved surface.

A patch of fog dissipated, and her heart sped up, her breaths rapid.

She lay in a coffin.

Sweet Christmas! She breathed deep…and gasped. Pressure on her chest, a boulder crushing her.

Tried again. Couldn't breathe. *Breathe!*

Had to get out get out get out get out.

She pushed at the sides, pounded the roof over and over, choking out a scream, twisting, rocking. *Getout, getout, getout!*

Above, a shadow grew to monstrous size. A horrible screech.

The coffin lid disappeared, the blue fog dispersing.

"Breathe," the deep voice demanded, backlighting the man who blocked the sun.

Cool, crisp air filled her lungs, and she gulped it down faster and faster.

Blackness quivered at the edges of her vision.

The man leaned over her and cupped her shoulders. "Slow down and breathe."

Apollo—the angles and planes of his face beautiful and terrible —whose strange hair fell forward in a long braid, as his black eyes bored into hers, asking…

No!

Arms slid beneath her, lifting her.

Her chest rose up and down, faster and faster and…

The Kestrel stared down at the limp woman in his arms. He had raced through the forest at a speed few could match, run for miles, fixated yet again on the disparate elements the Alchemics had used to create him, to create all the CastOuts. Along with man, he was hawk and tiger and other creatures—the Alchemics did that, combine different species with humans to create a new being. Yet he felt incomplete, for he was a man but not a man. He wished to feel whole.

When he had heard shouts and screams, he pushed his body faster to find a clearing awash in blood and a glass cylinder atop a hovercart. Three men sprawled on the ground, dead, one of them his Clanmate, Calix. Kes had last seen him hauling a lasecannon.

The fogged capsule—he recognized its purpose—encased a Made One. A dead Made One. He drew his sword. He would smash the abominable capsule that held the female, one constructed as her prison and death sentence. Her ending pained him. The Alchemics had done this to her, both created and destroyed, and it hurt his soul. Each breath he took made him angrier and angrier.

A muffled scream.

He dashed to the cylinder to find her howling as she pushed at her prison's immovable glass.

Kes tried to unlatch the thing, failed, and he sliced his sword down across the lock. He threw open the lid.

She wheezed, but when he told her to breathe, her breathing sped up, and he had touched her, his fury at the Alchemics replaced by a sense of yearning. Strange, for she was skin and bones and nearly bald, her loose locks splayed around her.

May Father Sky guide him, for no reason he understood, she was his to protect.

Panicked eyes captured his, eyes the color of turquoise, the blue-green gem prized by the Cats. He slid his arms beneath her shoulders and hips and lifted her from the pod.

Her chest rose and fell like a bellows, her eyes rolling back, and she sagged, unconscious.

But she was *alive*.

CHAPTER

TWO

O *ne Month Later*

Kes leaned against the wall, observing Sybelle in the small cabin the CastOuts had prepared for her. Flooded with the natural light, the building stood beside a tall redwood, per her sisters' request. Yet the woman he had rescued from the pod lay as if dead.

Over the weeks the sleeping woman had been with the CastOuts, the Wolf Clan doctor had visited several times, their own healers carrying out the doctor's instructions and intravenous feeding schedule. Marcos, their chief healer, had worked on Sybelle with unceasing attention, as well.

But she slept on.

When Kes had brought the fragile Sybelle home, he had prayed to the Fates she would survive. In four weeks, she had gained weight and her color was good, but Sybelle had not awakened.

Beside the bed sat her two sisters, who visited several times a week, one or the other or both, and today they spoke to Sybelle in soft voices his acute hearing easily heard. His friend, the CastOut

4

Luciana and Sybelle's primary caregiver, sat a small distance away from the pair.

Kitlyn and Breena talked of their life in the circus and their circus friends, as well as the people, animals, and life on their farm in Maine, along with something called a "sensei."

"We are Made Ones," Breena had said. "We're young again, Sybs. All new bodies! Which is very cool."

Kitlyn talked about Eleutia, and how it was parallel to their Earth, while the coywolf who accompanied her rubbed his cool nose across Sybelle's cheek.

With that, Kes had gone on high alert, an absurd reaction. No creature in this room would hurt the woman on the bed.

Nothing seemed to affect the somnolent Made One.

His heart thumped.

She would not die. Could not die.

As always, he kept his feelings close. When Luciana or another CastOut was present, he remained silent. But when alone with Sybelle, Kes spoke of life on Eleutia and how he wished her to see his world and its beauty. How she could reunite with her sisters, meet him, the Clans, and the CastOut community. He wanted her to know him.

The woman drew him, and though her features were comely, his feelings were akin to...what? He did not know, but an inner yearning demanded she awaken *now*.

She did not.

"I can't wait for you to meet Rafe," Kitlyn said of his friend, the Wolf Alpha. "We are in love, so amazing, and we're married, Sybs. They held a mating ceremony, as the Eleutians call it."

Breena was Luciana's stepmother and the Cat Alpha's mate, the Alpha another friend and comrade. Gato would blush to hear her drone on about his fine qualities. Her two bonded cougar cubs crouched beside her on the floor, the black female licking Sybelle's feet. He knew the sensation well, and it made him laugh.

Terras often made him laugh, as well. Now, the one-winged peregrine walked up and down Sybelle's body, pricking her lightly with his talons in hopes she would awaken.

His companion's efforts failed, too.

At Kes' behest, their techs videoed the conversations, and Sybelle would have a record of her sisters' visits when she awakened.

Luciana glanced at him, and he moved to the bed to turn Sybelle. They exercised her flaccid muscles often. When she awoke, she would have the strength to rise from the bed.

The sisters and their creatures stepped aside, and he lifted Sybelle with care and rolled her onto her belly, turning her head so she could breathe.

Luciana approached and began to massage Sybelle's back.

"What has Marcos told you?" Breena asked.

"Our healer says no physical reason exists for her to sleep," he said.

"A month is a long time," Kitlyn said.

Too long.

Sybelle's lips moved, a tear rolling down her cheek, but she spoke no words.

The woman was trapped, living in some unreachable land.

The cubs were sniffing about the room, and Breena called them to her side "I've got to go. The kits need to hunt and Bartholomew has to be with them."

"I have to leave, too." Kitlyn stood. "The Alchemics' new tithe on WolfHome's laseblasters is ridiculous. Jerks. We're going to withhold our monthly meat and produce delivery. That should stick it to them."

"I will keep you both informed," he said to the sisters.

Kitlyn straightened, her face serious. "If we're not here when she wakes up, please don't steamroller her."

"Steamroller?" he said.

"Sybs is a pleaser," Breena said. "She relents when she should assert her thoughts and feelings. Be kind."

"And gentle," Kit said.

"I could do no different," he said, ushering them out the door.

Once they and the vid tech had left, he and Luciana completed Sybelle's exercises, and she excused herself to see to her vegetables and flowers. The sisters had voiced Sybelle's affinity for plants, and Luciana had filled the room with growing things.

To spark Sybelle, Kes must conjure a new and different action.

The chair beside the bed creaked as he sat. "Enala was old when she found me, a cranky woman who taught me much."

Few knew his origin story, but if it would help Sybelle, he would tell it. Reciting the tale, he recalled one of Enala's abilities—dreamwalking. One of the CastOuts had the same ability.

Ohtli, at ten years old, was a prognosticator and a dreamwalker. An ability worth investigating.

Sybelle awakened surrounded by her beloved gardens in Maine, the scents redolent in their richness. Such a relief, for her dreams had been strange, filled with unnatural places and odd events that bore no relation to the life she lived with Bree and Kit.

The gardens were about to produce, beautiful blooms, herbs, and vegetables. A smaller raised bed sat beside the flower garden where she had planted herbs for seasonings and medicinal purposes. She loved reading the old cottage remedies and medical journals about early medicines and often wondered if they were as powerful or even more so than their modern counterparts.

Today, the trees seemed restless, as if they wished to *move*, though the sun blazed and the sky was bluer than a jay's feathers.

Yet she felt their fretful spirits calling her home.

She was home.

Though her fifty-two-year-old bones protested, Sybi kneeled and began to weed the flower bed, a pastime she loved. She was giving them room to breathe.

A man stepped from the wood, the tall pines draping him in shade, and beside him, the shadow of a child, his large hand wrapped around hers.

The man struck her as strange, though his jeans and t-shirt looked normal. Yet light intensified his black eyes, eyes so probing, he seemed surreal. She pushed to a stand, staring, needing to understand.

They could be there to hurt her or to hurt all three sisters, though she doubted it. Friends of Bree's or Kit's? Or perhaps hikers who had lost their way?

Her anxiety ramped up, her abdominals contracting.

The smartest thing would be a retreat. If she backed away now, she could race to the house and the security of her siblings.

She raised her hand to her forehead, shading her eyes to see better.

The man was beautiful, with blue streaking through his long rust hair. Yet he remained frozen.

And were those swords crisscrossing his back?

Awaken, Sybelle, the man said. Yet his lips hadn't moved.

Sybi pinched herself and felt nothing.

Both relief and disappointment trickled through her.

An odd reaction, but she *was d*reaming. The man and child were not horrific, though lately most of her dreams had been just that.

No more. She pushed and ripped at the fabric of sleep that bound her to the dream.

Dammit, she *would* wake up.

A soothing blanket of darkness surrounded her, and she blinked twice. Her eyes were indeed open and they gradually adjusted to the glow of the dim lamp beside her.

She closed them again, exhausted. She was free from pain, and she… Her name. What was her name? Fog cloaked her mind, and her hands scrabbled against what felt like fur, her breaths harsh. A tear tracked its way down her cheek.

She could not remember her own name.

And then she did.

Sybelle Yennenga Balážová.

Sybi wanted to sit up, but she waited.

Memories of those odd dreams rampaged through her. The pod, that cursed imprisoning coffin where she had heard voices but had fallen back asleep without the strength to make sense of the words.

She touched her cheek. Warm and soft. Too soft. Softer than she remembered her lined, middle-aged skin. She ran her hands across her body.

What the heck? Her breasts were three times their normal size. Ridiculous. Creepy. She still must be wandering the dreamscape.

This was stupid. Sybi pinched herself hard.

Ouch.

A breath of sound.

Sybi cut her eyes to the right. Beside her bed sat a beautiful, black-haired woman reading a book. She scanned the room and caught the outline of a man shrouded in darkness, standing statue still. The faint light limned his enormous height and breadth, the muscles of one arm large and defined.

Like the man in her dream. Sybi almost snorted.

Was she dead and he a god? Ridiculous, as her amorphous spirituality never contained a man silent as a graveyard.

She shook her head. Odd not to feel her chin wattles. Her hands smoothed beneath the white free-flowing shroud she wore. Her waist was small, her curved hips lush. Curves were not part of her human anatomy, but Bree's specialty.

Her sisters. Alive. They must be.

But, no. They had all fallen into that crevasse in Acadia National Park.

Dead.

Then why did that pinch hurt? And why was her flesh humming with life?

Maybe that was how being dead felt.

Except...

Something plunked onto her feet, feather light.

Sybi froze. That did not feel like dead.

She bit her lip, hard. Pain. And the coppery taste of blood.

Alive then.

Which raised about two-million questions.

Where was she? Why was she here? Something was very strange and wrong.

A deep breath to calm herself. She was alive and indoors, where walls surrounded her and sage scented the air.

Sybi squinted. The thing that had plopped on her feet had two black eyes that *glowed*. It stared back at her and tilted its head. A bird.

Its footsteps left pinpricks as it crept up her legs, across the white sleeveless dress, and upward.

A falcon.

Lala! The flightless peregrine she had rescued who followed Sybi everywhere.

"Hello, Lala," she said in a rusty voice.

Lala nodded and took several steps forward, close enough she could make out detailed markings. No, not Lala, but...

"Forgive Terras. He is still young."

Terras.

That smokey voice had come from the man in the corner, his sound resonating with familiarity.

Another light clicked on.

She lay on a cot, warm pine walls and shuttered windows surrounding her, and the peregrine standing on her belly.

The young woman beside the bed put down her book, her bright blue eyes concerned, while the man remained where he was, the light washing across him and his strange rust and slate-blue hair woven in a single braid. He was huge and imposing and quieter than a whisper, and yet his hair sparked an elusive memory.

The dream in the gardens. The man and the child. He had the same blue-and-rust hair, though this man's was bound in a long braid.

Terras continued his walk up Sybi's chest.

"He cannot fly," the man said. "And he is insatiably curious."

Lala was that way, too, though she was aggressive with everyone but Sybi. "I thought he was mine, my rescue peregrine. Who are you? Where am I? Why am I here?"

The woman peered over her shoulder. "Kes?"

The man shoved from the wall and approached. Except for the sword and knife, belted on opposite hips, his clothes reminded her of the Wild West—beaten leather pants and an embroidered vest above a long-sleeved, dark green t-shirt.

The closer he came, the wider her eyes grew.

"Who are you?" she said.

"My name is Kestrel."

Kestrel, his eyes like a raptor's, though his nose was no hawk-like beak but a bold aquiline.

"Who are *you*?" she asked the woman.

"Luciana." Her smile wobbled, worry darkening her eyes.

Kestrel squatted beside her bed and took her hands in his. Warmth spread to all of her, and though his palms were roughened, his grip was gentle.

"There is nothing to fear," he said.

"I'm not afraid." The situation was too looney for her to be scared.

"I see that."

His smile transformed his hard face into one so handsome it hurt, his black eyes bright with warmth.

"I am not sure how to explain." Kestrel's voice was low and slow, a baritone sax played on a summer night where couples danced in the moonlight.

The echo of the voice wove through her and said many things— that he understood, that he cared.

How strange. In her later years, few but Kit and Bree knew her, as all three had distanced themselves from the world because of their Huntington's disease.

The peregrine reached her neck and nuzzled, his feathers downy soft.

"Why is it so hard to explain?" She touched the pommel of Kestrel's sword. "Why are you wearing this?"

Kestrel's head tilted, she'd swear in imitation of the peregrine now perched on her chest. "For battle."

Oh. Battle. Right. "Let's go back to where I am, okay?"

"It is complicated," Luciana said.

Sybi pushed herself up, the peregrine hopping to the bed. Except for a few markings, Terras could be Lala's twin. She gathered the blanket around her and pressed her back against the wall. Movement felt weird. *She* felt weird, her body fluid and humming with strength.

"What's going on?" she said.

The hand he placed on her shoulder shot a sense of wellness pumping through her. Which unnerved her even more.

Terras' eyes were glued to hers, and she held out a hand. It shook, dammit. The bird hopped onto her palm.

Luciana stood and smiled. "I have a soothing drink for you, Sybelle."

They knew her name.

Sybi set Terras on the bed. She might be parched, but she had no intention of drinking anything. "No, thank you."

A visceral memory slammed her. She was falling again. Falling. "Kit and Bree… We were hiking. The ledge disappeared and we plunged into an abyss."

Luciana glanced at Kestrel, and the trace of pity in her eyes worried Sybi.

Her pulse raced. "Are they here? Are they all right? Please tell me." She lurched forward and clutched the man's forearm. He was solid. Unwavering. Eternal.

Sweet Christmas, her fanciful ideas had always prompted teasing from her sibs.

His large hand covered hers. "Kitlyn and Breena are well. They are here, but not here."

Sybi squeezed her eyes tight. He was making no sense.

"They visited you while you slept," Luciana said. "I am your sister, Breena's, stepdaughter, as Gato is my biological father. We have videos of them talking with you when they visited."

The woman's words rang with truth. *Thank the goddess Kit and Bree were alive.* She bit her lip hard to stop her racing pulse and runaway thoughts. Bree was the one who had panic attacks, not her.

Through clamped teeth, Sybi said, "Please continue."

"They are on Eleutia," the Kestrel said. "*You* are on Eleutia."

"Your sisters visited," Luciana said. "But they are not in our village now."

"What is Eleutia?" The whole scenario was like one of her stories, tales she turned into comics of derring-do and dashing deeds, maniacal villains and warrior women. Of fantasy lands. But this was real.

"I don't understand where I am or what's going on." She crossed her arms and dug her nails hard into her flesh to stop her chatter. "It sounds like you're stonewalling."

"I will show you." Kestrel scooped her up, blanket and all, and headed for a door.

"I can walk!" she said.

"We are not certain you can," Luciana replied.

With his arms around her, she couldn't help the thrill that coursed through her. Of what? Security and safety, nothing romantic about it. She peered at his chiseled face, with its dark brows and black-black eyes.

A man that beautiful would never see her as desirable. She was the mouse of their sister trio, brown-haired and gray-eyed, the one who scribbled and drew her romances on the page.

With care, he carried her through the door and pressed on the light in another paneled room where a floor-length mirror rested against the wall. He strode to the mirror. "We brought this for you. To see."

"See?"

"Look."

Sybi stared, then burrowed her face in her hands. "Absurd."

"Look again," he said.

"I saw," she said, her words faint. "But that's not me." The woman in the mirror looked like her protagonist in *Rhiannon*.

"You are like a sweet syr emerging from the nest. Growing. Becoming. Your song bright."

"What's a 'syr'?"

"The Eleutian bird with the most beautiful song."

The image touched Sybi. She smiled, a shy one.

"May I call you 'sweet syr?' It suits you, the woman you are and the one you will become."

Surprised at what she saw as an endearment, she bit her lip. No one had ever given her an affectionate nickname. She breathed him in, his scent sage and citrus and musk. She liked the name, liked that he called her something special. He said she was growing, becoming. She liked that, too. A blush touched her cheeks. "Yes."

He bent his head to hers. "The image in the mirror is you, sweet syr."

What she had seen did *not* make sense.

Bree would look. Kit would look, too.

"In a minute."

"Look," he repeated.

One last breath, and... "Please put me down."

He set her on the floor, cool stone beneath her feet, and on mincing steps, she turned to the mirror.

That face. Gone were the wrinkles of fifty-two hard years of living, and she stared at soft cheeks full with youth, plump lips, and shapely brows—her face of thirty years ago. Almost.

Her eyes, not their normal gray, but *turquoise*. And her hair...

She threaded her fingers through the platinum and gold strands, all hints of mouse-brown gone. "What did you do? How did you *change* me! My eyes, my body, my hair."

"*We* did not." Kestrel stood behind her, easily a foot taller than her five-foot-five.

"Then who did? Why? What do they want from me?"

"The Alchemics," he said. "Our Eleutian scientists brought you and your sisters here."

"And where the hell is Eleutia?" she said. "And why did they do that?"

The man hesitated, then said, "Eleutia is a world parallel to your Earth."

Though his jaw was tight, his eyes bore compassion.

A parallel world, eh? Sybi bottled her sigh. "Turn around, please."

Once he moved, she dropped the blanket and whipped off the gown.

Her laughter erupted. She couldn't help it, given the visual confirmed what her hands had felt. Her coltish body had been transformed into Jennifer Lopez curves.

Stars afire. Her breasts were like the boobs she drew for Marvel comics. But not for the women of *Rhiannon*, her own graphic novel. A deliberate choice.

"This isn't my body."

Welcome.

Oh! Now she was hearing voices in her head. No, not voices, but a singular one echoing like a chorus, vibrating and expanding into hundreds, thousands, millions. She had heard that voice before.

Sybi threw the gown back over her head, smoothing the sides. "You can turn, Kestrel."

In a swift move, she drew his knife and pricked her finger. Yep, real blood. Large breasts, platinum hair, turquoise eyes—like a fantasy creature she had never wanted to be.

With a twirl she returned his knife, hilt first, a remembered move taught to her by the circus knife thrower. How did this not-her-body remember that twirl?

"You are calm now," he said.

A talent that transcended her shyness—projecting calm when all she wanted to do was scream. "I don't like how I look. Whoever did this to me, it was *wrong*."

"Yes, it was." Kestrel's blast of anger made her jerk. Fury glinted from his eyes, beyond anger to lethal.

A scary man. "My body belongs to me. No one else."

"Agreed. Rest assured, your flesh will not be tampered with again."

Cold comfort. Their scientists had done this, felt she needed "improvement." Insulting. She liked her old self, where she could walk through life like a shadow, reserved and quiet. Sybi preferred the silence. The hush.

This body would be noticed. *She* would be noticed. "Who the hell are these Alchemics who changed me?"

"Our scientists belong to the Alchemic Clan," he said. "They create new technology on Eleutia. In recent years, they have specialized in biological experimentation such as you have experienced."

"How dare they?" she said.

"They dare much." Again that lethal gaze.

"Have they tampered with my emotions and thoughts, too?"

He frowned. "Not to my knowledge."

In a burst, fear galloped over her—suffocating in the coffin, *can't get out*. She choked.

Kestrel rubbed circles on her back.

"They put me in that coffin," she said. "Didn't they?"

"Yes."

More malleable than Kit or Bree, Sybi enjoyed the river of life pushing her this way and that, setting a course unknown. The man rubbing her back was like the river rock that parted the water into differing streams. "Damn them."

"My fervent wish," Kestrel said.

"You are *sure* my sisters are safe and healthy?"

"As I noted earlier, we will show you the vids." Kestrel nodded, his long plait of hair swinging forward, with its strands woven of steel blue and rust. Sybi doubted it was a dye job. Fascinating.

Luciana entered the room with clothes and boots. "I thought you might prefer these."

"Thank you!" Sybi stepped behind the mirror and changed into panties, a short green tunic, and flowy brown pants, then pulled on the socks and boots.

"A bra?" she called.

"We do not wear them," Luciana said.

Great. Welcome to jiggle central. She moved from behind the mirror to face the pair.

"I am Breena's friend and she has spoken of these bras."

A friend of Bree's? Her heart hammered with excitement. "How is she? Where is she? What is she doing?"

"The Kestrel will explain." Luciana winked. "He is our Alpha."

"Do not use that word." Kestrel's voice was soft, but threaded with steel.

Luciana's lips twitched as she fled the room.

Alpha, eh? Kestrel peered down at her, and she fell into those black-black eyes, mysterious pools luring her with secrets and desires. She could almost feel the tenor of them, some alluring, others whispering "danger." More than Kestrel's hair was different from others. She wanted to open him up and have him tell her his secrets.

He'd spoken, and she'd missed it. "Pardon?"

"You were transported here to save our world." His face remained severe, as if he were utterly serious.

A world saver. Right. She would not insult him by laughing out loud, but sweet Christmas. Of all the implausible things she'd heard that day, that was the most absurd. "And how am I supposed to do that?"

In the distance, a bell clanged.

"I will return." He and Luciana sped out the door.

Come. Now.

That voice in her head again. Calling. Incessant.

Too bad. She wasn't answering. Sybi finished tying her boot laces and walked outside into the dappled sunshine, the screen door slapping behind her.

COME NOW.

Sybi's skin tingled, alive with champagne bubbles. She took a step. Dammit, she didn't want to. She fought, rooting her feet in Mother Earth.

COME NOW!

Sybi ran.

CHAPTER

THREE

Kestrel raced toward the blaze, still shaken from his meeting with the sweet syr. When he had first looked upon her in the pod, a bolt of connection had hit him hard. One he did not understand, one that shook him, though he had chosen to ignore it. He must ignore it. Pumping on the speed, he raced toward the fire that could devastate their encampment. As leader of the CastOuts, he was the first of first responders.

Their connection had not abated while she slept, but had grown stronger. He needed to comprehend why.

The closer he got to the blaze, the hazier the air became, its smell acrid. Shouts and calls rang through the redwoods, sparks floating toward the sky. He halted, Luciana and dozens of others arriving behind him to stare at the fire threatening their homes and the forest as it ate up a redwood.

He began the change.

"Kestrel!"

He halted as the child Declan raced toward them accompanied by Marcos. Declan was a cloud bringer, and Kes ran and scooped the boy into his arms.

"Are you sure, Declan?" He carried the boy back to the blaze eating away at the aerie perched high in the trees, the redwood's trunk wreathed in flame.

"Yes, I am sure," Declan said in a quivery voice.

He hugged the child, then raised him high in his arms.

Around them, villagers poured streams of water at the hungry blaze, yet the fire did not abate.

Declan lifted his chin to the sky and sang a few notes. A few clouds above shifted, but nothing happened.

The insatiable fire lept to a second aerie.

Kestrel ran a hand down the boy's face. "Do not feel pressured. Take all the time you need."

"I cannot do it," Declan said.

"Perhaps," Kes said. "And perhaps you can." He nuzzled the boy, trying to impart strength and belief into the small child. "You can."

"Yes." Declan opened his mouth to sing and poured his heart into his song.

Above, a trio of clouds darkened, coming together into one thunderous boom as sheets of water poured from the sky.

"Well done!" Kes said.

"But look," Declan said in a plaintive voice.

The fire continued its ravenous path to the top of the first aerie and ringing the second redwood's trunk, licking its way upward to the home above.

The abnormal blaze was so odd he wanted to taste it, know it, understand it. A foolish notion prompted by his own strangeness.

Declan tucked his head into Kes' shoulder. "It will not work because my rain will not put it out. I can feel the fire's power."

A woman's face appeared at a window in the second aerie. Xento, who was chair bound.

Kes hugged the boy, then put him down beside Marcos.

"Coming, Xento!" he shouted, hoping the woman could hear him above the cacophony.

"Kes, no!" Marcos shouted.

Kestrel backed up to get a running start, then ran to the second building, propelled off it to a nearby redwood trunk, then leaped to propel himself to the first burning building, and off that to reach Xento's window.

He clung to the window frame with one hand while his other arm reached around Xento's waist.

"My hover chair!" she cried.

"Replaceable," he gasped. "You are not."

Flames licked his feet and legs, but he ignored the torment to pull Xento from the window and out of the burning building, and she wrapped her arms around his neck, sobbing.

With a leap, he pushed them out and down, plummeting fifty feet to the earth below.

As Sybi trotted through the village's stone and wood buildings, the voice in her head quieted, yet the compulsion remained. A demand, really, and now a humming had begun. *Humming.* Sweet Christmas, what next?

She passed the chandler's shop, a large meeting house, and various other village buildings that, oddly enough, felt familiar. Her feet even seemed to know the path she walked.

At the wood's edge, Sybi paused to breathe in the cool, crisp air, and she stared down at the small village. Her eyes took in the community with a sense of having been there, the idiocy making her shake her head.

The buildings, the trees, the paths—the familiarity increased her unease, coupled with the compulsion to follow the voice.

Her situation was real, she was real, here was real, and not because of a bitten lip or a knife prick. Her gut and heart told her so.

Sybi was being fanciful, which was often her modus operandi. That served her well in her job with Marvel, where for years she sketched cels for the company's comic books. Her long-distance work was deeply satisfying, yet she had refused a full-time job that would necessitate a move.

The scents of pine and sea drew her, and she again entered the redwood forest. As she walked the forest floor, whispers replaced the humming, some high-pitched, others rumbling like a bass drum. The murmurs held words, not that she could catch them, and yet they lapped at her consciousness like a gentle surf, their timbre excited.

Beneath the whispers, the compelling voice rose, the one from the casket and cabin, its call insistent.

And the forest itself? Though she had never seen a redwood in person, her familiarity with the wood and the trees was disconcerting. The path led to the Pacific Ocean. She was certain.

Why? Why was it she could picture that ocean and coastline? A niggle tickled her mind, but she failed to catch it.

The treesong grew louder, the voice implacable. Her fear galloped, her heart racing.

She would figure this out, and understand *where* she was and *who* she was. She would learn exactly what had happened.

Gathering her tattered nerves, Sybi followed the call.

Patches of snow dotted the earth alongside sprouts of green, buds near waking, and ferns ready to unfurl.

A familiar and welcome peace descended, as it always did when she walked a forest. She pressed a hand to the bark of a giant tree, its warmth and life tingling her fingers.

Hum, a rum tum.

That bass hum was familiar, too—welcoming—just as some trees on Earth had done, though she had never told her sisters, not anyone. It was as if she had walked this ground many times, her feet knowing the way, too.

Hard stop, and Sybi laughed. *Rhiannon,* of course. Each splash page and speech bubble she had drawn for her graphic novel echoed the world now surrounding her.

How had Kit and Bree reacted? They were here, too, Kestrel had said. Stars alive, she hoped Breena had avoided a panic attack.

"Sybelle!"

She ran from the shouts behind her. No one must find her until she answered the voice's call.

Kes thudded to the earth with Xento in his arms, rolling so he took the brunt of the fall as pain shot from his feet up his legs. But he managed to hold on until someone took the woman from his grasp before he collapsed in a sprawl on the forest floor.

The fire had melted his boots, his feet blackened, while burns scored his legs, his pants in tatters. Agony threatened his consciousness, the world wavering. He held on.

Nearby, a hovercraft appeared with a massive lasecannon that shot flames.

What the fark?

A stream of dirt poured from the gun toward the fire.

To his shock, wherever the dirt hit, the fire winked out. The cannon swiveled back and forth as one of the two manning the craft kept reloading the chamber with soil.

Marcos knelt beside him. "You are in agony, my friend."

"Declan? Xento?" Kes said through clenched teeth.

"Both fine. Now hush." Marcos skimmed his hands across Kes' body from the tip of his head down to his blackened toes.

"Father Sky save me from your healing." His will was iron. He would not pass out. But Marcos' healing was more painful than the flames.

"You must relax," Marcos said.

Kes snorted. Having heard that phrase countless times, Kes found it both humorous and challenging as he suffered Marcos' attentions. His fingers dug into Mother Terra, begging for the strength to endure.

After many sweat-soaked minutes, Marcos rose, calling several men to him. "Carry The Kestrel to his aerie."

"I can walk, you farker." He struggled to rise.

"No." Marcos held him down with a hand on his shoulder and leaned close. "Your pride is showing."

"Fark you," Kes hissed. But he allowed the men to lift him.

As Sybi ran through the wood, she sensed the presence of her followers diminish, and she paused atop a rise to catch her breath. Once her panting eased, she noted how the wood had grown silent, the voice in her head muted.

Before her, beyond the bluff, an endless sea roiled, waves tumbling one after another beneath a sky of cerulean blue dotted with fluffy clouds. The hush had deepened, giving her the cold creeps, and while the voice calling her held warmth and welcome, this hush chilled her bones.

A warning. She turned in a circle, discomforted by the strangeness, reluctant to go on.

But turning back was the coward's way.

The men carried Kes toward his aerie, Marcos accompanying them, Kes in a haze of pain.

"Kes?" Luciana appeared beside him and took his hand.

"Go to the Made One," he said, his words more hiss than speech.

"I wish to go with you." Her blue eyes flashed. "You are badly injured. I can help."

"No."

"Kes, the trees are talking, many of them. I believe it relates to Sybelle, but I cannot understand their words."

"Go to her." He squeezed her hand. "I am concerned."

"All right." With a frustrated "harumph," Luciana left.

When his bearers reached his aerie's great room, he directed they lay him on the sofa, though Marcos grumbled the bed would be better.

Kes shot him a look that clenched Marcos' jaw and flared his nostrils as the healer set a chair by the couch. "We should call the Wolf Clan's medical doctor."

"No." Kes healed unnaturally fast, as did several of the other CastOuts. He knew it and so did Marcos. "Do your worst."

Marcos growled but went back to work.

Fifteen minutes later, the vidscreen chimed with a call. He barked "On!" And the screen lit with the face of Gato, his friend the Cat Alpha mated to the Made One, Breena.

"What in creation happened to you?" Gato said, brows raised.

"Fire. Marcos is treating me." With each breath he took, the pain lessened.

"Shote," Gato said.

Marcos rose, his face dotted with sweat. "I have done all I can. Give yourself at least fifteen minutes before you scamper off."

The healer was furious, but he pivoted and left, closing the door quietly behind him.

Kes angled to better see the screen. "Water would not put out the blaze."

Gato pursed his lips. "I have heard of this, of unstoppable fire, though I cannot remember where."

"You will," Kes said. "Two of our techs appeared in a hover and blasted it with dirt. That worked."

"Odd. What caused the blaze?"

"I do not know, but rest assured I will. What is the purpose of your call?"

"Are you aware," Gato said. "that all three recent Made Ones arrived on Eleutia in unusual circumstances?"

"Kitlyn appeared in the mountains, buried in ice, yes?" Kestrel said.

"Correct. Breena in our territory, but alone and wandering. Need I say Sybelle's appearance was fraught with danger? Each should have landed in a safe and comfortable harbor, as all other Made Ones before them had done."

Kes knew all three women, their personalities at odds with other Made Ones pulled to Eleutia. "Perhaps these three are unique for a purpose."

"My thoughts as well," Gato said. "Before Neela was killed by the Alchemics, she said they used the same process of extracting the trio's Earthian Essences and infusing them in their renewed flesh. In her reports, it seems our spy Calix pointed out the Earthian sisters to the Cabal of Eleven. As specified by our laws, all three were dying. Neela said all proceeded in the usual fashion, the Alchemics expecting each woman to arrive safely." Gato's voice hardened. "All to have Eleutian children because the Alchemics convinced our Clans that would save our species."

"The Alchemics' lies are legion." Kes chuffed a sour laugh. "Considering the Alchemics deliberately caused the decline in our female births, Made Ones are yet another of their twisted experiments. Yet unlike the other Made Ones pulled through, the three sisters are not submissive."

"No, they are not," Gato said.

"I suspect that difference was unintended."

"As do I. Other differences strike me, as well. Note how two of the sisters have mated with animal Clan Alphas. No other Made One has done so."

"True," Kes said, ruminating on his connection with Sybelle. Gato knew his discovery of the Made One had prevented his attendance at Gato's celebration and the Compass True gathering. His gut tightened with an increasing ache to see her.

Another odd feeling. No one, not even Rafe or Gato, nor Luciana or Marcos, provoked any desperation to be with them. Seeing them gave him pleasure, true, but he never *longed* for them.

His isolation as a youth made connecting with others a challenge, and again he cursed the long-dead woman whose edict kept him separate from others on Eleutia. Enala had fed and clothed him, taught him sums and strategy and much more, for which he was thankful. But her warmth was nonexistent, and she never, ever touched him. He occasionally caught her eyeing him with revulsion. His upbringing had warped him in fundamental ways, as had his creation and birth.

Months ago, Mother Tree had mind-spoken to Kes, an unprecedented event. Mother had said, *The third sister will save our world.*

Guard her well. With Sybelle's discovery, all of Eleutia's plans neared that perfect moment when Compass True's strategies to overthrow the Alchemic despots would converge. Eleutia would at last rid itself of the Alchemic yoke and the Cabal of Eleven, including their despicable leader, Fukkes. The Cabal's restructuring had changed the very fabric of the Alchemic Clan from friends and benign researchers to a Clan that performed grisly experiments, demanded excessive tithes, and perverted that Clan's once-noble mission.

All that would soon end. Compass True's major remaining challenge was to locate the power source within Alchemic City which enabled the city to fly. Once destroyed, the city would be grounded and the animal Clans would attack.

He and Gato discussed plans for destroying the power source once they found it, then disconnected. He stretched, then gingerly rose to his feet, breathing a sigh at the diminished pain. Marcos and his abilities were incomparable, even if his friend was a stubborn goat.

He ached to see Sybelle and buried the longing, the desire unsettling. Instead, he drew a mug of troff and entered his weapons room, the drink's warmth a calming balm. With disgust, he lifted his burnt scabbard and tossed it aside as he unsheathed his sword and unstrapped his braces. A relief. Burns dotted his chest, the worst of them almost closed. He placed the sword on the large wood table and gathered his oil, cloths, and steel wool.

Luciana was with Sybelle, the sweet syr fine. If he went haring off to see her, he could further damage himself. A drop of sweat fell to the table, and he swiped it away. Still shaky.

Focus on the blade. From edge to hilt, it appeared undamaged, and he began the soothing process of cleaning it.

How Sybelle had looked at him, her eyes probing as if to exhume his secrets and drag them into the light. Her gaze had been so forthright, he had almost blurted his truths out as gifts for her to assess. Father Sky, that terrified him. For the first time since his birth breath, he hoped he would be enough.

A slam at his front door, and Kes laid down his sword. From her scent, Luciana was in the great room.

"Luciana?" he said, entering the room.

Her hands squeezed open and closed. "The Made One is gone."

Fukkatsu, Comstat of the Cabal of Eleven, simmered with fury as he sat in their meeting chamber within Alchemic City.

"Something is going on with the CastOuts, Fukkes." Gabin paced back and forth, back and forth.

"Stop that!" Fukkes barked. "Sit! You are making me dizzy." Of late, his fellow Cabal member had lost much of his scientific fervor, particularly after the death of the Compass True spy, Neela. He was becoming soft.

"I am aware the CastOuts are brewing something, Gabin," Fukkes said. "All because of The Kestrel, I have no doubt."

Gabin slumped into a chair. "We had him. We *had* The Kestrel. And he slipped through our fingers."

The CastOut Alpha had been within their walls, having traded him for the Cat Alpha's sniveling brother, yet The Kestrel had vanished, his escape unprecedented.

Decades earlier the Cabal had demanded The Kestrel be cast out, and the Falcon Clan had done as required, sending the three-year-old alone into the wilderness. He was expected to die. He should have died. Yet he had lived, and sadly, unbeknownst to them, their most successful experiment had slipped from their grasp.

At the time, they had not seen, did not know or understand the child's abilities, which was why they had released him to the Falcons. Their creation had faded to a distant memory. But the child's power had grown in endless ways and to immense proportions according to their spies, though details were few. But all said The Kestrel was unique.

And when they had finally reacquired the asset? Within a day, they had lost him.

"That was weeks ago, Gabin. You must get past it. As you are well aware, we have put new measures for his capture in place." Fukkes rubbed his face. He needed his afternoon massage and shave. His suspicions about Kestrel's escape remained private, though Fukkes was certain he had help within Alchemic City. Now, he needed all Cabal members on point.

Instead, he was forced to suffer Gabin's hysteria. He would like to leave the man on Eleutia to suffer the planet's doomed fate.

But Gabin was one of them, a member of the Cabal of Eleven, and he would become one of Earth's leaders along with the rest of them.

Gabin waved his hands. "Well?"

Fukkes' raised a brow. "Well, what?"

"How did The Kestrel escape?"

"The residue in his cage was inconclusive." Fukkes shrugged.

"Was it his excrement? Was he showing his contempt for us?"

"That idea is comical."

The chamber door swung open and the nine remaining council members poured inside.

A chime. Five minutes until the blank vidscreen coalesced into the faces of the Overseers, men and women of incomparable age whose purpose was to study the galaxy the Earthians called the Milky Way and their attendant parallel worlds.

What the Cabal was about to initiate was against Overseer policy, and they would keep that secret until each member transported their Essence into a prominent Earthian leader.

Another chime. As Comstat, Fukkes' sat in the center of the semicircle. Center or not, he always drew Overseer scrutiny, and he collected himself. No hint of their plan must escape.

Sybi closed her eyes, squeezed them tight, then opened them. Nothing had changed. Beyond the bluff, between a knoll and the cliff edge, lay a small dip in the land shrouded in mist. What a perfect setting for one of her stories. *Too* perfect.

Back on Earth, she had drawn the exact same landscape.

A shadow stepped from the wood, maybe ten yards to her left, the monkish figure cloaked in a patchwork robe and hood. The figure turned its head toward her, but its face remained shrouded. Tall, taller even than Kestrel, it lifted an arm, palm open, its long bony fingers extended to her.

Shit! Sybi stumbled backward, heart racing. And froze.

She tried to take another step back, but couldn't move. Like the creepy Nazgûl in *Lord of the Rings,* the thing glided toward her. Her throat tightened, her breathing rapid, and she pushed against her invisible imprisonment. Not even a budge.

If she were closer to the forest...but she wasn't. Only a single redwood draped its shadow over her.

She wiggled, trying anything, but failed to move.

The figure paused, but its hand beckoned as if saying, *Come to me.*

With a massive push, Sybi forced one hand to rest against the redwood's thick trunk. A small triumph as her fingers warmed, and strength and comfort poured into her. But she still could not escape.

She couldn't blink, but could she speak? "Hello."

Silence.

"Who are you, sir?" Her calm voice belied the terror ricocheting around her insides.

The specter said a word she didn't understand.

"Can I help you?"

Silence.

It flowed closer still, shadows danced over glimpses of a bony face, the edge of its robe never touching the ground. A Nazgûl had pierced Frodo with its terrible sword. This creature could do worse to her. Would it harm her? Take her? Kill her?

Sybi gathered her strength and with a mighty push stepped backward.

Except her only step was in her mind. Trembles rolled through her body now dizzy with fear.

Two feet away. Beads of sweat dripped into her eyes.

That cadaverous hand reached closer, mere inches from her face, its flesh an odd patchwork of uneven, multi-colored skin as if sewn together like Frankenstein's monster.

"Sybelle!"

Warm hands grasped her shoulders from behind. Kestrel.

He turned her to face him and ran a hand down her cheek. "We have been searching, sweet syr."

No longer frozen, she rested her head on his chest, terrified to look back at the wraithlike figure. "I'm sorry I worried you."

"You are unharmed?" he whispered.

"I'm fine." She forced herself to peek over her shoulder at the thing that had so terrified her. Only emptiness remained.

"Why did you run?" Kestrel said.

She pointed. "Did you see the cowled figure standing there?" A billion dollars said he hadn't.

"A figure?" Kestrel said. "All I saw was you."

Maybe those Alchemics had altered her mind. Her head hearing voices, her eyes seeing spectral creatures. Even the trees' voices. The worst was the *familiarity* of it. She could not voice her frightening thoughts to Kestrel. He'd see it as lunacy.

"Come," Kestrel said.

He took her hand and led her down a neat path where buildings high in the trees threaded like strings of pearls. The day had begun to blur into night and lights winked on above them like fireflies. Some homes swooped and curved through the forest, while others had the look of lavish cabins and still others circles upon circles. Often, staircases and wooden bridges connected one home to another, some buildings small, others large. Domestic sounds—running water and churning pumps—peppered the night, and cooking scents made her mouth water. Her stomach rumbled.

"You are hungry," he said with a smile in his voice. "We will eat, and then I will show you your home where you can rest."

She nodded, breathing deep, her nerves settling, his presence mantling her in safety and warmth. Logic said not to trust those feelings. And yet...

Kestrel led Sybi up a gentle winding staircase and across a suspended bridge to a largish building amidst the trees. They entered a vestibule of white walls and a redwood ceiling that led to an intimate lounge where tall windows looked across the forest to the sea beyond. Groups of twos and threes sat in comfortable chairs at stone-topped tables. Voices quieted and heads turned to stare at the two of them.

Kestrel waved a hand across the room, his face carved in stoic lines, and nodded. The diners dipped their heads and all began to talk and eat once more.

He led her to a table in a corner and sat her in the chair facing the windows. Kestrel took the seat opposite her and tapped the table, activating a holographic menu. "What would you like to eat?"

And wasn't that totally sci-fi? Reading the unfamiliar dishes, she spotted a BLT. "Bacon, lettuce, and tomato?"

"Yes."

"I'll have that, please."

He grinned, his face transforming from stoic hardness to one of joy, and she smiled back.

"My favorite," he said. "Your sister Kitlyn introduced sandwiches to the Wolves, and now all Eleutia is obsessed with them."

"When are my sisters coming to visit?" she said in a quiet voice. "Or can I go see them?"

He leaned forward, braid swinging over his shoulder, elbows resting on the stone table. "Kitlyn is mated to Radulfr. I do not doubt you will see her soon, as well as your sister, Breena, Gato's mate. Both women are considered Alphas themselves. Once our lead healer, Marcos, confirms your health, you may go anywhere you wish."

"You use the term 'Alpha.'" She avoided calling him that, given his reaction to Luciana. "Like clan leaders?"

"Yes. There are trials which each man succeeded in winning to become such."

A lightbulb moment. "How come I understand you, your language?"

"The Alchemics imbedded a disk behind your ear, as they do for all Made Ones. It translates, as well as enables you to read the common language used in the Northern Quadrant."

Another invasion of her body, though this one was useful, at least. Temptation called. She shouldn't. She really shouldn't. "Luciana called *you* Alpha."

His face darkened, his jaw tight. "I lead the CastOuts by default since I am the one who organized our Clan. But I have competed in no Alpha trials. I am no Alpha."

Sounded like splitting hairs to Sybi, and she wondered why it bothered him so much. "You used the term 'mated' regarding my sisters' relationships. What does it mean?"

"Bonded is a better word. The bond is similar to our relationships with our animal symbionts."

What the hell? "Animal symbionts?"

A red light pulsed on the holo screen.

"Would you like a drink, as well?" he said.

The menu offered drinks called troff, drass, kamla, and others she didn't recognize. "Water, please."

Kestrel tapped the table's holographic buttons. "I also ordered you some troff, a warming drink flavored with mint. Non-alcoholic."

"Thank you."

Perhaps the obvious subject change was the public nature of their discussion. Or it could simply be him. "Let's get back to the animal symbionts, please?"

He nodded. "Animals of different species are the Clans symbionts. The animals share power, cunning, scenting, nurturing, and other qualities with their human Clanmates. Humans share their intelligence, reasoning ability, self-awareness, and other qualities with their animal counterparts. Is Earth not the same?"

"No. Well, only in fiction."

"Eleutia has been thus for millennia."

"So all of Eleutia's animals are symbionts?"

He shook his head. "Many are simply animals, with no self-awareness or sharing power."

"I assume you're symbionts with hawks?"

"I am of the Falcon Clan."

"But a kestrel is a hawk."

His lips twitched, and he nodded.

A server appeared with their food, drink, cloth napkins, and utensils.

Sybi dove in, and her first bite returned her to Earth, back to the circus, back to long, long ago. Delicious.

Kestrel bit down as well, and he ate three sandwiches to her one, his drink fizzy and clear, like her favorite birch beer. He sipped it slowly, and she was tempted to ask for a taste. A furtive glance around the room. The few staring dipped their heads.

Bursting through silence was always hard for Sybi. She licked her lips. "What are you drinking?"

"It is called kevitt." He held out his glass. "Alcoholic. Your sister…"

"Has issues with alcohol. Kit and I do not. May I?" She held out her hand.

He nodded, handing her the glass, and she sipped. "Oh, my, that's yummy."

"Yes."

The kevitt's flavor teased her senses in sweet ways, with savory hints, though she could not identify the ingredients.

Kestrel squeezed her forearm. "Tell me about the creature in the woods."

While Sybi chewed, she brought up the stranger's image. "He seemed mysterious. Almost a cliché in his patched, hooded robe. I got glimpses of his face, but never really saw it. He stretched out his hand toward me, and it was odd, a patchwork of skin, multicolored, some patches rough, others smooth. I wish you'd seen him. You probably think I'm nuts."

"No." His black eyes burrowed into her. "I did not see, but I believe that you did."

"Thank you, Kestrel. Who or what was he?"

"I do not know. No CastOut. In this season, none would dress that way."

"CastOut," she said. "You use that term for your Clan, while the others are named for animals. Why?"

Kestrel chuffed a breath. "We who live in No Land are cast out from our animal Clans at birth or as young children because of Alchemic law and what the Alchemics term our 'defects.' We are unlike other Eleutians, though we have symbiont animals as well."

"What do you mean by defective?"

"We CastOuts have gifts."

The sweet syr fascinated Kes with her curious mind, yet his frustration grew at her hesitant tone. Perhaps she was afraid of him, or of angering him, though he did not understand why. He must explain better, given the confusion on Sybelle's face. Yet he could read her well. She was expressive, with eyes that melted a man with warmth no color change could mask.

"Many Eleutians are connected symbiotically to mammals or birds," he said. "Those born to the Alchemic Clan do not. When an animal clansman joins the Alchemic Clan, they leave that part of their lives behind."

"How sad. You told me you're of the Falcon Clan. No Hawk Clans?"

Smart. "Not on this continent, but Clans often contain differing genera, species, and families, though our Falcon Clan consists solely of birds of prey."

"Including owls?"

"Yes."

"Can you talk to them?"

He could, though most could not, and he deliberately left his answer vague. He nodded. "Their 'speech' is different. Hard to explain."

"Because you can talk to them, you were cast out?"

"No." An unfamiliar sensation, perhaps anxiety, made him down his kevitt in one long pull. She was stressed, and he wished to take that away. He always had answers, yet he had none for this *feeling*. "We CastOuts are biologically different. Earlier at the cabin, when you peered out the window, did you see the three-armed girl at play?"

She shook her head, but her fingers danced together, and then apart, and then squeezed into fists. He blew out a breath, reaching a hand out to cover hers.

Fark. Touching her felt like lightning brushed his skin.

"As with the child with three arms, some of our differences are observable," he continued. "Many others are not. We CastOuts are both blessed and cursed."

"So is that why I'm here?" Brows drawn together. "Because I'm different, too?"

Her hand beneath his curled upward and clasped his tight. He gently squeezed back. "No and yes." He did wish to explain, but not today when his mind filled with conflicting feelings about this woman, feelings that unsettled him, ones where he took her into his bed...and she died. So he projected calm and safety and gave her a smile. Sybelle would always be safe with him.

Sybi relaxed. Whatever he had done soothed her, and she read concern and care in those black eyes. "The term 'cast out'...well, it has a negative connotation." Again, awareness buzzed her brain, but the damned thought wouldn't be harnessed.

"True," he said. "We count that as a point of pride."

She smiled. "If you're good with the name, so am I."

"You seem less impulsive than your sisters." His braid almost dipped into his kevitt mug, and he flung it over his shoulder.

"I'm more of an introvert than either Kit or Bree." Sybi shrugged.

"And yet," he said. "You are calm, seemingly unafraid. I did not expect this of you."

She withdrew her hand and rubbed her palms over the cool water glass.

"We Eleutians," Kes said, "are more familiar with the parallel world of Earth than you are aware of ours. Eleutia is unknown to yours."

Not to Sybi, but a parallel world to Earth...

On Earth, when her parents led their circus around Europe, she had been the circus bookkeeper, though unbeknownst to them, she had also illustrated comic books in secret. Back when the circus was still active, Bree and Kit knew about her work for Marvel. Her parents did not. So loving, yet they would have taken over, and she smiled at the memory of them from long ago.

To her, illustration was like Kit's riding or Bree's trapeze work. Stuck at work indoors all day, when she wanted to be outside in her gardens or the woods, she had needed something to occupy her besides numbers. Though not a physical activity, her drawings were about life and death, love and loss, and so she lived through them within her cramped office inside a circus vardo.

"I prefer the silence of exploring the woods and fields. Growing stuff."

"Today you entered our woods alone." His head tilted as if in confusion. "Were you afraid at the cabin? Running from something?"

Sybi stared at the way she had lined up all her cutlery. Geesh. "I am afraid, but not in the way you think." She raised her face, wanting to see his reaction. "I wasn't running from something, but to it. A voice in my head compelled me to come. It lured me, urged me on." She chuffed a breath. "It's really hard to describe. But I *had* to obey."

"I see."

He didn't look at all surprised. "Do you know about something like this?" she said.

"I may. Eleutia has many things an Earthian might find strange. Have you felt the trees?"

"Yes!"

"Do they speak to you?"

"Not speak, really. At least not so far. But I hear sounds from them, and I get feelings from them, too. But..."

"Yes?" he said.

"On Earth, I felt the trees and plants. I could tell when they were ill or sad or happy. But today I heard Eleutia's trees humming. You're not surprised?"

"No. Come, it's time to see your aerie."

CHAPTER
FOUR

Sybi and Kestrel walked a path through the forest on their way to her aerie when they passed a large low building on the village's edge.

"Is that a large dining hall?" she said.

"Yes, as well as our meeting house."

Like The Gathering in *Rhiannon*. She froze. Ridiculous.

Past the meeting house, a fork appeared in the path. "My aerie is that way, isn't it?"

His head tilted. "Yes. What made you say that?"

"Just...certain places around your village... Never mind."

She was glad he let it pass as they walked on. The village green was filled with abundant flowers and plants, walking paths, and benches for resting and contemplation. Her heart pounded. Eleutia had taken on a surreal hue.

"Was there ever a battle in the meeting-house?"

He halted, swiveled to face her, brow raised. "What makes you ask?"

"Please answer. Please."

"There was, fairly recently."

Her mouth dried, heart racing. Near where they stood, another branched path wound around a massive redwood. Sybi pointed. "There's a general store there or a market."

"Yes." He crossed his arms over his chest, frowning.

"I didn't make it that far, but the Pacific lies beyond the forest, doesn't it?"

"The Pacific?"

"The ocean. The sea."

He nodded. "The Titanus."

Sybi sat on a bench and stared at her hands.

"What's wrong, sweet syr? You are pale. Shall I fetch Marcos?"

"No. Not for this."

"What is 'this?'"

How could she say aloud what she was experiencing—a surrealist painting come to life. He would think her mad. Not just him. Bree and Kit would, too, the idea ludicrous. Saying it aloud would give it a certain truth, and yet she hesitated. She liked Kestrel, and she didn't want him thinking she was not right in the head. But maybe she wasn't.

"It's nothing, Kestrel. Let's go. I'd like to see my new home."

They walked from the village green into the shade of the redwoods and took a right-hand fork.

She could see it, dammit, knew just what her aerie would look like, inside and out. They passed many homes high in the trees, strung together like Christmas lights, with bridges, ladders, and ramps connecting them. A world above. A world she knew. A world *she* had created.

He stopped before a treehouse surrounded by balconies and with a distinctive domed cupola like an upside-down bowl. The cupola was small and charming and duplicated the one she had drawn for *Rhiannon* atop the aerie that housed her female protagonist.

"This world," she said, terrified to say the words. Yet she must. "*Your* world matches the one I created."

"Explain." He tilted his head.

At least he hadn't laughed. Rather, his face was open, his eyes sparked with interest.

"I wrote a graphic novel," she said.

"What is that?"

"Comic books are drawn stories with speech balloons for dialogue. Most are serialized. A graphic novel is longer than a comic book, with both illustrations and narrative. Rather than installments in each issue, most graphic novels are entire stories."

"And you are saying your graphic novel is set on Eleutia?"

"The world I created, I called Rhiannon. I dreamed it." Dreams so vivid, she often forced herself awake and sketched what she had dreamt. When she had drawn *Rhiannon*, the world felt real to her, tactile, with an overload of sensory impressions. When that first cel emerged from her pen, she'd had a flare of recognition, as if she'd seen it before, been there before.

At the time, her reaction confused her. But she knew only too well as the Huntington's took possession, the disease often muddled the brain. How could Eleutia be the planet Rhiannon, given that world had been all in her imagination?

Sybi leaned against a tree, and it hummed a soothing melody. She squeezed the bridge of her nose, trying to gather herself. She was living inside the comic-book panels she had created. "The trees, the buildings, the aeries—I recognize them from my novel."

"Do you recognize people?" he asked.

Not Luciana nor Kestrel. Her male lead, Barac, was blond and could fly though he had no wings. But when she'd looked in that mirror, she saw her new body resembled *Rhiannon's* female protagonist. "Not really."

"And what was in your world of Rhiannon?" he said.

"It's bursting with life. Flying horses and floating cities, unicorns and phoenix birds."

Kestrel stiffened. "I have never seen a unicorn."

"Your saying Eleutia has all those creatures?" How amazing and marvelous to see it all and have it be real. "Truly?"

His eyes grew distant. "All exist, though the unicorn has eluded me."

"I'll draw you a Rhiannon one." Sybi grinned. "They're much like horses, though more fragile, with a spiraled horn on their forehead."

"I would like that very much."

"I still can't believe those mythical creatures are real on Eleutia. I want to see them! Then I can draw them from life!" An electric excitement sizzled through her.

As a jobber for Marvel's comics division, her projects had run from Thor to The Silver Surfer. She had pitched Marvel *Rhiannon*, named for an enchanted Welsh deity. Her bosses had gently rejected it, but they had encouraged her to revise the book, promising to review it again. She was hopeful.

Her creation. *Her* world. Yet this world looked nearly identical. "Rhiannon might feel like Eleutia to me, but it has to be some kind of wish fulfillment or something."

"Does it?" he said as he climbed the stairs.

They stepped onto a redwood deck, and when Kestrel swung open the door, he invited her to enter first.

Oh, my, how lovely. Windows filled the good-sized room high amidst the redwoods, like the aeries in *Rhiannon*. She walked to a window and peered outside, and the trees' humming within her grew, warm and joyful.

Sybi breathed deep, then followed Kes on a tour of the aerie. Her new home held four perfect rooms—a large great room, a separate bedroom with a large bed, a bath, and a den. In the den, a wooden straight-backed chair sat against a table ideal for sketching and wall shelves above it held pads, paints, pencils, and other art supplies. Odd-shaped plugs sat at differing heights, one by the table, hinting the CastOuts might have a computer she could use. The brightly upholstered club chair would be perfect for reading or snoozing.

Her very own studio.

Sybi was giddy, and she whirled on Kestrel. "It's wonderful. Beautiful."

"I am pleased you like it."

"I do. So much." Like a fantasy come true. Which left unexplained why her aerie was exactly that. Her protagonist, Elona, was not a Nomad—the name she had given people in Rhiannon who were different from others, like the CastOuts.

Sybi wasn't a CastOut, true, but she was different from everyone on Eleutia except for Kit and Bree. She chuckled. She wasn't much like them, either, with their vibrancy and confidence.

Sybi and Marie, her long-dead youngest sister, had been most similar—both quiet, reserved, and near-invisible except to Kit and Bree. The sisters still used Marie's "hand talking," as the ten-year-old had called it before her death. Marie and Sybi would hand talk for hours, in perfect harmony with one another.

Then Marie had gone, felled by an illness that galloped through her small body. Sybi's heart sighed at the tragedy and the terrible irony of it all. Marie was the only one of the four sisters who did not carry the deadly Huntington's gene.

Sybi's hand reached for her chest, the pain familiar when she thought too hard on Marie. Her sister's gentle nature and sweet soul were here, alive within Sybi, and she massaged her sore heart.

"Are you well?" Kestrel said.

"Yes." She smiled up at him. "Just lost in memories."

"Will you draw for me?" Kestrel held a large pad and pencil, which he set on the table.

"You want me to sketch now?"

"I do." He leaned against the wall and crossed his arms.

"Shall I draw you a unicorn?"

"*All* of Rhiannon."

She laughed. A mighty task, and though his face was stern, his eyes were as warm as a banked fire, their warmth for her. Unsettling. Sybi took her needed tools from the shelves, sat and lifted the pencil, and began to sketch. Kestrel pushed from the wall to stand beside her, his eyes intent.

As she drew, time lost its meaning, and she leaned back after the final stroke, exhausted. "I did a sort of compilation from my novel."

Kestrel angled the pad and stared. Long minutes later, he pointed to the upper lefthand corner showing the city that floated above Rhiannon. "This is Alchemic City."

"In my novel, it's the Golden City."

He moved his finger to the drawing's center. "This is Mother Tree." He gestured toward the lower right corner. "And here you have drawn CatHome, which is where Breena and Gato hold sway." He gestured to the lower left. "Where you drew the wolf and the circular building is WolfHome, where Rafe and Kitlyn reside."

"You're saying all I drew of Rhiannon is on Eleutia." Ridiculous. Talk about wish fulfillment. "How could I possibly see that, draw that?"

"We will discover how."

"The place where my Nomads gathered." She pointed to a building near the center of the sketch. "This is the CastOut meeting and dining hall, isn't it?"

"Yes," he said. "Other buildings you drew are true, as well. As are our aeries, dens, and nests."

"What about the flying horse?" There were many in her story, but she had drawn her favorite—golden and huge, he reminded her of the sunrise.

"Not horses, but a mistral," he said. "Daybreak, I suspect, the largest, most powerful mistral in the Northwest Quadrant. Eleutia's most precious creatures. Their bones are the strongest material on Eleutia." His lips twitched, eyes dancing with humor. "You have even drawn the conical knobs behind their ears, which are highly useful in battle."

She gestured to the phoenix rising from the ashes in *Rhiannon's* village of Pepla. "And the phoenix bird?"

Kestrel stared at the bird as if captivated. He blinked and nodded. "We have phoenix birds, though they are rare. I see you have drawn Terras." He pointed to the single-winged peregrine.

"No." She grinned. "That's Lala, my female peregrine who couldn't fly. I thought it would be fun to put her into the story."

His finger traced numerous images, hovering above them so as not to smear her pencil lines. "Would you do another sketch of your Golden City for me?"

"Happy to." She flipped a page on the pad and began, putting as much detail into the battlements, towers, and crenelations as possible. Yet when she began to draw inside the Golden City, a place she had sketched many times, she couldn't see it in her mind. She shook her head.

Odd, as if a fog lay over the city's interior, resisting her efforts. "It's strange, but I can't visualize inside the city."

"Not important. You are fretting. Do not." He took a seat in the upholstered chair and leaned back, appearing deep in thought.

"I'm sorry," she said, her typical response to guilt at not performing.

He sat up. "Please, Sybelle, do not be. Your value is far beyond your sketching."

A kindness she appreciated. "Should I continue?"

"Perhaps when the fog lifts." He puffed out a breath, and his fingers curled into a fist. "I belong to Compass True, an organization created to overthrow the Alchemic yoke and take back our world."

His words shocked her. "Why?"

"The Alchemic Clan's power has grown over the last two centuries or so, as our female birth rate plummeted among the animal Clans. They began to experiment on our species, to hold tech over our heads to control us, to affect laws to constrain our clans. With each century came more demands, stranger experiments, and more cruelties until we now are but puppets to their masters."

"How awful. But why are you telling me this?"

Kestrel blew out a long breath, his fisted hands unfolding. "Once we succeed in ridding Eleutia of their control, we plan not to destroy the clan but to neuter them so they no longer hold sway over us. To do that, we must find the engines that power the city's floating mechanism. By doing so, the city will remain stationary long enough for our forces to attack." His smile was grim. "The Alchemics do not wish for this war, and they will evade any attack. Mistrals are relatively few compared to the Alchemic might, and the hovercraft they have "gifted" us are too few and cannot match their city's speed. So we are unable to engage our enemy."

"If you destroy their energy source," she said. "The city will be grounded."

"Yes. Our spies within Alchemic City have yet to find the source. Once your mind sees clearly within the city, you may be able to pinpoint that source."

Sybi jerked back. "On Rhiannon..." She paused, breath held, wondering if Kestrel would find her idea nonsensical.

"Continue." He leaned forward and brushed a hand across her cheek.

He'd surprised her with his touch. Even if he did think her crazy, she had to try, almost smiling at Bree's constantly quoted Yoda expression—"there is no try, only do."

"On Rhiannon," she said, her words measured. "I called the floating city's power station the Golden Chamber."

"So you drew a power station." Though his face remained stoic, his eyes burned like black flame.

"I did." Sybi pointed to a rectangular half-buried block on her compilation sketch. The block's glowing golden lines radiated outward. She'd placed the building far from the immense city it powered. She couldn't remember why she'd done that or its exact location, which bothered her. How could most of Rhiannon be clear in her head, but have parts she couldn't picture. "That is my Golden Chamber."

"You have placed it far from the city."

"Because..." Sybi shrugged. "That's what I did."

"Why is it buried?"

She bit her lip and tried, finally giving up. "I can't remember why.

I can't remember where I should put it on my map, either. It powers the Golden City's flight."

Kestrel didn't move, his stillness absolute. Yet his shock quaked through her.

"I mean, the story's just my creation," she said. "At least, I thought it was."

He pointed to the sketch. "You set the chamber far from the city, on the margin of your drawing."

"Right. It's not in the city. That much I do know. But I can't picture where it belongs on Rhiannon, dammit." She squeezed her eyes tight, trying to redraw the chamber on Rhiannon in her mind. Stars afire, she could not see *where* it rested. "I am absolutely sure of one thing. My Golden Chamber is outside the floating city."

He closed his eyes. "Do the characters in your story enter the city?"

"They do, but..." It took her a minute. More than a minute. So much of *Rhiannon* was crystal, every cel and panel she had drawn. She saw blades of grass and stretches of desert, yet she couldn't *see* inside the city. Ridiculous—she had set several scenes there. Even worse, she couldn't picture her characters' faces or which ones were in the city scenes. "I don't know why everything's so fuzzy, but I can't see it."

"It does not matter now." He rose to stand over her again, his index finger rubbing the back of her hand. "You have done well."

Kind, but this time he failed to soothe her.

"Hello?" came the voice from outside the studio.

Kes went to see who it was while she stared at her sketch, willing her mind to picture what was hidden.

"Hello, Sybelle," Luciana said from the doorway.

Sybi mentally shook herself, rose, and pasted on a smile. "It's good to see you."

Luciana took her hand and squeezed. "Kes texted that you were being introduced to your aerie. How do you like it?"

"It's perfect," Sybi said, some of her joy returning.

Luciana's eyes twinkled. "I'm glad. I thought to come help you settle. Shall we get to work?"

Kes left a troubled Sybelle with Luciana, who would help the sweet syr arrange the aerie to her liking. As he returned to his nest, he could not stop thinking about a power station, one with the requisite energy to float and fly Alchemic City. The station should sit somewhere within the city itself. And yet... Sybelle had drawn the energy source *separate* from the city. Astonishing.

Sybelle's "Golden Chamber" could be of immense importance.

He called for a Compass True council vidconference session in thirty minutes and the responses were typical—complaints and whining. But all would attend. His message made certain of that.

While he waited, he shaped his words and how much he would reveal about the power station to the council members. Though he would tell Rafe and Gato all, he would keep Sybelle protected. As important as his information was, the sweet syr was more so. He trusted few. Though no spies existed on the Compass True council, he was wary of its individual members. Some were ruthless, others filled with avarice, and anyone might hurt or covet her. Confident in his word choice, he called his two friends and filled them in.

At the appointed time, a bell chimed and a screen coalesced. And then another screen and another.

When a mosaic of Compass True members filled his three screens, he pressed a button to greet the council, but one of the members—the disrespectful Falcon—started in on him.

The Falcon Alpha despised him, in part because Kes was the far more powerful Clan member. Rafe had told him the Falcon was jealous, the emotion eluding his grasp, but the Falcon's constant sniping was a gnat buzzing around his head. Already the man's face was flushed as he launched his vitriol before all the members were in place.

"You missed our meeting at Gato's fete," the Falcon said with a sneer. "Where were you?"

"That is no concern of yours, Falcon."

"Could you not bestir your mightiness to join us as we voted to begin war?"

"War has already begun. Or have you not noticed?"

"You insulted the council!" Falcon barked.

Rafe pounded a gavel, as he was Compass True's nominal leader. "Enough. The Kestrel called this meeting for a purpose, not to listen to your petty verbal attacks, Falcon. Let us proceed."

The Falcon's furious silence and narrowed eyes promised retribution, but he settled back in his chair. Kestrel could not like the man and found him a fool.

"I have learned," Kestrel said, "that the Alchemics may use an external power source to fuel Alchemic City's flight. A source I believe is buried somewhere in the soil of Eleutia."

"Where did you get this information?" the Sequestered said in a firm voice. She was the newest council member, the previous Sequestered having been murdered by the Anti-Made Ones, an irrational cult bent on destruction. Because of the man-to-woman disparity on Eleutia, the Sequestered chose to disguise their faces and forms from others, the persistence of males desperate for partners overwhelming to them. Their retreat was one of the many sorrows following the decline in female births.

The Alchemics *appeared* to be attempting to raise the female birth rate by pulling a woman's Essence from a parallel world to Eleutia. That Essence created Made Ones such as Sybelle and her sisters, with Made Ones purposefully inclined to birth females.

But as Compass True had learned, the Alchemics had, in fact, *caused* that decline by poisoning Eleutia's water. That a Clan had deliberately sent their species spiraling into decline was the tipping point for war.

"I must keep my source private, Sequestered," Kestrel said.

"That is absurd," the Ferret said.

Rafe pointed his gavel. "You are out of order, Ferret. We all have sources we wish to shield for various reasons including their safety.

Think of what happened to Calix and Neela, both acting as our spies and both dead because of it."

"But this is huge," the Dolphin Alpha said. "Not some small factoid, but information that changes much in our battle to free ourselves. If we can destroy the power source, Alchemic City will be grounded. We will finally have a fixed location to attack."

Kestrel sat back in his chair and crossed his arms as the members argued about whether he did or did not have the right to remain silent. Irrelevant. He would never reveal Sybelle as his source.

Perhaps Mother Tree knew where the power station was located, as she and all her trees on Eleutia were interconnected. While Mother was not a god, she was the offspring of the Fates, a powerful being with near godlike attributes. Mother had shown herself to him, a great privilege, and she had only spoken to him once, telling him of Sybelle.

In Mother Tree's own circuitous way, she had foretold to Breena of Sybelle's arrival. He did not doubt Mother would speak to Sybelle. The question was when. Even more crucial, if the sweet syr asked about the power station's location, would Mother know the answer? If so, would she reveal it?

"Silence," Rafe said in a calm, assured voice. A pose, as Kes knew he boiled inside at the political maneuvering during these meetings. Rafe hated politics as much as Kes did.

Gato leaned forward, hands braced on his desk. The Cat was Alpha to the mightiest of the Northwest Quadrant's Clans and like a brother to Kes. He knew Kestrel's secrets and kept them close.

The Cat Alpha snarled. "The council is behaving worse than a cackle of Hyenas. Rather than harp on whether Kestrel should give us a name, we should be focusing on how to find this power source." He sat, tossing Kestrel a wink.

Kes's lips twitched. Of course everyone had seen that wink, not that Gato cared. His friend was ever the showman.

The Sequestered leaned forward. "Do you have any indication where the power source is located?"

"No," Kestrel said. "Not as yet. But my source may be able to assist in locating it. At present, its whereabouts remains a mystery."

The Southern Continent's Tiger rose and paced. The lean man had replaced his brother Tiger, killed alongside the Sequestered. The dead Tiger had been a fair and just man, but Kes had yet to get a good understanding of the new Tiger.

"So how are we supposed to find this Power Station?" the Deer First Commander said.

The Ferret stood. "Our hidden Ferret labs have focused on electricity. We can grid the planet looking for areas with high electrical emissions."

"Who is to say it's electrical?" the Falcon said.

The Bear chimed in. She was old, but her presence continued to command notice. "Do you have any better ideas?"

Rafe's gavel thumped. "Excellent thought, Ferret. We will contact all the clans, though I suspect the power station is in our Northwest Quadrant."

"Is that not a grandiose suspicion?" the Deer First Commander said.

"I do not think so," Rafe said. "Alchemic City is on or above our quadrant more often than any location on the planet. But even if it is not within our borders, with the other clans' help, we will find it."

"I have handheld electrical impulse wands or EIWs," Ferret said. "The searchers can use them."

"How soon?" Kes said.

"Within the week."

"Good," Rafe said. "We have a plan. We will send out scouting parties in a week—north, east, south."

"I will grid our Titanus sea," the Dolphin said. "Ferret, how long will it take to grid the land itself?"

The Ferret sighed. "Weeks."

CHAPTER

FIVE

Sybi twirled around the good-sized room after Luciana had left. The young woman had helped her settle into her aerie and been sweet as pie. They had talked, and Luciana had answered many questions about Eleutia and its people, creatures, and plants, the mistrals and other "mythical" creatures, the underwater Clans, and the Eleutian gods and demigods. Paralleling *Rhiannon,* no cars, planes, or trains existed other than hovercraft supplied by the Alchemics.

While Luciana had explained many things, including how hovercraft were extremely useful, the vehicles did not move very fast. Most startling was Luciana's use of the term "magic," which both surprised, and yet did not surprise Sybi, given the existence of flying horses and other mythical beings. Luciana commented that many on Eleutia considered magic to be explicable by not-yet understood science.

Luciana had also loaned Sybi what she called a "mobile" and shown Sybi how to work it, the device like a cell phone. She would have her own phone any day, Luciana assured her, once their techs cleared it of Alchemic listening "moles," a delicate task. Sybi had used the loaner to call Kit, who had linked Bree into the call. Hearing their voices had been bliss, with all talking about how they were, their mates, and planned visits in a few days.

"Why were we brought to Eleutia in the first place?" Sybi had said to Kit.

"Wait'll you hear. We were supposed to be broodmares, and have little girl children to save the species. Made Ones have a predisposition for female babies."

"You must have loved that, Bree," Sybi said, sarcasm lacing her voice.

Bree snorted. "Immensely."

"How could three women save a species?" Sybi said. "It sounds absurd."

"There are and were other Made Ones on Eleutia," Kit said. "Made Ones were all some bizarre Alchemic experiment. That Clan lives for their experiments. The paradox, of course, is that the Alchemics were the ones doping the water to inhibit female children's birth."

"Frankenstein experiments on a grand scale," Sybi said. "Evil."

"Very," Kit said.

"I despise them," Bree said.

Though Sybi had wanted to jabber on, Luciana had begun putting her aerie to rights, and Sybi would not let her do it alone.

She couldn't wait to show Kit and Bree around and wished "a few days" was today. The sooner they got to No Land, the vast tract of land between the Cats and the Bears the CastOuts called theirs, the happier she would be.

Once Luciana left, Sybi moved the coffee table to attempt her hatha yoga practice, wondering if this flesh would remember how. Forty-five minutes later, she walked through her aerie thrilled with this body, this not-hers new body, and the way it had flowed into the different poses with ease. She felt grounded, and whether it was from her yoga practice or the spill-over from drawing her novel, it mattered little.

Grounded. Sybi laughed aloud. Here she was, fifteen feet in the air amidst trees of unfathomable age who welcomed her with all-encompassing warmth. At times, their call was nearly irresistible.

Yet that commanding voice remained near-silent, muted, a background sonata to the trees' hum.

She entered the bath and turned on the shower, carefully hanging her clothes on the hooks by the door. The warm, lightly humid air across her naked body felt lovely.

Her new body felt normal and right as if she had always lived in this skin. All except for the superficial changes the Alchemics had deemed...necessary? Useful? What? Sybi turned to face the mirror. Her large breasts weren't awful. They just weren't *her*.

Had she been so imperfect in their eyes? Maybe they were tinkering. Kestrel said their love of experimentation transcended their often-imperfect results.

She showered, using the "blower" Luciana had shown her to whoosh herself dry. Kit and Bree must be as disturbed as she was by her physical changes, knowing how she preferred to remain in the shadows.

The dresser in her bedroom held fresh clothes, and beside it sat a hamper for dirty ones where she chucked what she'd been wearing.

But she did not dress. An odd sensation—like feathers up and down her spine—made her jittery.

She sat on the bed, folded her legs, and quieted her mind, seeing if she would again hear the voice's call. Unsuccessful, she sank deep into meditation, a practice she had done for many years.

Words came, soft, louder, then screams, distant and desperate.

She startled, her eyes flying open.

Scratching from the living room. Sybi donned the fuzzy robe, belted it, and went in search of the noise.

Scratch, scratch, scratch. Outside, then. Peering out the window, she saw nothing...until she looked downward.

Terras raised a claw and scratched again.

She opened the door and kneeled. "Hello, Terras."

He hopped through the door, padded across the great room, and lept onto a chair. Fascinated, she watched him climb the chair's arm. He launched and flapped, his wobbly flight taking him to her shoulder.

"I could have helped you," she said as she petted his downy-soft head. She appreciated that he had not dug his claws into her.

Then again, she shouldn't be surprised. Kestrel had said symbiont creatures were sentient, and Terras must be a symbiont.

"I'm glad to see you, too," she said.

Go.

One word. One syllable. *In her head.* Not the voices, but bell-clear and demanding. "Repeat that, please."

Go.

"Wait. I have to think." It made no sense to blindly follow Terras' command. Yet Kestrel trusted the bird. They were friends. And truth be told, she had always trusted animals more than humans.

"Where?"

Mother.

"My mother is dead."

Mother is not.

"I need clothes."

Why?

Because she would feel weird walking around the woods in a bathrobe. Terras wouldn't understand. After all, he was naked. "To stay warm."

Dress.

Sybi donned jeans and a tunic, socks, and boots, and she wrapped a cloth around one shoulder as padding for Terras. If she followed him as they walked, it would take a week to reach their destination. With the cloth in place, he could ride her shoulder and dig in his claws.

Back in the living room, she found Terras snooping. He was

peering under a pillow and then moved on to a sofa cushion. Lala was a snoop, too, and the memory made her smile. Thank heavens the three gals who worked on their horse farm would take care of the land and their animals. They had left the three Js their farm and all its contents and animals in their wills, with the provision all of them had died. Which was what had happened to their bodies on Earth.

"Shall we go?" she said to Terras, who seemed to understand her speech perfectly well.

His head bobbed up. The eyes—talk about a guilty expression. A red string from the pillow fringe hung from his beak.

"Shame on you!" But she giggled, ruining the effect.

Terras laid the string on the sofa and hopped across it, and she leaned down so his talons could clasp her hand and lifted him to her shoulder.

"You can direct me, right?"

He bobbed a yes.

Once in the forest, she noted the blessed quiet hum of the trees. As they walked, the woods' familiar scents and sounds welcomed her. It took a full half-hour to understand Terras' direction gestures since he'd stopped speaking in her head. Every so often, he would peer up through the towering trees to the blue-blue sky.

Poor fellow. His intense longing to fly hurt. Sybi wished she could sketch a wing that would come alive and let him soar into the skies.

The trees' warmth, their murmurs and sighs, swelled her heart. Though she had often felt the same on Earth, she had never told a soul. Funny how seldom she thought about her Earthly existence since she'd "arrived" on Eleutia.

Sybi missed the horses and other beloved critters at the farm in Maine. Lala, Tansy and Peach, their Sheltie pups. The sweet Js who helped Kit with her horses, all wonderful young women. Her sensei, Master Karen. Jimmy and Kasturi, virtual Marvel friends. Photos of her parents and circus friends. Their letters, too. Her iPad. Prized comics, especially her X-Men #1. Her full *Rhiannon* manuscript with its notes, research, and sketches was a great loss.

Heaven's goddess, her list was short.

At least money didn't concern her. Hundreds of years earlier, she had been told, the Alchemics' had begun creating Made Ones, where a woman's Essence was pulled to Eleutia and infused into her own youthful, recreated flesh. Those early Made Ones suffered from a lack of independence, and one reason was they had no money of their own. So the animal clans and CastOuts created the Made Ones' fund, monies that were banked for Made Ones upon their arrival.

In other words, Sybi was flush, something she and her sisters had never been on Earth.

Pondering what she missed from Earth, she suspected Kit and Bree's lists were equally brief. Though she was their trio's introvert, Bree and especially Kit had made a point of distancing themselves from others, in part because of Kit's horrific and disabling accident. Kes had shown her the videos from before she awakened, and Kit's and Bree's new bodies were that of their youth—whole and beautiful and not modified like hers.

She paused. "Terras, does my new body have the Huntington's gene?"

His black eyes stared at her, then he blinked. *No. You are perfect.* He shook his head. *Mother Tree is displeased with the tampering of your flesh.*

"So am I," she said, welling with relief. "Do you know Mother Tree well?"

He bobbed his head.

"Do you agree with her?"

More head bobbing, and she ran a gentle finger down his feathers. Terras nuzzled her as if in comfort.

They climbed the same rise she had earlier that day, to see the same shrouded dip in the land near the cliff edge, the tips of leafed trees poking above the mist. The fog wasn't normal, its tendrils curling into the forest like a living thing, while others spiraled up the trunks of nearby trees.

Creepy. The thought of walking into that curling mist gave her goosebumps.

Go.

Flaming goddess, Terras wanted her to stride into the ominous death trap. She sighed. "All right, I guess."

The first step was the hardest. The second not much easier. Misty tendrils curled around her body and across her face, oddly warm and luxurious.

Sybi wanted to turn and run.

"Sweet syr!"

Kestrel stood not five feet away, his eyes focused beyond her.

She turned to face him, relief flooding her chest, and breathed deep. Over her shoulder, she was unsurprised to see the land looking as normal as the rest of the forest.

Sybi sat, twining her arms around her knees.

"Where were you going?" Kestrel folded himself to sit cross-legged beside her.

"It sounds crazy."

His lips twitched. "We CastOuts specialize in what you call 'crazy,' Ma'am Sybelle. Tell me."

"All right." Sybi explained Terras talking in her head, the mist, and its curling tendrils. "So you arrive, and I turn to talk to you, and when I look back, it's all gone—the dip, the mist, the treetops. Well?"

"That was Mother Tree, Sybelle," Kestrel said. "She often talks to Terras, though only once to me."

His sweet syr was connected to Mother in a way Kestrel did not understand. Like Luciana, Sybelle had an affinity for growing things. The redwoods and other forest plants touched her as she walked, as they did for Luciana. Yet she was different from his Clanmate. He wished he could define how, a thing full of promise within him.

"Why do you do that?" she said. "Talk to me like you know me, like I'm a part of all this?"

"Because you are." He felt her inside him, a beautiful living

Essence that grew until his heart squeezed. Brave, with a willingness to dare the dance, Sybelle possessed a stillness he admired.

"How can you *know* that? Given that I'm from Earth, it makes no sense."

"Because I do. With certainty." Truth. But the questions would come now, the burrowing for information. The asking and the nods, when what they wanted to do was shake their heads.

Her hand moved to touch his forearm but stopped, and she bit her lip. "As if the feeling was instinctual. I know those only too well. But *why* am I part of all this?" Her arms spread wide.

He shrugged. "That I do not know." He knew about himself well enough—the result of another Alchemic experiment, Fukkes' experiment. That he was a patchwork of several Eleutian creatures besides human was never far from his mind. Those pieces were transformational, yet the sum of them failed to explain who he was. His aloneness pressed in on him.

Thanks to Enala's vicious teachings, much practice had gone into his ability to contain his emotions. But doing that with Sybelle was a daunting challenge. He simply had to look at her and his emotions leaked out. Her soothing presence made it a struggle to keep his reactions at bay. Yet he felt a quiet peace with her like no other.

He *must* remain distant, for she could ignite his prey instincts and his rage would burn. While his tiger nature was but a minor part of him, it would urge him to stalk her, to take her. He could hurt her. Kill her.

"Kes?" She rested a hand on his arm. "It's all right."

Calm stole over him, her understanding a balm. Rather than pry, her eyes were warm with concern for *him*.

He clasped his hand over hers. "Thank you."

"For what?" she said.

Her head tilted, her waterfall hair sliding across her shoulder like the Afródis river, and he lost himself in the gleaming golden strands, their ends curling like the fall's froth.

"Kes?"

"Mother may be gone for now, but she will return for you."

"What makes you so sure?" Sybelle said, hoping her question wouldn't distress him. His haunted expression had cut her, and she didn't want to stress him again.

"The mist, those tall leafy treetops, the land's dip—they are Mother's world. I have seen them before. She revealed herself, the mist, and her sentinels. Had she not wished to do so, you would have seen only forest."

"I see. Thank you."

At times, Kestrel spoke as if he was weighing each word, different from other CastOuts she had met. He might be a man of many aspects—Alpha, warrior, carer—but he was troubled, too. The thought disturbed her, and she wished to be a balm that soothed those stresses.

"I suspect Mother will soon return." He dipped his head and sniffed her.

She startled. "Are you *smelling* me?"

"Yes." He stood, fluid and fast. "Come."

He held out his large hand, callused, with a faint scar across his palm. She wrapped her hand around his, and that familiar warmth blossomed. Distracted, she remembered Terras. The bird was nowhere in sight. "Where did Terras go?"

Kes grinned. "A mercurial fellow, our Terras."

Mother, Kes' arrival, Terras vanishing... They reminded her of the surreal dreams she'd had drawing *Rhiannon*.

They walked, Kes stepping onto one of the nearby paths.

"Where are we going?"

"To your nest. I would like to see how your drawing of Rhiannon is progressing."

"Slowly." If only she could see *all* of it.

Gabin walked beside Fukkes across the circular courtyard flanked by glass enclosures containing many of their experiments.

To their left lived Eleutian Clan members whose DNA had been recombined with their symbionts and other animals. Some were like vegetables, while others had proved more successful. According to Fukkes, even the non-responsive had secrets to reveal. How they would divulge them, he could not imagine. Gabin sighed, wishing the Cabal had never come to this cursed planet.

On their right were the animal enclosures which held both symbionts, exotics, and mistrals for breeding, combining, and bone harvesting. At present, they held but a single dun-colored mare with a black curling mane, forelock, and fetlocks.

"Why wait to harvest the new mistral's bones?" Fukkes said.

"We should try breeding her one more time," Gabin said.

"Our mistral breeding program is a failure. The Cabal has accepted that. *I* have accepted that. Our captive mistrals refuse a live breeding, and if we artificially inseminate, somehow the fetus is always aborted. We leave this world soon, Gabin. I'm done with these absurd creatures. Harvest the bones. At some future date, from the comfort of our new home on Earth, we will find a way to transport mistrals there. They will have great value on that world."

Gabin nodded, but he would put it off. Fukkes saw mistrals as useless but for their bones. They were majestic creatures, and he was sick of the killing.

He recalled a time, centuries earlier when Fukkes had appreciated creatures and worlds for more than their experimental value. All had changed with the death of his wife and child. They were long, *long* gone. Yet Fukkes...

A squawk from the next cage. Alongside the single mistral was a rare caged gryphon, mostly skin and bones. It lay on its side, and though blind, the creature glared at them. Beyond that cell sat a glass enclosure filled with saltwater where a half woman-half fish bobbed, her iridescent tail swishing this way and that in languorous motions. The fish-woman's sharp, serrated teeth had ripped several Alchemics apart before they subdued her. She was a beautiful specimen.

At the end of the aisle sat a huge glass suite of rooms, empty. When The Kestrel had been traded for Gato's captive brother, Fukkes had locked the CastOut leader inside. Yet The Kestrel had escaped.

The Kestrel baffled even the Cabal, his loss a slap in Fukkes' face.

Though secretly pleased, Gabin hid his smile. "I say we leave now."

"Leave for Earth?" Fukkes said. "With our business unfinished on Eleutia?"

"It has become dangerous here. The Eleutians are plotting to be rid of us."

"Come," Fukkes said.

They turned a corner and stepped in front of two automatic doors, the noxious smell familiar and unwelcome as they swung open. Their largest lab held numerous stations for experimentation, and Gabin slipped a pair of noise blockers in his ears, the screams and cries of the test subjects deafening.

As they walked through the lab, few stations drew his attention until they came to a gurney with a recombination—a man to his waist and a tiger below. Could the tiger-man walk upright or not? That was Darva's experiment.

Recombination remained Darva's favorite pastime. Given she worshipped the Comstat, that made a pathetic sort of sense. When they stopped by her station, she fluttered like a hormonal teenager over Fukkes.

"Impressive, my dear," Fukkes said. "Do the legs function?"

Her lips thinned. "No, much to my fury."

The tiger-man on the table wept, which was typical. By this point in the making, all the fight would have leached out of the test subject.

"Carry on," Fukkes said.

"Thank you, Comstat." Darva bowed and returned to her specimen.

They exited the lab and strode through the supply corridor. More labs lay to their left and right, with two guards before the door straight ahead who bowed when he spotted them.

Inside, sat the underground chambers holding the machinery, capsules, and trino devices that would transport the eleven Cabal members' Essences to Earth. No one entered that area but the Cabal.

Instead of entering, they climbed the nearby staircase and walked through an arch onto the city's vast central plaza. Above, dark gray clouds sailed over the stone-paved plaza planted with flowers and bushes and dotted with sculptures and benches. Citizens strolled the plaza, as did others from across Eleutia, while Alchemic guards stood watch at critical points.

Today, their city floated over a roiling sea, the air pungent and fresh. Seagulls wheeled above, and if he were correct, several albatross. On Earth, he believed humans saw them as harbingers of doom. So much to explore and learn about the Earthians. He was eager to leave Eleutia.

One or two Alchemics waved but did not approach. Smart.

"Dear Gabin," Fukkes said. "You are concerned that the Eleutians are plotting against us." Fukkes grinned, crystal teeth glittering even in the dim light. "Of course they are, but let us be realistic. The animal clans' smaller brains are unable to sustain complex thought. Nothing will come of it."

"You see them differently than I do."

"I do not." Fukkes frowned. "Ever since Neela's death…"

Gabin clasped his hands behind his back and strode to the rail that overlooked the sea far below. *Neela*—quiet and sweet and a spy for Compass True, or so Fukkes alleged. "She did not deserve to die."

"She was a traitor."

"She was harmless."

"Be careful," Fukkes said. "Your affection is showing."

Gabin whirled. "My affection? A brotherly thing. No more."

"If you say so." Fukkes walked to stand beside Gabin and rested his hand on Gabin's shoulder. "So you continue to lie even to yourself."

If Gabin could toss Fukkes over the rail without repercussions, he would. But the array of cameras would record every moment of it.

It might be worth it.

He sighed.

He wished to arrive on Earth without further damaging Eleutia, whereas Fukkes had become obsessed with decimating the planet. In the centuries since they had arrived, the Cabal had evolved from careful and unobtrusive experiments to ones that twisted and mutilated the Eleutians. All because of Fukkes' hunger for vengeance.

Many years earlier, the Anti-Made Ones had infiltrated their city and destroyed dozens of Essence globes, the destruction unhinging Fukkes. Other Essences were replaceable. Not so Fukkes' wife and child, Mari and Xenon, their Essence balls damaged beyond repair.

Gabin's task was to inform their Overseers, men, women, and nonbinaries who ruled their home planet. They oversaw the many Cabals introduced to numerous planets, their missions intended for the good of science. Days of waiting followed, but when the Overseers finally spoke to him, they said to take no vengeance.

As if Fukkes would listen. As one of the Overseers' oldest and highest-ranking Cabal leaders, they held him in high regard. Yet they either ignored or failed to understand Fukkes' devotion to his family. Not that Gabin could voice that opinion.

Now, revenge on all of Eleutia and leaving for Earth were Fukkes' focus. Grief-stricken and incensed at the loss of his wife and child, Fukkes had begun those hideous recombining experiments with the support of the Cabal. That was not the worst of it, for Fukkes had crafted a hormone mixture and added it to the planet's water. Eleutia's female birth rate had plummeted from fifty to a twenty percent female-to-male ratio. Left unchecked, the hormone would end the species. A resounding success in Fukkes' terms.

Now, Fukkes wanted to speed up the Eleutian destruction and insisted the Keystone be brought to the city. Placing the Keystone in the desert, its power propelling the city's flight, had been a smart move. But given the heightened tensions, their power source presented a weakness the Eleutians could exploit. Once within the city, that shortcoming would shatter.

So much maneuvering, when all Gabin wished was to leave for Earth. There, his Essence would inhabit the comatose Pope's flesh, as all eleven Cabal members would become prominent Earthian leaders.

Neela's death had devastated Gabin and only increased his desire to leave. He was not delusional but had loved Neela as a man loves a woman. That Fukkes made him the agency of her death was yet another reason he visualized Fukkes tumbling into the ocean.

By taking over Earth, they would be flaunting the Overseers' directives. Once that was accomplished, the Cabal would be untouchable. He liked that idea.

"How long before the Keystone returns?" Gabin said.

"The crew has left the city for the reclamation of our power station," Fukkes said.

Gabin nodded. "That should take less than a day."

Fukkes moved to a battlement and leaned against its wall. "I have ordered the hover teams to fly at the slower Eleutian speeds." All hovers traded to the Eleutian Clans had a maximum speed of thirty-five miles per hour.

"Why?" Gabin was furious. More wasted time. "It will take them days to reach the station."

Fukkes' sneered. "Time is our friend, Gabin. Not our enemy."

"Why are you stalling?" Had he really said that aloud? Fukkes would ignite.

In a calm voice, Fukkes said, "The Eleutians can track and would take note of the faster vehicles. You fool, they could follow them to the Keystone."

"A team of hovers? Will *that* not be noticed?"

Fukkes shot him a disdainful glance. "I've taken the additional precaution of sending the teams on separate routes."

"How are you sure the Eleutians have tracking capabilities?" Gabin scoffed at the notion.

"They may be insects to us, but they have developed laboratories using our technology and, I suspect, manufacturing their own."

"Implausible," Gabin said.

Fukkes' full-on smile was a hideous thing to see. "Yet you say *I* underestimate them. You are the fool, Gabin."

CHAPTER

SIX

As *Rhiannon* emerged from Sybi's pen over the following four days, her frustration mounted. She had little trouble rendering the world she had created, as well as its creatures, though she did wonder at her drawing of Rhiannon's unicorn, phoenix, and daylight-blind Lamia. Kes said he had never seen a unicorn. Luciana's descriptions of Eleutian creatures had aligned with myths from Earth. Had Kes seen phoenixes and Lamias? She would love to see them, as well.

Today, she drew in furious bursts, but Sybi still could not *see* inside the Golden City, nor place the Golden Chamber that powered it.

Luciana had said many visited Alchemic City, and the CastOuts had images taken from outside its walls. But Sybi needed to see the guts of the place, its passages, buildings, and internal workings.

Even her own characters remained fuzzy, and whenever she went to sketch them, a mental "fog" obscured their faces.

Over the past days, she had been introduced to many CastOuts, including Luciana's beaux, the serious Asher, a kind of CastOut policeman called a Sgiath, and Asher's best friend, blind Pedro, a burly man with ink-black curls, a handlebar mustache, and a jolly demeanor. Pedro told awful jokes, and she had to laugh, yet behind those milky eyes lay a deep sorrow.

Yesterday she met Marcos, and the healer was nothing like Sybi had imagined. Huge and ebony-skinned, he resembled a tribal warrior, with epic dreadlocks and patterned scars dotting the right side of his face. He wore a sword at his waist, like Kestrel, and his deep, sonorous voice recalled James Earl Jones'. Though he looked fierce, Marcos answered all her questions with grace, humor, and compassion, and Sybi instantly liked the man, who was also Kestrel's second in command.

She had seen wonders aplenty, too—a Star Wars-like hovercraft that floated above the earth and a powered glider resembling a falcon that had flown overhead. An immense symbiont brown bear, who had bowed when he met her. Pedro in *flight*. He was making awkward circles above a grassy valley, while Asher stood on the ground and gave him commands.

Too much woolgathering, and Sybi got back to work. Yet the minute her pencil touched the page, a knock came at the door.

Not a surprise visit from Terras, who now perched on her shoulder. He had made himself at home in her aerie and visited often, and she wondered what Kestrel thought about that. She rose, and Terras hopped down and tapped his talon against her ankle.

"What? Terras, dear, I can hear the knock."

He tilted his head, and she would swear he was telling her to go faster. *That bird.*

When she opened the door, Luciana smiled. "Your sister is on the vidscreen at the command center in Kestrel's aerie waiting to speak with you."

"Great!" She grabbed a thin jacket. "I thought all the TVs, er, vidscreens could do face-to-face. Why not at my aerie?"

Luciana's lips thinned. "Security."

Sybi got it, and she shoved Luciana out the door, much to the girl's amusement. "Let's go!"

They walked deep into the forest until they came to an immense redwood with a trunk the size of a VW bus. Built around it was a large, multi-room aerie.

"We wait," Luciana said.

"For what?" Sybi bounced on her toes, bursting with anticipation.

"The lift." Luciana slapped a hand over her mouth. "I do not mean to laugh, but you are very excited."

"An understatement."

The wooden lift, dangling from thick ropes, arrived with a faint thud. She stepped onboard, gripped a rope, and waved Luciana to hurry.

The young woman shook her head. "Not for me. See you at mid-day meal."

"See you then!" The lift jerked, and Sybi looked upward as the platform ascended far above the level of her aerie.

Kestrel peered down from the deck, and when she arrived, he welcomed her inside. Outside, his aerie was huge, yet his rooms were not much larger than hers. He walked her through several, then down a corridor to the end of a hall where he waved her forward.

Banks of massive monitors filled one wall of the large room, while two men sat at computer stations beneath them. Sofas and chairs were scattered around the room, with a meeting table and more chairs pushed against a wall. Kestrel led her to a blank monitor that had to be eighty inches and nodded to the man beneath it working the controls.

"Go," he said.

As the man departed, Kes dragged over a large sofa. "Sit." She bounced onto the couch and turned to Kes. "When—"

"Back soon." He disappeared and returned with drinks, handing her one.

Kestrel was such an imposing figure, his whole demeanor stern. Yet the drink offer was typical of his subtle kindness, which both impressed and touched her. "Thank you."

"On," he said.

The screen coalesced, revealing a Mediterranean landscape with a swooping Frank-Lloyd-Wright-style building above cascading waterfalls.

"Sybi!" Bree screamed, filling the screen and waving her arms.

Sybi leaped out of her seat. "Breena! You look great!"

Bree stretched out her arms in a virtual hug. "All that, dear sis."

Sybi virtually hugged her sister back. "I've been dying to ask, but all our conversations have been with Kit. How is she, physically? I mean, the accident and all."

"Amazing," Bree said. "She's riding like a dream again, her body unbroken and strong."

Sybi sat back on the sofa. The thrill of Kit physically healed more than made up for her own disturbing transformation. "I'm so glad."

"So am I, Sybs." Bree raised a brow. "Um, you have a bird on your shoulder."

"This is Terras. A friend. He's taken up couch-surfing in my aerie."

"Why am I not surprised?" Bree said, her voice bemused. "He looks like Lala."

"Almost identical." Sybi scratched beneath Terras' chin, something he loved. "I thought you were coming here for a visit. Kit, too."

Bree looked annoyed and sighed. "We both have to wait. Gato and I were about to leave when Compass True messaged us."

"Kestrel told me about the rebel organization," Sybi said.

"Apparently," Bree said. "The Alchemics have begun tracking Kit and myself. Coming to No Land would draw their attention to you. According to the messages we've intercepted, the Alchemics think you're dead. Hooray! Compass True wants to keep it that way. They found three bodies and your smashed capsule."

"How can they think I'm dead?" Sybi said. "My body wasn't there."

"Drag marks indicated an animal had taken your remains. On a vid with them, when they told me you were dead, I even cried."

"Good playacting. I'm glad you guys knew I was alive." Kestrel had not only saved her but masked her escape.

Bree's face went blank. "Um... You look, er...well."

"I look *well?*" Her sisters had obviously seen Sybi's physical changes on their visits while she slept. Where was Bree's snark about her new looks?

"I look ridiculous." *Holy moly*. Bree was different, too, and not just her confidence. Her hair was its natural red hair, hair she *always* dyed black. Her boobs were natural, too, without their Earthly breast implants. What a refreshing change.

On Earth, Bree had been an enhanced size D, makeup on, nails polished. Always. She was breathtaking, but her enhancements were for all the wrong reasons.

Today, she was pure, unfiltered Bree. "You look lovely. It's obvious you're well and happy."

"Incredibly so." Bree winked as she turned from the camera and wiggled a finger. "Come here, catman."

A tall, longhaired man stepped into the frame and sat beside Bree, one arm draping over her shoulder. Bree's smile at her "catman" lit up the screen.

"This is Gato," Bree said. "Lucky stars, I'm happy as fuck."

Pure Bree, swearing like a sailor, with one of their mother's constant, oddball expressions her three girls emulated.

Bree's joy was one Sybi had never seen on Earth.

Gato swooped in for a long, lingering kiss, then waved to Sybi. "Farewell, sister. For now." He left followed by a black panther the size of a pony.

"*That* is Bartholomew?" Sybi said.

"Epic, isn't he? The cubs, Fortis and Audacia, are in lessons, or I'd introduce you."

"I can't wait," Sybi said and grew serious. "I've had some odd experiences since waking up."

Bree snorted. "That sounds like one of your understatements."

"Kestrel says I'm here to..." She cleared her throat. "...save this world."

"I'm not surprised."

"Why in hell is that?"

"Mother Tree says weird shit," Bree said. "When I met her... I told you a little about that already. Well, Mother Tree said 'She is here. She will come. Be at ease.' I had no clue what she meant, but the 'she' was *you*, not that I got it at the time. When Calix, a Falcon spy for Compass True, pointed us out to the Alchemics so they would pull our Essences to Eleutia, it was at Mother's behest."

Calix had died trying to save Sybi, a weight on her soul. "It's all seriously strange."

"Hell, yes. I have trouble wrapping my head around it."

"You're not the only one, sis," Sybi said.

Sybi told her about the floating man in the woods and how Terras talked in her head. She did *not* mention her attraction to Kestrel. Bree would run with it and have them instantly paired up. She scraped a hand through her hair. "I hear other voices in my head, too, like a chorus, but one."

"Mother Tree spoke in my head. Maybe it's her." Bree leaned forward, clasping her hands together. "Eleutia is this weird combination of science and magic."

"Do you realize Eleutia is Rhiannon?"

"Rhiannon? Your novel?" Bree startled, then grew quiet. "Holy shit. Yeah, you're right. I never saw it. Kit hasn't, either. Your lead characters, Barac and Elona, you're—"

"Don't say it." Elona transformed into a naiad at one point in her story. Sybi shivered. She might look like her, but she was no Elona. She told Bree about drawing Rhiannon for Kestrel. "The fog. I can't see my characters' faces anymore. Or inside the city. Or where the Golden Chamber is located. I don't understand why and it's driving me nuts."

A deep baritone said, "Mother."

Sybi twirled, having forgotten Kestrel was in the room.

"Mother Tree?" Bree chimed in.

"Yes," he said.

"So there's a reason," Bree said.

"Timing." Sybi got it. "It might be about timing." Mother had arranged their arrival. Now, for some reason, she suspected Mother was fogging parts of Rhiannon because the time wasn't right. Frustrating to be controlled like that, but some otherworldly plan was in place. Or was she fantasizing? "Tell me more about Mother Tree."

For long moments, Bree remained silent, then, "Mother is imposing, though she's small of stature. Like you."

"Very funny." Sybi stuck out her tongue, feeling like a teen rather than her fifty-two years. The thought made her giddy. No teen, but with her youth restored.

"Mother speaks with eloquence, and…" Bree huffed. "I'd have to say the only word I can find to describe her is 'profound.'" Bree went on to tell her about the sentinels, a carpet of flowers, and gems inlaid in Mother's trunk. "She's impossible to describe in full."

"I hope I meet her soon."

"Are you eating enough?" Bree said.

"What?" And Bree was off on her mother-hen routine she and Kit had perfected after Marie's death. "I am eating plenty."

Breena exuded confidence, a trait she had lacked for decades. That thrilled Sybi, especially since it came from within, rather than from physical enhancements.

"I love your new self-assurance," Sybi said.

"Even minus the big boobs and black hair? Ha! I've come to like me. And Gato calls my hair 'sunset.'"

"I'm so pleased, Breena. You're stunning."

"You're beautiful, too, Sybs." Bree sat forward. "But you don't feel like you, do you?"

Sybi shook her head. "When I look in the mirror, it's like I'm wearing a cosplay outfit."

A large, warm hand came to rest on Sybi's shoulder and

squeezed. For some reason, Kestrel's touch gave her the courage to speak her mind.

"People stare at me. All the time. Some try to touch my hair or bow. I'm uncomfortable with the attention. I'd rather blend."

"I know. I can get you some hair dye."

Sybi whooshed out a breath. "What would be the point?"

"Maybe you'd feel better?"

"I doubt it."

"Harsh, Sybs."

"I didn't mean... I would never..."

Bree snorted. "I'm pulling your chain. Stars alive, did you lose your sense of humor in the transition?"

"Har, har, har."

"What about clothes?" Bree said. "You're at a higher altitude, are you wearing enough layers? It gets cold in those mountains."

"The sweet syr is being well cared for," Kestrel chimed in.

Bree batted her lashes. "Oh, la la, the 'sweet syr,' is it?"

Sybi ignored Bree's implication. "Yes, *Mama hen*, I'm keeping plenty warm."

"Sarcasm doesn't become you, Sybs." Breena sniffed.

"Tough noogies."

Bree laughed. "How about exercise? You hate to—"

"I've been walking and doing my yoga and martial arts forms. Enough!"

A mew sounded.

"Fortis! Audi!" Bree said.

Two stunning cougar cubs prowled onscreen. One was tan, the other black, and they stood knee-high on either side of Bree. The tan one lifted his front paws to Bree's thigh.

"They met you, but you didn't meet them." Breena smiled at the tan cub. "This is Fortis." She scratched behind the ear of the black cub. "And this is Audacia, or Audi for short. I bonded with them soon after I arrived on Eleutia."

"Wow." Bonding. Mating. All strange. Like some shapeshifter

romance. Perhaps all the tropes on Earth existed on parallel worlds. Too big a thought. "Gato doesn't turn into a cat, does he?"

Bree laughed. "Sometimes I think he'd like to, but no. As far as I know, shapeshifting isn't part of Eleutia."

"Symbionts are strange enough."

"Right?" Bree said.

"The Alchemics aren't tracking me," Sybi said. "What if I came to CatHome?"

"It is unsafe for you to go," Kestrel said. "Not yet."

Sybi tried to hide her disappointment. "But I'll see you soon, Bree."

"We'll make it happen."

Bree continued to pepper Sybi with more questions about her wellbeing until Sybi cut her off. "I'm being cared for and treated kindly, Breena. I am *fine*."

Breena's cheeks flushed. "I know. I just worry. Gotta go."

Bree signed in ASL, Marie's chosen form of speech the sisters still used. *I love you.*

Sybi did the same, and each pressed a hand to her heart.

Keep the faith, Sybs. We'll be together soon.

Sybi signed, *Soon.*

CHAPTER

SEVEN

They talked with hands. Kestrel had followed the gestures but had yet to make sense of them.

As he had watched the sisters converse, he had felt an odd pinch beneath his breastbone. Uncomfortable, and he was not sure what it signaled. The CastOuts were his brothers and sisters, but he had no living biological family whatsoever.

He stepped forward. "Sybelle?"

She stood with her back to him, and he felt her sadness. That was unacceptable. Kes turned her to face him and smoothed his hands down her arms. "You will see Breena soon, Sybelle. Your Kitlyn, too. I will make it happen."

Her head was bent, and she nuzzled his chest, her sigh a stutter. "Thank you, Kestrel. I miss them."

"I understand your loneliness," he said. "Would that I could ease it."

"You're kind."

He gave her a slow smile, hoping she saw the warmth he felt for her, wishing he had the words to convey his feelings of care and protection for this bright, whimsical woman. So easy to lean

76

down and brush his lips across hers, to taste the sweet syr. A surprising compulsion, but Sybelle had given no indication she would enjoy the gesture. Instead, he stepped back and led her outside.

"You talk with your hands," he said.

"We do." Sybi explained about her sister Marie and ASL.

"Would you teach me?" he said.

"Sure, though..." she said, her eyes clouded.

"You hesitate."

"Not really. ASL was our secret language." Her smile blazed. "I think Marie would approve."

Sybelle tucked her hands into her pockets and began to walk, her stride fluid and purposeful. "ASL isn't easy to learn."

A test of his will and stamina... Learning from this woman who compelled his thoughts. His control would be strained, but he was confident it would not break. It never had. "I am up for the challenge."

The following day, Sybi began work in the CastOuts' gardens, so she and Luciana went to inspect the greenhouses. A wonder of design, the soft fabric "houses" meandered through the cathedral of redwoods, camouflaged by paint and the towering trees. When she stepped through the airlock door, lights woven on the interior of the curved arches made the space seem like daylight.

"The lights are timed," Luciana said. "They reflect the sun's movement, so they dim at nightfall and rise again at dawn."

Rows of pots marched atop tables, ones that looked like plastic, but were organic according to Luciana. Seedlings popped up from their loamy soil, and Sybi recognized many of them—mallow and goldenrod, willow and—she smiled—cherry tomatoes. The rows curved into the distance following the twists of the greenhouses as they wound through the trees.

"This is amazing," Sybi said.

Luciana dug her fingers into the soil of a rosemary seedling, closed her eyes, and raised her face to the heavens. "I can feel Mother Tree's life force."

Sybi stepped to the tomato plant and burrowed her fingers. Tingles skipped up her arm and across her shoulders, as if she had been numb, but was now awake. "Oh, my."

"Mother Tree's energy is everywhere," Luciana said. "Even in the air and the sea."

Sybi withdrew her hand, rolling black soil between her thumb and fingers, savoring the energy, the *clarity*.

As Luciana walked down the row, she touched a few of the plants, especially those who needed some extra TLC. "I thought we could start by repotting some of the larger plants. What do you think?"

"Excellent idea."

They exited the current greenhouse, and several minutes later came to another one and entered the same way. The damp air smelled of growth and life, like home. Here, the potted plants were larger, with vegetables on the right and herbs and flowering plants to their left. Luciana walked to a large group of nasturtiums, each in its own pot.

"Let's carry a few of these to the planting area," Luciana said.

Sybi lifted three heavy containers and followed. Halfway down the aisle, they came to a series of raised beds, many already filled with flowers and vegetables.

"Why don't you take the bed on the right." Luciana pointed to a raised bed black with rich soil. "I'll take the one across from you."

"Great." Sybi got down on her knees, placing the pots beside her. The floor, though appearing wooden, felt rubberized and comfortable.

"Do you want a trowel?" Luciana said.

"No. I'm good." Sybi wanted her hands in that beautiful soil and she began to make a hole for the first nasturtium she would replant.

The tingles began again, increasing to where they tickled her insides. She released the nasturtium's root ball from its pot and placed it in the hole, smoothing soil around the ball. Feather touches brushed her face and arms and neck. How lovely.

She blinked rapidly. "Wow. I'm really feeling Mother Tree. Is she a god?"

Luciana sat back on her heels, dusting her hands on her pants. "That is a good question. Mother Tree is so of the earth, I have never thought of her that way. Mother Terra *is* Eleutia, as is Father Sky. They are two of the five Fates, and Mother Tree is their offspring."

"Maybe she's what we call a demigod in Earth mythology. The five Fates are gods? What are the others?"

"The Fates of Air, Water, and Sorcere complete the five."

"Sorcere?"

"You Earthians call it magic. Sorcere represents all that we do not see or cannot know, the indefinable."

Funny how Sybi could relate to Eleutia's Fates. "I'm intrigued."

"They are benevolent, though along with giving blessings, each can wreak havoc. No, I would not call Mother Tree a god. She is more like... life's essence itself? Maybe? I never thought of her this way before, but to me, Mother Tree is the personification of life."

Luciana's voice was so soothing, like dandelion fuzz. Sybi had only caught a smattering of her words as she worked the soil and plants. Goddess rejoice, a euphoric feeling as if she could fly herself. By burrowing deep into the soil, colors brightened, the air redolent with incredible scents. Bliss.

"Sybelle?" Luciana said. "Are you going to plant the next nasturtium?"

What a silly question. Of course she was. Sybi giggled...which was dumb, and she wove her fingers back and forth through the soil, her body swaying. "Oh, this is grand." She flopped to the floor onto her bum. "Oops!"

"Sybelle!" A grip on her arm, and she was pulled upward, stumbled, and crashed into Luciana who managed to keep them upright. "It appears Mother Terra's soil affects you in a powerful way. Most unusual. Come."

"I don't wanna go," she said with defiance, having a wee bit of trouble staying upright.

"We will get something to eat," Luciana said. "Mid-day has started, and I hear they're serving stew, always delicious. Come on. We can join Kestrel."

"Kestrel." Sybi sighed. "He's beautiful."

"Yes, he is."

"I like him a lot." A hiccup burst out.

"We all like Kestrel."

Sybi playfully slapped Luciana on the shoulder. "Not like *that*, Luce! I mean like...you know. He makes me—"

"Do not say it," Luciana said in a stern voice. "He is like a father to me."

"Not to me." Sybi winked.

Funny, but as they stumbled through the forest, she would swear the trees were laughing. It was *hard* walking. Stones and holes would jump into the path, and she would trip. Sybi rubbed her hands together, still coated in earth, Luciana's hand beneath her arm. The happiness. Such happiness. A log attacked her, and she flew, face-planting on the path. *Oomph.*

"Fates alive," Luciana said, as she hauled Sybi up. "How will I ever get you back to the village?"

"By walking, silly."

"Father Sky save me. It is like you downed a barrel of ilaberry wine."

With Luciana's help, Sybi began walking again. *Oh, ho!* A huge rock jumped out, but she saw it in time and stepped around it. Sunlight sparkled on the redwoods' needles, redolent with fecund scents, and she marveled. The sounds of the sea, too, of crashing waves and gulls' caws reminded her of Acadia. Eleutia was so beautiful, like her Rhiannon.

She had seen no cement, no soaring towers of steel, nor highways with cars. This world was quiet, serene. There was magic here. *Real* magic, and it brushed against her as if alive—warm and comforting. She tilted her head back, the breeze a playful brush across her cheeks, the sky so blue, the flowers so bright.

Child.

"Mother? Where are you?"

I am here. I surround you, always.

"Why can't I find you?"

You will.

"Who are you talking to?" Luciana said.

"Mother Tree."

"Mother is talking in your head?"

"Yes. It's her voice I've been hearing in my head. And today she answered me. Isn't that cool?" Sybi hiccupped.

"I am sure it was."

A shadow on the path abruptly turned into Kestrel, and she bonked against him, almost knocking Terras from his perch on Kestrel's shoulder. Peering up and up, she stared at that stark face staring down at her as if she were the only living person on the planet. As if she mattered.

No man had ever looked at her that way.

She froze.

"What has happened to the Made One?" Kestrel said to Luciana.

"Hello?" Sybi waggled her fingers at him. "I'm right here."

He clasped a hand around her wrist. "You have been gardening."

"Playing with Mother." Sybi nodded solemnly.

"Mother Tree," he said.

"I had no idea this would..." Luciana's voice trailed off.

Kestrel nodded. "I will take her home."

"She needs to eat," Luciana said.

"Chocolate!" Sybi smacked her lips. "The colors are so bright!"

Kes chuckled and brushed his lips across Luciana's cheek. "I do not think food is the solution, though washing her hands may help."

Luciana sighed. "I guess her specialness extends to much."

"That it does," he said.

Fukkes stood in the Ocular, peering down at Earth to check on the eleven comatose bodies they had chosen for their Earthian existence. The planet teetered on chaos as their leaders fell silent, an unfortunate side effect of the Cabal's plan. While the Earthians' flesh lived, each Cabal member would transfer their Essence into their "new" Earthian body, the original's Essence destroyed.

From what he observed, the bodies were being well cared for, with numerous doctors and attendants exercising the flesh so it did not atrophy. Leaving their new bodies in the hands of Earthians was a risk, but a sound one.

He tweaked the dials on the Ocular to the small country of Iceland. A curious place with frequent eruptions.

Noise from the corridor, and he switched off the Ocular's screen.

A senior aide burst into the room. "Comstat! Comstat, this is important!"

Annoying, and highly unusual. At the Ocular, no less, a sacred space in Alchemic City, or it was to most Alchemics. Little was sacred to Fukkes other than Mari and Xenon's globe.

The Ocular was where they harvested the Essences from the dying or newly dead women to make Made Ones. He chuckled. At least, that was its original purpose.

His thoughts turned to the three wayward sisters. Problem children.

As the three had proven unsatisfactory, perhaps it was time to pull a few fit and healthy women from Earth to Eleutia. A challenging and interesting experiment considering the Overseers' deemed a Made One must be near death in their Earthian lives. The Cabal had always chosen malleable women who accepted the transition with ease. Many reveled in it. None had challenged the Cabal until the trio of sisters had arrived. All annoying women.

But perhaps a healthy Made One would react in unique ways to Eleutia. Maybe she would have a lover on Earth, and children. Fukkes pictured the woman's fury at being pulled away from them.

Learning she could never return? To never see her lover or children again?

Would her reaction be fury? Fear? Sorrow? A rich idea for research.

Ah, yes—the fellow standing before him, tremorous with excitement.

"Well?" Fukkes said.

The aide bowed and lifted the papers in his fisted hand. "Comstat, we have highly disturbing energy readings within the CastOuts domain.

"Explain." The aide was a verbal dawdler. "Be brief."

"We can measure the output," the aide said. "It will spike, and we catch it, but then it vanishes—poof!—defeating even our AI. Stranger still, we cannot decipher *what* is producing the energy."

Fukkes wound his arm around the man's shoulder and led him from the Ocular.

"Come," Fukkes said. "Let us talk in my rooms."

"Of course, Comstat." The aide quivered.

How pleasing.

Back at his rooms, he led the man to the dining table, and the aide spread the energy printouts across the surface.

"Do you see?" the man said, pointing to several dots on the printout.

Fukkes ran his finger across the readings. The energy source emitted more gigawatts than even an uncloaked Keystone. No Land had no shielding.

According to the marks on the topo map, the spikes appeared haphazard, with no energy trails left behind, vanishing from one location and reappearing in another. Teleportation made sense, yet the spikes were too intense for a single, biped teleporter.

"What could it be, Comstat?" The aide said.

An enigma. "Nothing to disturb us at present, but keep a close watch, understood? I suspect it is a creation of the CastOuts, perhaps a weapon to be used against us. Chart the thing's movements with more precision and discover a definable pattern. Once we under-stand the pattern, we will take it down."

"Of course, Comstat," he said, gathering his papers.

"Leave them," Fukkes said. "I wish to study them further."

"As you will." The aid bowed and backed out of the room.

Fukkes was fascinated by the energy surges, far more than he had revealed to the flunky. They appeared near the Made One Sybelle's landing point, her death staged.

He scratched his cheek. The woman lived, he had known that for days, though other Cabal members had yet to puzzle the pieces together. The energy surges must relate to her.

The question was how and why.

The Made Ones Breena and Kitlyn had proven disruptive. Kitlyn was intended to die, but she did not. She was also intended to mate with the Cat Alpha, yet instead mated with a Wolf, a powerful one of that eternally fractious Clan.

Worse, the second sister had mated with the Cat Alpha. That one was a willful bitch. Infuriating. Now the third sister... He suspected she would further complicate his plans, though he was unsure how.

Fukkes' frustration grew.

He despised things in threes. The number's natural harmonic resonance could transform the sisters into something new. From the moment of their simultaneous arrival, each had gnawed at his mind.

Ironic, for Fukkes had been impressed when their Alchemic Apprentice Calix had noted their suitability for transformation. Each had looked ideal, strong in their youth before illness and injury stole their health. Their renewed bodies would be marvels of engineering, and the Cabal had moved on Calix's suggestion and drawn the sisters' Essences from Earth.

If he had predicted their troublesome natures... But he had gone along with the plan. Been enthusiastic, in fact.

The third sister must have a connection to the odd energy spiking from No Land. The hours spent altering the woman's physical form—an enjoyable experiment—had been a wasted effort. Nothing for it.

Sybelle must die. *Soon.*

Mari's light in her damaged Essence ball drew him.

"Do you agree, my darling?" Naturally, Mari agreed.

The third sister's death would shove the two remaining sisters off their pedestals. Their mates, as well. Perhaps the CastOuts would suffer her loss, too. All in all, a delightful scenario.

As Kestrel escorted the sweet syr to her nest, he found her relaxed and jocular, even singing a few bars about a stairway to heaven. The Eleutian soil had made her blissed, yet it also eased a tightness in her, relaxed her.

Terras hopped from his shoulder to hers and rubbed his head against her chin.

As they walked, Sybelle chattered about her sisters, her Lala, the ponies she wanted to ride, and the mistrals she wanted to fly.

Terras told him that she was blissed.

"I know, my friend."

Ignore her, Terras said.

How could he? Her voice wove a melody to his soul.

Kes carried her up the stairs to her nest and stood Sybelle on the platform. He did not release her waist, uncertain if she could stand upright on her own. The platform's enclosure was normally safe, but in her current state, she might tumble over the side.

Sybelle stared up at him, a look of wonder on her face. That surprised him. Not her expression, but that he grasped it. He often struggled reading faces, the emotions expressed eluding him due to his childhood and youth with Enala. He had met no other human until he met Marcos in his late teens.

Yet reading Sybelle came naturally, though why she would peer at him in that way mystified him.

In a swift change, her face grew thunderous. "You kissed Luciana."

He opened his mouth to answer, but before he could voice a word, she continued.

"I mean, people on Earth kiss in different ways for a greeting, but in America, we generally don't kiss when we say farewell, not unless it's a relative or lover."

"Luciana is like a daughter to me."

Her brows beetled. "You're the same age!"

"No. We are not."

She took a deep breath, thrusting her hands onto her hips.

Her fury, contrasted with her unsteady body and unfocused eyes, charmed him.

"You didn't greet *me* with a kiss." She sighed.

Kissing was a natural thing, yet to the sweet syr, it seemed to be of great importance.

Like the click in a game of puzzler, he understood—by kissing Luciana, he had hurt Sybelle's feelings.

Had he kissed her, her scent filling his lungs, her flesh touching his, he would have desired more from this strange unworldly creature who created a powerful want inside him.

That want... An alien thing.

He understood sexual desire from his time with Urcel, but that had ended in disaster years ago. His mind grasped emotional love, had seen it countless times in others, had observed Breena and Gato's mating, a beautiful thing. But in his years on Mother Terra, no man nor woman had inspired that response in him.

And yet Sybelle... Given his makeup, he had no idea what acting on that desire would unleash. Or if his feelings resembled "love."

He must tread with care to avoid his desire for Sybelle becoming destructive. Enala had drummed that into him.

His foster mother had trained him to hold his hungers in check, to imprison desire and shackle want, her brutal ways successful. Enala said he was too powerful to release his emotions on the world.

But this want was different, more like a life-affirming call that...

"Say something," Sybi said.

"I do not want to talk."

Her eyes widened, and then she smiled and swooped in and took his lips.

When Sybi touched her lips to his, as gentle as spring rain, she lost all words.

Pleasure rippled through her, and he gripped her waist and lifted her so they were eye to eye. She wrapped her legs around his hips, her arms around his neck, and reveled.

He was solace and warmth, rebirth and renewal. Her lips parted and his tongue explored, as the world spun fast and emotion poured from him, cresting over and over. His steel arms clasped her close so she did not fragment into a million pieces of light.

Within her, a glowing tree limb formed and spiraled outward. She could *see* it. A hawk rose in the distance clutching a golden rope that wove of its own accord toward her branch.

They touched, an electrical jolt spearing her.

She shoved away from Kestrel and stumbled backward, gripping the platform rail. If the elements had completed twining, would she be *attached* to him? To Kestrel?

She clutched the rail in a death grip. "What *was* that?"

Kestrel cupped her cheek, and she leaned into it. "Come, sweet syr."

Comfort. Desire. Protection. "Kes."

"Come."

He drew her inside to the kitchen sink, and as if she were a child, he washed and dried her hands.

Terras hopped from her shoulder to the counter and peered up at her. *Why did you stop?*

She felt both euphoric and nauseated. "I don't know."

You do, sweet syr.

Wishing Terras would leave her alone, she squeezed her eyes tight. "I was scared."

Terras said no more, and she opened her eyes to see Terras atop Kes' shoulder as he made for the door.

"Kes?" she said, mind a muddle.

He didn't turn, but his hands fisted open and closed, his chaotic emotions piercing her fog.

"Get some rest, Sybelle," he said. "I will get you gloves so you can continue to work with the plants."

When he closed the door behind him, she was bereft.

Still shaken from Sybelle's kiss, Kestrel sat before the vidscreen for a conference with the Cats and Wolves, intending to devise a search plan for the power station.

Whatever had scared Sybelle during their kiss, he had felt it, too. A great power stirred within him, a part of him. And yet not.

Rafe and Kitlyn popped onto a screen and seconds later, Gato and Breena appeared on a second one. He greeted them, wondering how it would feel to have Sybelle by his side. As a friend, a partner, a lover. Strange ideas that had never entered his head. Why would they? He needed no partner.

"Kes?" Gato said.

"Humm." He pulled his thoughts to the meeting. "Any news about the power station's placement?"

"No," Rafe said.

"Given all the trees on Eleutia are connected, Mother might know its location," Breena said.

"*Poosha*," Gato said to his mate. "Mother is elusive. We cannot simply walk up to her and ask. She must manifest first. The only Eleutian she has spoken with is you."

"Mother has spoken in my head, and Luciana's, but never in a dialogue." Kes deliberated about revealing Sybelle's part. But as his closest allies and Sybelle's sisters, he did not believe she would object. "Sybelle has heard Mother."

"We know," Kitlyn said. "Mother Tree has called to her."

Kes nodded. "I do not know if Mother Tree speaks in words to

Sybelle."

"Mother is in her head?" Rafe said. "That is a powerful thing."

"I agree," Gato said.

Kes scraped a hand down his cheek. "After Sybelle's Essence was infused into her new flesh, I believe Mother remained with her in the Making pod."

"How strange," Kit said.

"Mother's powers blanket our continent," Rafe said.

"Perhaps beyond even that," Kes said.

"But Sybelle has not physically met her?" Gato said.

"No." Kes shook his head. Sybelle should be present, an omission he would correct in the future.

"Perhaps your sister can ask Mother Tree about the station." Gato looked at Breena.

Kes had thought the same thing. "I will suggest it. But we can ask nothing until Mother Tree appears to your sister. That may be today or in a week or a month."

"Soon," Kitlyn said as the large coywolf, Paulo, climbed onto the couch and curled up beside her, resting his head on her thigh. "It'll be soon."

Breena gave her sister a long look, then said, "How's the water situation progressing, Rafe?"

Rafe grinned. "Well. WolfHome was the first to drink the purified water. But we have spread word through our Compass True network, and many Clans have begun desalinating seawater."

"CatHome's desalination has been successful," Gato said. "We exclusively drink that water, and our troff and drass makers are using the desalinated water as well."

Rafe chimed in. "The mountains' ilaberry winemakers have been reticent, as they use their spring water for the kamla and wine. They have agreed to try collecting rainwater for the next two months as a compromise. From Tilde's tests, our rainwater does not pervert the opossum or mice reproduction or for that—"

"Well and good for rainy regions," Gato said. "But what about those living in arid locales?"

Kestrel's focus was off, his mind wandering to his sweet syr's kiss. *His* sweet syr. He thought of her that way. As if she belonged to him, not that he believed in ownership of others. And yet...

"You interrupted me," Rafe said to Gato, steel coloring his voice.

Gato's lids fell to half-mast. *That* expression he understood. His friend would either make a joke or shoot an arrow.

"Forgive me, oh great Alpha," Gato said.

Rafe burst out laughing. "Too much alpha-ing, eh?"

Gato began laughing, too, as did their mates.

Their laughter delighted him. These were people he cared for, and they were happy. "Continue, Rafe."

His friend gave him a nod, his eyes warm. "Tilde also learned another crucial point, a positive one about the poisoned water. Whatever hormone the Alchemics used to dose it, the effects dissipate after two weeks or so, and the hormone preventing female births becomes inert. Not that I am prepared to test that on our women."

"That's great news!" Breena said. "Though you're smart to hold off testing on your women."

Kes agreed. "Good to know. We CastOuts are using desalinated water as well, piping it up from the sea and pumping it through our settlement. Only our outliers deep in the forest do not use it, but rainwater instead." Either way, many CastOuts were unable to reproduce. Another Alchemic "gift."

A child. The want stirred within him. He did not know if he could father one or not. What creature would his hatchlings be? Kes shuddered.

"Kes?" Kitlyn said. "Are you okay?"

"I am well, Kitlyn."

Gato knew his secrets, while Rafe suspected. Though many CastOuts knew of his ability to fly, none were privy to all his parts.

He was unlike any other living being on Eleutia. *That* he knew only too well.

CHAPTER

EIGHT

After her incendiary kiss with Kestrel, Sybi had not spoken with him for days, and she'd only seen him from a distance. She was frustrated by their lack of interaction but understood ramping up for war was no simple thing.

Kes seemed to be everywhere—directing men building new observation platforms, discussing supplies with the head cook, observing the village's youth in drills.

She continued work on *Rhiannon*, struck by what emerged from her pen. Her sketches were not the same as in her original novel. While many of the illustrations matched, often people she did not recognize or mysterious buildings would appear on the page without conscious volition.

After supper, she hunted down Kestrel to show him what she had drawn. She found him in his aerie's command center, posed with two other men over maps spread out on a large table.

When he spotted her in the doorway, he walked over.

"What do you think?" Sybi opened her sketchbook so he could review her drawings.

"These are excellent," he said.

91

"Will they help?" she said.

"Yes."

"Here." She ripped out the pages and handed them to him, having made duplicates.

He took them in silence, but after a long pause said, "You kissed me."

She could say she had been drunk on Mother. A coward's way. "I wanted to."

"I wished to, as well."

Was that a glimmer of humor in his eyes? So hard to tell because the spark vanished as quickly as it had come. She smiled. "See you later."

"I am glad we did," he said as she turned to leave. "It was—"

"Kes!" a man shouted from across the room. "We have an Alchemic hover heading toward No Land."

"Go," she said.

Kes blew out a breath. "I must." He nodded and walked away.

Beneath Sybi's pen, a cluster of trees appeared, along with a woman in a wicker mask. She was new, and Sybi continued sketching to enter the zone where the magic happened.

A feather brushed her cheek. "Terras, behave."

The bird's touch had evoked her kiss with Kestrel, and she brushed a hand across her mouth. It tingled with memory. That kiss, seeing the glowing branch, the hawk holding a golden rope.

Was that vision from her imagination?

Perhaps. After all, she'd been soil-drunk, as Luciana called it. Yet her gut said it was real.

Terras began to walk across her sketchbook.

"Stop."

You are daydreaming.

Sybi scratched his back, between his shoulder blades, and she would swear he purred. She was tired, her days full. She'd talked with Kit and Bree daily, reminiscing and yapping about nothing and everything, thrilled to be together again. She'd also amped up time spent on her martial arts forms, as well as learning to wield a sword from Asher. But her biggest daily challenge was searching for Mother, her internal compass lending urgency. The routine had become rote—she would hear Mother's call and search the forest, never finding her. After thirty minutes or so, the call would fade to silence.

That first time Terras had accompanied her. When he was with Kes, Sybi searched alone, though when she returned, she would often find Terras prowling about her aerie. She never knew how he got inside.

Terras was a mystery, one of the few living things on Eleutia that remained opaque. He was a symbiont animal, true. But he felt like *more*, though she didn't understand what that "more" was. No matter, for Terras remained unique, Eleutia felt real, and Earth was becoming a dream.

Daily, she partnered with Luciana to work in the greenhouses, wearing gloves to avoid a repeat of her drunken episode, although she sometimes cheated. Only when she was alone and for short periods, Sybi would dig her fingers into Eleutia's soil and imbibe Mother Tree's energy.

Terras tapped her arm. "Huh?"

Out the window, the sun hovered bright overhead, Terras' reminder she was about to miss mid-day meal. Off she went, and both she and Terras enjoyed spending time with Luciana, Asher, and Pedro, as well as others, while Terras gleaned tidbits and crumbs.

Belly full, Mother Tree called, as she had been doing for days. Off she went, Terras atop her shoulder, and into the forest she was coming to know well.

Come to me, child. Come.

Mother's voice spiraled down to her very marrow. As it had in the pod. That voice, or rather a chorus of voices woven into a singular one, had kept her sane while enclosed in that glass coffin.

An hour later, she swiped a bandana over her face and neck, her body weary as she climbed another hill to the sea cliffs.

Marcos disapproved. The CastOuts' great healer worried for her as he watched her frustration grow. A wise, kind man, Marcos failed to understand her compulsion. Choice did not enter into it.

She might be tired, but the usual perfect peace wrapped Sybi in joy. She paused to breathe in the crisp air. The trees whispered unknown, but comforting words, while the ferns and other low growth would tickle her ankles or wave in greeting. A favorite madronis tree bent a branch as she passed, and she ran her hands across the smooth, cool bark.

Atop another rise, leaning on her walking stick, she watched the froth of waves below. Beautiful. A sigh. Time to head home.

Sybi began to descend when a man stepped onto the path. She jerked to a halt, Terras squawking his disapproval.

The man, built like a bull, wore tight-fitting jeans and a green t-shirt, and he carried a large pack of twigs on his back. He should be a CastOut she hadn't met, as intruder sensors ringed all of No Land.

Yet her neck prickled, and the trees' hum changed to discordant notes. The guy didn't belong. Or maybe she was being fanciful.

The man waved a greeting and headed toward her. Wary, senses heightened, she put on a smile and returned the wave. As he neared, his looks startled her further, he was that beautiful.

His long blonde hair was tied in a queue which emphasized the perfect angles of his face and his sky-colored eyes. Though her fingers itched to sketch him, she tasted ugliness beneath his pretty facade.

Then he smiled.

Shit! His faceted crystal teeth gleamed in the light shining through the trees. Her shiver was unavoidable, but she forced herself to stand her ground.

The man bobbed a nod. "Greetings, Made One."

"Hello. I'm—"

"Sybelle." His smile widened. "I Made you."

Another shudder. It wasn't just his teeth, but his whole

demeanor. Creepy as hell. "What do mean, you made me?"

He gestured like a courtier of old into a bow. "*I* drew your Essence from Earth. *I* created your flesh. *I* infused that Essence within you. It was *I* who gave you the spark of life."

The CastOuts despised all Alchemics, in particular the Cabal of Eleven who had created them all, according to Luciana. Alchemics had designed and performed monstrous experiments on pregnant women and their children, often without the child's or woman's knowledge. A tasteless drug here or a DNA tweak there, according to Marcos, born from women imprisoned in Alchemic City.

Despicable experiments. Yet when the Alchemics noted the "imperfections" of their failures, they forced the child's biological parents to cast their children into the wilderness. Most died.

The particular Alchemic standing before her was a smug bastard. "Why are you in No Land?"

"My name is Fukkatsu," the Alchemic said, ignoring her question. "You must call me Fukkes. Everyone does. I am Overlord of all Eleutia."

Stopping her snort in time, Sybi gripped her walking stick tight. He was here for her, and she doubted it was for a hug.

"You appear less aggressive than your siblings," Fukkes said. "That will make my work easier."

"Your work?"

His hideous smile reappeared, and she wanted to run screaming. She would not. *Kit and Bree, give me your inner strength.*

"Sad to say, you cannot live." Fukkes pressed a finger to his chin. "That is unfortunate, as the making process is long and tedious. But it must be done."

His focused calm amped up her fear, his chatty demeanor a sharp contrast to his lethal words. She began calculating her next move.

A laseblaster like she had seen on the practice field hung at his waist. A swift and deadly thing. If she ran, he would shoot her in the back.

No running, then. Not a chance would she make it easy for him.

Breena would know how to strike him with her walking stick, a favorite study Bōjutsu, the art of stick fighting. But Sybi was not adept at it, having focused on taekwondo, capoeira, and jujutsu. She might debilitate him enough for her to escape. Or she might die.

Great option. Not.

Sybi would keep him talking until a plan solidified. "Why kill me when you put so much work into making me?"

"Ah," Fukkes said. "But you see, I suspect you are the fulcrum, the pivotal point on which all Eleutia is depending."

Sybi laughed, though his words fell uncomfortably close to what Kestrel termed her purpose on Eleutia.

"I'm not special in the least," she said.

He winked!

"We believed you dead," he said.

Sybi took a step backward, and closer to the trees.

"But you are far more hale than a resurrected corpse," he continued. "We noted a strange energy coming from the CastOuts' cursed land, and here I am. Voila! Venturing to the source. And look who I found." He grinned.

Sybi forced another laugh. "Not me. I'm not any 'special' energy." Sybi took another step.

Talk, you bastard, talk. Most of her training was defensive, her comfort with attacking, nil. If she appealed to his gentler nature, though she suspected he did not have one, that might be a good stall. "You have a wife you love, a child you love. You're—"

"How could you know that?" His face mottled, mouth spewing spittle.

She jumped back. "I heard you talking with her, with Mari. That's her name, right?"

Fukkes eyes bugged. "You *heard?*"

Sybi had, in the pod. Not smart to mention that. Water over the dam and all that. "I did."

Shift your weight and relax your grip. Bree's oft-spoken words.

Dammit, she wanted to be rescued. But if Bree or Kit were here, they wouldn't hope for rescue. They would act. The stick was in her hand, and she prepared to strike.

As she began to swing the stick, he stepped close, too near for the stick to be effective.

"Impossible for you to know of them!" His blotchy red face purpled with fury.

"Is it?" she continued in a calm voice. One more step and she could take him down. "And yet I know your wife's name."

"My Mari and Xenon were damaged by those Anti-Made Ones. Irretrievably, and it's all because of you Made Ones!"

He struck swifter than a snake, his hands clamping around her neck.

Momentarily stunned, Sybi clawed at his hands when Bree's words pounced. *Sybs, squeeze his balls!*

"I had planned to shoot you," he said, increasing the pressure. "But this is far more satisfying. I so enjoy watching a life ebb."

Pain shot through her. Panic. Fear. No breath to catch.

Her arms went limp, Sybi closed her eyes as if she were about to faint, and sighed.

Her right hand shot between the two of them, finding its target. She crushed those twin jewels like there was no tomorrow.

Fukkes screamed, shoving her away so hard he fell backward. "You bitch!"

Sybi ran.

Her tunic grabbed from behind.

Shoving her hip to one side, she elbowed him, the momentum enabling her to swing her arm all the way around so she could grab his legs. She pulled them out from under him, taking him down.

She was free.

Run!

What? She twisted, running backward to see Fukkes flying through the air. He landed in a heap beside the tree line, and the pine who had tossed him gave her a bow, while *all* the saplings bent over the prone man, slapping him with their branches.

Stars afire. The sight awed her as mature pines bent into a downward arc closer and closer to Fukkes.

He pulled his blaster from its holster and fired at the trees. As a unit, they leaned back, and a sturdy sapling's branch smashed into Fukkes' hand, the blaster flying into the forest.

Sybi continued to back away as Fukkes reeled to a stand and staggered from the trees, face furious, crystal teeth gleaming.

"We are not done, Made One!" He thumped his chest and launched into the sky, the "wooden sticks" shooting plumes of vapor.

A jet pack.

She watched until he was a speck.

Dizzy with relief, she leaned against a redwood, who hummed comfort. She drew out her cell, and after a few fumbles, called her sisters.

"He *what*?" Kit said.

Bree's "that fucker" made Sybi smile. Just like home.

"Can you walk?" Bree said.

"My throat is killing me," Sybi said. "But I'm fine."

Kit scoffed. "Fine, eh? How about you call Kes or Marcos and get some help?"

"Yes, but, well... I thought of you guys first."

They laughed, and Bree said, "I would've done the same."

No, Bree would have called Gato, and Sybi shrugged off the twinge of jealousy her sisters always kindled. A small twinge, and she hated it as much today as she did growing up. They loved her and she, them. She was happy they had found life partners, even if it made her loneliness more acute.

"I'd better report in." She made a face. "They'll make a fuss."

"I know how you hate that, Sybs," Kit said. "But Fukkes could have killed you."

Not when surrounded by trees, it seemed.

Still shaken, Sybi fixed her mussed tunic and brushed off her pants. Twigs embellished her hair, and she finger-combed them out and re-plaited her braid.

The forest's hum again sounded serene, but it failed to soothe. No one had ever tried to *kill* her before, and she vowed to increase her time practicing her martial arts forms. Asher had offered to teach her knife fighting, as well as swordsmanship. She would accept.

Though her legs wobbled, Sybi pushed away from the redwood and searched for her walking stick. At the same time, she began to punch Kestrel's number into her phone.

Come, child.

Really? Now?

I am here...

The voice at her back, Sybi turned toward the sea, only to stumble. "Oh."

Where the land had been level moments earlier, it now formed a shallow bowl. No mist, but a circle of immense trees at least eighty feet tall towered above her. Strange trees, with smooth, poker-straight trunks topped by leaves like pom-poms, much like the African Adansonia digitata or baobab.

This was it—she was about to meet Mother Tree. She should be excited or scared or... Sybi felt numb.

Her call to Kestrel would wait.

Fukkes returned to the city with a sore shoulder, aching balls, and blind with fury. He stormed to his rooms livid at the lunatic vegetation that sprawled across this despicable planet. How dare it attack him? He ripped off the jetpack, then his clothes, and showered.

Still incensed as he dried himself off, he retrieved Mari and Xenon's box and withdrew the jagged half-globe where their Essences bobbed—two gray lights within the murky swirls.

Mari's presence calmed him, as did Xenon's, dampening his ire to where he could think.

Think he did.

Igniting the CastOuts' forest and homes could prove productive. This had occurred to him earlier, but the Cabal had vehemently nixed the idea, arguing it could alert the Overseers.

Cowards all. He was their Comstat, was he not?

He would burn the CastOuts alive. A joyful thought, enhanced by the bonus of eradicating their failed experiments. "What do you think, Mari?"

To hear her voice just one more time.

But she would not speak. Could not. She was...

A knock at the door.

"Go away!"

The knock came again, more insistent.

Could these people do nothing *themselves?*

He slipped on a robe and walked to the door, flinging it open. "What?"

Gabin stood before him, frowning like the pessimist he was and waving a torn piece of paper. "There is a spike in the energy again within No Land. One near nuclear levels. What do you say to *that?*"

Fukkes shrugged, his thoughts on the impending conflagration. "I am working on the problem."

"What can—"

"Get out." He slammed the door shut and sauntered to the cool-freeze, withdrawing a bottle of ilaberry wine, snagging a glass, and carrying both to the couch where he poured a hefty drink. Given the Overseers' watchfulness, he must be smart about his plan. A smile grew. Of course. Those energy spikes would make the perfect excuse, if and when the Overseers questioned him.

The situation called for Valdinine Fire.

The flame was unstoppable by water, and yet within sixty minutes, it self-extinguished. By the time the Overseers reviewed the vids, No Land and the CastOuts would be nothing but ash with no trace of the Valdinine that preceded it.

Oh, yes, he would burn the CastOuts to the ground, scorch the earth, and sear this planet to its *bones.*

When Sybi reached the monolithic trees, two of them bent their trunks to form a circular entry, a cool mist from within brushing her face. Without hesitation, she stepped inside, the trees closing behind her with a whomp.

Goddess alive, no. Smoke wisps curled upward, and the scents of ash and death overlaid the circle's charred landscape. Atop a central mound stood the remains of a small tree, its trunk bent, its few remaining branches charcoaled.

"Oh, no."

Sybi wiped her eyes, tearing from the acrid smoke, and walked toward the charred tree. As she moved across the ground, bones poked through the ash, remnants of animals caught in whatever had destroyed Mother Tree. Nearing what was left of Mother, she spotted a small creature's skeleton curled as if trying to protect itself from the flames.

"Mother?" She dropped to her knees.

Silence answered her.

Bree had described a beautiful flowering tree with waterfall branches and blue blossoms. The ache in her heart grew.

Memories assaulted Sybi, a kaleidoscope of them. Marie's terrible death. Her bullying from some circus folk. Kit's horrific accident.

Soothing murmurs rose, a surcease of sorts. Sybi blinked. "Mother?"

More memories...the pod, sharp voices, Kestrel's kiss, Fukkes teeth. She inhaled a sharp breath. Before her stood glorious Rhiannon, the beautiful world she had not created at all. Verdant fields and mighty seas, epic trees and rolling sands. Rhiannon did not *resemble* Eleutia. They were twins.

But her novel's ending was nothing like this charred, blistered earth.

Sybi opened and closed her hands as an overwhelming pressure built inside her, a raging conflict—reality battling illusion.

Seeing truth is often difficult, child. Your human eyes see, and you instantly believe.

A whirl of color.

Velvet grass covered the rise where she knelt, sunlight beaming down on the tree at its center mere inches taller than Sybi, its branches a fountain of delicate blue blossoms, while frangipani, eucalyptus, and jasmine perfumed the air. Glorious.

Sybi rose and took a step, and then another, laughter and whispers echoing in her head. She amused Mother and her guardian trees, it seemed. Standing before the blue floral veil, she raised a hand, one finger touching a glowing petal.

Come inside.

A shiver, then she parted the branched canopy to reveal the heart of Mother, and stepped forward.

A floral carpet rose to Mother's trunk, which was strong and healthy and encrusted with multicolored gems, her branches swooshing around Sybi like a fairy dance.

Mother was whole, not burnt as Sybi had "seen."

"You are well, Mother Tree?"

Yes, child. My sentinels protect me.

"What I saw..."

Was an illusion that will come to pass if I fall to the Evil Ones. Sit and find comfort.

"The trees saved me from that Alchemic, Fukkes." Sybi kneeled, bum resting on her heels, as Mother's floral bed cushioned her. "Can the trees destroy the Alchemics?"

The Evil Ones are clever. They never set their floating village among us, for they know we would destroy them. Millennia ago, when I was a sapling, all of Eleutia's trees could move at will across our world. Yet most remained rooted, and hence they became bound to Mother Terra and anchored in place. I see a question in your mind about the evil ones' power station. All I know of this is that no vegetation of any kind grows near the machine.

"What can I do? How can I help?"

Ah, Sybelle, always the caretaker, the helper. You have begun drawing our world.

"Yes. Well, Rhiannon, but yes."

Continue. Draw all, in particular their floating village. That will help at the end.

"The end?"

You will see. Your call will be answered. Did you know your Marie was mine, dear one, as are you?

"My sister? What do you mean?"

Two babes of two worlds able to bridge the scrim. World walkers.

"World walkers?" Sybi said.

You walk between worlds—Earth and Eleutia. We are parallel, and for you, the veil between our worlds is thin. You have walked Eleutia in your dreams, have you not?

"It seems I have." Remaining calm in front of Mother felt essential, yet this world-walker business was too weird, like living some Marvel plot point.

Sweet Christmas afire, she never wanted to be a special snowflake.

Sybelle.

Sound expanding, words yet no words. She pressed her hands to her ears, but the sound was *inside* her, demanding.

"Mother!"

Still here. Still waiting for your attention.

"I'm sorry." Sybi ran her hands across the cool grass, then flattened them on her thighs, trying to remain still and calm as her insides churned. "Are Kit and Bree world-walkers?"

No.

"Would you tell me about Marie, please?"

Mother trembled. *She is loved but had to pass from her physical Earthian existence, as she was not strong enough to sustain her fluid life. We grieved.*

Pain stabbed her heart. Sweet Marie. "I get why I'm here, sort of, but why are Kit and Bree on Eleutia, too?"

Mother trembled again, only this time she was laughing. *The rule of threes, kiddo. Only you can call, and when you do, you must be bound to the three.*

Sybi slumped back on her heels. This all was too strange and yet familiar, like a movie she'd seen many times. "Heaven help me, you sound like that *Matrix* woman, like... I can't remember her name."

The Oracle. What makes you so certain I am not she? Or perhaps you are The Oracle.

"Me?"

Was not Sybelle an ancient prophetess on your world?

It was Sybi's turn to laugh—Mother had quite the sense of humor. Her legs had gone numb, and she unfolded herself and crossed them in front of her. "So what am *I* supposed to do?"

The Fates demand you to seek the Kestrel. Mate with him.

The idea of Kestrel tied to her forever... Kit had explained mating and how the bond was a permanent, lifelong thing. Though Kestrel drew her in an otherworldly way, that wasn't love. Nor was it knowing a person or trusting them. She could imagine Kes' reaction. Any man would resent a lack of choice in their partner, and Kes would come to despise their irrevocable bond. Despise *her*.

Binding her life to another's terrified her, and being compelled by The Fates made her furious. Sybi would make her own choices.

"I can't, Mother."

Mother seemed to shrug. *When the time comes, you will. Ah, they track me once more. Off I go like Dorothy, eh? Scoot. You cannot be in the circle when I do so.*

In a daze, she hugged Mother, and the magical tree bent her limbs to embrace Sybi, the very definition of bliss-infused love.

Feeling a bit drunk, Sybi stepped back, prickles dotting her skin.

Hurry, child!

Sybi stumbled toward the sentinels' opening and when her feet hit the ground on the opposite side, a steamroller of energy flattened her. Pushing up, she peered over her shoulder, Mother and her sentinels were gone, the forest undisturbed.

CHAPTER

NINE

Kes and Marcos walked the fenced outdoor training ground, a large circular structure amidst the trees where the CastOut children could test their gifts in safety. Each child was accompanied by an adult CastOut, a spotter who could prevent any youngling's inadvertent self-harm or outward destruction. He and Marcos assessed the children each week as they learned to control their gifts.

They passed nine-year-old Pierce—his talent was causing others pain—who had progressed to where he could manage his ability, rather than randomly hurt others. By another redwood, four-year-old Ono flashed a smile. Unique glasses shielded eyes that x-rayed everything, and she giggled with glee as Kes picked her up and swung her around, a reminder that even CastOuts could play.

Pedro also worked with the children. Though he could not see, he was exceptional with them—a bear of a man with a gentle touch.

After greeting Pedro, Kes moved on, following the trail until he came to Broan's station. Marcos leaped from behind a tree, and Broan's porcupine quills sprouted. Fortunately, Marcos had stepped back, anticipating the boy's reaction.

"Farking Fates!" the boy shouted in frustration.

"Language." Marcos walked to the ten-year-old once the boy retracted his quills.

Broan crossed his arms wearing a mulish frown. "Sorry."

"You are making progress with your startle reflex," Marcos said. "You quilled too soon."

"An understatement." Broan kicked the dirt at his feet.

"It is not easy to master a fear response." Marcos rested his hand on the boy's shoulder. "You are moving forward."

The boy's eyes narrowed. "Slowly."

"Change can be slow," Marcos said.

"He is right, Broan," Kes said, walking up to the pair. "Mastering fear is no easy thing."

Watching the children work carved a hollow feeling beneath his breast bone, accompanied by the useless memory of Enala whipping him for one failure or another. These children were *loved*.

Marcos' hand thumped on Kes' shoulder. The healer knew and understood, and his touch comforted. He nodded his thanks.

They found Dorin, a Bear Clan cub with one-hundred times greater scent ability than his Clan members and symbiont siblings. The boy was but six, and Asher, who had issues with his extraordinary voice and hearing, was training him.

Most CastOuts were one-offs, and teaching them posed unusual challenges. Yet these classes led to sustainable lives.

Dorin had smoothed away the pine needles and other detritus so he could play his favorite game—ball and stars. He would bounce the ball and scoop up the stars. The child would play for hours while a patient Asher taught him to define and sort out scents. When not training, Dorin wore a filter in each nostril that edited out many. But once they taught Dorin's brain to differentiate and block scents, much as Asher filtered out sounds, they would count it a victory.

Marcos pounced on the boy, giving him a hug. All the villagers cherished the healer. Yet when Dorin looked at Kes, his eyes revealed fear. Kes was certain.

Kes crouched by Dorin." Are you afraid of me?"

"Not you, Alpha." The boy reached for Kes and he swooped him up.

He was no Alpha. Kes set the boy on his feet, took a knee so they were at eye level, and gentled his expression. "Tell me what you fear, Dorin."

The boy shivered. "I smell."

"A valuable gift," he said.

Dorin stomped his foot. "*No.* What I smell is bad, and I am scared."

"Let Marcos and I help. What is scaring you?"

"I do not want you to get mad at me," Dorin said, lower lip outthrust.

"Dorin," Kes said. "Whatever scent is scaring you, it is all right. Marcos and I will not be angry if you tell us." The child was six, for sky's sake. "Knowledge matters, and since the smell frightens you, I would like you to share that knowledge." A chill washed through him.

"I smell smoke. A lot of it."

Kestrel's battle ice descended, his mind clearing of all inessentials. "Can you show us the direction?"

Dorin nodded and pointed north.

In the far distance, his hawk's eyes spotted a curl of blue smoke wisping upward on the edges of No Land.

Well...*that* was different. Having flattened like a pancake as Mother disapparated, prickles raced across her flesh, her tongue thick, her head woozy. She was drunk on Mother.

If she didn't sober up, she'd never find her way back to the village. She scrubbed her hands up and down her arms and face. What time was it? Had hours passed? Or merely minutes? She was *starved.*

Sybi sat up. Surrounded by the forest—no trace of Mother—she breathed deep. From behind a tree, two wide eyes peeked out and blinked. A gray rabbit with enormous ears, their insides pink. Too adorable.

"Hello, Mr. Bunny! Or is it Mrs.?"

Climbing to her feet, she wobbled, disappointed when the bunny hopped away. She began to walk, leaning against trees, shaking her head to clear it, and feeling as if she was getting more and more drunk. Giggling as she passed a madronis, the tree dipped a leafy branch toward the ground where dappled light shone on her walking stick's bronze head. She retrieved it and hugged the tree in thanks.

"Wish you could teleport me home." Crap. Her words were slurred.

The stick helped. Sybi was happy to be alive, near euphoric. Too euphoric to unravel Mother Tree's words.

Did it matter? Naw. She wanted to sing and dance, draw and paint. "Wheeeeee!"

She twirled and whirled, flailing against a redwood in drunken delight. Reason had left the building.

"Onward!" She pointed her stick forward and grinned as she wove through the wood, uncaring of her destination, soaring even higher with the forest's welcoming voices. Some trees touched her, while others bowed, and the mighty redwoods projected such love her eyes burned.

But moments later, the air sharpened, the trees trembling, their treesong a jagged, dissonant melody. In her head, shrieks. Distant, but powerful.

She looked north, toward the source of the screams. Fear gut-punched her.

The fear wasn't her own.

The trees, the forest, it was terrified.

Propelled to near-sobriety, she swallowed hard, noticed animals scurrying beneath leaves, deer flew by, and squirrel, running in mad flight, and to her left, a raccoon, frozen, a statue of terror.

Sybi forced herself to stay calm because something was *very* wrong. Think. Think. She'd find Kestrel, Luciana, the villagers. They needed to know something bad was happening. She ran around a large redwood and headed for the path.

The acrid scent of smoke bit her nose.

Fire.

The forest was burning.

And the mind-splitting screams began.

Kestrel glided above the treetops until he found the fire's source. As he had suspected, this was no normal forest fire, not with the smell of phosphorus soaking the air, a loathsome garlicky smell. He dropped lower. A flaming gel-like substance stuck tenaciously to bark and leaf, much like the fire the day Sybelle had awakened.

Since that day, he had learned much. Valdinine Fire was tenacious and far more deadly than any natural blaze. The gel clung to where it landed, devouring all in its path, and was unaffected by water until it burned itself out.

They had done this, but why? And why now?

The Alchemics never wanted open engagement, which was why they moved their city when attacked. Perhaps Sybelle or Mother Tree had been the prompt. Or an incident unknown to Kes. The "why" mattered little.

All he cared about was saving the forest and the lives within.

He turned, banked, and flew home, transforming to human on arrival.

Marcos, Asher, and Luciana met him, as did the fire marshal and numerous Sgiath, and they discussed methods to douse the fire.

Back in his aerie's command center, he deployed the bulk of the Sgiaths to protect the village. It was possible the Alchemics would send ground troops as well.

"Done," Asher said.

"We must get the children out," Luciana said.

"Yes," Kes said. "We have sounded the alarm for all to return to the village. We cannot use water. It will not defeat the gel."

"We need to deploy Urich to the command center," Marcos said, waving a hand. "Our comm equipment must be protected or we will be in trouble."

"We can take it to the underground lab," Asher said.

"Too much time wasted hauling too much gear," Kes said. "Peter and Elmer can protect the village."

"Their shields will hold." A tear dripped onto the fire marshal's cheek. "Who would possibly—"

'The Alchemics, of course." Marcos said, bitterness souring his words. "When they offered the Bears gelfire to eradicate the cyst-worm infestation, the Bears refused. No Clan would unleash such a vile destroyer of life."

"Sand will douse it," Asher said.

"Shall we haul it from the desert?" Marcos frowned as he stared at the map of No Land. "Not enough time before the fire spreads."

Like a chime of crystal, Kestrel saw the way.

Luciana screamed and fell to her knees in agony.

Kes!

The cry pinged Kes' mind. Not Luciana, but Sybelle.

"Call Sybelle!" he barked.

Marcos did so, but shook his head. "Voicemail every time."

Asher held a weeping Luciana, and Kes knelt before her. "What is this, Luciana?"

"The trees' fear and pain." Her hands slapped over her ears. "It is in my head."

His sweet syr must feel the same. Or worse. "I must go," he said to Marcos. "Here is what we do."

As Kes laid out his plan, a buzzing sounded from above. He raced outside. Far in the distance, a clump of small flying machines buzzed the skies, too small to be piloted by a human. He watched in horror as a machine sprayed the forest, exploded in a fireball, and dropped to earth to enhance the conflagration.

Blind with fury, Kes transformed and took to the skies, soaring until he flew far above the metal machines. As he dove toward them, the cluster differentiated into singular entities spraying liquid death.

He attacked, ripping them apart with beak and talon before they could release the gel. But there were too many for him to effectively destroy, and Kes streaked back toward the village to fly above the treeline in search of his sweet syr.

His Sybelle searched daily for Mother, and Mother Tree had recently appeared. He knew that much. But *where*?

Back and forth, again and again, searching for Sybelle as flames crawled nearer to the village. Sybelle must be terrified, alone, with screams of pain echoing inside her. Where was she?

Sybi lay prone on the forest floor, her cheek resting on a bed of moss, legs sprawled across exposed tree roots, the forest's wails of pain and shrieks of fear draining her. But her ears heard waves crashing against the shore. The cliff face wasn't far.

To live, she must leave the forest and head toward the sea to her left. How?

Impossible to stand. She couldn't get to her hands and knees without collapsing in mental agony. Accompanied by the trees' horrid screams, she stretched out her arms, wrapped her hands around a tree root, and dragged herself forward. Next, she dug her fingers into a clump of moss and pulled. Again and again. She aimed for the waves, fingers digging, toes pushing, inching forward with blind purpose. Staying still meant death.

The acrid smell worsened, as did the choking smoke. Tears bathed her face, her eyes nearly useless. With dogged determination, she pushed and pulled toward the cliffs. The cliff path, rocky and barren of trees, would not burn.

Animal screams mingled with the trees' shrieks, a horrific symphony. She coughed, choked on the smoke and the pain.

The sun dimmed. A cloud. Or maybe a plume of smoke.

Sybi reached forward and pulled again, slicing her knee on a jagged rock.

There. A break in the trees, and in the distance, the sea.

She could do this.

For a moment, a sea breeze cleared the bitter air of smoke.

Pushing up on her palms, she moved to get her legs beneath her and stand. A spike of pain sent her to her knees.

She crawled again.

Redwoods and madronis, ferns and bluebells would burn. So would rabbit and deer, cougar and coyote, bobcat and mouse. All would die.

Coughing, Sybi rested her forehead on her arms. Too much.

Yet she was close, the sea louder.

She forced her fisted hands to release each finger and grip the soil, to pull forward again, and she managed to reach a promontory high above the sea, where the sun beat down and the waves crashed. Behind her, flames ate the stately redwoods that had stood for thousands of years.

Shelter. She'd find a protected spot. Perhaps she'd climb down the escarpment. Slowly, of course, but a necessary gamble.

Black clouds boiled overhead. She squinted. No, not clouds, the sky so blue it hurt her eyes. *Birds.* Hundreds and hundreds of birds soared and swooped above, with one far above the others plummeting straight downward. As the bird came closer to where she lay, it grew and grew. So large, she could barely take it in. Gods in heaven, what was that thing?

She froze.

A cloud of dust momentarily hid the Suburban-sized hawk that landed in a clump of tall grasses by the cliff's edge.

She blinked repeatedly as the dust settled, yet the hawk failed to decrease in size. Wait. Was that *Terras* riding the hawk's shoulder?

The bird folded its wings and walked from the tall grass on *human* legs. Its muscled arms were anthropoid as well, though its chest and hips were fully feathered, its magnificent steel-blue and russet head of...

Sybi sucked in a smoky breath.

Kestrel. Whether bird or man, he *felt* the same even with his round avian eyes. His beak was a startling yellow with a curved black tip, his feathers the colors of his human hair. Or would it be vice versa?

This *form* was one of Kes' secrets, and he had revealed it to her. A precious gift. Though his legs and arms remained human, from head to stunning tail feathers, he was all bird, his wings and back that gorgeous blue and russet dotted with black.

Goddess alive, he was glorious.

He lifted his arms toward her, palms up.

Sybi took both hands, and he pulled her to him and held her close for long, long moments, his soft feathers against her cheek incredible. Then he tightened his arms, black eyes bright, and leaped into the skies.

Too overcome to appreciate the magic of it all, she nuzzled his feathered chest as the screams and pain melted away.

As Kes flew far from the conflagration, his sweet syr began to relax.

Thank Father Sky he had found her in time.

She began to pet his neck, the only human to ever dare touch his feathers. Where her fingers stroked, he tingled. An odd reaction, new and fresh. He liked it.

Kes' ability to compartmentalize had served him well over the years. His Falcon brothers and sisters, the CastOuts, the Alchemics, running the camp, preparing for war—all fit well into separate compartments. That was how he lived his life.

Until Sybelle.

When thoughts of his sweet syr intruded, the compartments jumbled, his attention blurring from that of fire-and-war to her. As if she was his center, his compass. Had it begun when they had kissed—the tug a living thing that reached for him, only to stop when she had pulled away. Another strangeness he failed to understand.

Kes dove toward Singing Rock aware of how desperately he wanted her. Her energy. Her life affirmation. Her touch. More. There was more, but this jumble of feelings remained just that, a jumble.

Singing Rock appeared and he plunged.

When Kestrel landed them feather gentle and stood her on her feet, Sybi closed her eyes to revel in the silence.

Long moments later, she took in the enormous rock where they perched, its towering spire ending in its "fist" where she stood, a stone giant challenging the skies. Forest surrounded the pillar, and far in the distance, smoke smudged the blue sky.

A whooshing sound made her turn. The man Kestrel stood near her on the rock, proud, wearing loose cargo pants, naked from the waist up except for his baldric, his bronzed chest sweat-sheened in the afternoon light. He was breathtaking.

Beside her on the rock, Terras hopped onto her shoulder and began to croon.

"Thank you," she said to him, unwilling to broach the elephant on the rock. "How did you know?"

"I saw Luciana's pain and heard your cry."

She hadn't cried out. At least, not aloud.

He strode to her, folding her in his arms, and she wound her arms around his neck. "Thank you."

They stood for long moments, silent, breathing each other in, and she pressed her cheek to his heart, its beat soothing. His scent wove through her, rich and earthy.

Had she ever felt this secure? This cherished?

"I will always keep you safe, sweet syr," he said, nuzzling her hair.

When he stepped back, she spotted three blue-steel feathers that poked from his now-human hair, stood on tiptoe, and brushed her fingers across a silky surface. A feather fluttered to the ground, and she picked it up, tucking it into her jeans' pocket.

"You should be with your people," she said.

"*Our* people. I am where I should be."

"What now?" A sudden awkwardness pushed her hands into her back pockets.

Terras squawked, as if in on some joke.

"You will soon see," was all Kestrel said.

He strode to the center of the spire's fist and dropped to his knees, placing his palms on the rock, forehead touching its surface, eyes closed.

Sybi had no idea what he was doing, but sat beside him and waited as he remained that way for more than twenty minutes. When he finally rocked back on his heels, hands on thighs, back bowed, brow dotted with sweat, he appeared exhausted.

"Are you all right?" she said.

He nodded, eyes unfocused.

Sybi looked to the east. The fire had grown, but a huge iridescent bubble arced over the CastOuts' village, with another smaller bubble to its left. "What are those, Kes?"

He stared east, unmoving. "Peter and Elmer. Each can throw up shields the Alchemics have yet to breach. They will protect our village and the comm lines if the fires near."

"Can other CastOuts do that?"

"Not that we know of."

He closed his eyes, lips moving as if in prayer.

In the silence, she searched for Mother Tree but found herself popping with too much nervous energy. She ceased, unsurprised at Mother's silence, for the air had turned electric, her skin itching with prickles.

Kes released a long sigh.

"Kes?" she said.

"Now we wait."

"For what?"

He shook his head.

"Did you do magic?" she said.

"No." Lines of exhaustion were carved beside his lips, his eyes bloodshot.

"You don't look well," she said.

"I will be, sweet syr."

"Can others transform, I mean, like you?"

"Not that I am aware of, though Pedro can fly."

"I know him. He's Asher's best friend, a big, burly guy. He's also—"

"Blind. Yes."

"Does he become a bird like you?"

"He retains his human form."

Far in the distance, bursts of flame shot from the forest, greedy for more to consume. Her breath hitched. "Kestrel...the forest."

"Patience, sweet syr. We can do little, but my friends can do much as you will see...*now*." He leapt to his feet and pointed.

To the west, a black smudge darkened the sky, undulating closer and closer, like a giant wave too large to comprehend. The smudge became a cloud, its sinuous movement seeming coordinated as it swooped and dove in a majestic dance.

She didn't have Kes' eyesight, but she'd swear the cloud began to differentiate.

The vast rippling cloud closed on them and became thousands, perhaps millions, of birds—hawks and eagles, sparrows and finches, colonies of seagulls and murders of crows.

Helmeted men were woven into the flock, as well, riding gliders that resembled falcons. She had seen a glider before, but far distant. They came closer, and she saw large pouches dangling from each bird's talons, with larger sacks strapped to the gliders.

Kes raised his arms in greeting. "Stand back, sweet syr."

One minute he was human and the next—half-man, half-bird. Even her enhanced eyes hadn't caught the change.

"You're going with them," she said.

He nodded.

"You'll take me with you."

He shook his head, stalked across the rock to Terras, and extended a wing.

Sybi ran after Kes. "I have to come, Kes. I have to see. *Please.*"

Terras hopped on to Kestrel's wing and climbed to his shoulder.

He does not want you in pain.

Kes bent his knees for takeoff.

"Please, Kes," she said, voice soft, knowing he would catch her words. "I need this. Take me with you."

He nodded, exhaling what sounded like a chuff of frustration, then folded her into his arms and lifted off.

The swarm followed Kes' lead, and though screams of pain and fear grew in her head, but this time Sybi was better prepared and managed to push the agony to the background. Horrific music, but tolerable.

Kes steered the swarm toward the fire, the avians blanketing the skies, and with each stroke of his incredible wings, the air warmed.

The Alchemics had done this, and she bet the man called Fukkes was the assault's engineer. They were fools, for this sudden attack on the CastOuts would only amplify Eleutia's anger and resentment, adding fury and fodder to the impending war.

Cocooned in safety, Kestrel's strong arms about her, she rested her head on his shoulder. Though the pain in her head increased, it had a cottony feel, as if the mass of birds and men surrounding them was some sort of buffer.

Smoke curled heavenward from numerous spots in the forest, the air thick and rancid as they neared the blaze. Many acres had been eaten by the fire. Amongst the trees, the remnants of numerous CastOut aeries teetered, charred and broken in the murky light.

The birds' murmuration widened, yet their mass still blackened the sky.

Kestrel stiffened, perhaps summoning the energy to blast orders to his avian troops.

All will be well. Terras, in comforting mode.

Kes lifted his massive hawk's head, and a voice boomed inside her. *RELEASE!*

His mental command shivered through her as both birds and men dropped their sacks, and a torrent of sand fell to the fire below.

The sandcloud boiled up and around them until she could barely breathe, and she squeezed her eyes tight.

Moments later, tree and animal shrieks faded to tolerable levels, the sand settling so she could inhale and open her eyes.

The fires were gone revealing the charred devastation below. Smoke curled from hundreds of charcoaled trees, while birds who had kept their sacks divebombed to douse any flickers of remaining flame.

A man on a powered glider maneuvered close, and he and Kes had some silent communication. How Kes had the strength she didn't know, her body an ache, her mind fogged with exhaustion.

Kes continued to coordinate the effort, as birds and men made repeated swoops across the fire-scorched land.

We are done! Many thanks.

The swarm scattered toward their nests, aeries, and homes far and near, while Kes headed toward the CastOut village. What was left of it.

TEN

Rafe, Alpha of the Wolf Clan, and Valdos, soldier of the Bear Clan, climbed the hills near WolfHome, hunting a rogue bear, their Wolf and Bear senses activated. Rafe and his trusted friend, also a member of Compass True, would catch the brown bear and return it to Valdos' Clan or, if it were irretrievably injured, would end its suffering.

The bear had attacked a child playing in his own garden, and only the mother's quick thinking had saved the boy. Given the current abundance of berries, fish, and small forest mammals, no logical reason existed for the bear to leave his mountain home and go after a child. Unless that bear was injured or ill. Though rare, bears had been known to contract rabies.

He and Valdos tracked the animal to land farmed by a wine maker but struggled to find signs of the bear's passing.

"Let us take a break." Rafe leaned against a tree, drew a bottle of drass from his pack, uncorked it, and sipped. "Ah. I needed that."

Valdos had already hunkered down, removing a jar of ale from his pack. After downing a good portion, he snorted. "Have you heard the latest about the Anti-Made Ones?"

Few knew Rafe was Compass True's leader, and though he would not lie to his friend, he would not admit the knowledge. "And what is that?"

"They say the Anti-Made Ones have joined with the Alchemics against our animal clans. To 'purify' Eleutia and begin anew."

"Begin anew?" Rafe knew Valdos' words to be true but was curious what the man had heard. Though the Antis were few in number, they had a large presence, causing much chaos and tragedy.

"We are impure, have you not heard?" Valdos said. "And so they will cleanse us all from Eleutia."

"Which makes no sense."

"Agreed." Valdos shook his head. "My cousin Gregor is an Anti. The man was always a nutter, but before the Antis, he was not a murderer."

"Painful, that, about your cousin," Rafe said.

"Both for him and the rest of our family. He is no longer welcome amongst us." His voice rumbled with pain. "We were once close."

Rafe had nothing to add. Others had voiced similar tales with the same sad ending of incomprehension and estrangement. He slid back into the silence as they packed up and again began to search for spoor and other bear sign amidst rows of vines thick with purple fruit.

A prickle on his neck, but he continued on, though he sensed eyes on them. Whoever watched could be friend or foe...or bear. A hand signal alerted Valdos to the watcher's presence.

His and Valdos' animal natures had a keen sense of smell, and the scents of bear and blood were expected. The acid sting of pure Alchemic was not.

Valdos' eyes widened, telling Rafe he had smelled the same.

A gust of wind carried the sounds of grunts accompanied by the wet rip of flesh. Valdos frowned and cocked his head, holding up a finger.

The day had warmed, and sweat trickled down Rafe's back. He

swiped his sleeve across his upper lip, then signaled Valdos to split up and circle the creature, the scents now overpowering.

The bear lumbered into view—a massive male with a huge hump feasting on a woman. When the male spotted Rafe, it hunched, protecting its kill, its brown eyes glowing an unnatural green that promised death.

No choice but to kill the animal.

Valdos lifted the lasebaster Rafe had loaned him, his distress palpable.

Rafe nodded and mouthed, *I'm sorry*.

Valdos closed his eyes as if imploring Father Sky and Mother Terra. He opened them, sighted the bear's head, and fired.

A bright clicking, but no lasefire erupted from the blaster.

What the fark. Their weapons were checked daily.

Rafe raised his spear, while Valdos tossed the blaster, drew an arrow, and lifted his bow.

The bear charged, evaded the arrow, and leapt for Rafe.

But Rafe had stepped back far enough to throw the spear. He aimed for the heart and the point landed dead on, plunging deep into the flesh to reach its target. Valdos' second arrow pierced its eye, thrusting into its brain.

Dead, the body continued its forward trajectory. Rafe side-stepped, and the bear missed him. The spray of blood did not.

"Farking Fates!"

Two hours later, Rafe stormed through the armorer's hall lit only by braziers and down the corridor to the chief armorer's office. Rafe was sticky and stank, his stomach roiling at his own smell, but he was so furious he had ridden directly to the armory while Valdos had gone to clean up. In his hand was the lousy blaster that had failed to fire.

He swung the office door open to find Talos sitting in near dark, the light of a single candle the only illumination.

"What the fark happened with this blaster?" he shouted. "It failed to fire, and—"

"I am aware," Talos said in a calm voice. "Why are you covered in blood?"

"Bear, one the Alchemics interfered with." Rafe found his calm and went to sit in the chair opposite Talos.

The chief armorer waved him off. "That chair is an antique."

"Shote that." He thumped down. "We were hunting a rogue bear." He held up the blaster. "And nothing."

The huge man with white hair crossed his massive arms. "You do not know."

"It seems not." Rafe raised a brow.

"All WolfHome tech. Or rather, all tech not created in our labs has gone dead."

"Fark me." The Alchemics had begun countermeasures.

"What of the rest of Eleutia?"

"In our Northwest Quadrant, only WolfHome is affected."

Rafe thought for long moments. "From our spies' information on the Alchemics' power reserves, I am fairly certain they cannot simultaneously disable *all* the Clans' tech. Too much power is needed. So they are doing the next best thing. We have prepared for such a scenario."

"And we are managing. The Cats' tech is up, as is the Bear Clan's."

Rafe nodded.

"But the Bobcats on the Western Shores and the Finlandia Owls are down as well."

Rafe began to laugh. "Those shoting prick-faced assholes."

Talos raised a brow, lips twitching. "Are you well, Alpha?"

"Of course. This show of 'strength' will only serve to further incense the Clans. Tell me more." Rafe removed a pile of paperwork from the nearby hassock, dragged it over, and changed seats. "Do not say this is an antique, or I will shoot you."

Talos winked, laughing, then sobered. "Our generators came online as planned, with the exception of the Keep.

"Can we fix it?"

"Our techs are working on it. Most homes have no power, and it has only served to make our people more furious."

"I assume the infirmary and other critical sites are covered."

"They are."

"If the Keep cannot be brought online, we will make do."

"True, though cold food and colder beds fail to appeal," Talos said.

"We have survived worse than this, Talos."

The armorer frowned. "Perhaps they *can* disable the entire planet."

"They cannot, or they would have already done so. This is their answering salvo to the Kestrel's escape, to dousing the No Land forest fire, and other 'slights' they perceive. A demonstration of power. Rest assured, my friend, this display will not go unanswered."

Since their return from the fire, Sybi had spent a long, exhausting week in the infirmary. Though she gave thanks her aerie had not been damaged, much of No Land had been, along with the trees and animals. Though CastOuts had been burned, thankfully none had perished. Along with about a dozen or so personal aeries, the fire had destroyed an outer command outpost, the CastOuts' fleet of six falcon gliders, and their museum holding rare and precious art and archives.

Because of the rolling tech blackouts that stretched across Eleutia, the CastOut village remained on high alert, as did all the animal clans. Most were not affected, but the nearby Wolves, the Mid-Quadrant Bears, the East Coast Bobcats, and dozens more on other continents had gone dark.

Each day, whenever she had a moment to herself, Sybi worked on *Rhiannon* with a new certainty her sketches would lead her to the Alchemics' power station. Too often, her mind fogged when she tried to sketch it, but she continued. Her mind *would* reveal the location locked inside her, and she would be damned before she gave up the quest.

The village was a hive of activity, and along with her infirmary duties, she continued to practice her sword training with Asher, her martial arts forms, and her yoga practice, along with the planting at the greenhouses. Though she only saw her friends at meals or in passing, Luciana, Asher, Pedro, and Marcos' camaraderie brought her great joy. Terras would appear, too, most often in the infirmary while she worked, and she saw Kestrel, though they had little time to talk. The same was true for Kit and Bree, as busy or busier than she.

Mother Tree was safe but remained frustratingly elusive.

Given the fire, the infirmary and morgue proved inadequate to hold the many injured, and the CastOuts had set up a new, larger infirmary to augment it. A dour man named Enoch was in charge, while the Cats, Wolves, and Bears had sent additional medical doctors and healers to assist. Thankfully there were few two-legged burn victims, but many animals had been injured in the fire. Cries of pain, fear, and sorrow rang in her ears long after she left the building.

Once the fire was out, the CastOuts left the forest to itself, saying Mothers Tree and Terra would heal the earth and growing things. Much to Sybi's relief, the remaining trees had stopped keening, settling into a faint sorrowful hum, and as days passed, they soon resumed noting joy in the rays of sunshine and the fall of rain, as well as grumbling about pesky bugs.

After a week of drawing *Rhiannon*, Sybi was sick of it. A first. She pushed the pad to the side and reached for another well-used one. Flipping to the first clean page, she drew Kes in his bird form, his splendid markings imprinted on her brain. She sketched him with his wings furled and unfurled, in flight and resting, dipping the crown of his kestrel head and preening his tail feathers. He was unlike any "changling" she had imagined, for in his bird form, his still-human legs wore leather pants, and the baldric filled with knives, throwing stars, and other weaponry crossed his naked chest. And his sword, of course. She smiled—he wore the thing as if it were a third arm.

Sighing, her pencil stilled. She missed his conversation, his sly jokes and his caring nature. The way Kes had held her when he had found her, how she had felt safe and warmed from within. Not spending time with him made her feel hollow and heartsore.

She tore the sketch from the book and pinned it to the wall amongst her many studies of the CastOuts' leader. As she surveyed them, her smile grew. Beneath her pen, an astounding superhero had emerged—The Kestrel. Fierce and formidable, yet kind, too. Along with her sketches, she had begun The Kestrel's storyline. She wished she could show her creation to the gang at Marvel.

Lifting her pen, Sybi turned to a fresh page and began to draw the murmuration's flight toward the blazing fires. For a moment, she chewed her knuckles, then her pen flew across the paper and time lost its meaning.

Minutes or hours later, she sat back and stared at the drawing.

Oh, yes, that was good. Very good. She took a deep breath, pleased, only to realize she was no longer alone. Kes was here, his perfect silence betraying his presence. No one did quiet better than Kes.

Exorbitant joy washed through her, and she set her pen down, wove her emotional strands tight, and rose. "Hello, Kes." She wanted to say how she had missed him, but that would sound lame. "Let's go into the living room."

He nodded, then continued to stare at her with his usual intensity. His ubiquitous scarred leather pants were forest green today, rather than brown or black, but his steel-blue tunic embroidered with umber stitching looked new, his fierce gaze familiar. But beneath that simmered concern.

"Is something wrong?" she said as she washed up at the kitchen sink.

He paused before the arched opening to the great room and blinked, his head tilting to the side, as if in confusion.

"Let me get you something to drink. Have a seat?" She gestured toward the sofa.

The man was in a mood.

He'd taken the armchair overlooking the forest with a vista of the sea. Not the sofa, his usual seat. She brought him some drass, setting it on the side table, and sat on the sofa with her own mug.

Kes was a straightforward man who quickly came to the point. Usually. What was making him hesitate?

"The drass is from a batch made at CatHome," she said. "Bree sent it over."

He nodded. "It is good."

Then nothing. Her old friend hesitation kept her silent, which was stupid. Seconds passed, pressure building. A wood pencil lay on the coffee table, and she swiped it up and began to pick at the wood, wanting to say something, anything.

Kit would talk to him, whereas Bree would sit in his lap and say, "So what's got your knickers in a twist?"

Fuck it. She set down her drink, rose, and slid onto his lap, wrapping her arms around his shoulders. When she rested her head on his chest, his muscles tightened. He felt more marble than man. "What's wrong, Kes?"

At least he hadn't thrown her off his lap.

After endless minutes, he relaxed, his arms sliding around her waist to hold her tight.

"I do not understand," he said. "You have seen my bird form, yet you have said little."

He was magic come to life. "I found your hawk form beautiful."

"To my knowledge," Kes said in a stilted voice. "I am the only Eleutian who can transform into another creature."

Unique. Singular. Alone.

"A great talent," she said.

He stood, setting her on her feet, and walked to the picture window that overlooked the village, pressing his forehead and palms to the glass.

The man was hurting, and she stepped toward him, then hesitated. He was special, a one-off, and she was plain vanilla.

His eyes had gone silver, eyes he had worn battling the fire.

"You're a man of secrets and magics and wonder."

"Not a man, Sybelle." His hand sliced the air, his disgust palpable.

Sybi smiled. "Of course you are. An outer change to a hawk doesn't make you *not* human." She was human, though the Alchemics had recreated her flesh, and she wore large breasts, blue eyes, and blonde hair.

"I am not simply a bird but other forms, as well." He exhaled slowly.

Someone had laid this terrible burden of non-humanness on him, of alienation, and she was incensed at this unknown person or persons. "The Alchemics changed us both. So what? They altered all the CastOuts. It doesn't mean we're not human." She laid a hand on his chest above his heart.

His hand rose, almost touching hers, then he dropped his arm by his side.

"Whatever shape you assume," she said. "Don't you see, you're still *you*."

He tilted his head. "How do you not find my altered state horrifying?"

"How can the man who saved me from the pod and the fire ask that?" Did she dare? "You're the man I kissed, the man who held me tight when I was so scared. You've comforted me when I was in pain and eased it. You are The Kestrel." *And I am coming to adore you.*

That sense of him reaching for her came again.

"I must think on your words, sweet syr." Kestrel nodded, turned on his heel, and left.

The following day as Sybi was rolling bandages in the infirmary, Enoch breezed through the door with a grin. He stood beside her, his mood making her squirm, his interest near predatory.

Along with other volunteers, Sybi assisted doctors and healers in caring for the injured, struggling with the terrible suffering and pain experienced by the many creatures and humans. No natural-born nurse, her time at the clinic was a challenge. Even so, she persevered.

Enoch didn't help when he would poof in and make merry. Often dour, he seemed a man out of step with any emotional intelligence. The man and his gift were a mystery, and though he was perfectly amiable, she wished he didn't single her out so often.

"Ma'am Sybelle." His grin widened.

"Good day, Enoch."

"You look lovely," he said.

Gods alive. "I dress for our patients. In a cheering way."

"And you succeed! Have you refilled the medical supply closet?"

"I have."

"Carry on!" He grinned and waved as he disappeared out the door, his movements lithe, almost balletic. That could hint at his gift, but asking him outright was not done. Even the friends she had queried were in the dark.

As she walked through the largest ward, a soft breeze from the open windows cooled the room. Beds and slings were filled with animals—deer and cougar, raccoon and bear, coyote and wolf and avian—all burned, many with broken limbs and other more severe injuries. All were in pain.

At the far end of the room, she forced a smile to her lips and warmth into her eyes and began with a burned sparrow. They'd splinted one of the bird's wings and a paste covered the burns on his back and other wing. The small creature panted as she checked his water, food supply, and the cleanliness of his dressings and bedding. Last of all, she looked the sparrow in the eye and stroked a finger across an unharmed patch of feathers, murmuring hopeful and kind words. Whether the latter had any effect, she didn't know, for while some of the patients were symbionts, others were merely their animal kin.

Terras often joined her to soothe the fragile creatures on pallets strung around the room. Even with the open windows, the work was hot and sweaty—no air-cooling. The CastOuts were storing energy in anticipation of the Alchemics shutting off the tech.

The CastOuts were, officially, an unacknowledged Clan, though all Eleutia knew of their existence. Yet Alchemic pride demanded all support the convenient fiction of the CastOuts' non-existence.

No Terras today, and the ward took her an hour. After a drink and a quick sandwich, she headed to the human ward. The injured were all adults except for a little girl named Ohtli, who was perhaps seven. The fiery chemical gel had landed on her legs, and she was temporarily wheelchair-bound, her legs suffering third-degree burns.

Yet Ohtli was a cheerful soul, her optimism unflagging, even while enduring the pain of the healers' chants and doctors' treatments. Visiting her always brightened Sybi's day, though as with Enoch, Sybi had no idea about Ohtli's gift.

Sybi saw Kes often, as each day he appeared in the infirmary and spoke with each patient, human or animal. Luciana told her of his many duties as Alpha, which had increased since the fire. Though he abhorred the title, he knew his place as Clan leader and never missed a day in the wards.

Sybi watched him, she couldn't help it, and the way he elevated the wards' tone and tenor. She would swear his visits helped heal. As with all the infirmary workers, he would greet her, make a kind but perfunctory comment, and move on to another worker or patient.

Days passed, and the wards began to empty. Most patients were healed enough to return to their homes, the forest, or their Clan. Three had died, and Kes was there, too, performing a ceremony alongside Marcos and others for the departed's journey into the beyond.

Ever since their conversation about humanness, he'd been distant. That distance was driving her nuts, her heart a constant longing for the man. She'd like to shut him in a room with her, only her. A closet would work, too.

He had said he "needed to think" when they'd last talked. His thinking was taking way too long. She would make a move soon, dammit.

On Thursday, or what the CastOuts called Tongerdi, Sybi leaned over a huge stone sink scrubbing used medical tools before she put them in the autoclave. She startled at an odd sound—giggles, coming from the human ward.

Sybelle finished washing, wiped her raw hands dry, then followed the sound. Ohtli. Of course it was. The child sat in her wheelchair facing the side of her bed where an array of dolls spread before her in a row. How totally adorable.

Ohtli spoke in a low whisper, and the conversation between the chestnut-haired girl and a blue-haired doll might be one-sided, but sometimes Ohtli would have another doll answer. Her pals were quite a crew—a dolphin, a blue-and-bronze stuffed bird (obviously Kestrel), a snake-skinned human-looking doll, the blue-haired one, and a dapple-gray horse with wings and a glittery silver mane. A mistral.

"Hello," Sybi said, approaching. "Looks like you're having a party."

"I am, Ma'am Sybelle!" Ohtli leaned back in her chair, smile wide. "Come join us for kamla."

Sybi curtsied. "I would be delighted, m'lady."

"Oh, we are not formal here," Ohtli said with gravity and pointed to each doll. "This is Annie, Orfris, Kestrel..." She giggled. "Parfa. Blane. And Pegasa. She's real! I saw her once."

Sybi sat beside the dolls and lifted the glittery Pegasa. "Yes?"

"She belongs to the Cat Alpha, Gato, though Gato's name is really Náshdóítsoh. I finally learned to pronounce it! He has two mistrals. I have seen his mate ride the one named Bellerophon. I bet Ma'am Breena's ridden Pegasa, too. She's lucky!"

"She is." Sybi pictured Bree flying the skies. A thrilling image. "You're very observant, Ohtli." Beyond a seven-year-old, her manner and speech appeared older, too. "And very grown up."

"I am almost teenaged." A flush dotted her freckled cheeks. "I know I look younger than ten, but The Kestrel says my body will grow into my mind's age."

"I don't doubt it," Sybi said. "You know, I've never seen a mistral, not in real life, and I can't wait. Breena is an excellent rider and my sister Kit is even better. Have you ever been on a horse or mistral?"

Ohtli beamed. "Oh, yes! I have a special rig and everything. But I've only ridden horses, and our old mistral who no longer flies."

"I'll ask Gato and Bree to take you for a ride on Pegasa or Bellerophon. Would you like that?"

The little girl's striking blue grew wide. "Yes. Oh, yes, Ma'am Sybelle."

Sybi slapped her thighs. "That's settled then. Once you're up and about, you will ride a mistral." She hoped Bree didn't kill her for offering this.

"If I was stronger, I would be a trick rider like Ma'am Kitlyn. Instead, I think I'll be a horse trainer. Horses like me a lot."

"Do they? How wonderful." She had told Ohtli about the circus years and their farm in Maine.

"You know your sister and Gato were mated here, in our village." Ohtli giggled. "That's a very special thing, but theirs was funny, too. They ran out of their nest and Gato was naked! They thought we were being attacked, and well, we were, but it was all okay, but Gato thought they would die, and they ended up mating."

"Wow," she said, unsure of a response to Ohtli's humorous rendition. Sybi could conceptualize mating, but for all her imagination, the feel of the experience eluded her.

A shadow darkened the door. Kestrel.

Ohtli waved, then whispered. "He comes every day and makes me happy."

Sybi leaned down and kissed Ohtli's cheek. "Time for me to return home, but I'll see you tomorrow. We're good to go?" She punched out her fisted hand.

Ohtli giggled and they bumped fists. "Good to go."

Kes stepped inside and she walked over to him. "How are you?"

Those black eyes of his drank her in. "Busy. Too busy."

"Ohtli said you visit every day."

"The wards are a high priority."

"She thinks you're special. She even has a doll that—"

"Come, for only a moment." He led her into the corridor. "Her foster mother made the doll at the child's insistence. I had no say."

"It's an honor."

He frowned. "It makes me uncomfortable."

"Ohtli admires you." She shot him a quirky smile.

He chuffed.

"You speak to everyone as equals and give each consideration. You're straightforward and tell the truth. All your people admire you."

His jaw tightened.

Nothing about Kes was fake, including his humble reaction. He really didn't see his admirable qualities. He knew his Clan members looked to him for advice, protection, and leadership, but had no understanding of how they revered him. A curious layer to a man adept at so much.

"I'll leave you—"

"Do not..." He pinched his lips and sighed.

"What is it, Kes?"

"Ohtli... She is a prophetess. They are rare, but all the females follow a pattern. Once her bleeding comes on, she will see in detail the remainder of her life, like a *scannán*."

"A movie?"

"Yes."

"So Ohtli will *view* her own future." Sybi tried to imagine seeing her life that way. And failed.

He nodded, his eyes pools of pain. "She will watch her death, and if she follows the path of other prophets, watching her death will end her life."

The thought was horrible. *Rhiannon* had a prophetess, too,

though she did not die. She was also part of Sybi, as was each character on the page. "Does Ohtli know?"

"We hope not, but I suspect she is aware. She is very bright."

"She is. And sweet. Is there no way to help her?"

"In the past, we made many attempts to save prophets. We have given them the medical kind of anesthesia, as well as our healers performing spells. We have tried to talk them through the visions, and Marcos has worked with several. Though he is the greatest healer in the Northwest Quadrant, not one has survived."

"What about meditation or hypnosis? They helped Kit deal with her terrible injuries after her riding accident, to distance her mind from what had happened."

"Hypnosis. I suspect Marcos has attempted this, but I will make certain. For you and for the child. How is the re-creation coming? We hope that your vision of Rhiannon will see that which our spies have not. The power station locale, a solid plan for attack, or other details Compass True will find useful."

"My fog is clearing a bit. I've seen inside parts of Alchemic City. I'm hopeful."

During the hours she had sketched, one of the areas she saw was Rhiannon's prisons, glass cages populated by the men, women, and creatures of her story. She avoided thoughts of the glass cell she had drawn holding a man with blue-steel and bronze hair.

CHAPTER

ELEVEN

Kes sat beside Marcos awaiting the vidscreen conference with Gato and Rafe. The left screen coalesced into Gato and his sister, Arina, who sat beside him. Kes admired the Cat's fierce, white-haired First Commander, though not her vinegary tongue. She and Marcos...

"What is *he* doing here?" Arina said, eyes flashing as she pointed at the healer.

For no reason Kes could grasp, Arina did not care for Marcos. The healer did not like the woman, either. Marcos did not move a muscle, though Arina's voice held a cutting edge. Which was *her* problem. "As you join your Alpha, Marcos accompanies me."

"He is no warrior," she said, jerking her chin toward Marcos.

Marcos chuckled a deep laugh that had terrified many an adversary. "And you know that because...?"

"You are a healer, man," Arina barked.

"I am that," Marcos said. "As well as a warrior. And what else are *you*, First Commander?"

Gato's hand swiped the air. "Enough." The Cat checked his mobile. "Rafe is never late for these meetings."

"He will be here," Kestrel said.

As the words left his mouth, the screen on his right cleared to show Rafe and Maximus, the Alpha's spymaster.

"Do not," Gato said to Arina. "Greetings, Radulfr. You called this meeting. Why?"

Thundering hooves on the stairs of Sybi's aerie. Lucky stars, what now?

A fierce pounding on her door.

"I'm coming! I'm coming!"

Flinging the door open, she gaped at Breena and Kitlyn, along with Bree's adorable puma cubs. The three of them squeed and pressed into a giant hug, making a cub sandwich of Audi.

The cub screeched, and the sisters jumped back, laughing, Sybi taking Bree's and Kit's hands and tugging them inside.

"You're here!" Sybi said. "I can't believe you're here!"

More hugs all around, then she waved a hand across the great room. "Do you believe I live in a treehouse?"

"It's perfect for you." Kit's eyes scanned the room while Bree bounced around peeking out windows.

"What a great view," Bree said. "Your fantasies come to life."

Laughter bubbled inside Sybi. So true in many ways. She stroked the cubs, then waved to her sisters. "Sit, sit. I'll get something for us to eat and drink."

Fortis and Audi, who had been prowling the aerie beside Bree, jerked their heads up, a string of Fortis' drool plopping onto the floor.

"They're hungry." Bree tossed her cubs an affectionate look. "They're *always* hungry."

"I'll find something for them," Sybi said over her shoulder.

"We couldn't stand it anymore," Kit said. "Not seeing you in person. Rafe has a meeting, a first without me. Lately, he's always around and has been watching me like a hawk."

"Ditto," Bree said. "Gato suspected I'd come, so he forbade me. And here I thought he knew me so well."

Sybi took a hunk of fish intended for dinner from the coolfreeze for the kits and assembled a platter for the girls. "Will you get in trouble?"

"No," Bree said. "What will Rafe and Gato do, spank us?"

Kit sent a sly glance to Bree. "You might like that."

"Not my cuppa, sis." Bree waggled her fingers.

Sybi held up a bottle of kamla, and both nodded. "How did you manage to sneak out on them?"

"Both are on a vidcall with Kestrel." Kit's smile was the cat's stealing the cream. "We took Moonrise and Pegasa to be fast."

Bree rolled her eyes. "Over the centuries of declining female births, Eleutian men have become, shall I say, overly paternalistic."

"And paranoid," Kit chimed in. "I've studied the histories. Women were often warriors, too. But no more."

"That will change," Bree said. "The leveling of the birth ratio has already begun. That warrior spirit remains within many of our women." Love shined from Bree's eyes. "We're here. Finally."

"I'm so glad." Sybi's heart was so full she felt it would burst.

"So are we." Kit's soft smile was familiar and so welcome.

"We're not defenseless," Kit said. "Along with the cubs, Paulo, WolfHome's coywolf, insisted on accompanying me."

"Bartholomew wasn't so gentle." Bree snorted. "He demanded I bring him or he would tell Gato. The big cat ran the whole way. I swear, he's faster than a jet."

"Where are they?" Sybi settled the cubs with their fish and a water bowl, then laid the tray of cheese, crackers, veggies, hummus, and three precious chocolates on the table by the sofa, then sat.

"Lounging on your deck." Kit squeezed Sybi's hand as if checking she was real. "Protecting the territory. Protecting you, us, and the cubs."

Her sisters were really here. She pressed fingers to her eyes, not wanting to cry.

Then time flowed as they talked about their physical changes, the peace of their Huntington's being gone, the joys of mating with Rafe and Gato, the beauties of Eleutia, and the horrors of the Alchemics.

"I told Bree my graphic novel was Eleutia," Sybi said. "Did she tell you?"

"She did," Kit said. "I was blown away. Neither of us saw it."

"When I visited Mother Tree, she called me a world walker. She said Marie and me—"

Kit's eyes sharpened. "Marie?"

Sybi nodded. "Mother said we were both world walkers, but Marie didn't have the strength and died. Her passing made Mother sad."

"I miss our sister." Bree's hand dug into Audi's fur, the cat leaning against her in an act of comfort.

Kit nodded.

"But you are both part of it, too," Sybi said. "Though I'm not sure how it all works. Our presence on Eleutia is a scheme of Mother's and others to rid the planet of the Alchemics."

"Some scheme," Kit said. "We haven't had Alchemic tech for days. It's pretty grim at WolfHome."

"They're such pricks," Bree said.

"Did Gato and Rafe tell you about the power station?" Sybi said.

Both women nodded.

"A little," Kit said.

"When I drew Rhiannon on Earth," Sybi said. "I drew the inside of the Golden City, which is Alchemic City. The Golden City had a power station separate from the city, too. But when I'm sketching now, much of the city's layout, as well as the power station, is foggy to me. I can't *see* my own creation."

"Why, do you think?" Kit said.

Sybi shook her head. "The fog has cleared a little inside the city." She drew a long breath. "I saw prisoners, including Kestrel. The idea of him being imprisoned..."

Kit and Bree looked at each other, then each arched a brow, something Sybi had never been able to accomplish.

So typical, them jumping to conclusions where her romances were concerned, just like at home. With both of them here, she *was* home. "I like him. I'm... I'm becoming entangled with him, all right?" She shoved a slice of cheese into her mouth, afraid she might reveal too much. Then they would be off on some sisterly scheme to match her up. "I like Marcos, too, and Luciana and Asher. Enoch, sort of. He's an odd duck, in charge of the infirmary where I help out. A decent guy."

Breena grinned. "Let's go back to that word 'entangled,' shall we?"

"Bree, stop," Kit said. "You know Sybi's uncomfortable talking about that stuff."

"And...?" Bree said.

"Have some consideration," Kit said.

Bree got in Kit's face. "Get over it, starchypants."

Kit flicked her arm. "No, you get over it."

Sybi laughed, ignoring the tears streaming down her face. So typical.

"Oh, crap," Bree said. "Sybs is crying."

Sybi rushed to hug them both, squeezing their waists and kissing their cheeks. "I needed this. I needed you. So much."

"We needed you, too," Kit said. "Without you, we didn't feel complete."

"I want to hear more about this power station," Bree said.

"The station must be outside Alchemic City like it is in *Rhiannon*." She just had to recreate it on the map she was drawing for Kes.

"The fog...," Kit said, tapping a finger to her lips. "From what you've said about Mother, maybe she's deliberately creating it."

"A timing thing?" Bree said.

"Mother Tree is in your head, right?" Kit took a slice of cheese, carefully laid it on a cracker, and popped it into her mouth.

"Sometimes. The trees' songs are always with me."

"Perhaps Mother," Kit said, "wishes to intentionally reveal the station's location."

"Possible," Sybi said. "Whatever the cause, I won't stop trying until I locate it."

Fortis crawled onto Bree's lap, and she stroked the cub. "I've told you, soon you'll be too big to do this. You weigh a ton."

Sybi would swear she heard the cub laugh.

Kit popped a chocolate into her mouth and closed her eyes. "Bliss. I have an idea how to help with your sketching."

Which was when Terras stalked through the open door like he owned the place. The cubs stood, backs arched, muzzles drawn back, hissing. His disdainful look accompanied his leap onto Sybi's knees, then he climbed up her right shoulder.

"This is Terras, my peregrine friend." She stroked his downy feathers.

"He looks like Lala," Bree said. "*Just* like Lala."

"Too coincidental," Bree said. "Something's going on."

"It sounds crazy," Sybi said. "But I think Lala was Mother Tree's avatar on Earth. The birds' resemblance is too coincidental."

"There is the sex difference," Kit said.

"True." Sybi nibbled an olive. "And yet..."

"From what you've told us about Mother," Bree said. "I don't think it's a coincidence at all."

"I agree." Kit bit into a carrot. "Hum."

"You said you had an idea, Kit?" Bree said.

Kit's deep green eyes lit with fire, and she squeezed Sybi's hand. "Let's sit in our circle. Perhaps that's what Mother Tree wants...needs?"

"Now?" Bree slid a chocolate into her mouth.

"Now." Kit winked.

The trio slid to the floor and into their sister circle—legs crossed and hands clasped—and sank into their meditation.

Arina and Marcos continued to glare daggers at one another, though Kes had no understanding of their animosity. No matter. Many people perplexed him. "Continue, Rafe."

"I have news," Rafe said. "From Phila."

"Our spy in the Alchemic's tech department, correct?" Marcos said.

Rafe nodded. "As you know, Phila is a high-level tech, her talents much admired by the Alchemics. Two days ago, one of the Cabal, Gabin, took her to a large enclosure within the city with several angular buildings the size of homes. Phila said the place was odd. High walls surrounded the twin structures, and the area could only be accessed through a tunnel. As they emerged, she saw the homes surrounded by grass, and Gabin took her inside one."

"So far, it is pretty banal for the Alchemics," Max said. "There is more."

"Inside one of the homes," Rafe said. "Gabin asked Phila to use some of the displayed tech and guess their purpose. Her lapel cam filmed the proceedings. See for yourselves."

Rafe signaled Max, who dimmed the lights, then lowered a viewing screen.

The vids had no sound, but Phila's actions were enough to get clear images of the strange tech and other sundries set in various workstations. A machine with odd markings on the buttons. Phila pressed several buttons and indecipherable markings appeared onscreen. Another station held a wand-like machine with a small brush on one end, and yet in another, clothes racks held unusual garments—a shortened tunic that would barely cover a woman's breasts, what could only be a jacket but one with sparkles covering it, and an odd cut-out shirt with a scooped neck and no arms."

"What could this mean?" Arina said.

"That wand with the brush is truly odd," Gato said. "A new weapon, perhaps?"

Rafe shrugged. "Phila does not think so. She suggested it might be a shoe polisher to Gabin, but the Alchemic only laughed."

"The items are not Eleutian," Kestrel said.

"No, they are not," Rafe said. "I believe they are from off-world. Look at this one."

Darva, a high-level Alchemic Kes had met, sat at a station holding a metal cross. On the desk lay an open book, the words unreadable.

"I believe," Rafe said in a strong voice. "These objects represent the Cabal's next move."

Once Sybi had grasped her sisters' hands, breathing deeply, as they had done many times before, electricity thrummed through her, the trees' background humming sweetening to a beautiful melody. Images and people floated through her mind, and she observed, then brushed them aside.

The background increased in depth, a new voice resonating with a thousand others.

Bree cleared her throat, a momentary distraction Sybelle eased away. Kit's hand reflexively clenched, and that too she pushed off to focus only on the treesong and the deep serenity.

In her mind's eye, rolling hills of sand appeared in a barren, parched landscape unbroken by rock or trees or any vegetation. She floated above the undulating sand, noting the occasional desert mouse scurrying to its hidey-hole and the snake slithering to its burrow. The hum rose until it trembled through her flesh, and she whirled and twirled above the dunes, dancing above a platform where golden rays reached from a central sun.

You must go for the dance. You and The Kestrel.

Sybi gasped at the words. Mother's words. She opened her eyes. "Did you see it?"

"See what?" Kit said. "All I saw was some giant tree *smiling* at me!"

"I saw the Ents," Bree said, rubbing her eyes.

"From *Lord of the Rings*?" Sybi said.

Bree nodded. "Treebeard and his cohorts were attacking Saruman's stronghold. What did you see?"

Starstruck, Sybi smiled. "Something even better. Mother said I must 'go for the dance.'" With Kes.

"What's that supposed to mean?" Kit said.

"I think I know."

Sybi raced through Kestrel's aerie and into the large command center.

Banks of huge screens covered one wall showing a black-clad Gato and a petite white-haired woman, with Rafe and an adonis on another screen, while Kestrel and Marcos faced them.

Marcos swiveled his chair and walked over. "Can I help you, Made One?"

"I need to talk to Kes."

"He is busy with—"

"I think I've found the power station." She clasped her hands tight.

His eyes widened.

In an instant, Kes stood before Sybelle, hands resting on her upper arms. "Are you well, sweet syr?"

"I'm fine. We found the station."

"Come, join us." He pressed a hand to her lower back and steered her to one of the observation chairs facing the screens. "We?"

She leaned close. "My sisters came and we did our group meditation."

"Where is the station?" he said.

"In the desert."

"Which desert?" From the monitor came the voice of the gorgeous woman who sat beside Gato.

"Arina," Gato said, his tone steel.

Guess her whisper had failed. "I don't know the desert's name, but it's east of here, on this continent."

"How can you possibly know that, Made One?" Arina demanded.

"I just do." She shrugged, unwilling to let the acerbic woman cow her.

"It must be the Tihja," the man beside Rafe said.

Even over the vidscreen, Arina's disdain was palpable. "That desert is nearly one thousand miles of sand and nothing else."

Sybi leaned close to Kes, uncaring if the council heard or not. "I'll explain later."

He nodded as Marcos and Arina began sniping at each other.

"*Enough.*" Kes' growl shut them both up.

"Sybelle," Rafe said. "Can you pin down coordinates?"

"I can show you the general area," Sybi said. "It's hundreds of miles on my map of Rhiannon, which mirrors Eleutia."

Arina snorted and leaned toward Gato, speaking in a whisper.

"To find the exact spot." Sybi raised her voice. "I'll have to go to the Tihja to 'see' its location." As Mother had directed.

A chorus of "no" rang through the room, though Kes remained silent.

Sybi shrugged. "Gotta go." She and the girls had predicted this very reaction, and she headed for the door.

"Made One, wait," Marcos said. "Please."

"Those are my terms." As she spoke, she glimpsed another vidscreen showing...an electric toothbrush? She halted. Too bizarre.

Kestrel rose to his full height. "I will keep the Made One safe. She goes."

Pleasure bloomed at his belief in her, yet she found the toothbrush fascinating. She walked closer to the screen as more images scrolled by. *What the hell?* "What's with the Earthly show?"

"Earth?" Shock bloomed on Marcos' face.

"Yes." She pointed. "That's a Christian cross, a religious symbol, and there's a muscle t-shirt. A calculator. An iPhone. All common. And that..." She pointed. "Is an electric toothbrush. They're all from Earth."

"How can you be so sure?" said Rafe.

"Pause it, please." She pointed. "That's an Apple iPhone. See the logo?" She moved closer. "And that toothbrush has Oral-B on it, which is the manufacturer."

Gato leaned forward. "Clothes, tooth scrubbers, and mobiles. The Cabal has no use for these on Eleutia."

"If," Rafe said, "as we have speculated, the Cabal is from another world, perhaps they are planning to leave our world, their Essences destined for Earth."

"That is a huge leap, Alpha," Arina said.

"It is not." Kes stood, his presence commanding. "The rolling tech blackouts disturb us, but not enough to provoke war. Even if they tried to bring all the tech down at once, I am not convinced they can. The blackouts are a stalling mechanism. A distraction. The Alchemics do not want full-on war. Each time we have challenged them, they fly their city away. I agree with Rafe. The Cabal plans to depart Eleutia for Earth."

"Thousands of Alchemics?" Rafe's companion said.

"Ah," Gato said. "But what if only the Cabal of Eleven's Essences were to go, the blackouts keeping us under their thumb until they leave. A distraction as The Kestrel said."

The handsome man beside Rafe chimed in. "That makes sense. They cannot transport Eleutian items to other worlds, thus they will be hampered before they have set up their laboratories."

"Why are they unable to bring goods from Eleutia?" Arina said.

"Phila does not know," Rafe said. "She suspects the Cabal does not know, either, though it is rumored they have tried many times and always failed."

"To practice, maybe?" Sybi said. "To be comfortable in their new environment?"

Marcos nodded. "I can see that. The Cabal are planners, as we know."

"It makes perfect sense," Kes said. "To practice with the unfamiliar so as not to stand out when they arrive."

"They're going to blow up Eleutia," Sybi blurted out. "Or something like that."

"What?" Arina said.

"*Rhiannon*," Kes said to Sybi, his expression dour.

Sybi nodded. "In my novel, the villains aim to destroy the planet Rhiannon." She gave a quick synopsis of the book's plot.

When she finished, Gato rose to lean forward, hands fisted on the table before him. "Our Compass True timeline for war must change."

That night, Sybi awakened in a cold sweat. Again. Ever since the fire, nightmares had troubled her, dreams of screaming trees, burning creatures, and a pulsing white light that both terrified and compelled her.

Knowing she wouldn't get back to sleep, she staggered from bed, the moonlight bright enough for her to cross to the living area and press her hands on the window where Kes had placed his the previous day.

Kes. If he were here, he would comfort her. Above all, he was a protector. She stuttered out a breath wishing she was more to him than a woman to protect.

Lights speckled the black, aeries stirring awake.

When she had spoken of her nightmares of the fire to Marcos, he'd suggested a calming tea. While it soothed her, the tea failed to quiet the screams of the dying.

Outside, a light bobbed downward from her neighboring aerie's staircase. Once on the ground, the light danced closer to her home, and she saw it was held by Jeff, partner to Miraelle and father to a teenaged boy.

From the darkness, a woman flew into his arms, and their impassioned embrace startled Sybi. She sighed, disappointed yet unsurprised. Just like on Earth, Eleutians stepped out on their partners. Only some were mated on Eleutia, but many, many romantic partnerships existed without the physical bond.

The pair began to speak, and shameful as it was, she cracked the window to listen.

"Kahu found a large eggshell," the woman said. "It was very old and he said it was a part of The Kestrel. It might be magic."

"Foolishness," Jeff said. "Our Alpha was birthed in Alchemic City, not hatched."

Sybi gasped.

Jeff jerked toward her aerie, and she jumped back. He shook his head, took the woman's hand, and led her further into the wood.

The cliché was eavesdroppers never heard good of themselves, but had she learned something about Kes, a thing that boggled her mind?

At the stove, she filled the kettle and set it to boil. Though animals and humans could be symbionts on Eleutia, the human half of the equation was born in human form. Or so she'd been told. Her thoughts whirled. As Jeff had said, foolishness.

Before the kettle shrieked, she snatched it up and poured the water into the mug that held the herb-filled infuser, the aroma of Marcos' blend calming her.

She returned to her bedroom, set the tea down, and scooped up her mobile. Four a.m. She took a sip, retrieved a book, and slid into bed.

A History of Eleutia lay on her lap. According to Kit, the writer, Yuan, was an elder at WolfHome, as well as The Fates' Paladin, whatever that meant. She turned to her bookmarked page and began to read a chapter on the Dakos Wars.

Thoughts of Kes swirled in her head. She had some understanding of the compelling man who was The Kestrel. The fact that he was only part human disturbed him. The man saw himself as not fitting in, as lacking. Kes lacked nothing. How could she help him see he was far more than the sum of his disparate parts?

Wishing she could call him, but knowing she shouldn't, she flipped the phone open and punched in his number.

"How may I assist you, Made One?" Kes said.

"I just wanted to hear your voice," she said.

"Why?"

"I've been having trouble sleeping."

"Would you like me to visit your aerie?"

"I—

Come to me, child.

Sybi sat up with a jerk. Kidding, right? "Um, no. But thank you. I'll see you tomorrow."

Come to me.

Mother wasn't kidding.

Trees blurred as Sybi ran, the landscape changing from healthy trees to charred and broken ones, their life force extinguished.

After Fukkes and the fire, and even with Mother's command and the trees' oversight, she wore knives and carried her walking stick.

She paused to catch her breath, the call echoing in her head. The wind sighed, curling around her, making her shiver though she had donned jeans, a tunic, and a fuzzy jacket. A deer's blackened corpse lay a few feet away, rigid and charred, and she ran again, needing to see Mother's beauty rather than the Alchemics' destruction.

Finally, breathless, the sentinels loomed above her. The closest sentinel bent its silver-barked trunk, the one flanking it mirroring its movement, to open the window which allowed her to enter Mother's domain.

Inside, Mother's light was dim, shadows melting across the verdant grass toward the small tree that glowed in the feeble light.

Sybi fell to her knees. "I'm sorry, Mother."

Mother trembled.

"Are you...laughing?"

Perhaps. What are you sorry for?

"The destruction of the forest and her creatures."

Not your fault, kiddo.

"You're sounding like that Matrix woman again."

Mother's leaves quaked with laughter accompanied by a bright ringing the sentinels echoed. Joy began at the tips of Sybi's toes and fountained upward, and she began to laugh, too.

My tree children will return, growing strong again, as will the forest's plants and creatures.

"But the pain, the suffering."

We endure, Sybelle. Remember this. Myself, Father Tree, our children. We always endure.

The intense weight of Mother's tactile words rang alarm bells. "There is a *Father* Tree?"

The sentinels clattered and clacked their branches, while Mother remained silent.

"Mother?"

Mother's sullenness was like caterpillars crawling over her flesh. She rolled her shoulders trying to erase the awful sensation.

The flowers draping Mother's limbs changed from healthy blossoms to limp brown ones. *You have seen him.*

"Not that I'm aware of."

A cloaked figure in the wood?

Sybi startled. That first day in the forest, when she had been following Mother's call, the Nazgûl-like creature had floated from the wood, his hand outstretched. *That* was Father Tree? "He can walk around?"

At times. When he bestirs himself.

Mother's tone was bitter, unlike herself, with an underlying note of sorrow. "Does he visit you?"

We are estranged.

Estranged? Such a mundane expression, yet rife with feeling. Could a god be estranged? But Mother Tree was not a god. No, Mother was more a Greek dryad or naiad, a demigod, as she and Luciana had discussed. A powerful demigod connected to Mother Terra.

The metaphysical had always called to Sybi, far more so than to Kit or Bree. Marie, on the other hand, had been fully on board.

"Why are you and Father Tree estranged?"

It must be, for now.

"You're sad."

I am, child. I am.

"Is there nothing you can do about your estrangement?"

Mother remained silent.

"Mother?"

The sentinels sighed, in concert with Mother.

The gears of the Fates, of time and of place, must be placated. If I voiced the words you wish for, the balance would be overset. We near the tipping point. You are the factor of change, Sybelle. To affect the change, you must transform, something you have already begun. All must fit and align, for the tiniest facet can affect the whole.

"I see," Sybi said, thinking of the butterfly effect. Mother sounded like a million books and movies where a deity booms an opaque pronouncement. Though, she admitted, Mother did not boom.

The laws of our world conflate with those of yours and all other worlds, as well. Immutable. Do you see? Even the smallest creature can change the course of the future.

Shock rippled through her. "Galadriel said something like that to Frodo in *Lord of the Rings*. Fictional words authored by an Earth human."

Are they? Mother laughed until her flowers, blooming once again, shivered. *Tolkien was a world walker, too.*

The best Sybi could do was try to process what Mother had said and hope that led to some kind of understanding. Any kind of understanding. "Kestrel and I will find the power station to disable it."

Mother's trunk bent as if to nod. *Bring Terras.*

"We will."

Bond with The Kestrel.

"I wish you wouldn't ask that. I can't, not when I don't really know him."

You will.

Longing and desire wove through her when she pictured a life with Kes. They'd have children, black-eyed ones sporting a feather or two. Little ones to laugh with, to play with, small mirrors or herself and Kes, but their own beings, too.

An image burst in her mind of a freckled, red-haired girl giggling as she chattered to a sapling that bent to her hand. The child's eyes were deepest black, and she wore loose blue pants and a red sweater Sybi somehow knew she had knit for her daughter. "The child is mine."

Time grows short. You must decide.

"Decide what?"

Go.

The sentinels began to sparkle like fireflies, as did Mother, and Sybi stepped from beneath Mother's boughs and out the sentinel's circle.

And she was alone, the forest clear, with Sybi standing within a clump of soft ferns.

TWELVE

As Sybi returned to her aerie, a man glided up the path toward her.

"Hi, Enoch," she said.

"I thought you were at the infirmary," he said as he approached.

"It's not my shift, but if you need me, I'm happy to come."

His eyes softened, and he tucked a strand of loose hair behind her ear. "Not necessary."

Was he hitting on her? "Is there a reason you were looking for me?"

"Yes." His cobalt eyes darkened. "I need—"

"SYBELLE!"

Enoch snorted. "Does he always shout like that for you?"

"No." She chuckled, relieved Kes was nearby. She liked Enoch, but something about him didn't sit right with her. She cupped her hands around her mouth. "I'm here, Kes!"

"I will see you tomorrow." Enoch pressed a hand to his heart and bowed.

"You wanted to ask me something?" Sybi said.

"No." He did a one-eighty and walked into the forest.

That bowing thing unnerved her every time, and she wished people wouldn't do that. Though no one touched her, at least not as Enoch had. His hair tucking had felt uncomfortably intimate.

A quick shiver made her jerk. They would leave in search of the power station in several days. Though she had sketched plenty of secret missions for Marvel, going on one in real life...

She laughed at the thought. Nowadays, "real life" was pretty surreal.

Kes emerged from the wood, and she again felt the thrill. She waved.

As he often did, he approached and stared down at her with his usual intensity.

"Hey, Kes." She smiled up at him.

Though he didn't return her smile, his eyes warmed. "We leave tomorrow."

So soon. She'd better woman-up for this adventure. Kes wore a distracted look as he followed her into her aerie to choose weapons. Together they reviewed the gear she would take, including her sketch pad and pens. His nearness and her nerves made her reach out to touch him and she pulled back just in time. Not the moment. Oh, but the man defined temptation.

After a deep breath, which didn't help because his scent was catnip, Sybi focused on the knives she would bring for their mission. Kes' odd preoccupation changed to anxiety when he stepped away from her, body taut, face intense.

"I wish..." Kes wanted his sweet syr to understand, to know all of him. He could not say the words.

"Hum?" she said.

He found it increasingly hard not to touch her. "The spear?" He pointed.

"I'm not ready for it." She began sharpening a knife.

From the moment he had seen Sybelle's withered form in that pod, trapped and unable to breathe, she became his sweet syr. But he never forgot that Sybelle was more than that, and he found her as fascinating and clear as an ice-cold day where snow whispered from Father Sky to Mother Terra.

For the first time since he had hatched, he wanted another living being to understand him. The idea was foolish. As a unique entity, who could possibly know him?

Yet he wished for closeness with his sweet syr. He had seen how Luciana and Asher interacted, much like Gato and Breena or Rafe and Kitlyn. He wanted that intimacy, though he had never experienced that deep emotional connection with anyone, not his brother and sister Falcons or his carer, Enala, she of the hard hand and harder heart.

He recalled a feeling, one he experienced with his birth mother and father before he was torn from their embrace at three years old. But he was unsure if that was wish-fulfillment or truth. Yet when thoughts of them arose, a pang of longing would hit him, though he no longer could picture their faces. Minus those three crucial years, he suspected he would be eternally frozen. Enala's spoken desire.

That remembered affection compelled him to seek, to hope. Yet cared little for understanding or acceptance, though he felt a closeness with certain CastOuts such as Luciana.

His inability to accept himself troubled him, for if he could not, how could Sybelle? His mind, usually composed and orchestrated, spun in circles like a drunken bee.

Kes walked to Sybelle's sleeping chamber and again reviewed the weapons on the rack he had made for her. He lifted a throwing star. "Take three of these."

She shook her head, continuing to sort clothes. "I'm terrible with them. I've got knives and the sword Marcos gave me. I've been practicing with both, and Asher has been teaching me, too."

"Has he." A spurt of annoyance tightened his gut.

"I wanted to surprise you. But the stars..." Sybelle shook her head.

"Accepted," he said, enveloped by her persona—her scent, the sweet arc of her brows, the smile that beamed at seeing him, her strength, masked by the illusion of softness and pliability. Not illusion, in truth, for she possessed both of those attributes. Her strength—so different from his—was of the tensile kind, much like the elegant madronis, pliable, gentle, until a mighty wind blew, and the tree bent in the wind. Much as the madronis did, Sybelle would grow stronger with each gust of wind, her purpose, her goal fixed. He felt that strength to his bones.

Kes strode to the living area, needing to physically distance himself for a few moments, and began the journey to center himself. He wanted to hold her, to breathe her in, and be one with her. He was unsure she wanted the same.

For he was not a man, but a fusion of many creatures. True, she accepted his kestrel form. But he suspected she would fear the others. He refused to imagine his sweet syr afraid of him.

At the sink, he ran cold water, wet his hands, and scrubbed his face, wiping it dry with a towel.

Walking to the expanse of windows, Kes again thanked Father Sky and Mother Terra for his two human parents who had gifted him his most valuable attribute—his heart. They had taught him by example to care for others, to appreciate differences and enjoy similarities, and to be kind to all. When necessary, he set those teachings aside, but they remained his lodestar, and he did his best to follow their example.

His hand fisted on the glass that overlooked the village proper.

"Kes?" Sybelle called.

"One moment, sweeting." He needed more than a moment.

Most in his egg clutch had not survived their emergence from the shell, though two more hatchlings had lived, "disappointments" like himself. They, too, were returned to their biological parents and Clans, only to be cast out at the Alchemics' edict. Once he had grown and after forming the CastOuts, he had searched for both men until he learned they had perished years earlier.

He had never met either man, but knowledge of their deaths

nourished that seed of loneliness within, blossoming to a dark shadow he had been unable to banish.

Fark. To focus on the negative was to become weak.

"Kes?" Sybelle called again, a note in her voice that prompted him to return.

Upon reaching the doorway, he watched her, enjoying the play of thigh muscle as she reached for a sword.

"Let me." He strode forward and lifted the sword from its place on the wall, handing it to her hilt first.

"Can I help?" Her words, spoken with what he imagined to be affection, made him freeze. "You seem distressed."

"I am not." A lie. His conjectures were hijacking his good sense. He nodded, pointing to the closed carry pack. "You have finished?"

"Almost. I need to check my pen and paints to make sure I've packed the right ones."

"Of course."

She beamed him the indefinable smile that soothed his heart.

His sweet syr eased him. Shoting miseries. What would she say when she learned he had been hatched, not birthed, or the pain he experienced when he took another form, *the* form, a shape so useful and so painful it took a mighty effort of will to change? Three times he had effected that change and each time he had prayed to Nixana for death, the pain even beyond the suffering he had known at the Alchemics hands.

He had borne the pain of that change by a hair's breadth, and he prayed he never had to bear it again.

Sybi slipped a rogue pen into her travel bag and straightened, becoming aware of Kestrel's utter stillness and concentration. His *aloneness*, as he stared at her with a tight jaw and distant expression.

Kes had said he wasn't distressed, but he was.

With intense longing, she raised her hand, stopping again before she touched him. "Talk to me, Kes. Tell me what troubles you."

She had prepared a whole conversation—how she admired him,

was drawn to him, wanted to be with him. About to spout the words, they all sounded lame to her. She hadn't had sex with many men, and even on those occasions...well, the act had not met expectations.

The men had messed up. Or she had messed up, her messes usually from dithering. Like now.

Kes was an immense presence filling any space with his power. Yet isolated. She ached to replace that isolation with warmth, light, and connection.

"I want you, Kes." Shit, that sounded lame, cliched. "I..." Fuck it. She wound her arms around his waist and nuzzled into his chest.

He wrapped her tight, and it was good. Better than good.

He lifted her so they met eye-to-eye. "Are you sure?" he said, voice a husky rumble, eyes a bright silver.

"Are *you* sure?" Sybi sensed a hint of hesitation.

"Let us try." He put her down and reached for his vest to remove it.

"I'll do it." She stood on tiptoe and lifted it off one shoulder, then the next. Sybi tugged his shirt upward.

He pulled it off, then he removed her tunic top, and they both stood bared to the waist and drank each other in.

A flash of embarrassment at her pendulous breasts. This wasn't her, not this body at least, and she wondered if he would have enjoyed the sight of her unenhanced flesh or if it would have disappointed him. Not that it mattered—this was the *real* her now, even if it didn't feel that way.

They continued to undress each other with care, their hands both tentative and reverential.

Finally naked, he took her breath away. Even Apollo would be jealous of his granite thighs, steel abs, and shoulders bound by perfectly sculpted muscle.

He smiled and turned playful as he touched her everywhere, licking her shoulder, sucking her nipples, questing and delving as she did the same.

Touching him...the joy of it made her giddy.

Sweat beaded his forehead, his arms, his belly slick with it, trembling from restraint. Sybi wanted him to break apart with passion.

He lowered her onto the sofa. "Yes?"

"Most definitely yes," she said, her voice a throaty rasp.

He covered her with his body, his cock straining against her belly, his silvered mica eyes reflecting the sun streaming through the picture window.

Sybi wanted him inside her now...except... "Shit."

He froze. "What, sweet syr?"

She tucked her head. "Nothing important."

He raised her chin with one finger. "Tell me."

She grimaced. "With this new body, I must be a virgin again. It'll...well, it'll hurt the first time. It's not a big deal."

He tilted his head. "I do not know this 'virgin.'"

Really? "I assume with this new flesh, I'm un-breached sexually. When your cock enters me, you will rip the hymen. It'll pinch, that's all."

His brows crashed together. "I have never heard of this."

Talk about a mood killer. "It's a piece of flesh across my vaginal channel." Now she sounded like Dr. Ruth.

On his feet so fast the breeze gave her a chill, he took his phone from his pants' pocket and called.

"What are you—"

"Hush." He spoke, then flipped the phone closed beaming a broad smile. "You have no hymen. Women on Eleutia do not."

"Who did you call?" she screeched. "They'll know...you know, *know*."

His confused expression said he clearly did not understand.

"Whoever you called will know we're about to make love." She felt the burn of a blush creep from her neck to her face.

"I called Kicks, the Wolves' female medical doctor." He twitched a lip. "Our villagers all assume we already have done so."

"You're kidding." She pushed up on an elbow.

"Sybelle. This is about you and me. No other."

He was right, of course. And she was being idiotic. She opened her arms wide. "Make love to me, Kes."

He slid back on the couch beside her, and a lock of blue-steel hair drifted across his eyes. She pushed it back.

"Stopping now would be a great challenge," he said.

He proceeded to make mincemeat of any awkwardness as he kissed her from the crown of her head to the tip of her big toe, until she writhed beneath him, blind with urgency.

He slid inside her as if they had made love a thousand times and with only a mite of discomfort and no pain.

Home. Kes felt like home, like hearthfires and down coats and the scents of pine and fir.

He paused, pressing his forehead against hers.

"All right?" she said, unsure of the Eleutian protocols.

"Too much." He sighed a breath and another, and then he began to move. "I will not come inside you."

"All right." Pregnancies were rare among CastOuts, yet the thought of a babe thrilled her, remembering that red-haired little girl. She and her sisters had avoided conception, never wanting to pass on the Huntington's gene to their children.

But then her thoughts splintered. Sweet heavenly goddess, a thousand fireflies danced within her, the pleasure so divine and delicate tears sprang to her eyes. Kes was silent, but his breaths, his hands, his lips told a different tale, one of climbing a cliff with her, stroking her upward, guiding the way.

Oh, Kes.

Near. She was so close to that incandescent place. With him. Only with him.

He drew in a gasp, one that pinged her intuition, one that said Kes was conflicted. Yes, he wanted her. That was obvious, yet his vibes shrieked hesitation.

Inside her, a movie unfurled, her glowing oak branch reaching outward and his fierce hawk spiraling closer, the hawk clasping the golden rope that stretched toward her branch. Bathed in pleasure, she watched the golden rope reach for her branch. Utterly beautiful.

The hawk wobbled.

No matter what he said, he was not perfectly onboard with the bonding, even as his words and actions urged them on.

Wait.

Yet her hands tightened on his forearms, her hips perfectly mirroring his.

Oh, sweet Christmas, it felt so good. Kes felt so good. So true, as if he were meant to be hers.

But what if it was a sham? What if the bond was Mother's construct, determined by the Eleutian Fates, by *their* will and not hers or Kestrel's. The bond could be a prison for both of them. Was she about to mate with a man who, deep down, didn't want her? She was uncertain. Too uncertain.

Though she knew much of Kes, she didn't know what he feared, what he loved; what angered him, what pleased him. She wanted to know him in the deepest sense, and then *choose* the life she wished to live on Eleutia. She *had* to choose, and she wished to choose Kes, but...

To be compelled by some predestined thing disturbed her.

Be honest, Sybs. Kit's words rang in her mind.

If she were honest, she wanted him to *choose* her—minus the bond, irrespective of any compulsion or fate. Just her.

She wanted him to love her.

Goddess help me, she was a walking cliché.

But that was her truth.

Untangling herself, she rolled off the couch, breathing hard and blinking madly, her eyes burning.

"Sybelle?" he said, pushing upright as if in pain.

She skittered away.

"I do not understand why you fight the bond."

Her golden man held out his upturned palm, callused and strong, his eyes soft.

Bree had told her what happened and how the bond tied two people together for life.

What if they bonded, and he tired of her or saw their bond as a prison. What if she reacted the same way?

His hand dropped and he sat up. "Mother Tree spoke to me once. Many years ago. Mother said I was fated to bond with a world walker. That as one we would defeat the Alchemics. You are that woman, and I fail to see why bonding is wrong."

His frustrated voice upset her, and she took another step back. "It's not wrong. It can be very right, like Kit's and Bree's bonds. I want that, too. At least, I think I do. But a lifelong mate is a huge commitment."

She whooshed out a breath. "In my other life, on Earth, I was dictated to a lot. It was my fault. I was malleable, I wanted to please, when I sometimes should have said stop. I never did. This is a new life for me, a second chance, and I don't want to be that weak person. I want to be proactive with my decisions."

He rose and stepped toward her.

"Don't, please." She held up her hand.

"Why? Our mating is a natural thing that occurs when two people connect so deeply they bond."

"Kes, please see, it's too new, too strange. I'm not ready."

His jaw tightened. "Your flesh says you are. What I see in your eyes—"

"Perhaps they do, but I have a mind, too, and a heart. Maybe even a soul. I want to choose. All of me, not just my body."

He relaxed, his eyes kind, and cupped her cheek. "Like your sister, Kitlyn."

Sybi had learned of Kit's victory and her choice. A tickle of joy— maybe she wasn't so different from her eldest sister after all. "Yes, like Kit."

He drew closer, still respecting her space, and she couldn't help leaning forward. He should be hers, *was* hers. Yet she couldn't. Not yet.

Conflict and intensity pulsed from his eyes, jaw tight, muscles rigid. He was waging battle...against himself.

He nodded, and Sybi released a breath.

"I will be patient, my sweet syr with her crystalline song."

Sybi smiled. "Crystalline, like a bell."

He started. "Would you rather I called you Bell?"

Her laughter erupted. She couldn't help it, and she felt bad. "No, not Belle. *Never* Belle. I'm might look like a Barbie, but I refuse to be a Disney princess, too!"

Sybi was always a terrible packer, a joke among the sisters as they lived a nomadic life with the circus for ten months a year. Kes had been gone for hours, and it had taken that long to finalize her packing. Her go bag was all set, but she dithered, adding more socks and removing some panties, then scooped up the pile and laid everything onto the couch in the living area. She surveyed the bounty as she began to stuff it into her pack.

A knock at the door, and in breezed Kes.

"I'm almost ready," she said without looking up.

He raised his brows. "It does not look like it."

"No, but I really am."

Sybi retreated to her bedroom, returning with a heavy sweater, and jammed it into her bag. It barely fit, but those chilling air currents at high altitude would make her bones ache.

"We go to the desert," he said. "You have packed your winter sweater. Why?"

"Because it's going to be cold."

"Your fleece jacket will be adequate."

"But if you're flying us to the desert—"

"We do not fly."

"Why?" She set the sweater back on the couch.

"I fly few places. Too risky. When I fly over No Land, the Alchemics may suspect it is me. Were they to fire a missile, I would retreat to the village, where Peter and Elmer protect us. The

Alchemics know this. If I leave our borders in flight, their missiles might find me. I cannot risk that happening with you along. Rest assured, when war comes, I will fly the land."

"War." Sybi shook her head, frowning.

He nodded. "Soon. Once we have disabled their power station, the Alchemics city grounded and unable to fly out of range, Compass True will destroy them."

As expected, Terras came along for "the ride," according to Kes. Their trio traveled far from No Land, heading south and to a lower elevation, Sybi got why she didn't need more clothing. For the cool nights, they used warm blankets, but each day grew warmer.

Except for his comment about the sweater and help with her weapons, Kes had not interfered in her packing, nor had he mentioned their aborted lovemaking. Sybi couldn't stop thinking about the latter.

He led her down paths and up rocky hills, through the forest, and across meadows. The land welcomed them, and its song nourished her soul.

At the forest's edge, a long, undulating plane stretched before them with abundant grasses, shrub trees, and sandy soil. The weight of their undertaking pressed on her. Would they survive or were they on a suicide mission?

Leaving the forest, as they walked the more Mediterranean land-scape, Kestrel handed her a light cloak.

"These will camouflage us from any Alchemic flyovers as we walk." He slipped his on, and she did the same, and she prayed their cloaks hid them as Galadriel's elven ones had done for the Fellowship.

Her "new" body was incredibly fit, unnaturally so for the athletics she had practiced on Eleutia, her clothing comfortable, her boots the same. Rather than a trial, the journey fascinated her. One of the pleasures of the lowered elevation was treesong from the new varieties of vegetation they passed. Grasses bloomed with blue and purple, while cholla, milkweed, and other succulents were abundant, as were glorious orange poppy. Many cactus' songs held deep bass staccato notes, while the mulberry, juniper, and fig trees chimed high languid ones. Trees often bowed as she passed, and she thanked them and drew a hand across their bark, acknowledging her appreciation of their welcome.

When they came to an olive grove, the trees sang a chorus of greeting. Beyond, she spied the outlines of CatHome's primary town and its nerve center, Catamount. Sybi wanted to visit Bree, the cubs, Gato, and Barth, but their journey was too crucial to interrupt with personal matters.

As the first evening star winked in the sky, they stopped.

"We will pause here for the night," Kes said. "This is the farthest edge of CatHome territory."

A grove of manzanitas surrounded the glade, and Sybi pulled her pad and pens from her pack. Her sketchpad was her constant companion, and she had drawn landscapes with plants and trees and animals they'd come across. She slid onto a rock and opened her pad.

Kestrel stared down at her, a faint smile on his lips. "Perhaps now is not the time."

"How come?" She completed a line and looked up.

At the grove's edge, Bree and Gato held hands as they, the cubs, and Bartholomew walked toward them, her sister grinning like a smartypants.

CHAPTER

THIRTEEN

Bree drew away from Gato and began to run toward Sybi, who mirrored her sister.

After many hugs, Bree pushed back, looking at her, a smile rippling her face. "You didn't think we'd let you pass through our territory without a visit, did you?"

"Kes knew?"

Bree laughed. "Of course. The man is a good secret keeper."

Sybi waggled a finger at him as he spoke with Gato. "Shame on you, Kestrel."

Though his eyes remained on the Cat Alpha, his lips twitched.

"The Kestrel arranged it all," Bree said. "He's the one who insisted it be kept secret."

That man.

Though their visit was short, they had time to share stories and laughter. Gato was a devil, full of sardonic humor and innuendo, and it was obvious he and Kes were great friends. The Cat even allowed Terras to walk across his shoulder, this devil of a man who obviously loved Bree to pieces. Sybi liked him immensely, and she adored the cubs and Barth, as well.

Too-short a time later they were back on the road, and as the days passed, the terrain segued from rolling desert hills and scrubby forests to a more arid one when they arrived at a promontory. Their perch overlooked a strange, alien topography reminiscent of movie locations.

"We stand on Fates Peak." Kes stretched his arm across the land before them. "Before us lies the Druzy Badlands, and beyond that the Tihja desert where we will find the power station."

The vista chilled her. Jagged summits, bare of any vegetation, plummeted into deep, shadowed ravines again and again, like rows of serrated teeth. The wrinkled landscape rippled for miles before blending into the hazy distance.

A spectral wind moaned, a perfect accompaniment to the disturbing landscape.

"Come," Kes said.

She paused, resettled her pack.

"Sybelle?"

Scanning the spectral land, an overwhelming fear gripped her heart and stole her breath. Of the land and its perils, of their quest, of danger, of death.

Warmth at her back, then arms surrounding her, holding her tight. "What is it?"

"I'm afraid."

"I know." He nuzzled her. "You are not warrior born or trained. Be at ease, sweeting."

"I'm not sure how."

"Your fear will sharpen your senses. A good thing." He chuckled. "I am here, which I admit sounds arrogant. But I have fought many battles. Mother Terra feels our presence, and Father Sky, as well. I will do all in my power to keep you safe."

"I know you will. And I'll do my very best, Kes."

"I know that, too," he said.

As they began their descent, Sybi almost laughed aloud. This mission was well beyond her comfort zone.

They trudged up high peaks and down valleys, and Kes helped her up a particularly steep climb, his face shadowed by his cloak's hood. Sybi flashed on Frodo and Sam crossing Mordor. They'd been victorious, and she kept that thought close.

Crossing the valleys, scrub brush clung to soil dotted with rocks and boulders so immense it took long minutes to walk around them. Sybi began to sweat as a broiling sun turned their trek into a footslog.

Kestrel was making a decent pace, and she matched him, but it was obvious he slowed his steps for her. She wished she could have ridden Kes or they could have taken a hovercraft, but Alchemic eyes were everywhere according to Kes and Gato. Big Brother watching.

Once they had disabled the power station, and she had no doubt Kes could, all Eleutia would be unleashed on the Alchemics. The consequences to her sisters, to herself, to Kes most of all, added to her fears. From Luciana, she'd learned how the Alchemics wanted Kes for more experiments. The thought made her ill.

All too soon, the heat turned intolerable, all vegetation disappearing, while the wind increased. As the crests and valleys gradually flattened to sand dunes, the air changed, with sour scents burning her nose like the charred remnants of a forest fire. The Tihja desert was unnaturally barren, with no vegetation to rustle in the wind nor small desert animals to skitter away as they passed. Only the wind howled its unceasing chorus.

"This desert reminds me more of the Earthly Sahara. Did you say it goes on for a *thousand* miles?"

Kes nodded. "The Tihja covers much of our northern continent, east to west and north to south."

"Eleutia's parallel to Earth," she said. "So the topography should be the same. On Earth, this would be our Midwest and Southwest where the buffalo and antelope roam, America's breadbasket, where corn, wheat, and other grains are grown and, in the south, cactus and Joshua trees, sagebrush, and scrub. Why is this so barren?"

He hefted her over a small boulder, Terras bobbing on her shoulder, then vaulted over himself. "We do not know. Tales from long ago speak of a land filled with vegetation and animals as you describe, where shaggybuff foraged and deer herds played. Rabbit, antelope, more. Now, it is sterile of all but the hardiest small creatures, sand, and rock."

"No one knows why?"

"Rumors exist of explosions, volcanos, and seismic rifts, but those are more speculation than truth. Others say Eleutians waged a war so terrible, it destroyed the land."

Sybi walked on, slipping her canteen from her waist to sip as she walked. The place felt haunted by the spirits of the dead, near-tactile memories of humans and animals and plants, malevolent and painful. Oppression pressed on her, and she ran up a small rise only to see more of the same—endless, eternal miles of emptiness.

That evening, they ate their meal beneath the minimal shelter of a dune, Terras having stalked off to hunt. He might not be able to fly, but he managed, though what he found to eat in this stark place she couldn't imagine.

"While in the Tihja, we can light no fire," Kes said.

"We have plenty of energy bars."

"Yes..." He grimaced, his voice almost a growl. "Plenty."

"You don't like them."

He shrugged. "They are what they are, practical and unsatisfying."

Hours passed, the temperatures plunging, and Sybi donned her fleece. Even so, she shivered.

"Come," Kes said, arms open. "You are shaking like an aspen before a storm. I will warm you."

She snuggled beside him, his furnace of a body keeping her toasty, his hold one of safety and care. Her eyes drooped.

"Sweet dreams, Sybelle."

"You, too, Kes."

He nuzzled her cheek as she drifted off.

The following day they pushed on long after the sun had set, yet her strength remained, and Sybi found herself enjoying the time alone with Kestrel.

He was brave, resolute, and even witty in his taciturn, spare way, and they bantered and joked, though getting Kes to laugh aloud was nearly impossible. But his eyes smiled often, and that was enough.

Eleutia was changing her. Because of *Rhiannon*, it had always felt like home, but now it felt *more,* the weight of her purpose pressing on her, but in a good way. As if her actions mattered, as if *she* mattered.

Her sisters would laugh. She would, too. They always said how important she was to those around her, but she never believed them. Yet the events on this strange world had subtly altered her self-image.

As they traveled, she had felt a push toward one direction or another, using some inner compass that must have been given to her by Mother Tree. Kes always took her direction, never questioning, amazing her.

When they halted the day's march, stars spangled the night sky, so close she could grasp them, though a bitter wind whined. Sybi pushed down the bandanna she had worn during a brief dust storm and rinsed the day's grit from her mouth. After brushing her teeth, she wiped her face with a dampened kerchief, taking care with their valuable water. They ate minus a campfire, and without light, she couldn't sketch. Yet Rhiannon's power station flashed in her mind, crystal. When they found it, would the real one look like Rhiannon's, which emitted a low hum and pulsed with light?

She skirted a boulder to take care of business, returning to find Kestrel already bedded down.

"Come, sweet syr. Let me warm you." He opened his arms.

She slipped into them, and he gave her a delicious, full-body hug. Her eyes searched for Terras, but was on one of his nocturnal hunts. He hadn't lost weight, so he must have found something to eat.

Kes slept as if dead, but she didn't doubt he would wake in a flash if danger was near. She snuggled close, breathing him in. He was such an understated man who hid his feelings well.

As they traveled, he told her stories of the Dakos wars and his childhood Falcon family. Of forming the CastOuts and how Marcos had become his First Commander. Of building luteons, a stringed instrument, and playing them as well.

On Earth, she had loved to sing both with her sisters and for them. Never in public, of course. Wouldn't it be fun to sing while Kes played? Perhaps he sang, too.

She'd learned much about his past, yet he never spoke his feelings aloud. But she often sensed them, for his eyes whispered what he would not or could not say, his body language doing the same. The laughter in those black-black eyes was a beautiful thing to see. Occasionally, she felt a powerful emotion concealed behind his stoic demeanor. Sorrow or joy, fury or love, strength or vulnerability. Sometimes, she felt him as a pillar of loneliness. That, most of all, made her heart hurt.

Few looked Kes in the eye, either out of fear or respect. Those actions must reinforce his feelings of separateness. Yet she felt connected to him in many ways, ways that only increased over time and their journey.

Perhaps she should take the leap and bond with him. He'd welcome that and had given her the choice, not pressing her once on their trip.

What more did she need? Maybe her fear of the unknown held her back.

He wasn't unknown, not any longer.

That wasn't the issue. Not really. Though it was clear he wanted her, her childish wish was for him to see her, to value her, to love her. Absurd. He was bottled up so tight, she doubted he'd ever open up for love to enter.

But she could love him, couldn't she?

Those carousel thoughts were for another day. Tonight, Kes was warm and cozy and cuddled up with her. That was enough. With a sigh, she closed her eyes and slept.

Two days of grueling marches and freezing nights later, Sybi stumbled, and Terras squawked at her abrupt halt.

"Wait," she said, choking out the words.

Intense pressure squeezed her chest, like a heart attack, and she dropped to her knees and flipped open her sketch pad.

Rhiannon's power station, the Golden Chamber, sat in a bowl surrounded by immense rocks with a blinding blue sky that arced to the horizon. Before her, the same sky blazed, but all she saw were miles and miles of desert where sandy valleys and rises continued to undulate in all directions. Not a boulder in sight.

So what. Eleutia was teaching her to trust her senses. "We're near, Kes."

He studied the terrain for long moments, hands on hips. "Where?"

"Let's try over that ridge." With no logical reason, she pointed east. That felt right.

He gave her a hand up and tugged her into the shadow of a boulder. "I will scout."

"I'm coming," she said, eyes narrowed, jaw firm.

Though he did not sigh, his exasperation was plain. "Follow behind me. Leave all but our weapons and canteens here."

Terras hopped from Sybi's shoulder to his, and Kes removed a laseblaster from his carry pouch and handed it to her. "Fire as needed."

He was gone, across the dune and up the ridge, so swift Sybi would have to run to catch up. She checked her knives, tightened her grip on the blaster, and ran. Near the apex of the ridge, she crouched low, scanning for Kes and Terras. A moment of panic before she found the pair, they blended so well into the land. She dropped to her belly and crawled to where Kes lay, Terras beside him, and peered over the ridge.

Below, down the ridge's steep incline, the land formed a bowl peppered by immense boulders where three floating silver cubes formed a triangle around a large plot of earth.

The power station.

Minutes later they crawled to the valley floor and flattened themselves mere yards from those faceted silver cubes the size of VW busses. Beneath her belly, the earth hummed.

Within her, a pressure valve released. The station. Now all they had to do was disable it. Piece of cake, right? Her fists clenched. "It's there, Kes, under the earth."

He nodded.

"There must be an entrance," she said.

"Look to the right of the middle cube."

A thin rod pierced the surface, painted the sandy desert color. Kes' eyes had closed, his face slack as if in a trance.

Waiting on Kes, she wiped her sweaty palms on her pants.

His eyes opened. "Those cubes and what is within are not of Eleutia."

"How do you know that?"

His nostrils flared. "I feel all that lives on our world."

"How doesn't that overwhelm you?"

"I can filter that sense in and out like Asher does with his hearing."

"But they're not alive, they're metal and—"

"Life forms exist within those cubes. Alien life forms."

The air changed, as if a thunderous storm were brewing, heavy as those weighted blankets people seemed to love.

"They come," he said.

"Who?"

"Three Alchemic hovercraft. Though they are miles distant, they head this way. We must hurry."

He stood. "Stay beside or behind me."

The faceted cubes trembled. *Shit!* This was like some sci-fi flick she had never wanted to see. Any minute, the cubes would open, lotus-like, in slo-mo, and...

The cubes exploded.

Kestrel leapt atop Sybi, pressing her into the sand as he blanketed her. Shrapnel flew and screeches rose, horrible sounds. And the smell, so vile her stomach heaved.

Seconds later he rolled off her to a stand, Terras somehow still atop his shoulder.

"Oh, Kes!" His back was bloody, scratched and scored in a dozen places, blood running down his forehead into his eyes.

Sybi pushed to her feet and wiped the blood from his eyes with her sleeve. "Can you see?"

"Yes." Sword and blaster at the ready, Kes moved forward toward...

"Goddess in heaven, wait!" Her hand grabbed his.

Three identical creatures stood before them, near Godzilla-sized, and she had trouble comprehending them. Their leather-like plated bodies were a light leaf green with random red streaking from head to tail. And those heads! Alligator jaws wide, the tips of their mouths resembling staple removers, their shoulders wearing spikes, as did their tails, and their thin arms bearing large clawed talons.

Killing machines like living armored tanks.

Their eyes were the strangest of all—mushroom-like stalks that bobbed with eyeballs at the end, another yellow claw curving where their nose belonged. As if someone had combined a bunch of different creature parts to make a monster. Thanos they were not.

Unfortunately, their size didn't affect their speed, and they blurred to form a triangle around Sybi, Kes, and Terras, preventing their escape.

Fear did not paralyze her, oddly enough.

Instead, her mind blurred fast as a comet, and she tugged Kes' hand. "Look at them, Kes. How can you attack them? Goddess knows, those monsters might shoot flames or spit poison, too. We must strategize. Maybe they're stupid or have a blind spot. Let's run behind the rocks."

Focused on the nearest monster, he said, "Strategizing will only get us killed."

Her throat died to parchment. Kes would die, she would die, with Terras the only possible survivor.

Kes shook off her hand and fired his laseblaster at one of the creatures. The laser flashed, but the creature leaped, the laser blasting thin air. The creature closed in on them, mouth yawning wide, the two others mimicking its movements.

"Kes, change! We must fly!"

If Kes could fly them to safety... He cursed his flesh, his heart. Changing to hawk would take precious moments and see them either captured or dead.

The lead creature took another step, could easily reach them, yet it paused, as did the other two. These atrocities appeared hive-minded—what one did, the others mimicked. Perhaps waiting for their master's instructions.

If he had more time. He did not.

Sucking air deep into his lungs, seeing Sybelle's strong stance and quivering chin, he wished to dismiss the one thought of saving them, the singular action that might free his sweet syr from danger. Or kill her.

A squeak.

The monstrous trio stepped forward. They had either been ordered to close in or they were self-driven. It did not matter, the result would be the same.

After his recent, albeit voluntary, capture by the Alchemics, he had vowed to never again be in their power, his secrets too precious.

"Sybelle." He took his eyes from the creatures to focus on her.

She swallowed. "Yes?"

"Do you trust me?"

"I do."

From the corner of his eye, the creature to his left hurled an arc of spittle. Kes leapt away, pulling Sybelle with him. Though he was untouched, Sybelle screamed. The spittle had landed on her calf and was burrowing into her flesh.

In an awkward motion, he lifted her in his arms, dashing his canteen's contents across her blackened skin. Then he spat on the bloody wound and eased her to the desert floor.

"Better." She whooshed out a breath.

He wrapped his kerchief around her leg. "Trust me. Bond with me."

"Kes, why—"

The creature on the right reared back, preparing to spit, while the one on his left strode toward them, reaching outward with its clawed hands.

"Now!" he shouted. "We must bond *now!*"

Fukkes laughed. He stood before the massive vidscreen as if what he watched was a creature feature, as the Earthians called it. Except it was real, those fools were trying to destroy The Keystone. How delightful.

In the distance, his Alchemic hovers drew near, the vidfeed catching them on camera. His soldiers would either capture the culprits or the emaks would end them. Fun to observe.

Fukkes retrieved a bottle of kevitt, a personal favorite, and pulled up a club chair to make himself comfortable, the better to enjoy the destruction.

The image onscreen was too distant for great clarity and showed but two Eleutians, rather than an army. Those halfwits had mounted an absurdly small contingent to destroy the Keystone, a thing of elemental power.

Born on a distant planet his Cabal had been researching, the Keystone technology had been a gift of the planet's natives. They thought the power would be used to better worlds. He pressed a finger to his chin, lips twitching. Even with the advanced races, naïveté existed throughout the universe.

Movement onscreen. Ah, the lead hover neared enough to get a sharp image of the invaders.

The Kestrel. Of course. Fukkes fumed. He should not be there. He *needed* the man. But who was that...? A Made One, the same bitch who had tried to best him in the wood. She should be *dead*, not allied with Fukkes' worst enemy. He'd never thought The Kestrel a fool, yet the man had brought *her*, a woman with no exceptional abilities. True, her Eleutian flesh was stronger, faster, and more far-sighted than her Earthian body, but she had no special talents or powers. In a fight, she would be useless.

He leaned to the left, grin flashing. "What do you think, Mari? Will we finally have satisfaction?" With reverence, he lifted the jagged-edged Essence ball. Swirls of smokey gray wove within the broken globe, two darker gray lights bobbing around the space—his beloveds, Mari and Xenon, and for a moment or two, he watched those lights swirl and twirl. They gave him all the answers he needed.

He would observe the capture of his chief adversary, though the death of the Made One would be entertaining, too.

Yes! The emaks burst from their shells to attack. Delicious.

The Kestrel and Made One were conversing, then hugging.

Poor them. He moved several levers on the console, then pressed the button on his ear com. "I will not let the emaks kill The Kestrel, though they are permitted to wound him. Nothing lethal. You are to capture the man."

"Yes, Comstat," came the voice on the other end. "What about the woman?"

"She dies."

The creatures' eye stalks flapped as they stomped toward their prey. Almost funny.

Fukkes narrowed his eyes and leaned forward. Fire?

The lead Alchemic hover stopped.

"Get closer, idiots!"

They were too far away, and Fukkes had trouble seeing the action through the column of flame, which burst into a cyclonic conflagration, flames licking toward the sky an unholy blue.

A roar.

Then...

Kes could *feel* Sybelle, inside him, a being of liquid silver and beauty. She harmonized at his call as their two Essences twined together, becoming one. The bond.

A jolt had him bending backward, and he reveled in their joining.

Terras made his *kak, kak, kak*, the sound growing, amplifying through Kestrel's bones to ping his heart, encouraging Kes' flesh, his soul to open to all that was Sybelle. And he to her.

Incomparable.

Sybelle sagged against him.

In the distance, the lead Alchemic hover grew closer, while the creatures took another step forward. And then another.

"Sybelle."

She looked at him then, eyes wide, cheeks wet with tears. But a beauteous smile wreathed her face. "Oh, Kes, I *see* you."

He prayed to Father Sky, Mother Terra, and Mother Tree. *Make it so. Let her live. Let his sweet syr live.*

"Forgive me, sweet syr."

The Kestrel burned, Fukkes prey disappearing.

"Get close!" he screamed into the mic. "Show me the fire!"

"Yes, Comstat!" The man's shaky voice spoke of his terror as the hovercraft sped up. All knew how Fukkatsu dealt with failure.

By the time the flier reached the flames, they were doused, The Kestrel and the Made One vanished. Just as The Kestrel had done when the Alchemics obtained him in exchange for the Cat Alpha's brother. The Eleutians would call their vanishing "magic." Fukkes scoffed. A logical reason existed, and he would discover it. Perhaps they had used a transporter beam, though that was a stretch. More likely, they had a dissembler, a tool he had researched an eon ago. If that were so, they would be close by.

He checked another screen. Good. The emaks were foraging for grubs, their focus primordial—kill and eat. Such delightful creatures.

The lead hover neared what was now a pile of embers. An emak swiped at the hovercraft, bouncing it away to land beside the mound of blackened ash. That ash pile appeared identical to the one left by The Kestrel in Alchemic City. He had analyzed those ashes, their makeup remaining mysterious to him.

The cursed vidscreen lost focus, Fukkes slamming his fist onto the console.

"Focus, and get closer," he barked.

The ash glistened with opalescence, an interesting byproduct.

"Take a bag, go outside, and sift through it," he barked to the captain.

The man's eyes widened. "May I use the mechanical arm?"

"No!"

A long metal tube sprouted from the hover, and when its segments thumped to the ground, a soldier flew from the end to stand. He began to poke through the pile, which scattered like butterflies on a brisk wind.

"I find nothing but shiny ash, Comstat." The man reached for a handful. "It dissipates when I touch it." His hand uncurled.

Nothing. No remnants of metal, gears, or chips. Nor was his hand black with the ash. Nonsensical. Impossible.

Though...

Centuries ago, soon after the Cabal's arrival on Eleutia, an Alchemic had crafted a creature that could teleport, a skeletal thing part mistral-part human. The teleportation had been a surprising side effect of its creation, but the thing had died within a week. Though many had tried—*Fukkes* had tried—none had been able to replicate the effect.

Fukkes had heard no whispers The Kestrel could teleport. Could teleportation be another aspect of his many facets? The Kestrel was the only surviving being from his unique clutch of eggs. The only remaining hatchling alive.

He admitted his mistake—failing to understand The Kestrel's worth. Fukkes needed him, to own him, to study him, to split him apart and discover his secrets. To transport his Mari and Xenon to Earth.

Fukkes tapped the green button which would send a sonic beam that commanded the monsters back into their cubes. He did not press it, not yet. Punching it would contain the emaks and keep the hover safe. Yet he hesitated as a creature again batted the hover's side, resulting in satisfying screams within.

A distant sand cloud bloomed closer, the remaining two hovers sent to retrieve The Keystone. Really, the one in front of him but a backup.

Since their discovery on a distant world, the emaks had fueled his curiosity. Would they attack the hover?

Hum. He sat back in his chair.

Screams came over the vidscreen as all three emaks ripped the hover, its captain, and two controllers apart, eating all. How *remarkable.* The monsters devoured everything—metal and plas, fabric and flesh.

"Comstat." Darva entered, closing the door behind her.

"Hold," he said, annoyed. The center screen showed the two remaining hovers closing on The Keystone.

But the emaks...

He changed the feed to one of the nearing hovers. "Give me a three-sixty visual."

The soldier complied, and he leaned close to the screen, eyes narrowed.

"Again!"

His view swiveled in a complete circle.

Bits of shiny metal cubes lay scattered like confetti across the sands. The emaks were gone.

"Fucking idiots!" he barked. Eventually, the creatures would die of starvation. No time to hunt them down.

Darva rested a hand on his shoulder. "There are more where they came from, Comstat."

He swiveled his chair and graced Darva with a smile. "Indeed, there are."

CHAPTER

FOURTEEN

Sybi awakened to something poking her in the back. Severe cold and blowing winds scored her naked flesh, cold air biting her nose, and she shivered as she sat up. Woozy and muddled, she shook her head.

She was surrounded by the branches and brush of scrub pine. Hard to see much but glimpses of a rocky landscape beyond. Above, the sky blazed cerulean blue, her location ringed by mountains. Immense ones, their craggy peaks jutting toward the sun, the distant ones sporting blankets of snow.

A mountaintop. That was crazy.

She clambered out of the brush onto a rock and trotted to a scrubby pine. The tree bent her way, but its voice was different, incomprehensible, and unlike the trees by the CastOuts' village or any others she had sensed. The pine's branches offered some cover and comfort, and she sat beneath it, trembling with cold. A headache buzzed behind her eyes and her temples throbbed.

She and her sisters were hiking in Acadia, up the Flying Mountain Trail headed to the top of St. Sauveur mountain, the summer sun bright overhead, when...

180

Wrong. That was wrong.

A pulse of warmth made her jerk. Inside her. A bond. *The* bond. Her *mate.*

Kestrel! She had been with Kestrel.

"Kes! Kes!" She ran from beneath the tree, but only the moans of wind and her chattering teeth replied. He was not here. He wasn't anywhere.

"Kestrel!" she cried out again. "Kes!"

Her shivers increased, and she was too aware of the darkening sky. Of the sun sinking lower. Of the wind searing her skin.

Where was her mate?

Dizziness sat her on her fanny. Ouch. Pine needles were prickly.

The desert. Right. They'd been in the desert hunting the power station when monstrous creatures had closed in as an Alchemic hovercraft neared.

They had been doomed.

Her headache thundered, producing a groan, but she must remember what had happened.

The bond helped—clasped in a hawk's talons a tether of golden rope entwined with a glowing leafed oak branch. She could *see* the living bond within her, a thing of fiery warmth and beauty. Of home. Of Kestrel.

He had taken her into his arms...warmth turning to pain, her screams. Pain consuming her. Eating her alive. Then nothing.

Until she had awakened here, on a mountaintop. Kes *must* be near, and it made sense to follow the bond. He might be foraging for food or he could be hurt or worse. Sybi again pushed to her feet, teeth a-chatter.

The grove where she stood was small, circled by dark pines and rocks that jutted this way and that, with moss dotting some of them. In the distance, she caught the gurgling of a stream.

Toes aching from cold, she pressed her hands to her face and breathed deeply, then strode for the water. Running would warm her, but tripping, falling on this rocky peak could be disastrous. Sybi rubbed her hands up and down her arms in a feeble bid to warm herself, and every few minutes called for Kes. She feared he was in pain or that he had woken up somewhere else. What if he had saved her, but not himself?

Without Kes... A different kind of pain lanced her, and her terror grew. He was a man who would risk all to save her, only to die himself.

Her heart fractured.

Stop. Kes couldn't be dead, for the bond was alive within her. He was now her other half, and if he had passed away, she would know. But if he were injured...

The whole bonding thing confused her, dammit. Would she feel his injuries? Sybi found the stream, a tiny thing, and she kneeled, her palm scooping water to drink. Satisfied, she searched for her mate until her feet grew numb and her hands stiffened, worried how to get warm on this strange mountaintop.

Circling back to where she had awakened, Sybi climbed a craggy boulder and peered around. Mountains were everywhere, an entire range of them, with an eerie mist blanketing them far, far below, hiding the land's topography.

She turned to survey her mountaintop. Pines screened her boulder, but in the distance, the land dipped to a round, unnatural shape. Sybi leapt onto a patch of mossy earth and headed toward the bowl, the only anomalous thing in the barren landscape.

The treeline of pine helped, and she followed it over rocks and scrub until she neared the dip in the land. She slipped behind a pine at the dell's edge and peeked beyond, her eyes widening. The bowl cradled an immense bird's nest made of pine boughs and branches, leaves and twigs and other detritus, and so huge three tractor-trailers could easily fit inside. Small bits of fluff—gold and red, gray and black—caught in the nest's weaving, fluttering in the wind.

Could it be *Kestrel's*?

Sybi maneuvered down one side of the small valley, taking care not to trip or fall until she reached the nest, so large she had to clamber down its branched walls to its interior. She made it with only a few bloody scratches to find bird detritus scattered across the surface, feathers and bark and moss, and even a few paper wrappers, colored string, and green velvet cloth. She scrambled across the nest's floor to pluck a bit of blue fluff between her fingers. Downy soft and the size of her hand, it was far too big for a hatchling. Too big for most any bird she could think of. Except for Kes. But none of his down feathers were bright blue.

The color was singular—the only time she'd seen it was on an indigo bunting. Needless to say, this feather was too large.

Sybi scanned the skies as she climbed from the nest, then hobbled over to the screen of pine and flopped onto the ground, her legs and arms nearly numb. She massaged them, then braced her back against the tree and as best she could and scooped up needles and leaves to cover herself.

Mother! Of course. Her worry for Kes made her forget Mother and her trees. When she smiled, her frozen cheeks ached.

Going silent and deep, she called. *Mother! Help me. I don't know where I am or how I got here. I need to get home.*

No answer.

Mother was a contrary sort, so she kept calling. As she did so, she petted the tree, which brushed a branch across her arm, its voice a low sweet hum resonating inside her. Yet she still could not understand the voice.

Dammit to heaven!

Perhaps she was on *another* parallel world, lost to Kes, to her sisters, to everything.

What would Cap do? Captain America had always been her favorite Marvel character, and he had transformed, too. But he also remembered what it was like to be weak, invisible, and discounted.

Damn. Her nose ran and her eyes teared from the cursed wind. She shook her head, her thoughts mushy.

Sybi was going hypothermic, she knew that much.

She dropped her head back against the trunk, and a lock of hair slid from her shoulder to her breast. Squinting, she lifted it. Brown. Her hair was mouse-brown with a few golden streaks thrown in. Huh. Peering down, she touched one breast. No more pontoons, but normal-sized...for her.

She lept up. And fell over.

"Fuck."

Getting her knees beneath her, she dragged herself to her feet and ran her hands down her body. *Holy shit.*

Her own, less-vivid curves had returned. She couldn't see her eyes, but she bet they were gray again, too.

Whatever had happened, her body was hers once more, not the fifty-two-year-old dying one, but the body of her youth.

How strange.

She must be hallucinating and pinched herself, hard.

Ow! Though she was colder than a popsicle, she laughed.

The *real* Sybi was back.

How? She didn't know or care, and even if she was delusional, the change felt good—great, in fact.

She sobered. She had no water, no food, and no warmth. She could be anywhere on Eleutia or not even on the planet.

But, oh, her reversion pleased her.

If she could build a fire... She began to gather fallen sticks and leaves that littered the ground. A sigh. Sybi had no clue how to do light one. Seeing some movie cowboy do it was not enough. So what. She would try. A few minutes later, her arms clutching her trove, the trees' voices rose to an excited pitch. Sybi looked around, then up, cupping a hand across her forehead from the bright sun. A speck in the sky grew to show a bird flying toward the mountaintop.

Kes! Her heart thundered, and Sybi stilled.

The bird neared. Not Kes, its wings beating in a motion unlike that of his hawk form.

Though disappointed, she watched the bird's approach as it grew larger and larger. The thing was huge, near the size of Kes, but it looked nothing like him. More like a giant parrot, maybe, though with its curling plumed tail and vibrant red and gold feathers, she had never seen a bird like it. As it closed on the nest, its gold feathers sparked in the sun, its wing embellishments red and turquoise.

The bird dove for the nest's center and pushed forward its immense talons that sprouted curved claws to grasp a landing.

Shit.

She dropped her bundle and slipped back into the pines. Scrubby and small they might be, but better than nothing.

The epic bird landed with a whoosh, settling into the nest in a side-to-side shake, its beauty astounding.

The bird began to preen.

Her frozen legs no longer supported her, and Sybi dropped to her knees. Even if she knew how, she couldn't light a fire with the bird nearby, its razored beak and deadly claws would rip her to shreds.

Slow and easy, Sybi drew her knees to her chest and rested her chin on them, huddling tight for warmth.

The bird stilled, and its head rose, then swiveled in her direction.

Sybi held her breath.

It went back to grooming itself.

Close. Too close. She blew out a breath. Night was coming fast, the pale moon rising. The breeze quieted, soothing pine scents surrounding her, and stars winked into the sky. She rested her cheek on her knees. Better.

In slow increments, her shivers decreased while a languorous warmth began at her toes. Restful. Like a vine, the absence of cold flowed up her body and twined her in comfort.

She sighed. Much better.

Her lids grew heavy as she kept watch on the bird and silently called for Mother and Kes. Nice. Just for a moment, she would allow herself to rest.

A squawk.

Her eyes flared wide, and she stared into two sapphire eyes lit with flame.

Sweet Christmas!

Its head feathers bristled, its wings outstretched, and it raised a red-bladed talon about to strike.

Too much. Way too much.

There she was, naked, on a mountaintop, and about to be killed by a giant bird because she had invaded its territory. She couldn't blame it.

But to never see Kes again. He wouldn't know what had happened to her, but *he* was alive. That was something. He must be, had to be.

Her eyes burned. Curses, not now. A tear dripped onto her cheek. Another followed the first, and then another.

The bird's head tilted, as if in query.

"I can't help it. So there. I miss him. I don't want to die, either, though it doesn't seem I have much choice."

The bird's talon thudded down, and Sybi shrieked.

But it had only taken a step closer.

She leaned back to peer up at its head.

It squawked, and her hands pressed against her ears at the deafening sound. She *could* punch it. A stupid move, and yet...

Sybelle would *not* end this way, waiting passive while the bird shredded her. Her hand scrabbled for a rock. All she felt were sticks and pine needles.

A stick it was, and she balled her fist around it, the other hand straightened in *dan Shuri-te*, the knife hand strike. Neither might hurt the giant creature, but she would not give up without a fight.

For days, Kes flew thousands of miles in search of his sweet syr, their bond fragmented and dimming. The bond's warmth would vacillate until he could not tell if it was real or a willful illusion. His avian friends searched, too, but none had found any trace of Sybelle. Emptiness yawned within him.

He pushed on, fearing his search's futility. No matter. He would find Sybelle alive or learn with certainty of her passing.

Days earlier, he had awakened at FalconNest, his birth Clan's aerie where he always rose during a rebirth. At first exultant, hopeful Sybelle had survived alongside him, now a terrible desperation propelled him.

Twice, Alchemic drones had almost spotted him, and he had climbed high above the clouds, eluding them to continue his all-consuming search.

Kes did not believe Sybelle was gone from this plane.

But if she were dead, he would soon be the same. Impossible to live in the world without his sweet syr.

Muscles near exhaustion, he wheeled toward the CastOut village. Over the days he had searched, he had lost near a stone of weight. Once home, he would rest and eat before he began his search again.

His wings faltered.

Fine, Sybi thought, straightening her spine. Should she leap up a tree? She snorted. As if the dwarfed trees could shelter her from an enormous bird. She had called to them, but they had not come to her aid.

Relax. Breathe deep. Prepare for the first strike.

Be like water.

Her sensei's oft-quoted words of Bruce Lee harkened far back to the *Tao Te Ching* and expressed a core principle of the martial art, Wing Chun. Stars alive, she was such a fangirl.

Be like water.

The bird's head inched closer.

Another tear slipped down her cheek. *Ready or not, here we go.*

The bird's pointed tongue flicked out and licked her tears.

She started. So did the bird, reeling backward.

It moved closer again, craning its massive head to lap at another tear like fine wine. Stranger still, a single wing patted her, then pushed her forward, nudging her until she stepped from the screen of trees toward the nest. The bird continued to prompt her down the nest toward its center.

Tired, cold, and very confused, she stumbled over mini-logs and across branches as thick as Kestrel's thighs. When she reached the center, the wing patted her downward. On legs of jelly, she flopped onto a large bed of moss.

The bird settled into its nest, then draped a wing over Sybi.

The warmth of a banked furnace enveloped her.

Divine.

The bird's odd behavior mimicked ones she had seen at Bird-sacre, the Stanwood Wildlife Sanctuary in Maine where she had volunteered in her later years. Birds of prey mantled over their food, protecting their kill from other predators.

Christmas. Was she its next meal?

The warmth sapped her worry, along with her will.

In for a penny... Sybi stroked the underside of the wing draped above her. Soft as silk.

The bird *purred*, its vibrations coursing through her.

Birds did not purr. Did they?

Woozy, she slid into her world of Rhiannon that now boasted the mighty warrior, The Kestrel. He was here, with her...

The power station. They had failed to destroy it. Marcos had said all would be lost if the station reached Alchemic City.

All would be lost. She had seen that oft-used phrase in the cels she drew and read. What exactly did it mean?

Silly thought. Sybi pressed her cheek to the bed of moss and closed her eyes, her mind lifting her imaginary pencil.

Ah, Rhiannon, where rhythms of magic rose and fell, and Kes flew her into the skies.

Kes attempted to bank for a landing on the village green. He faltered. Too much strain after too many miles, he had pushed his avian body beyond what it could perform.

His mind dizzied as he tumbled into a spin, leveling a cypress before he crashed onto Mother Terra. He boxed the pain and changed to man, normally an easy enough process. Today, agony.

Once finished, he lay naked and panting, covered in sweat as a chill wind burned his flesh. In the distance, heavy footfalls pounded, unlike those made by the two small bird legs that appeared in front of him.

"You made it," he gasped.

Terras tilted his head as if to say, *You are surprised?*

More footfalls and Marcos crouched to drape a blanket over Kes. "Talking to yourself, are we?"

"Later." He braced a palm on the ground and pushed to rise. His body failed to respond.

"Agon and Asher, take his torso," Marcos said over his shoulder.

Two other Sgiaths took his legs and the four men carried him to his aerie, Marcos walking beside them. A first. The indignity stung.

He was *never* helpless, and he loathed it.

They laid him on his bed, and Marcos sat in the chair he pulled over, then ran his hands across Kes, head to toe.

"Nothing is damaged past mending," Marcos said as he straightened. "But you have exhausted your stores and came near to permanently harming your hawk form. Your magic is depleted. You are to do nothing but eat and rest for three days. After that, you may begin a few light exercises that will help heal you."

Marcos and his pontificating. "When can I fly?"

"From your readings, I would say a minimum of two weeks."

"Unacceptable," Kes said.

"Truth, or you will damage your hawk form irreparably."

A day later, Kes felt as if he had eaten and slept enough for ten men. At least he could now stand and walk.

Desperate to find his sweet syr, the stiffness in his joints and persistent headache said it would take days of rest and food to enable flight. The powder keg inside Kes was about to explode.

Never had he been helpless, his magic not once failing him—he had thought it inexhaustible, fool that he was. Its lack and his own hubris shook him to his core.

Was this how his sweet syr felt, powerless? How Asher felt? Though the Sgiath was fearless, his talents made normal life a challenge. And Pedro? He could fly, but he understood the man's secret longing for sight. Everyone had weaknesses, but most CastOuts did their best to rise above their frailties.

He must rise above his and persevere.

Bewildered that his skin felt not his own, Kes left his sleeping room to see Marcos in the salon reading a book. Crossing the hall to the kitchen, he made several sandwiches, then pulled a flask of kevitt from the coolfreeze and downed it. He snagged a bottle of troff and two mugs and re-entered the salon with the sandwiches and drink.

His favorite chair stood empty and he slumped into it, glaring at the healer.

"Where is Sybelle?" Marcos said.

"I do not know."

"I see," Marcos said, looking him up and down. "You are not yourself."

Kes shrugged and took a satisfying chunk out of his sandwich.

"May I?" Marcos pointed to the extra mug.

"It's for you."

"What happened?" Marcos poured himself some troff.

"We need to convene the council as soon as possible," Kes said. "Sybelle and I found the power station. We could not deactivate it."

"What was it like?" Marcos leaned forward.

"Most of the station is underground," Kestrel said. "Our problem was not the station itself, but rather the three cubes that surrounded it."

"Cubes," Marcos said.

"Cubes the size of a hovercraft." Kestrel started on the next sandwich and his second mug of troff. "When we breached their territory, the silver cubes burst open and monstrous creatures emerged, ones not born on Eleutia."

"*Alien?*" Marcos said.

"Yes." Kestrel finished the second sandwich feeling almost sated. He lifted the third.

"And?"

Kestrel said nothing and finished the final sandwich, wiped his hands on the linen, and downed the remaining troff. Knots of pain troubled him each time he moved, but the physical was the least of it. The loss of Sybelle was unspeakable, their bond fading in and out, his mate perhaps dying or dead.

He reached for Mother Tree again in hopes she would answer. *Mother, I cannot find my sweet syr. Where is she?*

A thousand voices murmured in his head. *I cannot see or feel her. She is not on our landmass.*

Not on their northern continent. *Does she live?*

The mad chorus in his head howled. *I do not know.*

He closed his eyes. Even Mother could not feel his Sybelle.

"You must heal me so I can fly," he told Marcos.

The healer's eyes darkened. "I will do what I can. But your hawk form... Given weeks, I could affect change. Sooner?" Marcos shook his head.

"I do not have weeks." Kestrel's fury blazed.

His transformation to hawk was unprecedented, and a unique challenge even for Marcos' extraordinary healing abilities.

"Do what you can." He held Marcos' eyes for a long while. Though the Falcon fliers did not have the range to leave the northern continent, he could stop, recharge them, and continue. "What about our fliers?"

Marcos shook his head, laying a hand on his shoulder. "All were destroyed in the fire. Kes, what exactly happened?"

Nostrils flaring, Kes took a deep, deep breath. "I believed our bond would protect her when I burned."

"From what you have said, you had little choice. Sybelle may not have—"

"Do *not* speak the words." His sweet syr was *alive*. She must be, and she would have returned to...

Her "birthplace." Just as he always returned to Falcon Nest when he burned. That could be Alchemic City.

No.

He leapt to his feet grinning like an idiot. He *knew*. He knew where she was. True, the site would present dangers, but he *knew*.

"I must go," he said.

"You can try."

"I must."

"Where?"

"To the Anissa mountains."

Marcos froze. "Eight thousand miles away?"

Kestrel unearthed a fresh carry sack in his closet and began to load it with drinks, food, and clothing for Sybelle. He strapped a baldric around his chest, slipping his duplicate sword into its holster. He slid a laseblaster into its dedicated case attached to the leather strap holding the sack around his neck in his bird form.

"You cannot possibly fly eight thousand miles in your condition."

"I can and I will."

Marcos rose and gripped his shoulder. "What you will do is plunge into the sea or crash into one of those mountain peaks you're so fond of."

Kes shook his head. "I will fly in stages. It will not be—"

"You won't make it, and if you would be your usual rational self, you know that for truth. You must combine rest and exercise to regain your strength. Look at you, man, you have lost enough weight that your ribs stick out. Never before has a flight taken so much out of you."

The man should understand. "Do you think I am unaware? She will die if I do not reach her."

Marcos approached and laid a hand on his shoulder. "I know this, my friend. But I have an idea."

Sybi awakened on a crisp morning covered in fluff and leaves.

Maybe even some bark. The bird had done this, covered her to keep her warm. Now, the creature was nowhere in sight.

She blazed with thirst and rose to find that stream again. Every muscle she possessed ached.

Rather than go back to sleep, which had great appeal, she demanded her body emerge from its cocoon to climb the nest's gentle slope. Stiff and sore, Sybi headed for the wood and beyond toward the stream. Anything for a drink.

She walked through scrubby brush, each step a bit less painful, to the denser trees. Clusters of sulphurflower lined the path among other plants she could not name. At the far tree edge, a meadow rolled before her, a sea of yellow blanket flower, golden banner, and yellow stonecrop waving in the wind.

Her thirst, hunger, and chill fell away at the beauty before her. A different kind of nourishment.

In the distance, light glinted off what could be steel. Or water.

She stepped forward, a rock pricking her barefoot, while in the distance, a bird cried. *Her* bird, she supposed, but rather than a cry, it sounded like a song or a call.

The bird might be worried or it could need her. Thirsty as she was, she reversed direction and began to trot until she emerged near the nest. The bird's chest was puffed, its feathers ruffled as it sang, its head turned toward a speck in the distance.

Sybi's gut clenched. The bird's mate? He might not like her. Or maybe the Alchemics had found her. *Hells bells.*

The bird, for good or for ill, cawed with increasing excitement.

Retreat would be wise, and Sybi scrambled down the nest to her cocoon and burrowed inside, waiting and watching.

The speck grew. A man. No, two men, one lying flat atop the other's back, like an open-faced sandwich. She almost giggled, the image that strange. How their flight was even possible boggled her mind.

Closer still, and the giant bird's cacophony of squawks reached a fevered pitch of what sounded like joy.

Kes! It had to be Kes!

The two men neared the mountain peak. Kes laid atop...Pedro? He was the CastOut who could fly. And she would swear the man was smiling.

Sweet Christmas! Her heart soared, and she lept from her cocoon and clambered up the nest's sides.

Kes was here!

Her breath caught as they landed, with Pedro going vertical and Kes leaping off his back. Her body felt alive for the first time in days, joy lighting her from inside out. Though blinded by tears, she ran.

Kes stared as they landed, feasting on the sight of his sweet syr. Alive. Whole. Unharmed but for a few leg and arm scratches.

His legs weakened, relief nearly toppling him, but then the fizz of triumph surged. He tilted his head. Sybelle was different, though in his joy he could not pinpoint how. No matter. She was glorious.

Pedro had gone above and beyond, carrying Kes from the village to this far-distant mountain top. The man was now grinning as if he had caught the moon.

He should be, given his epic feat. They had stopped often for Pedro to rest, and at each stop, Kes felt more himself, his strength returning. Thank Mother Terra and Father Sky.

His Sybelle ran toward him, naked, and his strides ate up the ground as he neared her, the phoenix bird intermittently singing and squawking.

Then she was in his arms, cold and shivering, weeping and repeating his name again and again.

"Hush, my Sybelle. You are safe. I will warm you. You are safe, sweeting." After her weeping trailed off to sniffles, he eased her back and draped his sheepskin coat across her shoulders, fitting each arm into a sleeve, and buttoning it.

"You're okay?" Sybi said, looking up at him.

He read her heart in her eyes, that beautiful heart. "I am now." He and Marcos had planned the rescue carefully, with a grudging knowledge that at his current strength he was unable to fly the round trip. Pedro had stepped up.

By acting as Pedro's eyes and riding the man thousands of miles to the mountaintop, he had gained enough strength to transform and carry Sybelle home.

"It feels like forever since I saw you," Sybi said. "Though it's only been a day or two."

He raised a brow. "I have been searching for many weeks."

Sybelle scanned his face. "How..."

"Time is a strange creature. Perhaps your rebirth took far longer than mine." He wrapped his arm around her waist—by Father Sky that felt good—and steered her toward the phoenix bird. "Did she harm you?"

"The bird?"

Kes nodded.

"No, though at first, I thought she might," Sybelle said. "It was odd. She was attacking me, at least it seemed like that, and then she licked my tears. Isn't that weird? Her whole demeanor changed, and she steered me into her nest and covered me with her wing for warmth. What's wrong? Why did you fly on Pedro?"

His lips quirked. "He offered." Teasing his sweet syr felt...joyful. He took a breath and detailed his weakened condition, while he gathered courage for the tale of his making.

He had said he was well enough to fly, but he was unready to tell that story. Not yet.

"Did..." Sybelle paused, biting her lower lip. "Did Terras make it?"

He snorted. "That self-assured creature? Of course. He was irate I would not let him join our flight."

Two tears slipped down her cheeks, her smile impossibly beautiful. "I'm so glad."

While Pedro rested, Kes gathered wood, set rocks and moss into a circle, and made a fire. Once Pedro awakened, he accepted the troff they had brought, along with bars enriched with nuts and oats, and flavored with a few bits of precious chocolate. The phoenix settled into her nest and slept, and as they ate and drank, he forced himself to stop his Sybelle from drinking and eating too much after her deprivation.

"Kes?"

"Yes. I will tell you all." He kissed her forehead.

FIFTEEN

Sybi stared at Kestrel, the lines of strain fanning from his eyes and around his mouth disturbing. He had lost weight, too, his black eyes weary.

"You're bone-tired." She rested a hand on his chest.

"It will pass. I searched for you and my flesh gave out while my mind wanted to continue. I am much healed." He removed clothes from his carrysack and handed them to her.

Donning them, she held his coat out. He shook his head and again helped her into the warm sheepskin. Blinking rapidly, eyes burning, she prayed he would heal swiftly and well. "The power station..."

"We failed, but as it is now traveling to Alchemic City, we can do much."

"Those monsters were horrible, terrible things."

Kes nodded. "They can be defeated."

Sybi wasn't so sure but nodded. "What happened to us? I remember pain, and then I blacked out and woke up here, of all places."

"You did." He sighed, unsure how to begin.

"Kes?"

He petted the bird, nestled in her nest and content. g had sat up and was eating a power bar. "I understand now. Her blood runs through my veins." He pointed to the bird. "A mating bond is a mighty thing, our Essences mingling. That was what I had hoped for when I held you while I burned. With my Essence within you, after our conflagration, my blood, *her* blood, runs through your veins as well. You were reborn and awakened here because she is my mother phoenix."

"You did say *phoenix*?"

"Yes, though I doubt you can initiate the burn." He continued to pet the bird, who began to purr as she had for Sybi. "I have been a fool. Rather than thinking things through, I chased hope through the skies without rational thought to guide me."

"You have found me now. That's all that matters. How is any of this possible?"

Kes scraped a hand across his face. "The Alchemics brewed a stew to create me, and I am human, phoenix, tiger, hawk. For all I know, other creatures are part of my DNA. They created others similar to me, though I was the only one of our clutch to include the phoenix. When I burn, I return to Falcon Nest, the place of my human birth."

"How is any of that possible?"

"I do not know the science used in their creation of animal-human beings. It is twisted, certainly." His eyes softened as he stroked the bird. "They captured mother phoenix and siphoned off her blood, trapping her in a way she could not burn. But before they bled her dry, she escaped her bonds and burned to ash, returning here to her birth home. As you did."

Her eyes widened.

"When the alien creatures attacked and we bonded, I took you in my arms hoping..." He sighed. "I was correct about the bond, though incorrect as well."

"But what did *you* do? I can't remember."

"As I held you, I phoenixed, burning from within until all that remained was ash. I hoped our bond would..." His jaw firmed. "A massive gamble I despised."

"You hoped I would live through it, just like you do, and be reborn."

He nodded, his eyes a cauldron of fear and hope, grief and triumph.

"You knew I might die."

His lips thinned. "Yes. A grave risk, but the only one to take." He climbed from the nest to stand by its upper rim, hands on hips, jaw tight.

"The creatures would have killed us otherwise." She wanted him to see her eyes and walked to him. "You took a calculated risk, and it paid off."

He enfolded her, resting his chin atop her head, his voice choked. "Since that moment, fear has been my constant companion. I could not find you. I flew for many days, and yet..."

"You thought I was dead? You didn't feel the bond?"

He said nothing.

"Kes?"

"I did. But it trembled in and out, and I did not trust its truth."

She stood on tiptoe and kissed his chin. "I'm definitely alive. *We* are alive."

His arms tightened, but he remained silent.

"But look at my appearance. Why haven't you said anything?" She ran a hand down her hair, curling a lock in her fingers.

"You look fine," he said, head tilting in that bird way of his.

"Fine?" She was thrilled to again have her youthful Earthly body. She doubted he was. "I have my old body back, admittedly my young one—teeny breasts, brown hair, and I assume my eyes are gray again, too. Come on, Kes. *You* don't look any different after we flamed on, but I sure do."

Kes chuckled. "You feel the same."

Though she felt better than she had in months—she was her

physical self again, after all—she suspected Kes was disappointed at the disappearance of her flashy looks. He was being kind, but now that they were bonded, he was stuck with her.

She snuggled into the crook of his neck and sniffled. "I missed you so much. It was like the part of me that's complete when you're near became a gaping hole." She ran her hand down his cheek and stared into those fierce black eyes that glittered with both pain and joy. When she laid her cheek above his heart, peace enveloped her.

Until she realized how his body was tense, muscles straining. She raised her head, but he would not meet her eyes.

He gave her a quick squeeze, then released her and strode down the nest to the resting bird to stroke the bird's head. She cooed.

After two days' rest, they readied for the journey home, Kes' guarantees of his strength ringing in her ears. If he felt himself falter, he assured her, he would land. Nonetheless, she worried he would damage himself further in some mighty effort to see them safe.

Pedro was a jokester and had made friends with the phoenix, but Kes had remained troubled and silent about whatever bothered him. Sybi suspected her revised looks were the cause. Not that he would ever say so.

Kes surveyed the mountain peak, made their fires and food, and one night he and Pedro sang, with the phoenix crooning accompaniment. She hadn't joined in, shyness overcoming her. They spent hours with mother phoenix, often talking as if she understood. Sybi was convinced she did.

"We must fly," Kes said.

"Excellent," she said, her voice a little too cheerful.

She wrapped her arms around his waist, never wanting to let go. "I'm eager for home, but this moment feels precious."

He kissed her forehead, then strode to the center of the clearing near the nest. "The pants I brought you fit well."

"They're cozy." Lined with shearling, they felt heavenly.

Kes doffed his shirt, strapped on his chest baldric and sword, and began his change. Soon, he loomed over her in his epic bird form, the phoenix singing a trill of pleasure. Discounting his chest and legs, his bird form was larger than the phoenix, but not by much.

Sybi strapped on his harness, then hooked their bundle to its side with a carabiner. She double-checked both were secure, then walked to Pedro and touched his arm. "We're ready. Are you all set?"

"I am." The large man straightened, his sweet smile appearing, along with a flush that climbed up his neck. The flight had given him new confidence, his embarrassed pride obvious.

"Great!" Sybi kissed his cheek. "Thank you again, Pedro, for flying Kes. I'll call to you as we fly, so we'll always remain together. Kes says you should fly in his slipstream."

Another smile bloomed, transforming his long face into a handsome one. "I intended to do just that."

The phoenix. Sybi held her gaze. The idea that this magical being's blood now ran in her veins thrilled her. She had much to thank her "blood mother" for, and she scrambled down the limbs, sticks, and leaves of her nest to reach her. Sybi's heart thundered.

She knelt on the moss. "Thank you for giving me new life and for saving me here on your mountaintop."

The bird's faceted eyes glittered sapphire in the dawn light.

"May I pet you?"

The phoenix nodded.

She *did* understand, and that thrilled Sybi. As she stroked her crown, she said, "I'm sure you have a name. I wish I knew it."

The phoenix remained silent, but Sybi knew what to call her. "Farewell, Mother Phoenix."

In minutes, Sybi was settled on Kes' back. She strapped the tether around her waist and hooked it on its ring, then clamped the harness handholds.

They lifted off.

Flying long and hard, they rested and ate to recharge. Kes had not faltered, and the cliffs of No Land appeared on the third day, her heart soaring, her aches and exhaustion vanishing.

Home.

Below, a crowd awaited them, surprising her until she spotted Terras on Marcos' shoulder. Terras somehow knew when they would arrive and had alerted the village.

Welcome home whispered a thousand voices in one.

Her hands tightened. *Hello, Mother! I'm so very happy.*

As I said you would be.

Mother's smug tone made her laugh. Mother was a weisenheimer. But she kept that thought to herself as the forest chimed its greeting as well.

They landed on a grassy promontory banked by trees, and she directed Pedro so he could do the same.

The first to reach them was a woman who wrapped the depleted Pedro in a fervent embrace, her face wet with tears. Sybi lept off Kes and unstrapped his harness, lifting it and the carry bag into her arms, and backed away so he could change.

Kes strained and paused, his hawk's head bowed.

Oh, dear. Maybe the change was too much for him. "Wait until you're ready."

He shook his head, then strained again, managing to change into his man form. But he fell to his knees, pants bursting from his lips, body trembling. She dropped her bundle and ran, kneeling alongside him. "Kes."

"I...am...well," he said.

"I'm beginning to suspect that phrase." To her surprise, he accepted her helping him to stand.

Kes rasped a chuckle, flicking his damp hair from his face.

The villagers closed in, Marcos in the lead, while Terras bobbled atop the healer's shoulder. Enoch wasn't far behind, as were Luciana, Asher, and dozens more, engulfing them, with everyone talking, no one listening, and being submerged in the general joyful hullabaloo.

Home felt great.

Two days later, Sybi felt as if she had never been away, as if she hadn't been burned alive and emerged changed yet again. With Luciana's help, she'd moved her belongings into Kestrel's aerie. At first, she was reluctant. Giving up her own space was hard, the only people she had ever lived with were Kit and Bree.

But Kes assured her she could keep her original aerie, her own space, while he built her a studio in his aerie.

Which was why she was in her old home, sketching.

Alchemic City… When she first met Mother, she had emphasized Sybi should draw all, in particular Alchemic City. She failed to understand why given the power station was outside.

Soon the station would reach the city, much to everyone's dismay.

Drawing the city's interior remained a challenge. The thing was a floating monstrosity—a maze of tunnels and balconies and dead ends. As she sketched Rhiannon's Golden City, a mist would often close in, obscuring the vision. Though she was encouraged. The more she drew, the more the mists cleared.

Sybi wished Mother would explain, but Mother Tree said how pre-knowledge would change the Fates' intended result.

Which left Sybi's pens figuratively trudging along.

When she entered the zone, she sometimes saw horrible things, never sure if they were *her* fiction or reality. Tomorrow, the Compass True council would convene. She couldn't believe the members had taken two full days to agree on a time, the council's political and social maneuvering the same as Earth's.

The mating thing troubled Sybi. If she was in Kes' proximity, all she could concentrate on was *him*. And if he wasn't physically near, which was often for one reason or another, the urge to be with him plagued her. She wanted to trail him around like a puppy, and though she fought the absurdity of it, she often lost.

Luciana had reassured her Sybi wasn't going crazy. According to her friend, newly bonded couples struggled with an excessive sense of possession and an intense desire to be physically close. At least her feelings were normal, a slight relief. Yet her awkward sexual urges made her uncomfortable, and she continued to manufacture encounters with Kes.

Kes did not feel the same or he handled his impulses better. True, he had been preoccupied, as he had been on the mountaintop, but whatever the problem, he chose not to share. All she wanted was to touch him, breathe him in, hold him. If any of the bond's urges affected him, he masked them well.

At least visiting with Mother Tree had restored a certain balance, though Mother's self-satisfaction emerged often.

See, she had said in that smug tone. *It was inevitable.*

"Well, it's done."

Has he satisfied you?

She couldn't believe Mother asked that, asked about sex. *Sweet Christmas.* The question embarrassed Sybi, and she was even more embarrassed that they hadn't made love.

Mother had said their bonding had a purpose. *It sets in motion that which we planned. Time is needed. Our plan must ripen.*

"Who is 'our'?" Sybi had asked.

Thousands of titters sounded in her head.

Delightful. The trees and Mother found her hilarious. Not that Mother answered her question. Naturally.

Sybi went nuclear but moderated her voice. "Can't you give me any specifics?"

Sobering, in her tree way, Mother's flowering branches stilled. *We of the elements who have been tasked to heal our world.*

"Which elements, The Fates?"

Mother's boughs bent toward her, as if nodding. *Yes. Mother Terra, Father Sky, Mother Air, Father Water, Sorcere—*

Is Sorcere a Father or Mother?

They are both. There are others I cannot name, but Father Tree joins us, as well.

Father Tree. She assumed he was not one of the Fates and had demigod status like Mother. Perhaps their estrangement was part of the plan.

She would see Mother again soon, and perhaps more answers would be forthcoming. Maybe.

A beam of sunlight filtered into her studio, sending dust motes dancing, the open window allowing the pine and sea scents to swirl through the room. A refreshing breath later, she sketched a door leading to the bowels of Alchemic City.

A bird's chirping distracted her. Everything distracted her. She chewed her lip.

Kes was avoiding intimacy because of her new-old looks. She thought a lot about the situation. Maybe he was still physically recovering from his desperate search for her. No. Or, perhaps he was so driven by his mission to destroy the Alchemics, he thought of little else. That didn't fly, either.

Perhaps he'd lost interest. Dammit, that was the old Sybi's thinking, and she didn't believe it. And so she circled back around to her "new" looks.

But Kes was a man filled with craggy depths, not superficial ones.

He remained kind, courteous, warm...and completely asexual toward her.

Only her looks had changed. And yet...

Recalling Kestrel's conflict during their first aborted lovemaking made her wonder. Oh, he had wanted to bond, that was obvious, yet the hawk had wobbled, his hesitation real.

Pondering their relationship would drive her nuts. Simple. When she got home, she would ask Kes why he was not touching her.

Sybi returned to the safety of sketching. Her pencil flew as she sketched a... She reared back. A tortured Tiger Clan member appeared on the page, a man from the waist up and a tiger from the waist down. Her pencil blurred as she sketched his face, until she paused, breathless. Agony. He was in agony, bloody tears streaming down his cheeks as he wept.

She threw down her pencil, eyes burning, and squeezed the

bridge of her nose. No more horror. At least not today. Time to return to Kes' aerie. *Their* aerie. She gathered two pads and a couple of pencils from her supplies.

How the Eleutians would defeat the Alchemics with the station en route to the city accompanied by those monstrous creatures... Her imagination failed, the buzz of her mobile a welcome intrusion.

"Come home, Sybelle," Kestrel said. "Our vidcon with Rafe, Gato, and your sisters is about to begin."

She'd forgotten all about it.

Minutes later, Sybi hung her jacket on its peg, grabbed some cinnamon cookies, and walked through their aerie to the command center. The center oversaw their Clan's tech and observed and protected the borders of No Land, as well as being the site of sensitive meetings.

Most of the dozen monitors banking the room were silent and blank, while at three others, CastOut Sgiaths surveyed different No Land quadrants. One-way glass covered the windows, and permanent sound disrupters sat in the corners and on a central plinth. The place, often noisy, was nearly silent today.

Kes stood before two monitors tweaking dials like a maestro.

"Want one?" she said to him as she held out a cookie.

"No." He continued to calibrate the feed. FaceTime it wasn't. She stood on tiptoe, reached her hands to his shoulders, and kissed his cheek.

He startled, his face a frown, but his eyes warmed from remote to gentle. "Hello, sweet syr."

The urge to call him Big Bird made her giggle.

His brows beetled. "How am I funny?"

Not the time to explain *Sesame Street*. "Not you. Not really. I'll explain after the conference."

A war conference—her skin prickled, muscles twitching. The reality of guns and death terrified her. Imagining her Kestrel bloodied and silent... She shuddered.

The many tales of Kes, Rafe, and Gato fighting the dragon-like dakos had amazed her. They were warriors and knew how to fight. And hadn't she confronted those cube-creatures? And survived.

She could face monsters, sure she could. In truth, she'd like to get her hands on that horrid Alchemic, Fukkes.

Soon, the monitors melded into Rafe and Gato, both sitting in captain's chairs similar to Kestrel's.

"Are Kit and Bree coming?" she asked Kes.

Nodding, he pointed to two screens across the large room to see her sisters' faces. Sybi had thought the six of them would be on the same call.

Kes sat and swiveled his chair to face Rafe and Gato. "Welcome, friends."

His smile, so beautiful and rare, squeezed her heart.

"I will tell all to Rafe and Gato," he said. "Your sisters await you."

They did, but the separation was odd. Even so, she sat in a captain's chair before Bree's and Kit's screens, which were far enough from Kes so their conversations wouldn't overlap. Her sisters knew she was alive, they'd briefly spoken, and she'd told them about the bonding and her physical reversion. But today was the first they'd seen her, which she suspected was why they were staring at her, eyes wide and mute.

Sybi waited, then, "Well?"

"You look..." Bree said in a whisper. "Like *you*."

"How do you feel?" Kit's words tumbled over Bree's.

"What was the nest like?" Bree said.

"You're bonded!" Kit said.

"Guys." Sybi gave her beloved sisters a feeble smile. "One at a time."

"Sorry!" Bree said. "Are you cool with your transformation?"

Not a single CastOut had commented, and that pleased her enormously. She smiled. "I feel like me again." Kit and Bree wouldn't be disappointed.

"How did you escape those monsters?" Kit said. "Rafe knows, but the beast won't tell me."

Bree harrumphed. "Gato the same."

"I can't explain, either," she said. "It's Kestrel's tale to tell."

Bree whined. "Sybs!"

"Stop, Bree," Kit said. "Are you twelve?"

"Sometimes." Bree grinned.

A pause, and Sybi stared at her hands. "I think Kes misses the way I looked, you know, all the glam. That blonde hair *was* gorgeous."

"What?" Bree said, her skepticism obvious. "No. That other you wasn't you."

"Kes doesn't know that," she said.

"You are yourself, Sybs," Kit said. "You're beautiful, and Kestrel isn't a shallow man."

"No, he's not." Sybi snorted. "But beloved sister, I was never beautiful."

"Bullshit," Bree said. "Your beauty is a quiet one. You are lovely inside *and* out."

Sybi warmed, and she felt beautiful. In their eyes, at least. Ah, well. She took a deep breath. "Thank you both."

"What do you think of bonding?" Bree waggled her brows.

A blush heated her cheeks, curse it, not because of their bed sport but its lack. Luciana said bonded couples were like rabbits in heat. She and Kes were the least rabbity couple ever.

"Why aren't we in the Alphas' conversations?" Sybi said. "It feels off."

"I agree," Kit said. "Especially since we're Alphas, too. Rafe said it was so we three could talk, but I'm not buying it."

"I'm not, either," Bree said. "Gato mumbled something similar, but we easily could have talked afterward. Something's going on. They're scheming."

"We'll see about that," Sybi said, swiveling her chair to face Kes. "What plan have you three cooked up?"

The males grew quiet. Too quiet.

Kit disappeared from the screen, reappearing moments later beside her mate. "Rafe?"

The Wolf Alpha's expressive face roared "guilt."

"I will explain later," Rafe said to Kit. "Is it not time for Mimi's mistral lesson?"

Kit snorted. "Your sister won't mind waiting a few extra minutes."

Breena had left her screen, too, and now her arm wrapped around Gato's bicep. She gave him teeth. "I don't trust you. What have you three concocted?"

"*Poosha*, you must trust me." Those bedroom eyes smoldered.

If Kes ever looked at her that way, she would melt into a puddle.

Kes crossed his arms, his face a stoic mask, but his eyes danced with laughter.

Those three had plotted something dangerous and deliberately excluded the women. Talk about sexist. She leaned close and whispered to Kes. "You had better tell me what you guys are planning or else."

Kes shrugged.

A load of bricks hit her on the head. Sybi *knew*. "*You* are flying to the power station, right?"

"I plan to do so, yes."

She was coming to loathe that calm measured voice. "To attack it again. Alone."

Kes' eyes lasered Rafe and Gato. "I will fly a mistral and carry a collapsible lasecannon—"

"A *collapsible* lasecannon?" Gato leaned forward.

"We have developed one here," Kes said. "For the war."

"Impressive," Rafe said, nodding.

Sybi had to stop their absurd weapons discussion. "No. He can't. He drained his reserves searching for me and needs to regain his full strength."

"If trouble arises, I will phoenix," Kes said with a whisper.

"Bullshit." Sybi rolled her eyes. "According to Marcos, you can't. You're tapped out."

"You two might be whispering," Bree said. "But we can all hear you."

"What do you mean, 'phoenix'?" Kit said.

Sybi's eyes widened, but Kes just shrugged.

Rafe slid an arm around Kit's waist. "I will explain later, beauty. Point of fact, Gato and I agree with Sybelle. Therefore, as head of the council, I forbid it, Kestrel."

Kes' lips thinned. "Try."

"His flight to the station will not be necessary," Gato said. "Rafe and I will fly to attack it."

"Kes' expertise is needed with the ground troops, commanding them," Rafe said.

"But he's a bird!" Sybi blurted.

The Cat Alpha gave Kes the side-eye. "How observant, Ma'am Sybelle. He will not be *on* the ground but flying above our troops, as well as directing his avian brothers and sisters. That will give him the large picture, an incredible advantage."

Kes leaned back in his chair and crossed his arms, face serene, the conversation flowing over him like water slid across a rock. "I see your point," Kes said. "I do not agree with it."

"Don't the monsters spit burning poison?" Bree said.

"True, but a small issue we can manage, *poosha*," Gato said.

"You knew I would object," Sybi said to Kes.

"I did." He rose and stretched like the big cat he wasn't. Then again, he had said he was part tiger.

"So that's why you tried to put the three of us off." Kit's dour look had Rafe looking everywhere but at her.

Silence from the three men.

"Tell us," Bree said, her voice stiletto sharp. She poked her mate in the arm.

"The power station has moved," Kes said. "Two hovers and three alien cubes accompany it. Hidden as it was in the desert, we stood a chance of destroying it. Once housed within the city—"

"We can firebomb it and the city," Bree said.

Kes shook his head. "True, within the city the power station is vulnerable to assault, but the city can move at will, fly before any assault reaches them. If we wait until the station reaches its destination, the Alchemics will have time to plan further horrors. They will be unstoppable. Their great weakness is the station. We must destroy it before it arrives."

Rafe nodded. "Simultaneously, Compass True must gather its warriors to attack the city. You are the man to lead our forces, Kestrel."

"To finally rid ourselves of the Alchemic plague." Gato smiled, that devilish one where he looked demonic and way too much like Loki to Rafe's Thor.

The three were good men, fair and true. The idea of them hurt or dying horrified her. Yet war was war. People died.

Mother had said Sybi and Kes were the keys to victory, though Mother had never told her *how*.

"Nonetheless, I go to the station," Kestrel said.

A Sgiath rose to answer a knock at the door. The room went silent as Enoch stepped inside, the atmosphere wary.

Enoch's eyes darted across the monitors to alight on her. "Ma'am Sybelle, pardon the interruption."

"Is something wrong?" She rose from her chair.

"Ohtli has asked for you," Enoch said. "I thought you might come early for your shift and visit with her."

"Of course." She slipped behind Kes' chair, wrapping her arms around him, and whispered, "You can't phoenix again so soon. You *know* this. And your flying, well, it's not up to snuff. You told me so yourself. Don't fly to the power station. Please don't."

He rubbed her hand but said nothing.

Hoping Rafe and Gato could convince him, she bid her goodbyes, bussed Kes on the cheek, and joined Enoch.

"Is Ohtli all right?" She lifted her coat from the peg and slipped it on.

"I do not know." Enoch strode from the aerie like a man on a mission. "The girl is in much pain. Even Marcos cannot discover why."

Sybi soon sat by a sleeping Ohtli, Enoch standing behind them a few steps away.

The girl's eyes blinked open, and she smiled.

"I didn't mean to wake you." Sybi took her hand.

Ohtli's eyes warmed. "You did not."

"Enoch said you wished to see me."

Ohtli closed her eyes, her face twisted in pain.

"Ohtli!"

The girl clung to Sybi, who hung on tight until endless moments later Ohtli blew out a sigh.

Tears welled in Ohtli's eyes. "You made it pass."

Sybi wished that were true, but she had done nothing.

"The Made One did not do that, little Ohtli," Enoch said. "You did it yourself."

Sybi had forgotten he was here.

Ohtli shook her head. "Wrong."

Enoch winked, bowed to them, and left.

"I'm glad I'm here," Sybi said.

"So am I," Ohtli said. "I wanted to see the new you. Asher said you looked different. You do!"

"On the outside. Inside, I'm me."

"I know, silly." A giggle erupted, then she slid her small hand across Sybi's and clasped it. "You are so pretty. Prettier than ever!"

Sybi bent to kiss Ohtli's cheek. "That is very kind."

"I feel something coming for you," Ohtli said, clasping her hand.

"What?"

The girl frowned. "I cannot see it clearly, but it does not matter. You will be well. But after, you *must* see Mother Tree."

"Do you know why?" Sybi said.

Ohtli shook her head, then her body stiffened in pain.

Sybi hugged the girl tight, waiting it out. When it passed, she eased her back onto the pillows, though she continued to clasp her hand. Ohtli's small, delicate fingers gripped hers back.

The child sighed. "Your hands are magic. I can feel the Mothers in them. I am tired, Ma'am Sybelle."

The child's cheeks were sunken, and lines of pain radiated from her eyes.

"Sleep, sweetheart. But then you must eat and drink to keep up your strength. Please stay with us, Ohtli. Your joy and your sweetness are needed. You matter. You and the other children are our future."

Ohtli's lips curled into a gentle smile. "I will try, Ma'am Sybi. I will try very hard."

"Good." She stroked the girl's chestnut hair. "I wish I could do more, sweet girl."

"You will." Ohtli sighed, her lids drooping. "When the time comes, you will."

As Kes observed Sybelle and Ohtli, his throat closed tight enough to choke him. The bond was killing Kestrel, the imperative to mate near uncontrollable. He could not touch his sweet syr. When she had kissed him farewell, he had almost taken her there, on the meeting-room floor, in front of Rafe, Gato, and their women.

The urges before they bonded were strong, but now they had become unmanageable. So unmanageable, they terrified him. He was a beast, this frenzied imperative to mark Sybelle as his own. He could hurt her, or worse, kill her.

As a youngling, barely twenty seasons, he had been attracted to a girl his age named Urcel. A sweet creature of the Polar Clan he had met on walkabout, while he was learning to understand himself and his gifts.

They had kissed and touched and all was well, but when they

coupled, and he had orgasmed, he had gone up in flames. Her screams still echoed inside him.

Blisters had risen on her body as she ran from the bed shrieking in pain. Thank Father Sky Urcel had survived. But he had scarred her, inside and out.

In all his seventy-plus years, he had seldom made love since Urcel, fearing the outcome. Each time, he made certain to spend away from the woman and that had worked. But that was before he and Sybelle had mated. With it came the fierce, intractable desire to couple, to truly mate. He doubted he could withdraw from Sybelle, and if he flamed... Unthinkable.

Sybelle left with a kiss on the sleeping Ohtli's cheek and a squeeze to Kes' arm, and he approached Ohtli's bedside. As he sat, the child awoke.

"We must talk, Kestrel. I have things to tell you."

CHAPTER

SIXTEEN

Sybi walked through the forest to their aerie, having visited the market. Trees brushed their leaves across her cheeks and arms, while groundcover tickled her ankles. Their scents filled her with a powerful sense of belonging. Hard to believe that she had landed in a place she understood, one where she fit.

Kes had shown her his luteon room where he crafted the instruments. Much like an Earthly lute, the instrument had a deep, pear-shaped body with a fat round back, and a neck and strings, many more of the latter than she'd seen on Earthly lutes. There might be other differences as well, but she was no musicologist. His playing was equally lovely, as was his singing voice. She had yet to sing for him.

Each day was a challenge, each night fraught with anxiety over the coming war, waiting up for Kes until he took to their bed, big enough so they needn't touch. She liked bedtime. They would talk about their day, about the books they had read or the movies they had shared; whether he would practice sword fighting with her the following day or if she would show him another judo form; about a gown she had purchased for an upcoming celebration or whether

215

they would breakfast in the dining hall or at home. When she began to doze, as was inevitable, he would hold her, and her fears would recede. Yet he remained apart from her, separate. Even when he held her, intimacy seemed a distant memory.

All while a constant rumble at the back of Sybi's mind spoke of the violence to come. She hoped she was strong enough, brave enough, courageous enough to see it through.

Earlier, she had vowed to ask Kes straight out why he was avoiding intimacy. Yet she had not. When she arrived home from her forest walk, she would, even knowing she might not like his answer.

She slipped inside their aerie, laying her purchases on the kitchen island. Tonight she'd make cavatelli with red sauce, comfort food, the work a palliative for her constant ache for Kes.

The bond pulsed, pulling her toward the aerie's rear where Kes worked. He had beat her home, and much as she wanted to see him, she instead searched out a huge cook pot and whisk. Emptying the flour, tomatoes, semolina, and the other fixings from her bags, she laid them on the counter, then pulled over a bowl to mix the cavatelli's ingredients, which she did with speed. Spreading them in a single layer on lightly floured baking sheets, she took care they didn't touch each other. They would dry in about a half-hour or so, and she would pop them into the pot.

Kes strode into the kitchen. "Have you seen the oil for my sword?"

He had unwound his braid since she'd last seen him, and blue and rust locks spilled across his shoulders.

"No. The oil I use for mine just ran out, too. Can you use olive oil?" She held up the flask.

He shook his head. "It will turn rancid and attract dust. I need mineral oil."

"Sorry." He just stood there, tall and glorious, as if nothing was wrong, watching her with owlish eyes until her frustration grew and she stalked toward him, peering up, hands on hips.

"Why haven't you touched me?" she said. "Made love with me?"

Sybi caught a blink of surprise before his face hardened, and he clasped his hands behind his back. "The answer is complicated."

He was avoiding eye contact. This from the man whose fierce glare could stare down an army. Kes was pissing her off. Really pissing her off. His behavior, so different from his warmth on the mountaintop—as if he couldn't bear the sight of her.

Screw this. Kestrel was her mate, bound to her for eternity. He must feel the warmth and strength of their twined bond.

Sybi gave him the side-eye and turned away, making a show of checking on the cavatelli. "I believe I'm bright enough to understand your 'complicated' reasons."

Nothing.

"Dammit, talk to me, Kes." Using a second bowl, she mashed tomatoes for the sauce, adding olive oil, oregano, and other spices to the mix. *Heavens help her*, she was tired. Exhausted from her changes, their relationship, him.

She huffed. Her Kestrel might not be easy. But he was hers. *Hers.* She waved a wooden spoon and rounded on him. "Why, Kes?"

The room was empty.

"Fuckwad."

Sybi finished her prep work, put the cavatelli and sauce in the coolfreeze, and sat down to draw. Yeah, screw him. Restlessness made her toss down her pencils and turn on the vidscreen. A war movie. Just what she needed. "Vid off."

A bath might soothe her frustration. The taps were soon going, but she was too impatient for the tub to fill.

"Dammit." She flicked the taps off and stomped into their bedroom, pulling on her hiking boots and a warmer shirt. He had gone somewhere, but their bond would lead her to the frustrating man, and she would set things right. Somehow she would fix this.

A scratching at the front door. Terras, most likely.

She finished tying her boots and crossed the aerie, but before she could answer, she spotted a folded piece of paper on the floor, slipped beneath the door. When she checked, the landing was empty.

Please come to the far greenhouse. I have a problem and need your help. Luciana.

Sybi dropped the note on the counter, then shrugged on her thin jacket, "hearing" Kes tell her to take her knives. She sighed, but buckled the holster around her waist and slipped a knife into its back sheath, then another one into her boot. A slight drizzle made her grab her hat, and she left the aerie.

By the time she reached the farthest greenhouse, the drizzle had stopped, the air moist and rich with scents lifted by the small shower. She reached for the door. "Luciana?"

The air rippled behind her, and she caught a familiar scent.

A foul-smelling cloth slammed across her mouth.

She jerked reflexively, shoving an elbow into a cast-iron stomach, but grew dizzy, tired. Enervation oozed into her, blackness encroaching. She could not...

Sybi awakened as if she were pulling herself out of black sludge. She lay across a horse's back on her belly, wedged between the pommel and a man's crotch like a dead fish. The binding across her mouth was fresh, missing that redolent smell of whatever had knocked her out.

For whatever reason, she'd been kidnapped. She almost laughed aloud.

She might be screwed, but she wasn't done. No way.

The man hadn't killed her outright—always good news. Then again, he might torture or rape her—a bad-news possibility. She swallowed, throat dusty dry. Her stomach roiled and she started to cough. Her captor was oblivious, and the horse's hooves plodded relentlessly away from the village, the CastOuts, and Kes.

No one would know she was missing. Not for a while, at least, given the man had taken her from the farthest greenhouse. Kes wouldn't expect her for hours, no one would. She was on her own.

Sybi whimpered. She wasn't Bree or Kit, didn't have that fierce hardwiring. She would try her damned best.

Bree's favorite phrase chimed—*No! Do or do not. There is no try.*

Squeezing her eyes tight, she vowed to *do*. Just what that was, trussed up like a turkey, she hadn't a clue.

They rode for what felt like hours, and though her stomach flip-flopped and her fury rose, she dozed.

Sybi awakened when the horse stumbled. She groaned, her eyes sticky with grit. The sea roared in her ears, waves crashing to the nearby shore, the air damp. Above, gulls wheeled in a darkening sky. She stretched her neck to see beyond the tumble of rocks. A sandy beach with the sea beyond.

Though she tried to move her fingers, nothing happened, her whole body numb, yet aching. But her mind was crystal, zooming a million miles an hour, and she searched for trees or vegetation that could help her escape. None except for some seagrasses. Maybe they could flog her captor to death. Right.

The horse picked its way down the small verge to the water's edge, halting near a bowled rock holding a pool of rainwater. Her captor loosened the reins and the bay drank.

Sybi would like a drink, too. She couldn't even swallow, her throat too parched.

He touched her hair and she froze, then he fiddled with her gag until he could poke down the fabric. Something metal pressed against her lips, and she tipped her head back and drank, the water ambrosia. The canteen disappeared too soon, and she resisted the urge to spit her last mouthful at him.

They walked downward, nearing rocks that curved in a line far into the distance. She sighed. No matter what scenario for escape presented itself, a practical one eluded her.

The sun faded, the breeze promising a chilly night. When she lifted her head, night's first star winked into view. She wished upon it for strength and courage. She might be weary and beyond uncomfortable, but her captor must be tired, too, having ridden all day in the heat. A plus for her.

The horse turned onto a small dip along the shore, night shadows smearing the world.

An object slammed against her head, and she was gone.

Sybi surfaced on a sandy floor, covered in a blanket, head throbbing to the beat of the flickering light—a campfire inside a cave. Her captor, on his haunches, turned a makeshift spit and the smell of meat filled the air. She tried to scratch her itchy nose, but her unbound hands flopped like jelly. They hurt, too, but she squeezed them open and closed to get them working again. Each movement shot pain to her pounding head, which had started ringing.

But, no, that was not right. The ringing was beautifully pitched, a sweet, sweet sound. *Treesong.* In the distance, true, but the redwoods were singing to her.

If Mother could tell Kestrel where she was… Sybi called Mother again and again, but she never answered.

"I see you are awake," her captor said.

The thrill of recognition sizzled, then shock and disbelief. Enoch? "I am," she said, her words little more than a croak.

"Supper is on the way."

How could Enoch… True, she didn't know him well, but mercurial as he was, he was always kind and caring when dealing with patients. That he would kidnap her made no sense.

"Would you care to sit up?" he said

"Yes."

He removed the skewered meat from the brazier and set it aside. As he approached, she forced herself not to shrink away, though her skin crawled. His eyes glittered a little too maniacally for her taste. Whether he was crazed, angry, or on a mission, she needed to understand his purpose to effectively deal with him.

He lifted her by the shoulders to a sitting position against the cave wall, and she failed to stifle a groan, body aching like when she had the flu. Arranging the blanket around her, his hand casually brushed her breast. Pig.

"Are you warm enough?" he said. "It gets cold at night, especially by the beach."

Mr. Amiable. What a creep. But she was not Bree, not daring enough to return some snark. She nodded and shifted position. A rock or... Maybe it was her knife. Moving her shoulders and back, she hoped. No, only the rock. She wiggled her foot, but he had taken that knife, too. Not that it mattered. She had never stabbed living flesh. She wasn't even sure she had the guts to do so.

Dammit, she had to do something rather than sit like a lump.

"Food will be ready shortly." He offered a blinding smile and whispered in her ear, his voice seething with sexual undertones. "I have kamla and drass, and water of course. Which would you prefer?"

Like they were on a date. "Water."

"Water it is!" he said with great cheer, then bustled around finishing his preparations.

Stars afire, she wanted Kes to come. And yet she didn't, at least not until she understood why Enoch had kidnapped her. The rough cave walls were dry, with furs, food, and other accouterments stacked in a neat pile. Enoch must come here often.

Needing to pee, she convinced Enoch to give her some privacy after he lifted her, and she wobbled to the cave's mouth. Outside, he tied a rope to her ankle and followed, allowing her the privacy of a large boulder. With hands still half-numb, she managed to lower her jeans and crouched down to take care of business. The treesong grew in volume.

Tell Mother where I am.

Their song continued, but the trees did not acknowledge her words.

"Are you well, Made One?" Enoch shouted from the other side of the boulder.

"Just peachy!"

When she completed her task, they returned to the cave and she washed up. At the wave of his hand, she moved to sit before the fire, and he handed her a bowl of meat and the quinoa he had made in a fry pan. Strange as it was, he thrust a carrot at her. "We must eat our vegetables."

"That's what my mother always said." She bit into the carrot, hesitating when she speared a piece of meat. "Chicken?"

"Rattlesnake." He laughed.

Bile shot into her mouth.

I am here.

She clamped her teeth, preventing her startle. Not Mother. Not Kes. But Terras. Perhaps he would peck Enoch to death.

"Snake is quite tasty," he said.

"I'm sure it is." For the first time in ages, Terras was in her head. *You're in the cave?*

Yes. Is Kes here?

No. Well, swell. Now she was worried about Terras, too.

Your face still reveals all, Terras said.

What?

You need not worry about me.

She almost rolled her eyes.

"Do you not like the snake?" Enoch asked as if they were dining at the Four Seasons.

She grimaced. "You're working with the Alchemics, aren't you."

He grinned. "How could you think that, Made One? Though it is they who are coming to collect you."

Sweet Christmas. She had to escape before they arrived. "So you are only sort of working with them?"

In a flash, the point of a knife was an inch from her left eye. "I could always carve you up a little, nothing major, but if your one eye remains in your head, I do not think Fukkes would mind if I took the other. Eyes are quite tasty, you know."

He really would, and she was scared. Yet her gut said he was scared, too. Of Fukkes.

"I've met the Alchemic. My maker, or so he claimed. I doubt he would appreciate you marring his creation." *Oh, goddess, please do not.*

Enoch spat in her face. "If not for him, I would have killed you weeks ago. Since your appearance changed, he wishes to study you."

"What is *wrong* with you, Enoch?" she blurted out. "You speak of maiming, kidnapping, and killing as if they mean nothing."

"You *are* nothing." He shrugged. "You have no soul."

"You're an Anti-Made One." She shouldn't be shocked, yet she was.

"Correct on the first guess," he said, arms wide like a game-show maestro.

"*Why,* Enoch? You're a healer."

He backhanded her and she flew sideways, blood pooling in her mouth, her ears ringing.

"You Made Ones are abominations," he continued. "Constructs like yourself and the Alchemics' technology have ruined Eleutia. Now, they intend to leave our world. Finally. Once they depart, we Antis will take control and set Eleutia to rights."

Again, she clamped her teeth to keep from laughing. His words *were* laughable. Kes and others had told her how few numbers made up the Anti-Made Ones. It seemed their vile, fanatical group had malleable rules, ones that changed to suit their agenda.

She wiped her bloody mouth with her forearm and pushed herself up. Bree had told her how an Anti—a man Breena had trusted—had tried to kill her. The Antis might be both determined and pernicious, but their ideas of controlling Eleutia were far-fetched at best.

"When does Fukkes arrive?" she asked.

He checked his mobile. "Soon."

"Aren't you worried about The Kestrel coming for me?"

Enoch threw another stick on the fire. "Fukkes has plans for him, as well. If those fail, I will kill him."

"You will...?" She snorted. "That's very funny."

His cunning look gave her shivers.

His words are ridiculous. Terras' intrusion made her jerk.

Shush.

He is a bad one.

Sybi agreed. *But he's a loose cannon. Don't engage him.*

What is a loose cannon?

Not now, Terras! She could stall, would do so, but she wished she could get herself out of this mess rather than wait for rescue. That was wimpy.

Though Sybi had no weapons, she did have her martial arts. But her skills were more defensive than offensive. Even so, if he moved close to her again...

"What set you on this path, Enoch? You're a good man. I've seen it. You run our infirmary, for sky's sake. You're a healer, not a killer."

"So tempting to tell you," he said.

His sly, hooded eyes reminded her of night things, dark and slimy, and she shot him an innocent look. "Then give in to temptation."

"Did you know that your flesh on Earth is dead?"

"I'm well aware," she said, wondering what in Hades Terras was doing.

"When I planned to end your life..." He frowned. "Fukkes intervened. On your return from your feeble attempt at the power station, the Alchemics had never seen anything like you. Those alien emaks are killing machines, yet you and The Kestrel escaped them. He will not again. Stranger still, your appearance changed. Fukkes and that Cabal of his are now fascinated with you." He picked up a stick and poked her thigh.

"Stop it."

"Do you feel?"

"Of course."

He prodded her again, and she batted the stick away.

"Fukkes wishes to do further research on you." He removed his knife from its waist sheath and pressed its point to her thigh.

"Will you bleed?" he said.

Sybi froze. He was close enough for her to...

He cut her, then spun away in a sinuous move that should have been impossible, to go beyond her reach.

Pain blossomed, but she ground her teeth and narrowed her eyes. "What am I, your pincushion?" Enoch was playing with her, just as the Alchemics wished to do. Those men and women would poke, probe, and torture her like a lab rat.

He tossed her a cloth. "Bind it. The cut was merely a sample. Do not misbehave."

Fuck you. But she remained silent, unwilling to give him more fodder for his cruelties. Sybi bound her wound and sat on the sandy floor of the cave. She should be more terrified. Yet given all she had done and experienced on Eleutia—awakening in a casket, meeting Mother, confronting the monstrous aliens, becoming a part of mother phoenix—her "terror" button must have been reset.

Terras had gone silent and there appeared to be no escape, but the ring of her sisters' words strengthened her resolve.

Of course there's a way out, she imagined Kit saying.

Suck it up and find it, Bree's voice echoed.

Sybi summoned her courage, her old meekness a faded thing that nonetheless remained familiar and appealing. Easier to be passive. But passivity felt wrong, especially with the pulse of Kes strong within her, a vibrance that bolstered her nascent courage.

"What will your family think of your betrayal, Enoch?"

"I have no family," he spat. "They abandoned me because they saw me as a demon, an animal."

"They abandoned you on the orders of the Alchemics," she said. "What about your CastOut family? They love you and your work."

"*Family?*" He spat in the dirt. "CastOuts are abominations as well. Three-armed creatures, a flying blind man, the pathetic girl who is killing herself with her gifts—creations of Alchemic science. CastOuts have no grace, no humanity, no souls."

"But you're one of them." She kept her tone soft and caring. That he was a product of Alchemic science seemed to elude him. She had no clue what his "gift" was, but his CastOut status appeared diametrically opposed to the Anti-Made Ones' cause. Yet he embraced it. "How can you, in good conscience, turn me over to the Alchemics when I possess my natural form?"

"That is the point." He smiled, leaned back, and took another bite of rattlesnake.

"I don't get it."

"By the by," he said. "How *did* your change happen?"

She laughed. "I have no idea."

He set his meal aside and inched closer, grabbing her shoulder, knife again an inch from her left eye. "You *must* know. Perhaps whatever happened to you could change me back to a man."

"You *are* a man."

He squeezed harder, and pain shot down her arm. "*How?*"

Sybi growled. "I told you, I don't know! I woke up this way!"

Which was when Terras entered the cave and padded over to stare at Enoch.

"Fuck!" she said.

Enoch tilted his head and smiled at Terras. "What have we here?" In a lightning move, his blade flew, nearly decapitating the peregrine.

Yet Terras had sailed over a rock and out of reach. He began to groom his ruffled feathers.

Enoch rose like the snake they were supposed to eat and pounced on Terras.

"Let him go!" she screeched.

"He dies."

"Not a chance!" Sybi leaped to her feet, more like a wobble, and reached for a rock. Even if she failed to land a killing blow, her distraction could free Terras.

The earth shook. Literally. *Mother.*

Sybi crashed to her knees and Enoch tilted sideways, his hand shooting out to steady himself on a wall. Freed, Terras scrabbled toward the cave entrance, single wing flapping.

Enoch tore after him, and Sybi added their dinner's frying pan to her arsenal and ran.

At the cave's entrance, wind whipped the sand and debris in furious bursts, while high above the forest's smaller trees bent like limbo dancers.

Enoch closed on Terras.

"Don't you *dare!*" She pumped on more juice as she raced toward them.

"I will kill the unnatural bird." Enoch sprang, landing on his belly, hands clasping Terras in front of him. He rose to his feet and began to squeeze, grinning.

He would kill her friend before she reached them.

"Mother, help us!"

The wind gusted, picking up furious speed, debris clouding the air, and she flung the frying pan and rock at Enoch.

Sybi would swear the gusts directed the pan for it banged Enoch's head with a satisfying thunk, while the rock crashed into his arm. He staggered, but his death grip on Terras remained.

Vines slithered down the cliff face to wrap Enoch in a loving embrace, and Sybi snatched Terras from the stunned man.

The world stilled, the eye of a hurricane, and held its breath.

Terras cradled in her arms, she tried to control her joy. Terras was alive, and his ruffled feathers settled, his bead-black eyes focused on Enoch.

The vines had swaddled all of Enoch except for his head.

Dizzy with relief, she thumped onto her bum.

A pulse from the bond. Kes stood high above on the cliff's edge, arms crossed, face thunderous.

Mother, Kestrel is here.

About time.

The wind died, sticks, pebbles, and brush dropping to the sand. Above, moonlight revealed a bloody Enoch, a drained Sybi, and a chagrinned Terras, who tucked his head beneath his wing.

CHAPTER

SEVENTEEN

Sybi had cleaned and bandaged Enoch's cuts after Kes had knocked him out with brutal efficiency, unconcerned with the Alchemics' arrival. If they neared, Kes would smell them.

While Kes bound Enoch's hands and feet, she went to check on Terras, the very image of ruffled feathers and shame. Outside, Kes unsaddled Enoch's horse, tying his reins to a dead bush near the cave's entrance, then hefted a mobile the size of a landline from his pack and made a call.

"Come." He clicked off and turned to leave.

Terras hopped to Sybi and crawled up to his favorite perch on her shoulder.

"Kes." She sighed, frustrated at her sudden exhaustion. "We can't just leave Enoch and the horse."

Kes paused at the cave entrance, giving her his profile, but little more. "Several Sgiaths come."

"They'll put him in jail?"

He nodded. "After all is settled, he will be expelled."

"From No Land?" She shivered. "Will anyone take him in?"

Kes shrugged. "I doubt it. Not when they hear his crimes. Come, though I cannot scent the Alchemics yet, we must leave before they arrive."

She looked at Enoch one last time.

Gone! "Kes!"

He nodded, his eyes not on her but on the anaconda-sized cobra slithering from the cave. Kes drew his sword and moved forward.

"Don't!" Sybi said.

The snake flowed up the cliff, his body so massive she had trouble taking it in.

"This is what you call irony, is it not?" He slammed his sword into its scabbard with force.

Enoch reached the clifftop and slid out of sight.

"How is it irony?" she said, shaken from the sight of the massive snake.

"We never knew Enoch's gift," Kes said. "Now we do. When the Sgiaths arrive, they will find him."

"He could escape them, too."

Kes' lips thinned. "If so, I suspect our timber rattlers will object to his alien presence. With vehemence. Come. We return home."

Sore, scratched, and troubled, Sybi began her bath for the second time that day. As she soaped and rinsed, lolling in the steamy tub, her amorphous anger coalesced, not at Enoch but at Kestrel. She dried herself, threw on a t-shirt and loose pants, and hunted for the man to find him practicing Taekwondo forms in their wood-floored training room.

"I've been teaching you judo," she said, affecting a casual tone. "Where did you learn those?"

He completed the movement and paused. "Your sister."

"Kitlyn?"

"Breena."

"I see."

Sybi would make him notice her, make him end his indifferent pose and *react*. She doffed her linen pants and began her own forms wearing only her panties. From beneath her lashes, she watched his reaction—heated eyes, body taut, hands fisting.

Good.

She began a Sa Jang for no reason other than it came to mind, pushing away thoughts of Kestrel and welcoming her sensei's image in her mind. He had been old and wrinkled and sometimes forgetful, but Master Karen always remembered his forms. His teaching was impeccable, his eyes wells of knowledge.

"Stop." Kes halted in front of her, his hands banding her arms.

She breathed in his scent, a thrill arcing through her. "Why?"

He shook his head, released her, and walked toward the door.

She reached for him and grabbed his hand. "Can't we talk like regular people?"

"We are not regular people," he said over his shoulder.

"So what? We can try. Won't you try? I want to understand what's wrong, Kes. We need to fix us."

His nose flared, as if he were fighting a battle he knew he couldn't win, and turned to her. Warm arms slid around her waist, his breath hitching.

Peering up into his strong face her heart thudded. Working out their issues meant everything. A real relationship mattered more than even the bond. "You can tell me anything, Kes. You've listened to me, counseled me, comforted me. Let me do the same for you."

"Sybelle, your presence alone does that."

Sybi warmed from inside out. "I'm glad, but I need to understand, too. Don't you see, when you hurt, so do I? When you're frustrated, I feel it, too. Your pain and confusion, your hurts, I want to heal those as you do mine."

He squeezed her tight, holding on for dear life, his hard cock pressing against her belly. He desired her, and yet...

"You have seen me both skinny and curved," she said. "Mousy brown-haired and a brilliant blonde, plain and glamorous, so I—"

"Skinny? Mousy? *Plain?*" He leaned back to look her in the eye. "Never. You are the most glorious creature I have ever beheld."

Though his words stole her breath, she raised a brow. "Pouring it on too thick. I look nothing like when you first found me."

"What?" His confusion appeared genuine. "True, your physical appearance is somewhat different, but you are you." He examined her for long moments, face pensive, eyes warm. "And now your hair is the color of my wing splashed with gold, your eyes the calm before the storm, and your curves and breasts..." He paused, his gaze heating further, and cleared his throat. "You were made to fit my hands to perfection."

She tucked her head into his shoulder. She would not ask. She should not ask. She had to ask. "But your hesitation on the mountain when you saw me, well, I thought you were disappointed."

"Did you?" A spark in those eyes. "Foolish woman. I was, I am enchanted." He leaned down to brush his cheek over hers.

Her heart thumped. *This man.* "I'm enchanted, too." She stood on tiptoe to kiss him, but he turned his head from her lips.

"Dammit, Kes, why won't you even kiss me?"

Kes was afraid for her. Always for her. "More than my life, I wish to make love with you, my Sybelle. But I am...afraid." That she believed her looks did not appeal had shocked him. He found her natural beauty earthier, more real and true, but even if Sybelle's hair were green, her body bent, her eyes milky, he would love her still. How could he not?

"Please tell me why," she said.

With a sigh, he led her to the great room and sat her on the sofa. He took the chair, for touching her would lead to frustration. "I met Urcel many years ago when I was but an adolescent." He told her about the Bear Clan woman, and how he had burned her.

"You're afraid I'll burn up."

Terrified, in truth. Though why her face showed both wonder and confusion eluded him.

"How could you burn me?" she said.

He reared back. "I explained what happens when I experience a powerful orgasm."

"You have. But you've already burned me up once, right? I doubt burning will be a problem."

He froze. Yes, they had both phoenixed, but he did not believe it would be the same when they made love. Looking at those sea-storm eyes shamed him. She was pleading, begging, even. That was wrong.

"You won't hurt me, Kes."

His cock ached, but his heart ached worse. He longed to make love with his sweet syr and share their bliss.

She crossed to his chair and brushed her lips across his, sending shivers down his spine. When her hands cupped his face, he trembled, his eyes closed as feelings of bliss suffused him.

"Touch me, Kes."

His need burst free, yet he forced it back, images of a burned Sybelle holding his ardor in check. Instead, he kissed her with flutters on her cheeks, her neck, and her soft, soft lips. She tasted sublime.

"That feels wonderful," she said. "*You* feel wonderful."

"You are beyond my imaginings. I cannot express…"

"Show me, then."

"I will not," he said.

"Then I will show you." She pulled him to a stand, then removed his clothes, and then hers, and drew him down to the carpet of flowers and twining vines. They lay beside one another, naked, touching, exploring, savoring as their passion spiraled, and he entered her slowly, wishing to feel every inch, to watch as her expression of delight turned to urgency.

Her fingers threaded through his unbound hair, shooting sparks wherever she touched, their bond a pulse growing more fervent with each stroke of his cock. Sybelle neared completion, her cries and moans a song that spiraled him closer to the pinnacle.

Yet his fear remained, and Kes held back. She would find her bliss without him, and she would be safe.

"Oh, no," she said in a passion-drugged voice. "Not a chance I'm leaving you behind."

In a shocking move, she flipped them, so he lay on his back with Sybelle atop him. "Not a fucking chance, my love."

Her hands pressed on his chest, her arms straightening, her hips insistent.

Kes fought, tried to stay motionless, sweat greasing them both, her seeking their pleasure and resisting his own.

Sybelle sped up, and a groan erupted from his lips.

He could not, *should* not.

"Come." Sybelle peppered kisses across his mouth, his neck, his chest. "Come with me, my love."

The bond flared, and Kes' iron will turned to ash.

They came in a conflagration that went on and on and on.

Sybi's mouth refused to form words, her breath sighs as she descended from the peak. *Heavens above.* Kes' slick arms held her fast, cocooning her in warmth as he slid them to their sides, face to face, both wearing smiles, his eyes warmer than a summer sky.

Several fledgling feathers poked from his hair, and she brushed a finger over a downy surface. He shuddered. Oh, my.

She rested her cheek on his chest. He smelled of musk and man, and as she breathed him in, she laughed.

"Our activity did not strike me as humorous," he said, his words threaded with soft amusement.

"I agree," she said. "Ummm. But did you see our carpet?"

His head turned, eyes widening. "Ah."

Blackened and burned, it had not withstood the heat.

"Not a problem," he said in all seriousness.

"No?" She kissed his chin, that sense of oneness with him remaining, and scraped a damp blue lock of hair from his face, then nipped his earlobe. Perhaps he would want another go. His shiver forced her to kiss his chest.

"We will get a new carpet and plenty of sheets," he said, though his eyes sizzled.

Sybi licked his neck. "Ha! We'll need dozens."

"Agreed." Kes drew her closer and they talked no more.

The following day, far happier with the world than she had been in eons, Sybi joined Kes, Marcos, and Asher in the command room to meet with the Compass True council. The Sgiaths had not found Enoch, but she doubted he'd dare return to the CastOuts—they and the forest watched.

Prior to the meeting, Kes told her of Gato and Rafe's upcoming mission to find the moving power station and how his concern "rides me like a big cat, its claws dug into my back." Now, they sat around the table, Kes wearing his stoic face, but his eyes revealed his concern.

Both her sisters and their mates would attend today's meeting, then the men would depart for the desert. Her sisters intended to join Rafe and Gato in battling the creatures, not that they had mentioned that fact to the men. Sybi hadn't told Kes, either. She worried, sure, but the sisters' three mates wished to wrap each of them in cotton. Absurd. Kit and Bree were warriors, and she aspired to be one, too.

Outside beneath the towering trees, village members began to gather, some bringing chairs for the infirm and elderly who couldn't stand for long periods. A few carried signs urging the war all knew was imminent. Yet Sybi also tasted fear in the air. Each CastOut would play a part—the boy whose mouth could shoot flame, the nurse whose breath could kill, the Sgiath who could teleport fifty yards—and all the many others with talents, some obvious and some obscure.

They would use gifts disdained by the Alchemics and feared by the general populace, though each would make the choice to fight using their gift or to join the more traditional armed forces. Those with gifts like hers and Luciana's would command the trees, whose whispers had risen to near shouts. They despised the Alchemic hold, as did Eleutia's animals, symbionts and not.

Luciana joined them, and all took their seats around the council table. A dozen vidscreens lit up as distant council members signed on all across Eleutia. Mates such as herself sat around tables, on couches, or stood behind their partners, and her mantle of authority felt almost tactile, surprising her.

Rafe called the meeting to order, and she listened as different council members spoke, as tempers heated and passions soared. But to her, Bree and Kit's worry was obvious, and she was sure hers mirrored theirs. Kes could die. Rafe and Gato could die. Unthinkable.

Come to me.

Mother. Of all times. Mother Tree had been silent for days, and though Sybi visited where she had last seen her, she found only the forest floor.

I am in the midst of a council meeting for war. Sybi assumed Mother understood, for long moments passed while the Dolphin Clan Alpha held forth, though several private conversations were going on at once.

Come to me. Now.

Sybi leaned toward Kes, who was explaining *again* to the Ferret's Chief Armorer what had occurred at the power station.

"I have to go," she said to him. "Mother Tree."

He nodded, not missing a beat in his explanation.

She kissed his cheek, and he turned to take her lips with his.

When Sybi broke the kiss and whispered, "Later."

Fukkes twirled in his chair atop the dais, Mari and Xenon's bowl beside him on a bed of blue velvet, the gray-black smoke swirling in agitation. His darlings were excited, too.

He waited. Patiently. Gleefully.

The Keystone—what the Eleutian animals called a power station —was on its way, and when it arrived, they would decimate this disgusting world and all its revolting denizens.

Darva rushed into the hall.

He whirled toward her. "Do you have it?"

"Yes!" Darva thrust her tablet in front of him.

Joy filled him as he stared at the screen. A set of coordinates pulsed—the same CastOut energy source they had tracked numerous times had reappeared. Though its origin remained elusive, they had recalibrated the extensor to the precise pulse. That had taken weeks, but now they had done it.

He laughed hard and long. "Release the Kraken!"

"What?" Darva said, her look of confusion annoying.

The woman was so prosaic. "An Earthian joke you will understand in time." He gleefully twirled his chair to again face the console and his hand flew across dials and levers, giving the go signal.

"How long will it take for the strike?" she said.

"Not long. The energy will not escape us. Not this time." He pulled a final lever, his eyes following the launch trajectory. Fukkes was certain the "energy" had to do with that Sybelle, the Made One who had miraculously changed in appearance. The team had been instructed to capture her, if possible. If not, they were to end her.

Sybi walked through the forest, the trees silent. Worrisome. She began to run, urgency pushing her. By the time she reached the sentinels' canopy of mist, she was panting.

The mist parted, the sentinels opening for her, and she stepped through. Each time she beheld Mother Tree, awe suffused her.

Light flowed down from above splashing the translucent blossoms, today the heart-shaped flowers were a spectacle of peach and yellow darkening to orange or red. Like a waterfall, they cascaded around the small tree and ran in rivulets over the forest floor. Sybi parted Mother's branches. A multicolored carpet of flowers cradled Mother's silver-barked trunk, embedded with sapphires, rubies, emeralds, and other precious gems.

Hello, child.

"Mother." She closed the distance and sat at Mother's feet, crossing her legs.

Mother stroked her with flowers that felt like angels' wings. *I see you have met Ohtli.*

"You know her?" Sybi was surprised.

She is one of mine, a world walker like yourself, though she walks Eleutia's past and future, as well. Mother's voice held a smile.

"She's a wonderful girl."

Have the healer continue his mesmerizing work. There is hope.

"I hope you're right. I care for her very much." Encouraged, Sybi made a point to tell Marcos of Mother Tree's words. "The Compass True council is meeting. We go to war against the Alchemics." She brushed a finger over a peach flower.

You must remain strong for what is to come. Remember the three. Remember Father Tree lives. And remember that we endure, Sybelle. We always endure.

"I'm glad."

When the time is ripe, tap your fingers above your heart three times.

"Like this?" Sybi tapped to show her.

Yes, child. For you.

A diamond the size of a robin's egg popped from Mother's trunk to fall on a patch of moss.

Sybi lifted the stone. "Is it magic?"

Mother laughed, branches atremble. *A simple gift.*

The light in the stone captivated her. "Thank you."

You will endure, as well.

Would she? She felt strong, at least, stronger than she used to be. Her confidence had grown, too, and she had opened her heart to love. "But will I be strong enough?"

You will see, kiddo.

Warmth from Mother poured into her, lifting Sybi's lips to a smile. "I hear you, oh Oracle mine."

The sentinels clacked their leaves with laughter. They always found it humorous when she called Mother "Oracle." Mother chortled, too.

"I *will* be strong enough," she said, her joy full up.

Mother leaned toward her, brushing flowers across her cheek... and froze.

GO! Mother commanded.

Sybi toppled backward, the strength of the command flattening her.

GO!

She had done this before, and she remembered the drill. She dove out the sentinels' opening and...

RUN! screamed a bass chorus. The sentinels.

Run she did, though she twirled, running backward as the sentinels began to disappear, the mist closing in.

Movement from the skies and men in bulky black suits appeared. They wore jetpacks, along with huge machines hoisted on their shoulders.

RUN!

Sybi stopped. A man glanced her way, and she dove behind a redwood as the dozen or so men landed. The mist thickened, concealing Mother and the sentinels from view.

The men lifted their packs from their shoulders onto the ground, then uncovered them to reveal machines with long barrels.

With her mind, Sybi called Kes and Terras, her sisters, and Kes again.

The group unlatched small metal tubes from their waists, expanded them, and threaded them to the mouths of the machines. As if in a choreographed ballet, they hoisted the contraptions to their shoulders again and pressed triggers.

Flame streamed across the sentinels.

Mother's guardians shrieked in pain, the mist vanishing.

With flames licking up its trunk, the largest sentinel bent nearly in half to crush an attacker, while another swatted a man to its left and he flew into the treetops. But that wasn't enough to stem the flames, which raced up the sentinels' trunks and limbs to engulf their leafy tops, the massive trees writhing as they burned. A sentinel on the right crumbled.

This could not be. She had to stop them. Sybi ran toward the men, but trees lifted their roots and slapped her with branches. She stumbled, pushing at limbs, jumping across roots, but more replaced them until she could only shove and weep and shove some more.

The forest echoed with screams and shouts. *She had to get to Mother.*

Sybi kept pushing and pressing at the branches, but she couldn't find her way out.

Cloying black smoke was everywhere, making it near impossible to see, but she pressed forward one challenging step at a time. She ducked under limbs, climbed over roots, and batted branches that slapped her face and shoved her sideways.

"Mother!"

Yards behind her, a bellow. Then an answering one.

The trees' screams increased until a spectral shriek sent her to her knees, hands slapped to her ears.

Above, a dozen jet-packed men soared into the air, helmets gleaming in the sun.

Boom!

The explosive sound went on and on until...

The silence wailed.

The trees drew back, and she pushed to her feet, hands bloody, to lean against a redwood. The tree wept. So did she.

A cool breeze from the sea dissipated the scents of oily smoke and death.

"Mother!" She ran toward the sentinels, smoke curling from their blackened stumps. She still couldn't see Mother.

"Sybelle." Large hands clamped her waist. Kes, of course. "Do not go farther."

Unlike when the forest had burned, when the trees' pain and screams had immobilized her, the only sound was its lack, both in the forest and in her head.

"I must see Mother, Kes. She's alive!"

"Do not."

"I must."

He released her and she walked on. Within the charred ring of sentinels... Sybi blinked and blinked again, trying to clear the sight that replicated Mother's early trick, the one where she showed Sybi her own destruction. One hand slipped into her pocket to clasp the diamond. Warmth suffused her. Mother was alive.

"Sybelle, wait," Kes said.

"I feel Mother inside me."

He took her free hand in his as they approached the sentinels' husks, acrid smoke curling upward. The sentinels had laughed with her and Mother not an hour ago. She clamped the diamond tight. Mother Tree was special. Eternal. Invincible. She endured.

Some sentinels were bent at odd angles, while others had toppled, and a few had burned to the forest floor. Her eyes watered. Those towering guardians did not need to open for her, their killers had cleared the space.

Inside the circle, she hoped... Within, the carpet of flowers had blackened to ash. But Mother was alive.

Bile filled Sybi's mouth. All that remained of Mother Tree were charred branches and trunk, her silver bark gone, her gems vanished. Yet even this bare, Mother Tree remained extraordinary.

Mother was not dead, for her warmth brushed Sybi from within.

Sybi embraced her beloved Mother Tree. Silence.

And yet...

A warm pulse inside her.

An audible wheeze.

Mother Tree dissolved and Sybi held...nothing.

The trees hummed a song of mourning, and Sybi hummed along, desperate to fill the emptiness inside her, the place where Mother had lived. But no matter what she did, the desolation remained.

When the fire was properly doused, she returned with Kestrel to their aerie, only to flee to the studio Kes had built for her in their aerie. Her sketchpad and pencils lay on her drawing table, and she flipped open the pad and began to sketch in a frenzy, watching Mother and her sentinels appear before her strokes. She would use this study to paint them in all their glory. A memory. A tribute. A promise, perhaps.

Sybi dissolved into the work, but what she really wanted was to get so drunk she could erase the sight of Mother's protectors as husks and Mother's silver bones that were now dust. Sybi's body and clothes were still covered with that dust, and she didn't want to wash.

Grief was a frenzied creature. Turn left. Turn right. Up. Down. No matter which way, her despair was a dogged follower, an emptiness never filled.

Mother was well and truly gone.

As Sybi drew, her mind raced. *Where* had Mother gone? All that wisdom and beauty and power? She was so epic, too epic to become mere ash blown on the wind. Did she go to another continent? Another world? Another life?

Or was Mother simply gone-gone?

Kes' footsteps, then he loomed above her to watch her frantic strokes. His hands grasped her shoulders and he massaged them.

"We believe," he said. "Mother Tree is resting now, while Father Sky and Mother Terra heal her. She lives, Sybelle."

Sybi leaned back and brushed her cheek against his warmth. "What does that even mean? Mother is gone. She died. Burnt to a crisp."

"She will rise."

With her heart and soul, she hoped his words were true.

Now, they had Alchemics to defeat. Sybi raked her fingers through her hair. "For years on Earth, I lived with sorrow and grief. I'm used to dealing with them."

Kes stared at her with lambent, assessing eyes.

"Winter is coming." She returned to her sketching.

"Summer nears," he said.

"Not for long. And Rafe and Gato are about to be in a blizzard."

EIGHTEEN

Rafe winged across the Tihja desert atop Nightfall while alongside Gato flew his Bellerophon. Their packs held two CastOut collapsible lasecannons, laseblasters, and other weapons strapped to their mistrals and leathers. They were armed to the teeth, and he liked it. Forty-some years ago, he and Gato had flown side by side during the Dakos Wars. Now, they were about to face the Alchemics, with who-knew-what kind of weapons, not to mention three alien monsters. His blood sped, loosening muscles, battle-hunger drying his mouth.

"When did you last check the coordinates?" Rafe said into his earpiece, Gato wearing its twin.

"Fifteen minutes ago," Gato said. "We are on track to arrive in two hours."

A niggle of discomfort sped up Rafe's spine. Finding the power station's caravan felt too easy. "Something..."

Up ahead, a strange flying swarm darkened the sky.

"How are the lasecannon fuel reserves?" The black swarm veered in their direction.

"Our fuel reserves are acceptable," Gato said. "We have enough to take out the caravan, but it will only last so long before we must mix a new batch."

Rafe's blood sang, and he grinned, pointing. "I believe we first have battle beetles to contend with."

Gato laughed. "I suspect you are right."

The weather was fair with few clouds. A help. Rafe squeezed Nightfall's sides, who bulleted toward the approaching swarm, Gato paralleling him.

The mass of iridescent bugs, a good four feet in length, rather than their normal two-foot size, closed on them.

"They resemble those Breena and I fought," Gato said. "On the way to deliver Kes."

The beetles surrounded them from above and below, though they kept their distance and did not attack. Directed by the Alchemics, Rafe presumed. Their clacking mandibles were ear-splitting, while beads of poison oozed from their deadly curled stingers.

He and Gato pulled their cannons from the carry sacks, hoisted them onto their shoulders, and strapped them on, which gave them the freedom to fight two-handed. They drew their swords.

"They are as fast and deadly as the smaller ones," Gato shouted over the bugs' din. "Hold on the cannon fire as long as possible."

The beetles swarmed in.

Their swords flashed as they took down bug after bug, but it was never enough, as beetles poured from the skies, unceasing.

Rafe barked in pain as a beetle raked its claws over his shoulder, slicing his cannon's leather strap and scoring his flesh. The cannon tumbled off, and though he tried to catch it, it fell to the ground, a puff of sand rising. "Fark!"

Two bugs attacked, and he took both out swiftly even as his flesh blistered, the sweat dripping into his eyes hindering him further. He pulled hard on his Wolf nature and became a mindless predator, slashing, slicing, impaling one on the sword in his right hand, and stabbing another with the longknife in his left.

Not enough. Not nearly enough, even as the sky darkened either from the mass of bugs or from days' end. Rafe could not tell as blood streamed across his face. He swiped it away, and he and Gato fought on, his blistered shoulder aflame.

Rafe sensed his inner resources dissipating. He took another claw scratch, and he slashed off another bug's stinger before it got him, then stabbed his blade into its farking compound eyes. How many more bugs would it take to end him?

"Ideas?" Gato shouted after a bug crashed into his chest, nearly unseating him from Bellerophon.

A swift glance told Rafe his friend was in as bad shape as he— bloody, wounded, and nearly spent.

"For the Clans!" Rafe shouted, and they fought on.

Far below, dead beetles piled high in the sand, yet the air remained thick with the creatures.

Above to his left, two birds streaked their way. Two *huge* birds.

A beetle got in his line of sight, and he slashed its belly but not before another clamped its mandible around his wrist. His knife flew and he sliced the head off.

Above them, the bug canopy was so thick it obscured the sky.

A glow above the canopy, then flame cascading onto the bugs accompanied by high-pitched screeches, the beetles' canopy collapsing in disarray. A frenzied one knocked into his head, and his vision blackened. He clamped a hand around Nightfall's head knob as he swayed, blinking until his eyes cleared.

"Shote!" he shouted.

High above, Kit and Bree rode two mistrals, the pair shooting flames from throwers clamped to their shoulders.

Rafe sliced and slashed with renewed vigor, both horrified and overjoyed at his mate's arrival. Gato took out a beetle about to strike Rafe from above. His friend gave Rafe a snarky grin, and Fates alive, they both laughed. Those women. *Their* women.

Today was a good day to live.

Bree landed in concert with the other three riders, setting down by an oasis of blue water ringed by palms, and enough distant from the dead bugs they couldn't smell them, at least when the wind blew the right way.

The two couples embraced, and Bree found tears burning her eyes as she held Gato tight, so very tight. That had been horribly close. As it was, the men were cut and bruised, covered in blood, with terrible burns scoring their bodies.

The warm night offered barely a breeze as they removed their mistrals' gear and brushed them down, then fed and watered them.

Satisfied Pegasa and the other mistrals were comfortable, Bree lit a fire, boiling water to tend their mates' wounds, while the men cleaned off beetle guts and blood in the pool. Once done, and thanking the Fates both mens' wounds were superficial, she and Kit tended to their injuries. Only Rafe's shoulder needed more care, and he now sported a bandage the size of her thigh.

When the men drew aside to unpack the food, she pulled Kit aside.

"They're going to insist we leave," Bree said.

Kit agreed. "We'll threaten to follow if they don't take us along."

"Good idea. Gato is more protective of me than a mother puma."

A groan. "Rafe is the same, and it gets tiresome."

"It does," Bree said. "Gato's fierce paternalistic streak drives me nuts."

"I know, but I expect it. They're Alphas, after all," Kit said with a shrug. "And the men of Eleutia have been sensitized by the scarcity of Eleutian women. I hate upsetting Rafe. We seldom argue."

Bree snorted. "We argue all the time. It's like our sport, though we both enjoy the making up. I don't want to upset Gato, either, but it's sort of inevitable."

"Let's wait until their bellies are full," Kit said. "Rafe's always more mellow after a meal."

"I agree," Bree said, nose wrinkling. "Is that roast chicken, I smell?"

"They're cooking?" Kit's eyes were wide, her stomach rumbling.

"They're going to ply us with food," Bree said. "Then tell us to go home."

Kit straightened. "Rafe knows I have a cool head in battle, that I'm confident and competent. And yet…"

"Gato knows I'm the same." Bree harrumphed. "Come on. Let's get this over with."

They shared a companionable meal by the fire, and the men surprised Kit by not insisting they leave the minute she and Bree finished their meal. Rather, they discussed potential strategies once they found the station with its accompanying creatures. Once they finished the chicken and troff, she and Bree cleaned up, given the men had made the meal, a ritual she and Rafe followed at home, as well.

Should she and Bree introduce the topic of accompanying them to the power station? That felt odd. Maybe they assumed, now that the meal was done, the sisters would just fly off home.

"Why haven't they told us to go home?" Bree said. "They're scheming something."

"Yes, but what?"

"Not a clue."

Both women shrugged, and they shared a cloth to dry their hands, then returned to the fire.

Kit knelt by Rafe. "What about the pain powder we brought? Will you take it?"

"It dulls my senses too much." Rafe shook his head. "Do you need some? You fought fiercely today and what about…"

Kit ran a hand down Rafe's cheek. "I'm fine. We are fine."

He sighed, closing his eyes for a moment.

"Rafe," Kit said, knowing he was about to deliver a speech on why she and Bree should return home. "You have seen me in battle."

"Remember, you are not the boss of us." Bree's eyes glinted at her mate.

Gato began to laugh. "Ah, *poosha*, that may be the understatement of the century. Rafe, how much time have we lost?"

"According to my readings, the caravan has paused," Rafe said, lifting his tablet. "We only lost an hour, though it feels like an eon."

"We have one lasecannon, two flamethrowers, and a lasepipe. But given our task, our fuel is running low."

"We brought an extra batch," Breena said. "We can mix it up before we leave."

"Leave?"

Kit cleared her throat. "Leave for the power station."

The two men looked at each other.

"Don't," Bree said, wagging a finger at Gato. "Do not get imperious with us."

"When am I imperious?" Gato asked, with the hauteur of a king.

Bree burst out laughing, so hard she snorted, while Kit watched Rafe, who tried in vain to hold back his own laughter. Soon, all four were laughing, with tears streaming down Kit's cheeks. She didn't know if hers were from laughter or fear of Rafe's injury or death.

Either way...

"We invite you to join us on our mission," Rafe said, the words colored with reluctance.

"Wait." Bree held up a hand. "What?"

"Correct, *poosha*." Gato's gritted teeth signaled his equal hesitation.

"Seriously?" Bree said, her voice mystified.

Rafe snapped a nod. "Gato and I discussed this. We, um, tend to be overbearing when it comes to you two." He stroked a hand down Kit's arm. "You are my warrior woman, beauty."

"As Breena is mine," Gato said, muttering, "though why I could not have mated with a pliable woman, I do not understand."

"Because," Bree said. "You would have been bored in an hour."

That cocky smile of his appeared. "True."

"We have been wrong in the past," Rafe said. "As evidenced by your display today. You must make your own choices as to accompanying us or not."

Kit's eyes widened. Knowing Rafe, that choice of phrase was a deliberate one and echoed Kit's victory at the Challenge games, where she chose herself.

"You're serious." Bree took Gato's hand, and he threaded his fingers through hers.

"Yes," Gato said. "Though it sticks in my craw to admit it. But, yes."

"No objections, Rafe?" Kit said.

Her mate's eyes said he had many but would leave them unvoiced. "I cannot lose you, beauty."

Kit's lips wobbled. "I'm not willing to lose you, either."

Rafe flipped another stick of wood onto the fire.

"You will follow our orders." Rafe leaned back, his eyes boring into hers.

Gato glared at Breena. "Do you agree?"

Bree nodded, but her lips twitched. "We will."

Kit caught Gato's eye roll and let it pass, too shocked at their words to start a squabble.

"We are in excellent shape," Rafe said. "Especially since Breena and Kitlyn are uninjured. After we mix that extra batch of fuel the women brought and clean our weapons, we fly."

"Agreed," Rafe said, frowning. "Those beetles were abnormal, too large, and did you see their pincers? Unnatural."

Breena and Kitlyn removed the twin jars of fuel and began the mixing procedure.

"Let us do that," Rafe said.

"We've got it," Bree said, measuring out the powder.

Both men shook their heads.

"You remember the beetles, *poosha*?" Gato said, cleaning his sword of beetle detritus.

"They're hard to forget," she said.

Completing the mixture, Breena and Kitlyn got out the lasecannons and poured half the fuel into each cannon's reserve.

Finished, Kit washed up and sat beside Rafe, putting her arm through his and squeezing. "Why do they corrupt Eleutia's creatures?"

He leaned in and kissed her cheek, and she nuzzled his neck before he returned to the task of making his weapons battle-ready.

"I've never understood their twisted experiments," Breena said, helping Gato with his weapons.

"Nor have I. Only about two hundred or so years ago, with the current Cabal's ascension, were those types of experiments initiated. Before that, Alchemic scientists never tampered with humans or animals."

"Their new leaders were a sharp demarcation from the old," Rafe said, nodding to his mate. "Our picnic with Tilde and Max. Remember, Kitlyn?"

"It feels like years ago." Kit sighed, finished her drink, and returned the empty tumbler to Gato's carrysack.

"Months," Rafe said. "But it does feel that way. It was then I saw how the Cabal's corrupting experiments spoke to their otherworldly natures. No true Eleutian would contemplate such horrific actions."

"I see the same," Gato said. "Yet I remain confused by their purpose."

"We're their petri dish," Kit said, Breena nodding.

Gato raised a brow. "Petri?"

"It's a glass dish used for experiments," Bree said, saddling Pegasa. "All of Eleutia is their research dish."

"We suspect the Cabal plans to leave Eleutia for Earth," Rafe said. "Whether that is truth or not, that Clan acts like no Eleutian one. They have changed from beneficent bearers of knowledge and science to destroyers of our world. I believe the Cabal now despises all things Eleutian."

Soon, all four mistrals were saddled and weapons packed, the weariness on Rafe and Gato's faces hardened to battle readiness.

"As horrible as their experiments are, poisoning Eleutia's waters to inhibit female births was worse," Breena said. "The decline would have ultimately exterminated all human life on Eleutia."

"Except for the Alchemics, of course," Gato said with bitterness as he buried their fire beneath the sands and did a final check of the campsite.

They prepared to mount their mistrals with grim determination. Kitlyn knew what was coming—the next battle would either leave them alive or dead, victorious or defeated.

Rafe took her in his arms and kissed her silly, noticing Bree and Gato were doing the same. Drawing apart, she ran a hand down his cheek. "That was nice, my love."

"It was," he said, his voice husky. "Though I have many fears for you, I am delighted to again soar the skies with my Kitlyn."

"We'll win," she said.

"I will do my best and pray to the ancients and the gods for all our safety."

They lifted off.

Sybi got out her paints the CastOuts had gifted her, along with a set of beautiful brushes. Her paper. Colored pens and pencils. The mixing palette. All accouterments of her life as an artist.

A deep breath later, she began to finalize her sketch of Mother and the sentinels she would use as a study for her painting. As they surfaced on the paper, a powerful pressure built in her chest.

No point in breaking down.

She stuttered a breath, squeezed her lids, bit her lip hard.

Okay.

Her pens flew across the paper and the sentinels emerged in all their great height and breadth with their massive presence and delicate leafy tops. Beneath them within the circle, the carpet of grass and flowers grew from the forest floor. And finally Mother, her branches resplendent in flowers tumbling to earth like a glorious waterfall.

Sybi entered that dreamlike state where her art lived. The rhythms grew, frantic, frenzied.

Awakening, as she liked to call it, she leaned back in her chair, eyes closed. At times, her pen produced wonder from that manic-like state. Other times, the results were a hot mess. She chuckled.

Opening her eyes, she froze.

Mother and the sentinels were perfect. She had captured their dignity and strength, as well as a touch of humor.

But on the page facing the sketch grew a tree unlike any she had ever seen. More massive than a redwood and far taller, its odd branches began a few yards up the trunk.

She held the drawing up to the light, confirming her gut feelings. The tree was no figment of her grieving heart. She had never imagined anything like it. Was it real?

The trunk was part redwood, yet several limbs and leaves were oak, *Eastern* oak unknown to the West coast. Still others were maple and a few cypress. Silvery-blue eucalyptus and limbs wild as a boabs grew alongside them. Another bough resembled a banyan, including the fruit, and inches away grew the semi-tropical neem and the large-toothed aspen, both branched from a silvery beech limb. Many more unique branches grew from that singular trunk, like the coat of many colors.

The tree must mean something, and Sybi had her suspicions, though they felt more like hopeful wishes than real.

When Kes returned, she could ask him. But she didn't want to wait. Luciana might know, but she'd gone to help the Bears with their plantings for a few days. She would speak with Marcos, the wisest of the wise.

The healer had temporarily taken over Enoch's infirmary duties, so she knew where to find him. She ripped the tree's page from her sketchbook and left the aerie.

Fukkes waited in the large central courtyard within the exclusive Cabal sector of Alchemic City, pacing from the small apple tree to the large bronze statue of the ridiculous Mother Terra. He contained a smile that ached to split his face, held it off until he received news of the Made One Sybelle's death.

When their team had hit with their fiery blasts, it had taken but a few minutes for the energy source to silence. The vid feed worn by the shooters had stopped on landing for no discernible reason. That mattered little. Soon the powerful energy had winked out, as planned.

The contrary Made One was dead. Ha! All he awaited was confirmation.

He clasped his hands behind his back and kept pacing.

Darva was to meet him here, along with Gabin, and both were late. What to do about Gabin? He was to transfer to Earth with the rest of the eleven... Fukkes shook his head.

Gabin had grown sentimental and soft, as was obvious by his overwrought reaction to the woman Neela's death. Fukkes feared that infernal spy—traitorous and stupid—had twisted Gabin's mind.

A glint in the sky as the jet-packed troops returned, landing around him, filthy and smoke-blackened. All were wreathed in smiles but for the commander Toran, whose soot-blackened face was stolid as usual.

When Toran touched down, Fukkes approached. "Report."

Toran frowned. "We lost Garner and Kafkan."

Fukkes nodded, though he had no idea who they were. "And?"

"The trees are gone, Comstat, burned to the ground."

Fukkes froze. "Trees? What about the Made One?"

"Who?" Toran said.

Fukkes shook the man. "The source of that energy! You were to capture or kill her."

"As ordered, our Valdinine Fire destroyed the energy source, which was trees. Many large ones with a smaller tree inside their circle. I did not get a good look at the small one, for it burned fast."

Fukkes gripped the man's crisscrossed harness. "The Made One was the energy source."

Toran jerked.

Fukkes caught fear in the other man's eyes. Gone in a blink, but always satisfying. "Speak!"

"There was no woman, no man either, but the radiometer led us straight to those trees. They moved! Writhed as they burned!"

"And screamed," chimed in another soldier.

Fukkes shoved Toran away. "Dismissed!"

"Comstat?" Toran said, his voice with that touch of hesitance Fukkes enjoyed. "Any further orders?"

As he recalled, Toran was born on Eleutia into the Alchemic Clan, a good servant, and loyal soldier. But he had failed.

Fukkes laseblaster was instantly in his hand, and he fired.

Their Clan had no use for failures.

While Compass True gathered their armies, assuming Rafe and Gato would destroy the power station, Kestrel called the birds.

The eagles and falcons, the crows and ravens, the sparrows and finches. The gulls came, too, and a lone albatross, an old friend who greeted Terras with much joy. They met far out to sea to avoid the Alchemic blight, swarming the blue skies above navy waves that frothed and crested beneath them.

The Council had agreed to attack in three days' time, and Kes made sure the birds understood and would relay the message to all of Eleutia's avians. Would that all Eleutia's birds could participate. With a few exceptions, he would call the birds from the Northwest Quadrant, while others would alert the remainder of Eleutian avians.

As he spoke with his avian warriors above the roiling waves, Compass True council members were informing all—human and animal symbiont alike—that the call to battle neared. Much depended on Rafe and Gato, and he wished he could have accompanied them. But except for the avian Clans like the Falcons—some of whom could speak to their Falcon brothers and sisters—he alone could converse with all avians. An unintended Alchemic gift.

His strength, for days a sticking point, had finally returned in full, thank the Fates.

He had left Sybelle sketching back at their aerie, her world shattered with the death of Mother and the sentinels. Kes struggled to understand the depth of her grief, though he had comforted her as best he could. He was mournful for Mother's and the sentinels' loss, but accepted it, too. Having fought in previous wars, he understood how luck, destiny, or The Fates played a part. A toss of the bones could mean death...or life. He had seen that often enough in battle, when the soldier beside him was ripped apart by shrapnel or burned with Dakos fire, while he remained unscathed. Though they had won, many had died in that war, and he was thankful his friends Rafe and Gato had survived.

As he flew back to No Land, a weariness of the soul pinched. Battle was about to commence yet again. Blood and death. A soldier's pain, a mate's despair, a child orphaned. Often, as a creation of the Alchemics and a CastOut, one battle or another felt like a near-daily occurrence. The many years with Enala, the endless Dakos Wars, the noose of Alchemic overrule. Mother Tree's murder.

He dreamed of a time when life would prove less fraught with danger and death, so he could settle in peace with his sweet syr. He would bet his last korot Sybelle felt the same.

Diving low to feel the spray across his feathers, Kes listened to the song of the waves. On any other day, the world would seem glorious, yet today it was dark, his blood afire with impending battle.

Compass True's first wave would consist of the Northern Quadrant's men, symbionts, and a few women. Too few women. Odes had been hailed and artwork praised honoring Eleutia's warrior women, of which there had been many. Yet though female births were growing, correcting the imbalance would take time, with most women unable to take up arms due to their own fears or those of their Alphas' or partners'.

Knowing Sybelle, she would want to fight. Though the gentlest of the three sisters, Mother pronounced his sweet syr the fulcrum of change, putting her in danger. That emboldened her, while it tore at his heart.

In fairness, she'd had arms training and was a martial artist as skilled as Kitlyn and Breena. Emotion barreled into him. Even the skilled died, could be maimed. Having experienced her loss once, Kes was not prepared to feel that again.

He could lock her in their nest until the battle was won. Oh, that idea appealed.

Sybelle would *not* fight.

The ocean spray cooled his resolve, allowing sense to reemerge, disgust at his dictatorial thoughts leaving a sour taste.

Who was he to negate her choices? Nor would Sybelle forgive him for stealing them. More to the point, he would not forgive himself.

Spotting No Land and her mighty redwoods, he banked and began his descent as a red-tailed hawk bulleted toward him.

"I say we wipe the CastOuts from the face of Eleutia." Fukkes took a sip of ilaberry wine, one of the few good things about this backward planet. He had assembled the Cabal of Eleven and taken the podium in hopes of initiating Eleutia's destruction. "They and their brethren are malformed creatures we allowed to live for humane reasons. It is time for them to die. They are a threat preceding our departure. If the Overseers learn of our Eleutian research, they will end us all."

The seated Cabal members stared at Fukkes, some wide-eyed, others dismayed, while a delightful few hungered for the CastOuts' deaths with an eagerness he applauded.

Before he took his seat, Fukkes pulsed on the cooling system, the air grown stuffy. The autoair had broken down, but those assigned to fix it had disappeared. They were not the first Alchemics to vanish, though that mattered little. They were replaceable.

Gabin rose. "The Keystone will arrive in two days. Three days hence, we leave for Earth. Let the Eleutians do what they will with the Alchemics who remain. I see no reason to incite the Eleutians by destroying the CastOuts.

"No reason?" Efexx said. "Fukkes is right. They have been a carbuncle on my..."

"On your ass," another member said.

Efexx smiled. "An Earthian expression. I've been practicing, too."

"You sound like an idiot," Gabin said. "Your agreement with the Comstat is equally foolish."

"Is that so?" Fukkes said, burning Gabin with his gaze.

"There is no upside to their destruction, Comstat," Ilony said. "I agree with Gabin."

Another fool. Ilony was tall and sleek and regarded herself as a great beauty. Fukkes wondered how she would deal with the middle-aged, overweight prime minister she would inhabit on Earth.

The debate carried on...and on.

Boring. Fukkes sat back against the soft leather and crossed his arms. He still had time to acquire The Kestrel, a plan already in the works. Soon, he would prepare Mari and Xenon for the transfer to Earth, a complex procedure. In secret, he had brought an Earthian woman's and man's Essences to Eleutia, their physical bodies on Earth in comas. When the time came, both Mari and Xenon's Essences would be transported to Earth within the Kestrel's Essence, piggyback style. Risky, with both his son and wife inhabiting an alien Essence, but a good chance for survival. Which was why he desperately needed to capture that animal.

True, he could convey them within his Essence, but at severe risk to himself.

Many years earlier, he had studied the process using Eleutians as test subjects. All the Eleutians died with the infusion of another's Essence. All except The Kestrel, a child at the time. More encouraging, the creature carried another's Essence for a month, after which

Fukkes had extracted the foreign one. Even with the painful and often lethal extraction, the child had survived. It *could* be done. Mari and Xenon's relocation would succeed.

He tapped a finger to his chin, forcing his mind from the dangerous transfer and its perils.

A buzz in his ear. "Fukkes."

The so-called leader of the Anti-Made Ones, who was to retrieve Enoch's prisoners. He never forgot that the despicable group had harmed his Mari and Xenon while destroying dozens of Essences. His unique revenge included their working with him. Those tick-like creatures would die alongside the rest. "What do you want?"

"We have done as you asked, Fukkes, but our agent has gone missing."

"Done as I asked? You have the Made One and The Kestrel?"

"Not exactly. We arrived by boat, but both the Made One and Enoch have disappeared. The Kestrel was nowhere in sight."

Another failure. Fukkes massaged his forehead. "Go away." He clicked off. More trouble than they were worth.

The Cabal yammered away, divided on his proposal. He wanted to destroy the CastOuts himself, to wield the flamethrower, and watch the warped creatures writhe in pain and die.

If the vote did not go his way? He cared little, as he would still end the CastOuts. He didn't need the Cabal, not really. His thoughts on Mari and Xenon, he smiled, picturing them on Earth, in the flesh and real once again.

Soon, my loves. Soon.

Watching the redtail rise was always a thing of beauty.

Kestrel.

"Hello, cousin."

I report on the city.

"Good."

Many mutilated and changed creatures exist behind locked doors.

The grief in the redtail's voice moved him. *I know of this and will attend to it.*

He had always known of the many animals and humans used in the Alchemics experiments. He had been one of them.

Farewell. The red-tail soared. *I will await your call to battle.*

Thank you.

When the Eleutians began the city's destruction, those Alchemics not in the Cabal would be offered a choice to remain or an opportunity to flee. But the poor creatures locked in cells could not do the same. They had *no* choices and would die. He could not allow it.

Disturbed, he flew up the coast to the Titanus mountains that reared high above the sea in Bear Clan territory. Kes flew high, closer to the sun than he ever had, circling down and down to his secret aerie on a Titanus mountaintop of scrub and not much else. Few CastOuts knew of his hideaway. Nor did any of them know its purpose. At times, he needed to think away from those seeking his help or looking for protection or pulling for strategies, whether it was for rescuing a kitten from a tree or a mating issue. At his secret nest, he need issue no commands nor settle any disputes.

There, silent and alone, he could think.

After the war, he would bring his sweet syr here.

He landed and stepped inside, the usual detritus littering the floor, twigs, leaves, and whatnot. He had not visited for many months. Gifts hung from the rafters, across his pallet, on the floor— sparkling beads left by crows, a peregrine feather, a length of blue ribbon. He placed the gifts with the others, saying a prayer of thanks for his avian brothers and sisters.

The small aerie consisted of one room with a wood stove and a pallet, sparse because he ate and drank in his bird form.

After he transformed to man, he swept out the nest and doffed his pants, his mind's chaos seething and unnatural. He was a warrior. He knew the decision he should make—to forsake the prisoners. The price of war, of victory, compelled that answer.

Yet, he could not.

Sitting on the bed, he grew quiet. He crossed his legs and rested his hands on his thighs. Here, in that between place, voices and pictures often came to him of a past not his own. On occasion, strange future events in which he participated would appear. Most often, he heard only silence.

Kes leaned back against the redwood boards, closed his eyes, and prayed for illumination.

CHAPTER

NINETEEN

Sybi found the infirmary almost empty, with few injured from the forest fires remaining. Marcos was digging through the supply closet, cursing, when she discovered him. After mutual greetings, she showed him her patchwork tree sketch.

He didn't recognize the tree. Next up, Luciana, once she returned from the Bears.

"Will you stop by Ohtli's bed for a visit?" Marcos said.

"She's still here?" she said. "Why?"

He shrugged. "Enoch's notes were clear that she must remain for another two weeks. I will give the man that, he was a fine note keeper."

"Aside from being a traitor and a giant snake."

Marcos' smile was wry. "Both such a surprise. Ohtli is restless. She can walk, but not far. Your visit will be good for her."

Sybi went in search of the girl, disturbed that she was to remain another two weeks rather than return to her family. She had never asked Ohtli about her foster parents, not wanting to be too intrusive, and the girl seldom spoke of them.

Ohtli was holding court in the animal ward, surrounded by a

pigeon, a deer, and an opossum, the last ones to recover. The child sat on the floor in the center of their circle and was running a hand across the deer's coat.

"Ohtli," Sybi said walking into the room. "Who are your friends?"

"This is Mama Obeth, whose leg was burned. She will be released tomorrow."

"She's very pretty." Unsure of protocol, Sybi did not ask whether the deer was a symbiont or not as she joined them on the floor.

The pigeon pecked Ohtli's hand, and the girl lifted it to pet the bird. "Polly is a very demanding pigeon, mostly because of her wing." But she said it with a smile as she pointed to the broken limb.

"Polly seems to be healing well."

"She is. But she has a week before she can go home to her nest."

"What's your opossum friend's name?" Sybi suspected Ohtli had named the animals herself.

"Lemul. A few more days, and he will be released, too." A patch on Lemul's back bore a white bandage.

"What a handsome fellow he is." Ohtli's wheelchair was not in evidence, and Sybi was curious how the girl had gotten to the ward.

"I want to show you something in my room," Ohtli said.

"Super," Sybi said. "Let's get your chair, and I'll wheel you back. We can go fast!"

The child's cheeks warmed to rosy, and she stared down at her hands.

"Ohtli?"

Ohtli crooked a finger and Sybi leaned in. "I would rather walk, but I'm a little tired."

"Who brought you here?"

"No one. That's why I'm tired." She flapped her hands, face fraught with anxiety. "But I think I have one more."

"One more?" Sybi said.

Ohtli disappeared.

Sybi rocked back on her ass. And that wasn't strange. Not at all.

She pushed herself up, said farewell to the animals, and went in search.

She found Ohtli sitting up in bed, playing with one of her dolls, her favorite, a red-haired cloth creature whose face had long been obliterated by the girl's touch. She scooched onto the bed and waited.

"How did you do that?" Sybi asked.

Ohtli shrugged. "I'm not supposed to tell."

"Oht-li," Sybi said.

"I'm not sure. I'm new at it." The girl picked up her doll, her expression smug. "Marcos knows when my animal friends will be released. Because I told him."

"Impressive." The child was stalling. Could she really teleport? Or was it something else, like turning invisible?

Her prognostication skills encompassed animals, as well as humans. That was interesting, too. Sybi studied the girl. A healthy glow brushed Ohtli's cheeks, her eyes free from pain. Perhaps Enoch had been wrong, and she could go home sooner.

Sybi gentled her voice. "Would you please tell me what just happened in the animal ward?"

"I should not." Ohtli ducked her head, clutching her doll tight.

"Okay." She must accept that, though she was dying to know.

Ohtli looked around the empty ward, eyes narrowed, then leaned close and whispered. "I can teleport."

"Oh, okay. Well, teleport. That's a cool gift." Sybi had met two other teleporters among the CastOuts.

"A friend, another teleporter, is teaching me. I think where I want to be, then I am. I could not do it until the fire. Or, at least, I did not *know* I could. That first time, it saved me from dying in the flames. I've been practicing ever since. Sometimes, I take her with me." She held up her doll.

"Do you? Impressive. And Marcos, does he know?"

Ohtli shrugged. "Maybe. He knows lots."

That he did. "I won't say a word. Why is it a secret?"

"Mama and Papa are not supposed to know."

"A secret." Sybi suspected Ohtli planned to surprise her parents, which was adorable. "And a lovely surprise for them."

"No. Kestrel said I should not tell because..." She shook her head. "Papa...well, Kestrel said I should not."

How strange.

Ohtli laid her doll beside her on the bed.

"Her name is Edda, yes?" Sybi said.

Ohtli gave her a shy smile and nodded. "She is tired today."

Teleporting must tire Ohtli out, too. "May I hold her?"

Cradling Edda, the child handed her the doll. Edda was seldom out of her arms, and Ohtli's trust squeezed her heart. Up close, Sybi saw the faintest hint of the doll's features, only its blue eyes vivid. "If you would like, I can sketch back her nose and mouth with my paints. And her freckles."

Ohtli shook her head, all serious. "She was my last gift from my birth mother before I came to No Land." The girl burned with surprising fervor. "Mama was pretty. With red hair and big blue eyes."

Sybi smiled, tearing up for the valiant girl with whom she had spent many hours. "You have those eyes."

"Do I?" Two red spots dotted the child's cheeks.

"Your eyes are as blue as the Titanus sea. Big and beautiful. *You* are beautiful."

"Not like Mama."

"How do you know? Remember, you're not fully grown."

"That is true."

Ohtli's words were filled with longing, her expression wistful, and Sybi ached for all she had lost. "You seem to be in good health."

Ohtli lowered her eyes. "Because of you."

"Me?" She had done nothing to heal Ohtli. "What makes you say that?"

"Your kindness."

Sybi snorted. "That's easy, Ohtli! You are very sweet and very special. I'm sure your foster parents feel the same." Most children in No Land were fosters, many never knowing their birth parents. "I'd love to meet them."

"They are busy," Ohtli said, her words fierce. "They have many important duties, and they come see me when they can."

Important duties? In all her many visits with Ohtli, Sybi had never once seen the girl's parents. Given the child's expression and too-fervent words, Sybi suspected they came infrequently, if at all. Which troubled her. She didn't know what their deal was, but she would look up the pair in hopes of understanding what kept them so busy they seldom visited their daughter. Perhaps she could sway them to bring Ohtli home.

"I love spending time with you," Sybi said.

"Me, too!" She pointed to the paper Sybi had laid on the end table. "What's that?"

"A sketch," Sybi said. "One of mine, and it's sort of odd. Want to see it?"

"Yes! I love your drawings!" Ohtli's eyes brightened.

Sybi held up the sketch.

Ohtli slipped out of bed, stretched her arms above her head, and let them flop to their sides. "It is strange."

"It is. I'm not sure why I drew it. Perhaps you've seen a vision of this tree?"

Ohtli slipped the paper into her small hands and walked to the window, holding the sketch up to the sun. "There is magic about it."

"Is there?"

"May I keep it?"

"Sure." She could draw another to show Kes and Luciana.

"It *is* weird." Ohtli giggled and slipped back into bed. "I like weird."

Sybi laughed and leaned close. "Tell you a secret."

Ohtli leaned forward, an unholy gleam in her eye. "What?"

"I like weird, too."

On her way home, Sybi replayed her conversation with Ohtli about her parents, and as she did so, her concern morphed into distress.

She switched her trajectory toward Ohtli's aerie, their chat troubling. An undercurrent of aloneness and loss had colored Ohtli's words.

The place was easy enough to find—Ohtli said they lived near the standing stone, a huge rock by the sea perched amidst the thick redwoods. Sybi followed the cleverly camouflaged path until a half-hour later she stood before Ohtli's aerie, no ladder in sight.

Far above, the aerie looked well-appointed and expansive, a grand thing sprawling across not one, but two redwoods. According to Ohtli, the girl's father was a merchant named Tifu who sold naturally felled redwoods across Eleutia. The trees were as highly prized on Eleutia as building materials, as they were on Earth, and from the home's size, the man did very well indeed. Ohtli hadn't told her whether her mother, Eleanita, worked out of the home or not.

A call box stood beside a nearby tree, and she pressed the green button and waited.

"Hello?" A woman's tinny voice projected from the speaker.

"Hi. I'm Sybelle, the Made One. I'd like to talk with you. Is now convenient?"

Most Eleutians frothed with excitement when meeting a Made One, and except for Enoch, she had been universally accepted in the village.

"Oh!" came from the speaker. "Of course! Shall I lower the ladder or the hoist? Do you need someone to carry you?"

Sybi shook her head. Until they met her in person, many Eleutians saw her as fragile, though those who had met Kit or Bree knew otherwise.

"The ladder will do fine. Thank you."

Once hydraulics lowered the ladder, Sybi climbed to reach the unusually high deck platform. Ohtli's foster mother stood beside the landing, hands clasped, wearing a black tunic and a green sarong-type skirt common to both men and women on Eleutia. As Sybi had climbed, the reason for the unusual height was obvious, its vista of the brilliant sea, wheeling gulls, and congregating seals on the rocks impressive.

"Welcome," Ohtli's mother said. The pretty brown-haired woman pressed both of Sybi's hands between hers. "We are thrilled to meet you. Tifu, my husband, will be home any minute. I am Eleanita, but everyone uses Nita."

"Thank you for seeing me, Nita. I'm Sybelle, but please call me Sybi." She smiled hoping to put the woman at ease. As with meeting any CastOut, she wondered about their special gifts. She never asked. All CastOuts were *people* first, with human emotions, strengths, and frailties.

"Please, join us for some ilaberry wine." Nita's smile was welcoming. "Whenever Tifu gets home, we always share a glass."

"I'd be delighted." They entered the aerie through the kitchen. Beyond was an immense great room filled with plush furniture, elegant drapes, and a huge vidscreen hung above the wood stove crafted to look like a fireplace.

Nita seated her and brought their drinks, the third mug she assumed for Tifu, along with a platter of tiny sandwiches and pastries.

A clatter at the door revealed a large man with a barrel chest, a long beard, and massive thighs entering the aerie. Though he had four arms, his tailored, Nehru-like jacket and flowing silk pants of muted grays fit him perfectly. He set his jaunty peaked hat on the kitchen counter and offered a broad smile, white teeth agleam, though he threw a questioning glance at Nita.

She bustled over and kissed him on each cheek, her pleasure obvious.

"Who is this come to visit?" Tifu boomed in a bass voice.

"We have been honored by the Made One, Sybelle," Nita said.

Introductions complete, Tifu sat beside Nita while she fixed him a plate of food and handed him his mug of ilaberry wine.

"What brings us the pleasure of your visit, Made One?" Tifu said.

"I'm a friend of your daughter, Ohtli."

"Are you now?" Tifu said, downing an entire sandwich in two gulps.

Nita quieted, shrinking back into the sofa.

"She's much improved, health-wise," Sybi said, injecting positivity into her voice. "Her burns are gone, and she's healed well and regained her health. In fact, I saw Ohtli at the infirmary less than an hour ago."

Though Tifu's smile was broad, the warmth drained from his eyes. "We are glad. We hated to see her suffering so."

Nita nodded but paused. She straightened, eyes narrowed, and tilted her head right then left. "You...I see a shadow in your belly."

"Pardon?" Sybi said.

Nita flushed, her eyes boring holes in the floor.

"Nita's eyes are like x-rays," Tifu chimed in.

"I see." Her words had echoed Marcos' concerns. She couldn't be pregnant, having had her period for the last six days. A tumor? Dear gods, she hoped not. She had enough of sickness for two lifetimes. She would ask Marcos to clarify, and if he could not, she would ask Dr. Kicks. The Wolves might have an X-ray or MRI machine. The issue was solvable, of course it was, just not right now.

"Thank you, Nita." Sybi plucked a cinnamon cake from the plate and nibbled, then spoke in an even, calm tone. "I'm sure Ohtli misses you and is lonely. Most patients have been released."

"Has the new infirmary docent released her?" Tifu said.

How could they not know? "As the new docent, I believe Marcos will release her in a few days." Something of an exaggeration, but still...

Tifu nodded sagely, Nita parroting him, though neither answered her question.

"You have a beautiful place here, so high in the trees," she said. "Your home is lovely." Now what? She was making a hash of this. "From talking with Ohtli, I think she's anxious to come home."

"We will look into this," Tifu said.

Sybi nibbled her lip. "Ohtli has mentioned how busy you both are. I could accompany her home if you would like."

Nita jerked forward. "We want her here. We do!"

The lie slapped Sybi on the chin. Perhaps lie-dar was yet another Alchemic gift. "Of course." Right. They were about as eager as a pineapple to bring their child him. She smiled.

Tifu's answering smile chilled Sybi. "In truth, Made One, we do not want the prophetess here. Her menses will come on soon. We do not wish to deal with her or that tragedy."

"Tifu!" Nita said.

He took his wife's hand. "It is the truth, and you know it as well as I."

"Marcos is valiantly working to stave off her death." Sybi could not imagine rejecting the sweet girl.

"It is inevitable," Nita said with a sigh.

"I don't believe so," Sybi said. "There is hope. Marcos has begun hypnotic treatments and..."

Tifu stood, his arm pointing toward the door. "We respect you, Made One, but you have no business in our affairs. In truth, we have requested the CastOut assembly untangle us from the child. Soon, she will no longer be our responsibility. There. Now you know. Goodbye."

Her urge to argue was huge, but she squelched it. Tifu was right. It was not her place to interfere. To her ears, their "untangling" had little to do with Ohtli's possible death. They were afraid of girl and her prognostication. Not uncommon, Sybi supposed, and she couldn't change that. Yet these people had raised the child. They were supposed to love and support her, but instead were turning their backs. Their reaction to her foreseeing must be why Kes had asked Ohtli not to talk about her teleportation talent.

Ohtli shouldn't return to a place where she was unloved. Sybi understood their fears, but she found them distasteful in the extreme.

Back home, deeply troubled by Ohtli's foster parents, and the hurt they would cause the child, she beelined for her studio and began to sketch, besieged by a furious frenzy for Ohtli's approaching pain and rejection. *Christmas and Hanukah*, how could they?

Her energy escalated to monstrous proportions and hours later, she ground to a halt and flopped back in her chair, stretched and shook her hands to relieve the pins and needles.

Sybi ached for a mug of kamla, her mouth parched. Returning with the drink, she flipped pages to find her first sketch. Her stomach heaved. She'd drawn the "enclave" Kes had briefly described, the holding cells where the Alchemics kept the prisoners for experimentation. She flipped through the sketchbook. Pages and pages of the enclave. One sketch showed two figures opening the door of a glass-enclosed cell, complete with a small square of glass bars on the door. Opposite it, a creature emerged from the door, a man-tiger. Sybi's heart thumped. The creature...person...she did not know what to call him, towered above the two human figures. On the next page, the man-tiger was running from the city.

Strange and confusing. Sybi continued flipping pages. The next sketch revealed a tall figure with rust and blue-steel hair, obviously Kestrel, key in hand as he unlocked another prison door. She stood beside him, her laseblaster facing outward. In yet another drawing...

Page after page showed different scenes, most containing herself and Kes. A few had a crowd running from the enclave, while others had speech balloons with words like "Help!" and "Run!" One thing was clear—whoever or whatever had compelled her to draw these cartoon cels, she and Kes were in the thick of things.

She dreaded going to Alchemic City. She didn't want Kes to go, either. She should rip up the sketches and toss them in the wood burner.

But that would not change what she had drawn.

If Mother were alive...but she was gone.

Kestrel flew to the CastOut village churning with indecision. His mind had tricked him, teasing images from long past when he had lived with the Alchemics. Would that he could unsee them, but the pain of those distorted men and women remained fresh as the day's sunrise. If he rescued them, his attempt failing and he was recaptured or killed, no one else could command the avians in battle.

The hours of silence had given him no insight, and though he was due at the command center, he must wash, his scent riper than a spoiled fish.

He found Sybelle in the living area, completing her yoga practice. She rose, swiping an errant curl from her face and smiled. "Kes."

In seconds, she reached him and wrapped her arms around his waist.

He pushed her away. "Don't. I stink."

"As if I care."

"You should."

"You look awful. Exhausted and sad."

"I need a shower." He stomped toward the bath.

Sybi dried her hands on a towel by the sink, having finished drying the dishes. How to help Kes. He was like a sealed can, with no opener in sight.

The man was seldom outwardly troubled. Today, his face was drawn, his expression dour. She flung the towel onto the counter. Even if it took a crowbar to open him up, Kes would not leave their aerie until she learned what was disturbing him.

Kes walked through the great room with purpose, hair gleaming wet from his shower.

"Hold it right there, buster."

He turned to face her. "What is it, Sybelle?"

Though he wore fresh clothes, his exhaustion weighted him like a soggy blanket. "Let me braid your hair."

Sybi held out a dining chair, and he sat, flipping his long hair over the chair's back.

"I'll get a tie." Back in minutes with a hairbrush and tie, she began to brush his enviable blue-and-rust locks.

"Be quick," he said.

"Of course." She stroked the brush down his wet hair, heavy from his shower. "What's bothering you?"

Silence. His default.

"I'm not letting you leave until you tell me, Kes." She tugged his hair. Not too hard, but to let him know she was serious.

"You are a pitiless taskmaster." He chuckled.

She leaned close to his ear. "Tell me, Kes."

"I do not know which way to turn, sweet syr."

Sybi began to plait. "Talk to me, my love."

He explained how he wished to release the prisoners prior to battle. And how he could not. "I must lead the avians in the coming battle. And yet, I wish to free the prisoners. I see no solution."

Tying off his braid, she led him to the sofa and took his hands in hers. Unsaid was if he fell during the covert operation, no other Eleutian could direct the avians. Kes *would* return to lead them. The other was unthinkable. "You're the cleverest man I know. You'll discover one."

"I know the answer. The prisoners must be sacrificed for the greater good."

Sometimes the greater good sucked. "You don't believe that."

He shook his head, unwilling to meet her eyes. "I doubt myself, doubt these feelings raging inside me. You have changed everything, my Sybelle. Unlocked me to see...differently. To feel things I have kept tight within. In past times, past conflicts, I was never uncertain, never in doubt, always saw the path as straight."

"You're evolving." She leaned forward and pressed her cheek to his. "Becoming more."

"I do not like it."

"I know." The large hands she held bore no scars, a product of his transformations. No, his wounds were all on the inside, from that awful woman who'd raised him, from his time with the Alchemics, from his otherness he saw as a flaw. "Your heart is so large."

"I had no heart before you."

"Untrue. Your caring and compassionate actions always told who you were and are. The CastOuts recognized it. You are their leader because of it."

He snorted. "I am their leader because I am the strongest fighter."

"No," she said, her words soft. "That's only a small part of it. You ache to free the prisoners. That feeling won't go away."

"I must leave." He rose.

She took his hand and tugged him onto the sofa. "Not before we figure this out. Who else among the CastOuts can fly?"

"Only Pedro."

"That's it!"

"Pedro is not the answer," Kes said, weariness in each breath.

"Think about the way you flew him to the mountaintop. Someone could ride him as you did, and direct both Pedro and the birds."

Kes stilled, then shook his head. "That will fail. I am the only one who can speak to the avians."

"What about the Falcon Clan?"

"They communicate only with their symbiont birds of prey. Hundreds of non-prey and non-symbiont species will join the assault."

"Think, hon." She massaged his shoulder. "Didn't you tell me all the symbiont avians can speak to their non-symbiont brothers and sisters?"

He stiffened. "They can."

"Whoever rides Pedro can give orders to the Falcons on their gliders. They, in turn, will tell their raptors, who will disseminate the information to all the avians. It can work."

"It sounds ponderous."

"It doesn't have to be. You could even have a Falcon glider

accompany Pedro. Whoever's riding him would shout commands to the accompanying glider."

His wry smile bloomed, his eyes clearing. "Or..." He pulled her into a tight embrace and whispered. "Pedro's rider could use an earpiece to communicate."

Sybi half-suppressed a laugh. "Okay, stick in the mud. That works, too."

Serene in the decision, Kes strode into the command center. Having been imprisoned by the Alchemics, he knew the enclave's layout. But the mission must be furtive, before their forces struck Alchemic City, which was what he told Marcos, Luciana, and Asher.

"Are the Bears ready for battle, Luciana?" he said before he dove into his plan.

Luciana nodded. "Very much so, Kes. They are most eager." Her sweet smile transformed to feral. "As am I."

"Good," he said. "Before we strike, I plan to release the Alchemic prisoners. Once I enter the city, I will signal." Kes pointed to a portion of the city map they had gleaned from spies and Sybelle's many drawings. "The prisoners are here. When you receive my signal, you will create a diversion within the city."

"Impossible," Marcos said, hands on hips, pacing. "*You* must lead the avians in the coming battle. If you fall..."

"I will not, Marcos. But, in the event The Fates choose that path for me, Asher will fly atop Pedro and direct them."

Asher jerked his head up. "Me?" His Chief Sgiath, a serious young man, shook his head. "I have not your expertise, Kes. Nor can I speak with the birds."

"Understood," Kestrel said. "But you are a visionary, a young one admittedly, but the Falcon and Hawk humans and their symbionts will comprehend your words, and pass along your orders to the flocks."

Luciana peered up at Kestrel. "It's a great risk." She glanced at

Asher, the man she loved. "I fear, but I believe Asher will do a fine job. You both must do as your hearts bid."

"I do not like it," Marcos said. "The Falcon Alpha can use a glider to lead the avians."

"I do not trust him," Kestrel said.

"You trust few."

"Truth, and you trust fewer, which is why Asher will do well. No, it is not ideal, but we cannot leave the prisoners to the Alchemics' tender mercies."

Marcos frowned, expression dour. "Mother Terra save us. Unfortunately, I agree."

"Have you word of my father?" Luciana turned to Marcos.

Kes' sweet Luciana knew loss and grief, torn from her loving biological parents, Gato and Derula, as even now her father flew on a dangerous mission. He prayed for Gato's and Rafe's survival.

"Not for the past two hours," the healer said.

Kes understood his mission would lead to more deaths, perhaps his own. But Luciana's strength was endless, her courage more so. He took both her hands into his. "Gato and Rafe will succeed. As will Asher and I."

"Since you insist on doing this." Marcos stormed over to them. "We can send many Sgiaths with you."

"I will need approximately thirty covert operatives, including our Sgiaths," Kestrel said. "You can draw them from other Clans, if need be, those who will suit and you trust implicitly. Let me explain. Once inside the city, a team of twelve will create a diversion, one which will launch before our troops bring the battle to the city."

He lifted a pen and sketched the sectors of a branching corridor. "This branch leads to the prisoners, which I estimate at about twelve."

Luciana looked up from the screen she was monitoring. "So few?"

"Many of their experiments have died, either during the process or after the fact. Twelve is an optimistic number. A second team will secure the area where the prisoners are held. That will ensure their captors do not kill or move them when they realize our intent. I and about six others, including a healer, will retrieve the prisoners."

"We have no healer to spare." Asher's brow furrowed.

"Then we go without one."

"Will six of you be enough?" Marcos said.

"There is no certainty in this, Marcos." Kestrel drew in a breath. "But I believe so."

Marcos shoved his dreads off his shoulder with an annoyed flick. "You cannot be lost. You are our leader."

"What I cannot do is leave those tortured men, women, and symbiont animals in Alchemic hands."

Asher shook his head. "I am not convinced. Word has it they have practiced terrible experiments. What if a prisoner cannot walk?"

"Then, fark it, we will carry them out." Eager to return to his sweet syr, he wanted this conversation done. He walked toward the door.

"And will you carry out more than one?" Marcos ground out. "How many? Two? Three?"

Kestrel sliced the air with his hand. "Enough. I have made my decision. You and Luciana will orchestrate the diversion from here, and Asher will direct the skies if I fall. Assemble the team, Marcos."

He stared at the three, their concern writ large. Marcos was frustrated but also fearful for him. Asher looked terrified and thrilled, but he also sensed the man's worried affection for him. Sweet Luciana's eyes were downcast, as if already preparing for the grief to come. He sensed her hope, as well.

That he saw their emotions with such clarity surprised him.

The back of his neck prickled, and he rubbed it. Sybelle and her love had opened him to this, perceiving others more fully. Yet now, their concern for him and the warmth he felt for these three, revealed them in a new light. He was not simply their commander, but their true friend.

Perhaps these feelings implied they were family—he and

Marcos, Luciana, and Asher. His family. Perhaps. One truth he knew —they were strong.

If the Alchemics ended him, they would carry on. A good thing.

Kes strode across the village green, acknowledging the waves and "hellos," his thoughts on Sybelle. His sweet syr would worry about his journey to Alchemic City.

Inside their aerie, he found Sybelle in the studio he had built for her in their nest, sketching away, hair flying around her face as she bobbed in time with her pencil and some internal song, her whole body alive. He watched her for long moments, mesmerized.

With a small sigh, she paused, squeezing her eyes tight, and leaned back in her chair.

"Sweeting?" he said as he approached.

Her eyes popped wide and she lunged for him, wrapping her arms around him tight. He hugged her back, feeling every inch of her from inside out, and rested his cheek atop her head. He was where he should be, in her embrace, his heart beating with joy.

After long minutes, Kes kissed her forehead, hands framing her face. "Are you well?"

She stepped back with a quizzical smile. "I'm not sure."

He tilted his head.

"It's as if something has possessed me. I've been sketching like a demon, more crazed than even my first days at Marvel. I drew this strange tree which I gave to Ohtli. Now..." She shook her head, took his hand, and pulled him forward. "I'll show you."

Kes eyed the loose pages strewn across the table, righted a few upside-down ones, then lined them up. He surveyed the group, stomach clenched. "I am in awe. You have drawn the prisoners' enclave within Alchemic City."

"But I've never seen this before. In *Rhiannon*...these images were never part of it. They're not like anything I've ever sketched."

"Did you not say that *Rhiannon* came to you in dreams?"

"It did," she said. "But I was awake as I drew these. Sort of."

However she had done it, Sybelle had drawn a map of the prisoners' enclave *in detail*.

"It is perfect," Kes said.

"I know you've been there," she said, eyes somber.

"I have, though I have not walked the entire enclave." He pointed to a section of her drawing. "This is the area I am familiar with, and I suspect the rest of your drawings are as perfect as this one."

Sybi stared at her sketches, looking away as she sat at the table, and lifted a pencil to doodle. "Like I said, it's not in *Rhiannon*. That was a product of dreams Mother Tree sent me. These are different."

"How?" He disappeared down the hall and put together a cheese board and drinks, then reentered her studio. "Kevitt." He handed her the drink. "You look pale, sweet syr. We can all enter a state that is much like dreaming."

Sybi was exhausted, but she also understood meditative states. "No, this was different, Kes. As I sketched, it was like I was possessed and couldn't stop until I finished, not that I had any idea when that would be. I was frantic with it." A deep breath calmed her, the strong smoky kevitt warming her belly. "Mother sent me those dreams for my novel, at least most of them. But Mother is gone. How do I know what I've drawn is accurate? What if it's not right?"

Kes massaged her shoulders. Bliss.

"Be calm, love," he said. "All will be well. I have faith in what you drew."

Sendings into her mind were creepy as hell, especially with Mother gone. "So where did it come from?"

"Does it matter?" he said.

"To me, it does." Sybi chewed a bit of cheese and finished the kevitt. She gathered the drawings and began taping them to the wall, fitting them together to become a map of the prisoner's enclave.

"I feel a little violated." As she began to clean up the tools of her craft, Kes moved to study the map.

"Wait." He eyed a single drawing with his usual focused intensity.

Kes was brewing some plan she would not like. Sybi grasped his hand. "What's going on, Kes?"

A flash of guilt in his eyes, just for a moment, but she caught it.

"In the morning, I leave with a troop for Alchemic City," he said. "We will release the prisoners, where near-simultaneously the battle for the city will commence."

By his tone, Sybi saw where this was heading. "Who's going with you?"

"A group of thirty."

"And me."

He donned his stolid expression, the mask that blocked conversation or pushed people away. *Not this time, buster*. "I'm going, Kes." She pointed to her sketch and the cel that held two people, The Kestrel and herself, unlocking a prison door. "See? I'm there in the drawing with you."

"You cannot come. That is not up for discussion." He stomped to his weapons room.

With a sigh, Sybi trailed after him. He was digging in his heels, by now familiar territory. Perhaps a different tack... "Can you explain *why* I can't come?"

"The danger is extreme, and though you have many skills, they do not suit this mission."

Talk about bullshit. Could he *be* more vague? Once he entered the beast's belly, death was a high probability. Damn her for helping him come up with a plan. She could fight him on going, put up a massive protest, but that would only upset him before he walked into danger. Kes would not give his consent. Instead, Sybi would figure out a solution on her own. "All right. I'll stay."

His face remained impassive. But mated as they were, his shock pricked their bond.

She shrugged, hoping she didn't seem to give in too easily. "While you're gone, maybe I'll sketch something else helpful." She smiled. Could their bond hint she had no intention of staying behind? Fingers crossed she had played it correctly.

Who or whatever sent those images of the prisoner enclave intended for her to be with him. Sybi would follow her mate.

Kes and his troop would fly, she suspected. So would she. As experienced a rider as Bree, Kit had offered her Daybreak any time she wished.

Her smile fixed, she watched Kes lift the taped sketches from the wall, fold them, and slide them inside his waist pouch.

"I hope they help," she said.

He nodded sharply. "They will."

And so would she.

CHAPTER

TWENTY

That night they lavished love and care on one another. Kes made her favorite meal, nardis waffles, while Sybi gave him a massage. He played his luteon, and they sang. Afterward, they made love slowly and with a focus that made her feel like the most precious being in the world. He was that to her as well, and she would not fall apart.

Eleutia was at war. She couldn't wrap him in cotton fluff. He was the CastOut leader, a Compass True council member, and a fierce warrior. Her desire to hold him close, to never have him leave her sight was natural, but she could not do that.

She couldn't help being terrified. She'd never been in a relationship like the one with Kes. He rocked her world, made it complete. He was her partner, her friend, her everything.

Her throat closed, her heart stuttering. The idea of him being gone from her life...

The following morning, Sybi stood with Kes on a bluff near Mother's ashes, the trees humming their low song of sorrow.

He wore his battle leathers, his long hair dyed black with two slim braids hanging on either side of his face. He'd also pasted on a black mustache and beard and wore glasses.

Crossed swords rested on his back, a laseblaster strapped to his leg, and he bristled with knives, throwing stars, and a garrote looped through his belt. Over all, he wore a billowing, full-length cloak that disguised his armaments. Immense and massive, he seemed invincible. No one was.

A group of men and two women on horseback surrounded them, some dressed as Alchemic soldiers, while others wore more conventional Eleutian clothing. All wore disguises.

"You're not flying?" she said.

He shook his head. "We will make the city in two days. Such a large flight would be observed."

Riding Daybreak, she could fly to the city. Mistrals often circled above it, and she would dismount well before she reached it. Flight was the one way to catch his group.

He bent to nuzzle her neck, and she wrapped her arms around his waist and hung on tight.

"I will return, sweet syr." He massaged circles on her back. "Believe it."

"I'm scared for you."

Kes leaned back, his eyes warm. "I know what you plan."

"Oh?"

"Sy-belle." He drew out her name, his smile indulgent. "You wish to follow me."

Their love warmed her. She would *not* lose that precious gift. "Follow you?"

"You have taught me much, my Sybelle." A mistral appeared high in the sky, the sun gleaming off his palomino coat.

"Daybreak," Sybi whispered.

"My ride to the city. He will fly prisoners out, if necessary."

"But..."

He took her lips in a possessive kiss, and she melted, tasting his desperation and regret and, most of all, his love. So much love. By the time Kes released her, Daybreak had landed nearby, furling his wings into his body and tossing his head. He was unsaddled, bore no bridle or reins. Terras, appearing from nowhere, hopped up to perch on Daybreak's rump. The mistral seemed unconcerned as he clipped the sparse grass beside his hooves.

The pregnant moment built until she blurted, "Take me with you, Kes. Don't leave me behind."

"You are always with me."

"Mother says we should be together, that we're a team."

"Mother Tree was not infallible."

Flames flared within his eyes, literal ones. The enemy would find him terrifying. Sybi only felt love, yet she could not keep him from leaving her.

Kes squeezed her tight, took a few running steps, and lept onto Daybreak's back, giving her a smile so beautiful it brought tears to her eyes.

"All will be well," he said.

With a bunching of massive muscles, Daybreak lept forward, the riders following.

All will be well?

Of course it would...when she went after him.

Hours later, Sybi had reached new levels of frustration. The Cast-Outs' hovercars were too slow, and she'd never catch up on horseback.

Light dappled the trees as she sprinted to Luciana and Asher's aerie. At the landing, immense pots of blooming geraniums lined the railing, a cheerful note that raised her spirits.

Sybi knew Kes would die unless she accompanied him, knew it in her gut and in her heart. Whoever or whatever had urged on her drawing wanted her with him.

Luciana opened her door seconds after Sybi rapped on it. "Is everything well?"

"No." Sybi stormed into the aerie. "I have a problem, and I can't find a solution. I thought maybe you or Asher could help."

Inside, Luciana's home was as green as the outdoors, plants everywhere, from ivy outlining the large picture window to gardenias blooming beside the door. She brushed a Dracaena Marginata, bubbles welling within her, all fizzy.

Luciana led her to a sofa dappled in a flower and leaf print, then tossed her an indulgent smile.

Sybi smiled, trying to put Luciana at ease, though the smile was hard won. "Is Asher here?"

"He and Pedro are practicing flying together." Luciana went to the coolfreeze and returned with mugs of troff.

Pedro. He might make time to fly her when Asher did not need him. "I have to get to Alchemic City. Right away." She took a deep breath and explained. I'm afraid..." The words stuck in her throat.

"You are afraid Kes will die." Luciana sat beside her and wrapped an arm around Sybi.

"Yes, if I don't join him. Pedro could—"

"Pedro cannot," Luciana said. "After working with Asher, he is too depleted to fly. And Marcos..." She shook her head. "He would not permit it, in any case."

Sybi wove her fingers together trying not to scream. "Pedro was a wild idea, I know."

"You could take one of the horses."

"I would arrive too late. The same for the hovercraft." She should have prepared a horse and directly followed. But she'd been sure Kes would fly.

Luciana's eyes widened. "Kes is strong. And powerful. He is magic personified."

Even magical beings die. Sybi rose to pace the living area. "I don't know. I don't even know where the drawings came from. I just know I *have* to go. Don't the CastOuts have a mistral?" She recalled Kes mentioning one.

"We do. Remus was once a great battle stallion, but he is very old. I do not know if he could manage the distance."

"It's worth a try." Sybi hugged Luciana. "Fingers crossed and all that."

Sybi headed to the horse barns, and with each passing minute, her fear grew. She had never set eyes on Remus. That Kes rode Daybreak and not the Clan's mistral said volumes. Detouring to the meeting house, she snagged apples and carrots from the communal dining hall and beelined for the barns. Entering, she absorbed the bustling activity heightened for a war where hundreds, possibly thousands, would die. Several horses' heads popped up, and she handed out carrots and apples, saving plenty for Remus.

Charles, the stablemaster, was a tall rawboned fellow with wire-rimmed spectacles and wild curly hair. He stood before a stall directing a stablehand to take a bay to the training ground, spotted Sybi, and bustled over.

"Greetings Ma'am Sybelle."

"Hello, Charles. It's busy today."

He waved at the chaos. "We are in a bit of a frenzy, my dear. These horses are trained for battle, but not one has seen its reality. Training and reality…" He shook his head. "Not the same."

"You worry for them," she said. "From what Kes said, you're a master, what I would call a horse whisperer. They will do well."

"One hopes." He removed his glasses and cleaned them with a blue kerchief.

"Could I see your mistral?"

His eyes brightened as he replaced his wire rims. "Remus will love a visit. He is restless knowing battle is imminent. Though he can no longer fight, he remains quite the fellow. We treasure him. Come."

Charles waved her through the large stable, down an aisle, and up another until they came to a huge box stall at the end of the row. On the stall's wooden door, about a foot above the floor, an odd tan snout poked out from a small hole.

Charles laughed, pointing downward. "That's Clarence, Remus's goat pal and ever curious." Snuffling horse sounds, then a clip-clop, and a huge grizzled bay head perched on the stall door, eyes milky but bright.

"Hello, Remus." Sybi approached the stall.

Remus' head lifted, and though his coat shone, it was patchy in places. Sybi blew in his nostrils, giving him her scent, then scratched the old fellow behind his ears. He wuffled his pleasure.

"He is ancient," Charles said. "One of the oldest mistrals in the Northern Quadrant. He fought valiantly in the Dakos Wars, yet even then he was no youngling."

"That was forty years ago, yes?"

"Correct. He fought beside Daybreak and Bellerophon, mighty mistrals but both younglings back then." He scratched the mistral's chin. "Remus here led the way. He taught those young stallions how to dodge and weave, when to soar and when to dive before an enemy spots them." Charles' eyes moistened, and he drew out his kerchief and blew his nose. "Only in the last ten years has age caught up with him."

"May I enter the stall?" she said.

Charles unlatched the door and they both entered. Remus was immense of course, all mistrals were, but scars crisscrossed his body and his hip bones jutted though he was obviously well fed.

"Can he still fly?" At the word "fly," Remus' ears perked.

Charles' smile held sorrow. "He would like to. He can, but only for brief periods. Ten to fifteen minutes at most. Come, I'll show you."

Remus strutted as Charles led him from his stall. Clarence and Sybi followed them down the aisle and outside to a close-cropped grassy paddock. Charles unhooked Remus' lead, and the mistral pranced, neck arched, steps high.

Easy enough to see the battle horse within the aging flesh. "You are a handsome boy!"

Remus trotted about and without preamble, his wings emerged from his body, the sight a first for her, a glorious one. Completing the emergence, he shook like a dog, as if settling into his winged skin.

His brown feathers tipped in black sparkled in the sun, at least she imagined they did.

"Ten minutes," Charles said to the mistral.

Remus nodded, and after much flapping of wings, he finally lifted into the skies, spiraling higher and higher until he touched the edge of a cloud.

"He is wonderful," Sybi said.

"Yes." But his eyes did not smile.

Charles was old as well, and she suspected he was remembering Remus' in his prime. And perhaps his own.

Sybi had been fifty-two when she arrived on Eleutia, not elderly in years, but very much so in experience and sorrow. She'd been given a second chance at youth and life. It mattered that she used her gift well.

The mistral began his descent on a wobble, then straightened and bulleted toward them.

"Showing off." Charles grinned.

Remus landed on another wobble, but was soon prancing on the grass again.

"Ready for some warm mash, old friend?" Charles said.

The mistral shook his head.

"Time to return," Charles said as he walked toward the mistral with his lead.

Remus pranced away.

Charles sighed. "Clarence needs his mash, too!"

The goat was presently chewing the paddock grass.

Remus hung his head and walked toward them slug slow, and the stable master hooked on the lead. Back at the stall, the mistral and Clarance dove head deep into their mash buckets.

"He did beautifully." Sybi ran her hand along Remus' neck as he ate.

"He loves to soar and dive, but his body is failing, and I must keep watch when he flies." As Charles talked, he stroked the mistral's flank and peered at Sybi with a proud smile. "Though his will and heart remain mighty, his nature as fierce and sweet as always, he cannot fly far."

As if Remus understood, and some said mistrals did, he rubbed his huge head up and down the front of Charles' shirt.

With apparent jealousy, Clarence the goat pranced over and head-butted her. She scratched between his horns, praising him.

Sybi laughed at the absurd animal who had begun to chew the edge of her tunic. If only goats could fly.

Walking home seemed to take forever, her mind churning over Remus. A fifteen-minute flight was far from getting her to the city, though the mistral appeared willing enough. Eager, in fact. He would fly her, and maybe Remus would make it to the city. Perhaps adrenaline would give him hours more air time. Remus was her best bet yet. They could stop, rest, and continue.

"Dammit!" She picked up a stick and threw it.

Could she really do this—take an old, tired mistral, saddle him up, and most likely ride him to his death?

Of course, she couldn't.

Four gleaming mistrals flew high in the cloud cover above the caravan. Kit guided Moonrise, peering down at the convoy, a huge flatbed hover-truck carrying an immense, rectangular object. Armed guards and a second hover accompanied the flatbed, along with three silver cubes the size of VWs floating around the convoy. The creatures Kestrel had described must lay within them.

Rafe flew beside her, while Bree paralleled Gato, who spoke on his earpiece to Asher.

Gato's drawn face transformed to a grin, he nodded and stood in his stirrups. "Arm yourselves. We attack."

Throwing stars and knives at the ready, Kit drew her sword in one hand and slipped her laseblaster into the other. "Set!"

Bree shouldered her flamethrower. "I'm good!"

"Good here, too!" Rafe said, cradling the lasecannon like a child.

Gato held the second lasecannon she and Bree had brought, and he nodded, his eyes raised to the skies.

A cloud of birds appeared in the distance, hundreds and hundreds of them, drawing closer to the caravan below.

"The flocks are Asher's work!" Gato said, and he held up a hand, eyes on the birds that now encompassed the four mistrals, though not a single avian touched them.

"Now!" Gato's lowered hand launched the birds downward, while the four mistrals bulleted toward the rectangular box.

Below, Rafe's initiating laseblast set off chaos, with the guards returning fire. The birds swooped and dove, pecking at Alchemic eyes, ears, and mouths, while others dug their talons into faces, arms, and legs. A Harris hawk clawed a guard's face, nearly ripping it off.

Horrible and necessary. Kit shuddered and steeled herself for the carnage.

Covered in pecking birds, a man toppled off the hover-truck, screaming as he fell, then a guard winged Gato in the arm, blood soaking his leathers. The crazy Alpha laughed and blew his assailant to hell with his handheld blaster as Kt shot another guard in the leg.

The silver cubes were nerve-racking. They hovered below in a triangular formation, bobbing like ducks in a pond and seemingly oblivious to the conflict.

Their group held back on the big guns—the lasecannon, lasepipe, and flamethrowers. Kit knew what was coming, yet when she tried to picture the monstrous creatures described by Kestrel, her imagination failed.

A cube cracked.

Here we go.

The two other cubes followed, and she tore her gaze from them to look at Rafe. His eyes seared hers, and the silent promises they shared meant the world.

With a boom, the cubes exploded, silver shards flying across the desert. Three monstrous lizard-like creatures emerged. And grew and grew.

Their plated bodies were segmented, their massive tails spiked to mean-looking points. Crescent teeth erupted when those immense jaws like staple removers opened.

She had never seen...would never see...was not prepared. Lucky stars. Kit shook in the saddle, unnerved.

Why couldn't Sybi have exaggerated her descriptions? Instead, they were more grotesque than she had imagined.

Their backs bore red streaks, adding another note of creepiness, along with a large yellow claw where their nose should have been and protruding eye stalks that waggled.

Kit trembled, glad her balance was perfect as always, or she would have slipped from Moonrise's back.

A deep breath helped. But not enough.

Her battle-hardened mate flew close, leaned sideways, and kissed her. Normal and real and grounding.

She snapped him a nod. "I'll be fine."

He grinned. "I know."

As the creatures tightened their triangle around the caravan, Rafe directed Kit upward, her focus on the monsters' eyestalks, a weakness she could exploit.

Thought vanished. Knives and lasefire flew, accompanied by the creatures' roars, spittle, and claws. That poisonous spittle could burrow through leathers to the vulnerable flesh beneath. The mistrals' coats somewhat protected them, and their riders had taken precautions. They were given oral analgesics, their bodies scrubbed with antiseptics, their chests, backs, and thighs covered with a thin coat of metal, a helmet, and a face shield atop their heads. But plenty of flesh remained exposed.

Their quartet fought on, but the monsters seemed not to tire, nor feel pain.

Minutes, hours passed. Breena swayed in the saddle, while

Gato's left arm hung loose, dripping blood. Rafe looked solid, his wounds minor, but his too-stiff body hinted at his exhaustion. One monster's spew had reached Kit's chin, and though she had doused it with water, it seared like Hades. Their injuries were draining their strength, including the scores of pin-prick burns from the monsters' spit.

No matter how long or hard they fought, their team made little headway in ending the monsters while the power station continued its journey, drawing closer and closer to Alchemic City.

They had melted several plates on two of the creatures, and one was limping from a laseblast to its leg. All minor injuries.

Kit looked to Rafe. They had to do something radical, try anything to stem the tide.

Moonrise was fast, one of the fastest mistrals in the Northern Quadrant.

The battle must end, or it would end them.

"Hail Mary!" Kit shouted looking at Bree.

If she swooped in on Moonrise while the nearest creature's attention was diverted, she could sever its eye stalks and flee before the monster got her.

"Kitlyn!" Breena shouted. "Distract them."

She'd bet anything her sister had a similar idea as Bree bulleted toward the lizard to their right. Kit zoomed in front of it, raising her blaster to pepper fire across its body. Pressuring the monster with blasts, she wheeled Moonrise around to attack its back, praying it would follow her.

It turned. *Yes!*

Simultaneously, Bree flew Pegasa so low the mistral's hooves nearly grazed the ground. Bree drew her saber and shot upward, piercing her sword into the hollow between its foreleg and chest, and dove deep.

An unholy squeal echoed through the high desert valley, like the wail of a thousand cats.

Bree and Pegasa sped toward the skies while the monster whirled, almost catching Moonrise with her tail.

The lizard teetered like a drunken barfly, toppled, and stilled.

On a shout, she raised her fist in the air. One down.

A creature grabbed for Moonrise's rump.

Kit squeezed the mistral's flanks, and they jolted forward, paralleling the monster. *One banana head, two banana heads...Now!* Moonrise closed on the creature, and Kit stood in her stirrups, leaning forward to sweep her sword across the creature's quivering eyes stalks.

"Well done!" Gato shouted.

The now-sightless lizard and the one other upright ran amok in circles. Still deadly. But hope glimmered.

Gato dived, firing his lasecannon at the blinded creature's head, exploding it in a satisfying burst of glop and gore. The lizard staggered, ran in a half-circle, and fell, a dust cloud encircling it like Saturn's rings.

Kit threw Gato a thumbs up. Two down, one to go.

In a shocking move, the hover truck holding the station blurred forward at incredible speed.

Lucky stars. No hover could move that fast.

"Go after it!" Kit shouted to the men.

"We've got this!" Bree said, blasting away at the final creature.

Both men gave them long looks, then dashed after the caravan.

CHAPTER

TWENTY-ONE

On Sybi's return to their aerie, she was half-crazed. Kestrel galloped ever closer to Alchemic City, while she was hobbled, with no clear path to get there. Tears of frustration burned her eyes.

Slapping together a sandwich, she leaned her hip against the counter and imagined herself growing wings. That would work.

Her mobile buzzed. She dumped her plate in the sink and answered. A new infirmary tech, about the location of fresh linens. Sybi sighed completing the call and padded to the sink to wash her plate.

A thud outside by the open window. Great. More strange sounds and weird shit. She pushed the faucet off, dried her hands, and peered outside. A loud susurration of breath. Disturbingly loud. Yet she saw nothing.

Sybi didn't need more hassles today. She really didn't. She strapped on her knife and sped down the stairs, walking the tree's circumference, footsteps silent as Kes had taught her. She paused.

The wood was quiet. *Too* quiet. Her forearms prickled, and she drew her knife from its sheath, her eyes scanning her surroundings.

Why was the forest so silent?

For the first time since Mother's death, the trees had paused their song of mourning. Why?

Her circle of the trunk nearly complete, she stopped. A mound of ash lay in her path. White as arctic snow, the pile reached to her waist. She lifted a small amount only to see it crumble and disappear, her palm clean.

The pile began to glow. "Holy shit!" Sybi lept back.

At Marvel, glowing lights always meant something. Sometimes good, more often, bad. The light, fanning from the center of the pile, pulsed like a beacon.

The pile could be some strange Alchemic device, made to explode and take out the command center, not to mention their home.

She should move away, the wise thing to do, but how could she? Sybi inched closer, close enough to feel the pile's heat, its pulse increasing.

Footsteps on the path.

"What is *that*?" Luciana said.

"I don't know," Sybi said. "Maybe an Alchemic device?"

Her friend inched closer, eyes widened to saucers. She took Sybi's hand and pulled her a good ten feet away.

"What do you think it is?" Sybi said.

"I... I..."

"Luce?"

"If...," she said, voice breathy. "If it is what I am guessing, you will see in minutes."

"*What* will I see?"

Luciana shook her head. "It is too absurd. I cannot voice it. Let us watch."

"Is it safe?"

A peal of laughter. "Not if I am correct."

Sybi didn't like this. Not one bit.

The glow expanded further. What if the pulse turned to flames and burned down their aerie?

She loved their home, but it was replaceable. The mighty redwood was not. Their aerie's tree was millennia old, its willingness to support their home a precious thing. Sybi could not grasp the tree's words, but she often caught its emotions—joy, sorrow, even laughter.

Luciana grabbed her arm. "Look!"

A flame arced upward through the ash, rising higher, a mighty whirling column.

"No!" Sybi screamed. "The tree will be destroyed!"

"Watch," Luciana said in a quiet voice.

A normal flame would have singed the redwood, making it scream and sway away from the fire. All the trees reacted that way, even the young ones flinging their branches from the flame.

Their ancient tree did nothing, its voice quiescent.

The column of flame grew and grew, searing Sybi's eyes.

Luciana gasped.

The fire began to morph, to dance like a living being. Many colors joined the golden flame—red, blue, and yellow until the flame burst into tongues and sparks of light, mixing into a whirlwind of even more colors.

"Do you understand?" Luciana said.

"Hell, no," Sybi said.

The sparks' frenzy increased, and its whirling soon surrounded the blazing column, swirling in cyclonic movement.

Sybi strangled a cry.

A huge creature emerged from the sparks, coalescing, melding to form...

"Stars afire!" The phoenix. *Her* phoenix, her blood pulsing with energy.

The bird stood before them, shaking herself as if wet and ruffling her feathers until they settled into a neat iridescent formation, her crest erect. The phoenix glared at Luciana, then clacked her beak.

"I had best go." Luciana backed up step by step. "Come with me."

"It's okay, Luce. I'll be fine."

Another clack. Luciana turned and ran.

Sybi swallowed, mouth dry, and cleared her throat. "Hello, Mother Phoenix. Welcome. You weren't very nice to Luciana."

Though the phoenix never spoke to her, she would swear the bird's sly look was accompanied by laughter. Then the bird leaned her immense head against Sybi's chest.

Oh my. Sybi stroked her, feathers soft as down, the scent of sage rising into the air. The bird's crested feathers settled, and with them, a feeling of peace mantled Sybelle. "Are you here for a, er, motherly visit?"

The phoenix lifted her head and blinked.

"Maybe you're here to fly me to Kestrel?" Communication had never been their strong suit, and Sybi wasn't sure what to do.

"Will you fly me?" she said.

No response. Goddess help her. Did she dare hop onto the phoenix's back? Reach for her neck? She imagined clinging to the phoenix bird hundreds of miles in the air. Terrifying. "Are we going to do this? If so, how?"

The phoenix continued to stare at her, silent as ever.

"Give me a minute. I need to change." Sybi hoped the bird understood she needed her leathers and weapons if they were to fly and moved toward the stairs.

From behind, Sybi was clamped in mighty talons and up they went like a bullet, her shriek alerting the entire village.

Once she calmed, Sybi was mesmerized as they rocketed through clouds high above the sea. Wearing only her linen tunic and pants, she shivered, a single knife her only weapon. She told herself over and over that didn't matter, her teeth chattering away. Her martial arts skills would help, and she was flying to Kes.

Sybi looked down, the vast sea far, far below. *Sweet Christmas, don't drop me.*

In what felt like minutes, the phoenix dove toward the earth at Mach speed and pulled to a halt, gliding to land in a small meadow surrounded by dense woods.

In the distance loomed the white spires of Alchemic City.

The phoenix ungracefully released her onto the meadow floor.

Sybi pushed to her feet and scanned the meadow ringed by forest. The grasses and flowers resembled No Land's, but the nearby trees were shorter and broader than those in CastOut territory. Cousins, perhaps, but they swayed toward her in greeting, a tall pine brushing its needles across her face.

"Hello, my friends." In turn, Sybi bowed to the phoenix. "Thank you, Mother Phoenix."

The great bird nodded, though she glared around the meadow.

Sensing danger? Sybi wished the phoenix would mind-speak like Terras.

The bird's crest rose to a bristle. Sybi whirled. A dozen humans and brown bears stepped from the trees to surround them.

The phoenix launched into the air, trails of flame following her long glorious tail. Moments later, she vanished.

Now what?

The men and women stood not ten feet away. They were universally tall, many bulked with heavy muscle, and bristling with weapons. All eyed her with aggression. To Sybi's left, a grizzly rose on its hind legs, towering above the humans. The bear stood maybe twelve feet high, larger than any images she had seen of Earthly grizzlies. The bear lumbered toward her, its belligerent growls increasing with each step.

Symbiont bears were sentient. Sybi forced herself to remember that fact. But the immense ursine stomping closer scared her more than those monstrous alien creatures ever had. Perhaps because those monsters were incomprehensible. This bear she comprehended just fine—death on paws, so close its shadow slithered over her and she could see the individual hairs on its coat and the shine of its damp nose.

Her heart sped. So did her breath.

The bear halted mere inches away, jaws tight, lips curled, teeth glistening.

Blackness throbbed in and out, and Sybi bit her lip hard and tasted blood. Fainting was not an option while those small black eyes examined her, drool dripping from its fanged mouth.

The Bear Clan were allies, she kept reminding herself.

The trees murmured in seeming reaction to the bear's aggression, the forest growing angry. The trees would try to help, but their speed could not match the grizzly's lethal claws.

A middle-aged woman stepped from the ring of warriors and walked to Sybi, gray-haired and tall as any warrior. Knucklebones jangled at her waist and claws sprouted from her baldric.

The bear grunted.

"Not yet." The woman turned to Sybi and glared. "Why are you in our territory, Made One? Eleutia is on the brink of war, and yet you appear with a phoenix, no less. Why?"

The woman must be nearing the end of her life, which was when Eleutians visibly began to age. Yet she was their obvious leader.

Sybi's fear deflated to manageable levels, and she noticed gray on the bear's muzzle, its one eye clouded, its fur patchy and sparse. The leader's bonded symbiont, she guessed, like Gato's Barth.

Given the city's proximity, some or all of this Bear Clan could be working with the Alchemics, though she doubted it. Luciana had just returned from a two-day visit, presumably here.

Yet she hesitated to speak of Kestrel's mission. Plausible lies escaped her, too. Hard to think with a twelve-foot bear looming over her.

Sybi would not flee. Prey ran, and she was not prey.

She must show them her strength.

A breeze wafted across her chilled flesh, the trees humming their support. She took a step back, out of the bear's shadow and into the sunshine. She'd swear the Bear's body strained to move forward. It remained in place.

She lifted her arms to the sky. The move was a risky one. Maybe even stupid.

"Bow!" she commanded.

The trees swayed.

"Bow!"

Awe filled her.

Amidst shrieks and startles, the trees circling the group responded, and trunks and limbs that should have been inflexible bent and bowed to the Bears. To her.

When Sybi looked up, way up to the bear's muzzle hovering above her, she would swear its eyes smiled.

Once the voices died out, the woman leader grinned. "I see you are not without allies, Made One."

"True," she said with a confidence she didn't feel. "I come in peace, and I mean you and yours no harm."

"I will ask again, why are you here?" the Alpha said.

Her sensei's words floated into her mind, how an elder was wrapped in wisdom and deserved her respect. The leader's eyes were warm and deep and boundless, filled with great humanity, which she guessed was why she retained her leadership long after her body had begun to fail.

Sybi turned in a circle, hands pressed together, and thanked the forest, which responded by shaking their leaves and needles as they straightened.

The woman warrior didn't move, standing before her, relaxed, timeless, with what appeared to be boundless patience. Should she trust her and these people?

"Forgive me, but I'm nervous." Hard to forget the huge bear nearby.

"As you should be," the leader said.

What happened next would prove whether her trust was well given or not.

Kes and his team rested on a huge grassy plain, the grasses tall enough to disguise their presence. Alchemic City reared before him, its spires reaching to the sky, its white walls and buildings gleaming in the late afternoon sun. The place was a thing of beauty, he supposed. But for all its pristine glory, its black heart colored his vision red.

On his shoulder, Terras made hacking sounds of displeasure.

They left the horses tethered at the edge of a wood, where they could graze, and by twos and threes, his team climbed the hill's narrow path to infiltrate the city. All were well-schooled in the plan, and he was confident in the expertise of the Sgiaths and the other Clansmen, all experienced in covert operations.

He followed last, Terras atop his shoulder. His entry would be the riskiest, for many Alchemics knew Fukkes' desire to imprison him. About to enter the city amongst a group of other travelers, words whispered on the wind. The birds speaking, but so frantic, Kes could not catch their meaning.

"Fark!"

There is a problem, Terras said in his mind.

"So it seems," he said to Terras. "What are they chattering about?"

We must leave.

Kes slipped from the group, garnering several looks, and walked toward the forest set far distant from the city's crested perch.

A crow landed on his free shoulder.

"What is it?" he said as they walked deeper into the gloom.

The crow pecked at his ear.

SHE *needs you,* Terras said.

"She" was only one being, and his senses heightened. "Where?"

Follow.

The crow flew, flipping and diving around trees as if to flaunt its expertise.

Kes ran, and soon their trio reached a small meadow lush with wildflowers. He halted, fear, anxiety, anger broiling within.

His sweet syr stood talking to the Bear Alpha, a woman he both respected and admired. But the Alpha's stance shouted aggression, her warriors bristling with weapons, their expressions fierce.

Kes was about to defuse the situation when a soft wind brushed his cheek. Impossibly, the trees bowed to the warriors in unison, and then to Sybelle. He smiled—his sweet syr's trees had shown the war party she had many friends.

He chuckled and Terras echoed his laughter. But as his fear eased, his temper escalated. He admired Sybelle's determination, but she was to stay home. He should not be surprised she was here, given his certainty Sybelle would try to follow him. He could not imagine how she had accomplished that, but she had. *Shote.*

Easy enough to slip away and enter the city, Sybelle none the wiser.

But he could not. He scraped his hands across his face, wishing to erase her here and place her back in their nest. Safe. But that was not reality.

His Sybelle would follow, and by following, she would put herself in terrible danger. If he flew her out, returned her to their nest, he would break cover, the Alchemics noting his flight.

Sybelle bowed to her trees, turning in a circle and voicing words of thanks. The trees straightened, then shook as if accepting her gratitude. More surprising, the ursine and human warriors bowed to his Sybelle.

As well they should. He donned his warrior face as he stepped from the woods' edge and walked toward the two women. The Bear Alpha spotted him first and waved.

His Sybelle whirled to face him, eyes wide, and her face turned bright pink. Then her blinding smile stole his breath. As it always did. She was not only happy to see him but overly proud of herself. How he adored her.

As he neared the two, Sybelle's joyful greeting transformed into guilt. She expected his anger. But then she shrugged, grinned, and ran toward him.

"Did you see the trees?" she said, breathless.

"I did."

So did I.

Terras loved her, too.

Her smile brightened. "I'm glad. I know you're mad, Kes, but I'm supposed to be here. With you. There's no chance you're sending me away."

"Agreed."

Her shock lasted but a second before he wrapped his arms around her and held her tight, her familiar scent deeply satisfying. When her slender arms slid over his shoulders, he shuddered.

She was safe and in his arms. For now. "How did you get here?"

"Our mother phoenix," she said.

He stiffened. "Impossible."

"No it's not. She did."

"A tale for later," he said. "You will do exactly as I say."

"Don't I always?" She squeezed him tight, stepped back, and winked.

"It is obvious you do not," he said, his tone light. He could not hold his anger close, not with Sybelle.

Her expressive face grew serious. "I'm supposed to do this, Kes. I know it."

"You have said." He wished to return her home. Now.

"Let's eat first. The Bear Clan invited us for dinner."

"We cannot. Our team is inside the city, dusk is upon us, and they will lock the gates soon. We must go."

Sybi and Kes strode toward the city unnoticed, and it surprised her how easily they joined a group preparing to present themselves at the guard station.

"Are you sure everyone's inside?" she said.

He nodded, his eyes scanning their surroundings.

A line stretched before and behind them, clusters of people chatting, some eating, relaxed and convivial. Birds perched on other entrants' shoulders, making Terras unexceptional. Many who passed the gates were Alchemics, but some were tradesmen selling their wares, while others bustled with deliveries and still others wore the Alchemic soldiers' uniforms. Most fluttered and fussed when they reached the station, and by the time she and Kes arrived at the gate-house window, Terras had hopped to her shoulder, and Sybi was sweating cannonballs.

Kes handed the guard their papers.

"These are for you," the guard said to Kestrel. "The woman cannot enter."

She was doomed, would be sent home.

"Apologies." Kes held out a second sheaf of papers.

He must have brought them on a hunch. Smart man.

The guard glanced from Kes to Sybi. "What's her animal?"

She almost blurted, *"I can talk, asshole."*

"Raccoon Clan," Kes said dryly and glanced at Terras.

The guard jerked. "Really? She is my first Raccoon."

Under her breath, Sybi harrumphed. Kes was being funny. Fricking Terras was sitting right there. Falcon Clan, anyone?

The guard passed them through, though he gave Terras the side-eye. Once beyond the gate, Sybi said, "I can't believe you brought papers for me."

His eyes scanned the city, but they held laughter. "I prepare for all contingencies, including you."

"Nice to know I'm a contingency," she grumbled. Smartass.

The city's graceful white spires and swooping architecture turned the atmosphere otherworldly, though the crowds were unexceptional in their tunics and loose pants or bandeaux tops and sarongs. Most wore cloaks and were bareheaded, though a few wore straw hats sprouting feathers. Bird clans? She wished she knew.

Most Alchemics dressed in black, white, or gray, according to Kes. Which coordinated with the austerely beautiful city. Not an animal in sight—no pet dogs or meandering cats—and Sybi wondered if animals were unwelcome in Alchemic City.

Numerous mobile machines, on wheels or hovering, sped across the pavers as if on important missions. The place was a sci-fi flick come to life, its parapets glowing in the last daylight rays.

Side by side they strode across the large courtyard, and as they passed a small arched doorway, Kes made a sharp turn into the shadowed entry, pulling her with him. Two others waited, an Alchemic soldier and a woman wearing jeans and a leather jacket.

Kes nodded, and without a word signaled them forward, walking with purpose.

"This is a workers' passage," he said to Sybelle in whispers. "One I believe safe if the map is accurate. The passage winds deeper into the city."

"What?" she said. "Did you memorize the entire map?"

"Yes."

"Wow." *Here we go.*

He took her hand as they walked with purposeful strides, the passage curving downward at an easy slope until they entered a tunnel, the slice of night sky disappearing.

Around corners and down another passage, then up a ramp, where they met two more members of his troop, both dressed as Alchemic soldiers. They passed an occasional door, but walked what felt like miles of tunnels and deep into the city until three underground arches appeared—one straight ahead, the others flanking it. Kes paused, listening.

"You," he said, nodding at one of the CastOuts dressed as an Alchemic soldier. "We go." Kes and the man disappeared down the left tunnel.

Time crept on sluggish feet. The three who remained wore severe expressions, their eyes scouring the halls for movement. Kes and the CastOut returned, much to her relief, and he waved them through the arch on their right. Another, shorter tunnel, and up ahead, light spilled onto the pavers.

They halted before a tall embossed arch leading to a circular courtyard, one of stone set in a spiral design. Lights illuminated the space to near-daylight brightness. Kes peered into the empty space, his raptor vision acute, while Terras drifted down from her shoulder to peek around the corner. He bobbed his head.

Nerves like fiery pinpricks rolled up and down Sybi's arms, and she rubbed them. Though Kes could transform, his "normal" body was all human. Now, she would see men and women manipulated into strange man-beast beings. She prayed she acted well when she saw them, not just on a sketchpad, but in the flesh. Kes lifted his shoulder pack and took a knee, removing a round disk the size of his palm. He pressed a numeric sequence and aimed the disk at the courtyard.

Sybi peered over his shoulder. "What does that do?"

"Scrambles their vidcams."

Holding pens lined the courtyard, a few of stone, but most were clear glass or plastic. Kes lowered the device, fiddled with a dial on the side, and again pointed it toward the pens. He took out a box that held what looked like an old-fashioned portable phone and keyed in numbers.

"We wait," Kes whispered.

Adrenaline made her breath speed, and Sybi began her mula bandha breathing, which would settle her.

An explosion and screams tore the air.

Kes nodded to Sybi. "Now."

They stepped forward, only for Kes to jerk her back into the tunnel's shadow.

"Someone comes. Hold."

He'd told her another team had eliminated the guards surrounding the prisoners' enclave. She hoped so. Their breaths sounded loud, any movement a boom.

A man bustled into the courtyard accompanied by a woman and an Alchemic soldier.

Fukkes. The bastard. First, he had tried to kill her, and now he wanted to confine her in one of those holding cells and experiment on her. All because her appearance had changed. Just the thought of it... Sybi squeezed her eyes tight.

As a child, she and Marie had seen *One Flew Over the Cuckoo's Nest*. Totally inappropriate for their age, but Mama and Papa were outside rigging the big top, and Bree and Kit had been practicing tricks for their aerialist and equestrian specialties. So they'd watched the movie unchaperoned, and as they did so, a growing sense of suffocation had squeezed her throat until...

"Sybelle?" Kestrel whispered.

"Yes?" That damn tremor in her voice.

He nuzzled her. "We will be safe."

"I know. Just a bad memory."

He lifted her hand and kissed her palm. His lips were warm, a comfort, dissipating the horrible shroud of fear.

A man in their company coughed. The woman sneezed. Another cleared his throat.

Fukkes strode toward a courtyard arch, but not before he tossed loud, scathing words at the woman beside him. When they cleared the arch, Terras squawked.

"Fukkes didn't seem to notice the missing guards," she said.

"A calculated risk. But the higher-ups seldom mingle with the rank-and-file."

The soldier who had accompanied Fukkes' remained and met up with a second one entering the courtyard. Both walked to a cell, the second soldier unlocking its door.

"Wait here," Kes said to the group.

In seconds, he disabled both Alchemics, pulling ties and cloth from his pocket and binding their hands, feet, and mouths, and waved their group forward.

They raced across the pavers, and Kes signaled the other three dressed as soldiers to wait outside, as if on guard. Kes and the woman hauled the two bound men into the cell, and Sybi rushed in after them. And froze.

A green viscous blob on the floor contracted and released its muscles moving toward them. The blob was the strangest thing Sybi had ever seen, and she'd seen a barrel full of strange on Eleutia.

A man stepped from the corner shadows. He wore the purple uniform of the Alchemics' elite officers, a laseblaster aimed at Kes. The blob changed course and began to climb the officer's leg.

Without taking his eyes or the blaster from them, he slapped the green jelly-like thing away with his free hand.

The woman in their trio took a step to her left, while Kes did the same to the right, challenging the gunman to take down all three. The officer's eyes narrowed, darting back and forth between them.

The green blob slid again toward the guard, while Terras screeched, running toward the soldier flapping his single wing.

In a motion too fast for her to catch, Kes threw his knife, and dived, bringing Sybi and the other woman to the floor as the blaster fired. The gunman toppled, the knife an exclamation point in the officer's eye.

Mere seconds had passed, she was dizzy from it, when Kes stepped to the fallen guard, moving the body away from the blob now colored more yellow than green, and retrieved his knife.

"Leitia, check his pulse," Kes said.

She did as asked. "Dead."

Sybi heaved a sigh, then walked to the blob. She shattered.

A man's face peered up at her and blinked. And it *was* a face, with full lips, topped by a hawkish nose, human eyes, and a forehead fringed with brown hair.

Its, *his*, lips parted. "Thank you," he said in a rasping bass voice.

Kes took a knee and brushed a hand across the man's cheek.

The face slid around its viscous "body" like a pinball.

Kes turned to her, his eyes haunted.

Sybi willed herself to be strong, but her lips trembled and her body shook at the utter inhumanity of what the Alchemics had done to this man.

"What is your name?" Sybi kneeled before the face.

"Gareth." He gave her a shy smile. His eyes were pine green with long lashes, expressive lips, and a dimple denting his chin.

"We've come to free you, Gareth." She touched a sprig of hair that flopped onto his forehead.

He chuckled, his deep green eyes wistful. "I cannot see how you will accomplish that."

While she spoke with Gareth, Kestrel and Leitia laid out a four-cornered net across the cell's cement floor.

"If you do not object," Leitia said. "I will lift you into the net and Kestrel will carry you."

"Leave me," Gareth said. "I have no body, can barely move on my own. What is the point?"

Sybi thought of the trees who gave her help and offered comfort. They couldn't move, either. Nor could Stephen Hawking, whose body had failed while his mind continued to blaze. She smiled at him. "It's worth it, Gareth. *You* are worth it. What Clan are you with?"

He grinned. "Meow."

Laughter bubbled up. "Gato and the Cats will be thrilled with your return."

"I'll be unique, that is for sure," Gareth said.

The woman's arms slid beneath Gareth, and she lifted the green "body" that draped across her forearms, settling him on the net.

"Okay?" Kes said.

"Yes." Tears coated Gareth's cheeks, his eyes locked onto Kestrel's.

From his carry sack, Kes took out two carabiners. He snapped one on a ring attached to the back of his baldric and the other on the net, linking each corner together. He lifted the sack and hooked Gareth on like a backpack.

Kestrel peered over his shoulder. "Can you breathe, Gareth?"

"Yes," Gareth said.

"This is doable?"

"Doable!" Gareth shouted.

Sybi imagined Gareth fist-pumping.

Kes retrieved the dead guard's laseblaster, then cut off the man's hands with his sword, wrapping each in a square of oilcloth.

Sybi swallowed hard, bile doing the mamba in her belly.

"Why?" she managed to say, praying she wouldn't heave.

"For the locks," Leitia said.

She had sketched keys, not handprints, and shook her head.

"We go." Kes stepped to the door, careful to avoid the lamplight. Night had deepened, and the courtyard lamps above each cell door cast shadows on the prison walls.

A silent communication between Kes and Terras, for the peregrine walked from the cell, and after she and Leitia exited, Kes closed the door behind them. It locked with a satisfying click. Kes hugged the shadowed wall as he glided toward the next cell, and they followed.

The remaining three of his troop gathered, and Kes gave them one of the severed hands. They, too, would begin releasing the prisoners.

At the next cell on the right, their group found a man with the head of a chimpanzee, his body human and about her height.

When they entered, the monkey-man screeched, jumping back against the cell wall.

"This is so farked up," Leitia said.

"Evil," Sybi said, the Alchemics' depravity beyond anything she had experienced.

Kes spoke soothing words as he eased toward the creature until he was near enough to stroke the monkey man's shoulder.

Monkey-man calmed, and Kes lifted his hand and put it into Sybi's.

She squeezed. "Hello. My name is Sybelle."

The creature responded by pant-hooting with excitement. He touched her hair, and she stilled.

"Come." Kes slipped out the door, and she followed, Leitia taking up the rear.

As they neared the next cell, the strangeness of their procession struck her.

How many prisoners were there? What other horrors would they or the other team discover?

Five cells later, they had released one female and two males, including a man with a zebra's coat and a woman with four breasts.

Both could walk, and they joined the second team, who spoke in whispers of the deformed dead they'd found before continuing their search.

Their group found two empty cells, while a third held the corpse of a hairless cat-woman. The sight of these tortured people nearly broke Sybi, but monkey-man's warm hand in hers grounded her. She stiffened her spine and continued.

Outside the cat-woman's cell, Kes tilted his head and nodded. "Our team surrounding the enclave will peel off in twos once we have completed the prisoners' release. The explosion accomplished much, and our second team found two more dead and released three more prisoners, two ambulatory and one to be carried. Several guarding the enclave will assist with carrying those who cannot walk and cover their retreat. Three cells remain."

Kes surveyed the group, face stoic, eyes fierce, but his grief and fury singed their bond. He handed each sentient and ambulatory prisoner a knife, and the group peeled off in twos and threes to make their way to Bear territory, where aid awaited them. The monkey-man and Gareth remained with their group.

Three cells more, and they were done. When Kes opened the next one, Sybi stifled a gasp.

The room reeked of feces and urine, and on a pallet lay an emaciated tiger man. His bony hips and legs were feline, but from the waist up, he had the body of a man, a handsome one, with blue-black hair and striking Asian features stark with exhaustion.

She'd drawn him, but her sketch had failed to capture the reality.

Tiger-man stared up at them from his pallet. "Alpha." The word was barely a breath.

"Cragon?" Kes froze.

The man nodded.

Kes took a knee beside Cragon's pallet. "We are releasing the prisoners. Come, we must leave."

Cragon shook his head. "My tiger legs do not function. I cannot even feel them any longer. I see you carry Gareth. I am glad. But you cannot carry me."

"We have others to help," Kes said.

"There is nothing for it. I am dying." Cragon was panting by the time he finished his speech, sweat running down his temples from the effort.

"No," was all Kes said. "Sweet syr, step to the door with your companion."

Sybi inched the monkey-man several paces back.

Leitia moved forward, but Kes waved her back. Still on one knee, Kes whispered to Cragon, then pulled a knife from his waist and sliced a small incision in Cragon's forehead and one on his tigered back paw. Kes bent his head and shudders jerked his body.

"Alpha?" Leitia said.

"Get back," Kes hissed.

Sybi would swear the woman jumped ten feet.

Kes' back was to Sybi, and she angled to see his face.

Tears ran down his cheeks, dripping from his chin to land on Cragon's forehead where he had cut him. Kes lifted the man's paw, his tears flushing that wound as well.

Cragon whimpered, and Kes slammed his hand across Cragon's mouth, muffling his screams.

A horn sounded. Kes froze, eyes shooting to the door. With his free hand, he drew his sword. A second horn, far distant. Kes remained still, then relaxed and removed his hand from Cragon's mouth.

 The tiger-man was unconscious.

Kes held up a warning hand. "Wait."

The wounds Kes had made began to glow pale blue, the light across the tiger-man's forehead spreading downward, the one from his paw flowing across his body and upward until the man glowed like a radioactive beacon.

Cragon's legs twitched, and in awe, Sybi watched muscles grow beneath the striped furry flesh of his thighs, his arms transforming to a tiger's forelegs, though his torso and face remained unchanged.

Horror contorted Cragon's face when his eyes opened. "You have taken my arms!"

Kes rose, face pale, lines of exhaustion bracketing his mouth. "Have I?"

Cragon's furious stare changed to one of wide-eyed wonder as his arms again became human, then morphed back to tiger. "I can change them at will."

Kes nodded. "As was intended. Now walk."

Though the man's uncertainty was patent, Cragon changed his arms back to tiger legs and slid his front paws to the earth, his hindquarters slipping from his pallet to follow. One wobbly step, two, then a more certain one. Soon, Cragon circled the small cell in his powerful tiger form. He rose to his hindquarters, towering above them all, stepped forward, and squeezed his eyes tight, his face red with effort.

Cragon's tiger legs transformed to human ones thick with muscle.

"Wow!" Sybi said.

Her Kes was true magic. Like the phoenix Fawkes, his tears healed.

Cragon was panting, hand pressed to the cell wall, but he remained upright. His eyes devoured her mate, shining with deep gratitude.

Kes nodded. "We go."

Thirty minutes later, only one cell remained.

Thank the stars. Sybi drew a shaky breath, exhaustion making her woozy. Her heart thrilled at what Kes and his teams had accomplished, but she couldn't erase the days' horrors tattooed on her brain. She'd seen many animal-human combinations, many awake and aware, but three were void of sentience, eyes glazed and empty, and nearing death. Kes had ended them with mercy, but a profound sorrow pulsed through their bond.

She bit down a sob thinking of the mermaid woman. Sinuous and beautiful, tail iridescent and scaled, they'd found her floating face down atop the aquarium's murky water, her long black hair aswirl about her head.

Sybi's footsteps dragged. Pausing to catch her breath, she centered herself.

Even Mother's death had not hit her as hard as this collection of horrors… Kes must have seen such sights and worse when imprisoned by the Alchemics. How had he stood it? His low persistent growls said he was as anguished as she with the days' sights.

A man with a human head and the body of an eagle; a huge four-legged lizard with a woman's face; another man with a mouth of clawed insectoid mandibles. More.

All dead.

Their group moved to the final cell.

"There has been a breach." Darva's hands flew over the controls.

A Cabal member eyed her with disdain. "Really?" the woman said in a slow drawl.

"I'm having trouble pinpointing the type and location. The birds flocking the city are setting off all the sensors. The kitchen explosion affected our oversight, as well."

The Cabal member narrowed her eyes. "*Where*, Darva?"

Darva wanted to scream. With the exception of Fukkes, all the Cabal members treated her as less. She had been born an Alchemic and was proud to be one.

"The following locations have disturbances," Darva said, pointing to the constellation of pulses on her screen. "The hospital, the armaments factory, the experimentals' enclave, and the dining hall." More lights lit up her board. "Now the soldiers' barracks." She was so frustrated, she ground her teeth. "See for yourself."

The woman snapped Darva a furious look but checked the board. "Send additional security to the enclave."

Darva winced at her scorn. "Already done."

When the woman stepped away, Darva swiveled to the screens showing locales across the city. People raced this way and that, some screaming, many flinging up their arms to protect their faces as flocks of crows, ravens, and seagulls dive-bombed the populace. She pressed a button on the com pinned to her shoulder.

"We need you," she said.

Fukkes reply was husky. "On my way."

A shadowed movement on the screen to her left. She looked closer. Someone hugged the inner wall of the enclave—a man with a hump on his back nearing an exit. Two women entered the frame behind him, one of them with a bird on her shoulder. One woman held the hand of...

Darva enlarged the screen. Was that a Made One? She laughed. *Oh, this would be delicious.*

CHAPTER

TWENTY-TWO

Their quartet was about to enter the final cell when a pair of purple-clad officers strode through the courtyard arch. Kes and Leitia made short work of them, incapacitating, binding, and locking them in a cell.

In the distance, shouts and screams pierced the air, while places around the city blazed with flame, embers and ash floating toward the clouds. High above, flocks of birds swarmed to dive-bomb the populace.

The temperatures had chilled, yet the city broiled as if burning alive.

Kes scented the air, then halted them. "Remain here." He raised the hand to unlock the cell door.

"Wait, Kes!" she said. "What do you smell?"

"Nothing good."

The cell was much like the others made of clear glass, yet she could not see a being inside.

"I don't like this," Sybi said, her feelings of dread expanding.

Leitia stepped forward, brow furrowed.

"Leitia wait," Sybi said, putting monkey-man's hand in hers. "I'll go with him."

Kes' mouth quirked on a sigh, and he brushed a kiss across her lips.

Sybi lifted her blaster and peered straight at her stubborn man. "I can do this."

Agreed, Terras echoed.

"You are impossible." Kes shook his head, but his eyes were warm.

"Love you," she said.

He pressed the severed hand to the lock and pushed inside.

Monkey-man screeched.

A sharp movement to her left, and Sybi blasted, just as an immense cobra struck at Kes.

Though her blast missed the snake, the monstrous creature jerked, its poison fangs closing on air rather than Kes.

The snake rose again, eight feet tall, its hood at least three feet across. But Enoch's eyes, black disks of hatred, stared back at her. In a blur of motion, he again reared to strike.

They blasted him to hell.

Shaken, Sybi ran outside and puked. If Enoch had struck Kes...

Kes closed the door behind him, and she reached for him, only to freeze. Droplets of venom had burrowed through Kes' leathers, bubbling blisters sprouting across his shoulder, fortunately not the one holding Gareth's net.

Sybi upended her canteen on his shoulder, which stopped bubbling, leaving raw burned flesh. "Kes."

"Go," he hissed.

She again took monkey-man's hand, and she and Leitia began to trot beside Kes, Gareth's net bouncing, Cragon padding beside them, with monkey-man at her side and Terras on her shoulder.

They raced through the archway, back the way they had come, to the tune of shouts and curses. The Alchemics had found the emptied cells.

They ran down the hall as footsteps thundered behind them. Up another corridor, Kes turned and pulled them through a door, slamming it shut behind their group. Shouts neared and Kes jammed the door with a sturdy chair.

They flew through an anti-chamber and down another passage that smelled of burning meat. A lead weight of exhaustion pulled at Sybi, monkey-man stumbling, but light filtered from a distant door. She pumped on the juice. Onward and upward, while pounding footfalls and shouts came from behind.

One more turn, up another set of stairs, and they burst into a packed hall where people milling about viewing paintings and sculptures amidst the outer chaos. Kes steered them to a side hall, through another door, and down an endless flight of stairs.

They arrived at a vast boiler room, noisy, humid, and hot, and she recalled sketching the room. That Kestrel remembered her map with such precision seemed impossible, yet he did.

Hooray, they were walking, rather than running, monkey-man panting hard, steps slow. Voices popped from somewhere, but they slipped to another aisle and continued on. It was too good to last.

An Alchemic stood at the far end of the row, laseblaster in hand. Cragon rose in his tiger form to his epic eight feet and growled. The Alchemic ran the other way.

Kestrel's pace never faltered even when the bright overhead lights blinked off, only a sprinkling of blue and green glows lighting the room. Handy, that raptor vision.

"Well done, Terras," Kes said.

She stared at the bird on her shoulder. "*You* turned off the lights?"

Terras bobbed his head, eyes smug.

"What *are* you, Terras?"

Mother's avatar. As was Lala.

If Mother's avatar lived… "Mother lives!"

Terras tilted his head to the side, a gesture that was both habitual and a good avoidance technique.

"Well?" She said.

Terras blinked, though she'd swear laughter radiated from that small body.

Monkey-man whimpered, breaking the moment.

Long minutes later, Kes' took her hand, and he stopped, pressing a finger to her lips. She nodded. Stygian darkness cloaked the corner where they stood.

Cranking sounds, huge gears turning, then spotlights aimed at the forest momentarily blinded her. The fur of a tiger's haunch brushed by, and Kes pulled her and Leitia outside, monkey-man trailing. He eased the door closed.

They stood beyond the city in an area piled high with boulders, a necessary climb to reach the tree line. When they left the walled city's shadow, they would be exposed.

Yet freedom blossomed, the air crisp and piney, with a soft sea breeze from the west. Monkey-man's alarming barks were distressing, but he'd calm once they scaled the boulders.

"That was intense," Gareth said from the net on Kestrel's back.

"I'll second that," she said.

Kes' fingers touched her face, and her heart expanded. As always, his comfort eased her.

"We go," Kes said to the group. "Terras."

The peregrine hopped to his shoulder from hers.

"Allow me to take point," Cragon said.

"I'll accompany him," Leitia said.

Kes nodded, and the pair scaled the rocks with ease.

"Come," Kes said. "Follow my path."

Monkey-man made several rough grunts, and she stroked his head in hope of soothing him. "It's all right. We'll be safe soon."

Up ahead, Terras rasped his kack-kack-kack.

Which was when the monkey-man wound an arm around her neck, elbow holding her firm, a blaster aimed at her head.

"Turn around slowly or I will shoot your woman," monkey-man said in perfect speech.

Kes did as asked.

Sybi could disarm monkey-man and extract herself, but Kes' slight shake of the head asked her to wait.

"Move, woman." Monkey-man waved his blaster toward the door they had exited. "Too slow and you die. Or perhaps I should shoot you in the leg. Or maybe your man's cock? That would be fun. You see, I am the bogeyman in the dark, the one who eats little children and enjoys it. I believe you are The Kestrel."

Kes remained silent.

"Fukkes knew you would come, and he gave me the task of capturing you. An important responsibility. But he didn't say I had to bring you in whole or keep the woman alive. I was a mere farmer once, and now look at me!" He smiled, his simian noises of pleasure revolting.

Terras vanished.

"How did the bird do that?" monkey-man said.

Kes shrugged, his eyes calm as a soft night. "No idea."

Monkey-man's elbow tightened on her throat as his fingers pressed a button on his collar. "I have them."

Time to make her move, but she must be sure the lasefire didn't reach Gareth or Kes, who continued to look unperturbed.

Catching Kes' gaze, she smiled.

She was fast, even faster than Kit. She swung her left arm around to squeeze Monkey-man's right elbow, hyperextending his right arm while her right arm hugged his neck. She kicked her leg, and down he went.

She thumped onto his back, monkey-man's blast hitting a boulder.

Kes bound his hands and feet, then straightened, lips twitching with humor, eyes bright with admiration. "Well done, sweet syr."

Satisfaction wove through her.

"I have seen Kitlyn and Breena fight," Kes continued. "You are their equal."

She ducked her head, cheeks pink. "Thank you."

"We must hurry. The Alchemics come."

Kes lifted her into his arms and she *eeped*. Swift as a cheetah, he ran up and across the boulders toward the screen of trees.

After the day they'd had, racing in Kes' arms was bliss.

Bellerophon and Nightfall were fast, far faster than the average mistral. Even so, it took Gato and Rafe a mighty effort to catch the power station before it disappeared around the massive escarpment that led to Alchemic City.

When they rounded the cliff, the caravan was far distant, hurtling toward the city perched like a bloated spider above the valley.

Below, the hover carrying the station blew plumes of dust into the air. But Gato could see the station, and they pushed their mounts closer. A little farther, they would be near enough, their cannon and flamethrower fully charged.

"Now?" Rafe said into the earpiece.

"Almost," Gato said. "Closer."

They flattened themselves on their mounts, hands clamped around their mistral's head knobs. Gato whispered to Bellerophon. "No game here, my friend. Life or death. Go."

"Now!" Gato fired his lasecannon, Rafe shooting the flamethrower.

Their cannon fire and flame fell a hair short. *Shote!* He pulled the fuel recharge handle.

Their mounts surged, straining, inching closer, riders and mistrals in beautiful harmony.

A screeching sound.

"What the fark is that?" Gato said.

"Bay doors opening," Rafe said. "I know that sound. A tracking missile. Go! I will lead it on a merry dance."

Rafe and Nightfall peeled away.

As Gato's range of fire neared, he again unhooked the cannon and hefted it to his shoulder.

An explosion pulsed through the air, pushing them forward, the cannon's charge almost complete.

Kit and Bree flew around the creature like buzzing insects.

Infuriated, it swiped at them with immense claws, and in a lightning move scored Pegasa's hindquarter. The mistral screamed, faltering.

Kit harried the monster, giving Bree time to land. The injury was bad, blood dripping from Pegasa's rump.

The monster spat, and Kit swerved, but her right hand flamed with pain, her knife falling to the desert floor. But she still had her blaster, and she and Moonrise dove and swooped, peppering it with stings, like a flea baiting a mastiff. Useless, but with Pegasa and Bree out of action, and Rafe and Gato gone, she must succeed.

She cradled her right hand and raised her left as she and Moonrise raced toward those waving eyestalks.

The creature's claws flashed out again and clamped around her waist, its grip iron.

Stars alive.

No escape, Kit widened her legs so Moonrise could flee, then stabbed the lizard on the soft flesh between its claws. To no effect.

The monster held her high above the earth, and she would swear it watched her face as it squeezed her tighter, its bulbous eyes bobbing with glee as it ended her.

Pain seared her spine, her waist on fire, only a sip of breath.

Rafe. Her death would devastate him, her grief at their future making her tears flow. Another tightening of those curved claws, and she groped for even a trickle of air, her vision clouding.

Boom!

Blood and brains rained down on her.

Breena!

Kit coughed, choking. The creature might be dead, but its grip was unrelenting. Headless, it tottered like a drunken sailor, swinging back and forth. It stumbled, and began to topple, its grip loosening at last.

She tried to hang on, but had no purchase, slipping inch by inch from its grasp to plummet downward.

If she landed on a roll, she might make it. The thought steeled her will. She could do this.

Kit fell down, down...

Hands snatched her from the air, and she thumped atop a flying mistral, pressed to a chest bristling with armaments.

"Ouch!" she said, clutched in a suffocating grip.

"When I saw you fall..." Rafe eased his hold, but only a tad. "I thought..."

"Sweetheart." She stroked his hair as her mighty warrior trembled, his head buried in the crook of her neck. "I'm all right. You've got me. You've always got me, love." Kit held Rafe's waist as she swung one leg over Nightfall's neck, settling into the saddle in front of him, a tight but perfect fit.

"I do, beauty," Rafe whispered in her ear. "What are a few broken bones, eh? Maybe a fractured skull?"

"You're impossible."

"And you are glad I am."

"Humph." She angled her head to kiss him full on the lips until they came up for air. "Breena!"

He pointed.

Bree flew into the sky paralleling Rafe's flight, Moonrise beside her. Pegasa's wounds must be non-critical. *Blessed stars, thank you.* "Is Gato all right?"

"He will be once I return," Rafe said.

Kit leaped from Nightfall onto Moonrise's back.

"Cute trick, sis," Bree said.

"My lasepipe's gone," Rafe said. "I need yours."

Bree unhooked the pipe and leaned toward Rafe, handing it to him with a snarky grin. "Of course. Boys and their toys."

After Kestrel set Sybelle on her feet, they ran over rough forest terrain for several miles, only halting when they were deep in a grove of redwoods. Gareth was well, Leitia too, and Cragon had disappeared into the wood, while Sybelle tended his burns.

Once Cragon returned, the five of them ate power bars while he unloaded a box from his pack, removing the advanced mobile. He unpacked the comm, eyeing Sybelle. White lines framed her mouth, her eyes weary as she slumped on a moss-covered log. He suspected her exhaustion was not from their physical danger, but rather grief for the disturbing creatures crafted by the Alchemics.

"Would you like another cup of water?" he said.

Sybelle stared up at him with wounded eyes. "Yes, thank you." She accepted the cup. "I see you looking at me, your eyes worried. I'll be fine."

"I have noticed you use those words when you are *not* fine."

Sybelle looked away.

"She is tough, your mate," Leitia said to Kes.

"That she is." He sat beside Sybelle, pulling her close.

"I've never understood how human beings can torture others, animal or human." She rested her head on his shoulder. "Observe their pain, their agony, and ignore or relish it."

"This happens on Earth?"

She sighed. "Too often. Can you picture Earth if the Alchemics ruled it?"

"I can." His voice hardened. "Do not fear. We will stop them."

A far-off explosion, a blinding light, and Gato prayed to Father Sky that Rafe had made it through. The silence grew, and minutes passed until he and Bellerophon were once again in firing range of the caravan.

Boom!

A huge missile shot straight toward him, its red nose arrogant.

He could shoot it down, his cannon fully charged, but that would mean precious minutes recharging, giving the caravan time to enter the city.

Calculations blazed through his head.

Shoot the caravan, the missile would take them out. If he shot the missile, saving his and Bell's life, the station would escape.

There was no choice.

Gato straightened, settling into the saddle, and lifted the cannon. Glancing left, he gave the missile blazing toward them a final look.

Forgive me, poosha. Our life together would have been sublime. But you will live. Of that, I have no doubt.

Gato aimed and fired, then urged Bell high into the clouds, even knowing the missile would follow and reach them soon. He pulled the lever to refuel the cannon, a rather futile gesture, then patted Bell's flank.

"You have been a great friend and battle companion. I am sorry."

The power station exploded in a blast of lasefire and Gato punched his arms skyward.

Sparks and ash rose into the air, drifting on the wind. On his cannon, the dial showed three minutes remained before firing.

The missile closed on them, its bloody red nose and white tail plume infuriating.

They could not win this battle, but he urged Bell into evasive maneuvers. Might as well stall as long as possible.

A shadow above.

Nightfall shot from fluffy clouds, zooming toward him. *Rafe had survived!* Lasepipe shouldered, his friend aimed and shot. The pipe's fire roared toward the missile, followed by a wild explosion that peppered his back with shrapnel, pain barking through him. *Father Sky thank you!*

Gato laughed. Pain was a manageable old friend.

They had done it. Destroyed the farking power station, the city grounded.

He and Rafe shared a grin, then dove to check on survivors.

As they neared the desert floor, worry niggled. Gato expected the explosion's vibrational energy waves to crash against him. He had felt none. Perhaps the station had been designed to contain a blast. Yet he wondered.

On landing, they dismounted, and Gato clasped forearms with Rafe. "A timely reappearance, my friend."

"I try." Rafe winked.

Gato softened, recalling what Breena would say. "No, you *do*."

"Yoda." Rafe snorted. "Kitlyn has talked of their *Star Wars* vids. Often."

"The women are well?" Gato said.

"Fine. All creatures dispatched."

"Thank the Fates."

"Come," Rafe said. "I doubt there are survivors, but we must check."

There were none, but he had little sympathy for the dead Alchemics who wished to destroy his world. They rounded the smoldering wreckage, Gato going one way, Rafe walking in the opposite direction.

Minutes later, they met up beside their mistrals, Rafe's grim face a mirror of his own.

"We should have anticipated this," Gato said.

"Agreed."

"I am eager to return to Breena," Gato said.

"As I am to Kitlyn," Rafe said. "We fly."

Fukkes giggled, thrilled with the explosion on the vidscreen. Sparks, flame, smoke. Delightful. He had chanced upon it while checking the screens with the three Keystone caravans.

The fools had blown up a counterfeit. As intended. The true Keystone neared the city.

"Almost time, Mari." He glanced with longing at her jagged Essence globe.

Every trap he had laid to recapture The Kestrel had failed.

Fukkes must infuse Mari and Xenon's Essences into himself to safely carry his beloveds to Earth. He sighed. A lesser being would not survive the transport to Earth. He would. Once arrived, he would re-infuse Mari and Xenon into the two comatose human being's flesh. They would rise, and he could hug them once more.

It would work. It must work.

When the Cabal departed Eleutia, only their Essences would travel, their current flesh dead. He pictured their arrival. Fukkes would become the United States president, the rest of the Cabal a film star, a member of England's royal family, the Pope, an Indian guru, more…powerful figures, each in their own right. Once they assembled, the Cabal would see their plans realized.

They would *own* Earth. No Overseer control. No countered orders. No rigorous rules, all of which stopped their essential experiments and the progress of science. The Cabal would craft a world of thrilling possibilities, Fukkes free, his beloveds beside him. Picturing a dance with Mari, a smile lit his face.

An Alchemic officer disturbed his musings.

"Comstat." The man saluted, then stood at rigid attention.

But his hands were white-knuckled, his eyes avoiding Fukkes. So sadly obvious.

He glared at the officer. "Report."

The man's jaw tightened. "The courtyard of experiments is empty of living subjects."

"Surely not subject 843297."

"Gareth is gone, along with the others."

Fukkes let out a disgusted breath. "After forty-three failed attempts at a mobile and sentient slug-man, the forty-fourth was a success. Thousands of research hours wasted, thousands of credits spent, of trials, of sweat, and of despair, yet you are telling me our creation is not in his cell?"

The soldier nodded.

What was the officer's name? Norito? Albert? Junus? All Alchemic soldiers were an amorphous collective who looked similar, acted similar, and thought similar. There was no "each."

"What of the snake-man?"

"Dead in his cell."

"And Chimphumus?"

Red crept up the man's neck. "Alive. We found him bound outside the walls."

"I was told he was a clever and lethal killer," Fukkes said. "He was trained by an elite detail as an assassin."

"He was, Comstat."

Useless. They were all useless. "The Kestrel did this."

"We believe so, according to the chimp, though the man's name was never spoken aloud."

Fukkes knew, and he burned. The Kestrel had released their test subjects, had scrambled the vidcams, had taken out the snake-man. Kestrel had contained Chimphumus. Yet with the chimp-man at his mercy, Kestrel had spared his life. Why not kill him?

No matter. A glance showed the Keystone nearing the south entrance, the city's massive doors swinging wide. The hover moved beneath the arch, and a sigh of pleasure escaped him.

"Find the escapees and those who rescued them," he said to the soldier. Not that it mattered. They were about to leave for Earth. "Kill them all."

"I will retrieve Gareth."

"Are you deaf?" he thundered. "Kill them *all.*"

TWENTY-THREE

Marcos moved from screen to screen, touching dials, pressing buttons, and voicing orders to reposition troops. They had come from as far away as the Southern Continent, as well as other distant points around the globe, most with their symbiont companions. Cats and Wolves, Bears and Gorillas, many more, including numerous sea warriors such as the Dolphins, though minus their symbionts. He worked beside Luciana and Asher, while down below, the multi-talented CastOuts readied, practicing their own specialties.

Peter and Elmer shot up shields to encompass the CastOut village. Aleana and Rad joined together, practicing their "emotional projections," as they called them, ones which would strike debilitating fear into any Alchemic in range. Even Ohtli worked her prognostication in an attempt to pinpoint where the Alchemics would first strike, another CastOut feeding her energy. All day, the girl had been away from the infirmary. Marcos' skin crawled—more was at work with Ohtli than he could perceive.

CastOuts were innately secretive, due to their circumstances at birth. Yet given Ohtli's open, sunny nature, she was being unusually circumspect. He worried.

While he and Luciana coordinated Compass True's ground-troop movements, other Clans buttressed their efforts. How Luciana's strategic mind coexisted with her empathetic soul eluded him.

Luciana leaned toward him and whispered. "I wish Asher could fly a mistral, rather than Pedro."

"Why?" He had expected this but dreaded it nonetheless. "You do not believe Pedro capable?"

"It is not that," Luciana said. "But Pedro is no trained soldier. Why not a mistral?"

"Mistrals might be semi-sentient, but they do not comprehend commands the way Pedro will."

"But what if Pedro panics and flees?" Her eyes widened with worry.

"My dear friend," Marcos said. "The pair will be fine. Pedro has trained, and neither he nor Asher will engage in the fight itself."

"They will be a target," she said, lips thinned.

"I understand your concern." He squeezed her shoulder. "Remember, the birds will protect both at all costs."

"If they can." Luciana returned to her consoles.

Their command center might be fixed, but if the Alchemics moved their city, another Clan's headquarters would take on the command role. At present, he and Luciana had coordinated the troops to surround Alchemic City.

They waited on their Alpha's "Go!" when Kes' troop had released the prisoners and the power station destroyed. Once done, the armies would begin the assault.

The sep mobile rang. He snatched it from its cradle and put it on speaker, also melding Asher into Kes' call.

"Our mission is complete," The Kestrel said. "The prisoners freed."

A thrill of joy rocked him. Yet fear, too. A first salvo, that was all.

He had participated in many wars and loathed each and every one. "When will you arrive?"

"Soon. Once I return Sybelle to the village's safety, I will join the avians."

"Sybelle is with you?" He was truly shocked.

"Yes."

Marcos turned to his companions. "How the Fates did the Made One..." Seeing Luciana's flushed face, he lasered her with a fierce stare. "You knew."

She nodded, her guilt writ large. "Long story."

He shook his head, voice desert dry, and hid his smile. "I look forward to hearing it."

"Has the power station been destroyed?" Kes said to Marcos.

"We have yet to hear from Rafe or Gato."

"Signal me when we are free of the station." Kes disconnected.

Marcos sent a prayer to The Fates that it would be soon.

Breena scanned the skies for Rafe and Gato's return.

"Do you think they got it?" Kit said.

"Hell, yeah." Bree shaded her eyes and pointed. Two specks dotted the clear sky spiraling on a downward path. She reached for Kit's hand and squeezed.

"It's them!" Kit said.

They ran toward the men as they landed, and Bree thrilled to feel Gato's arms around her again.

He held her tight, whispering words of love and comfort. He might be filthy, bloody, and weary, but Bree was home. She burrowed deeper into his shoulder, clutching his waist, confirming he was real and safe.

Finally disengaging, she looked up, her smile fading at his anger.

"What is it?" she said.

He took her hand. "Come, *poosha*. Rafe and I will explain. I need a drink."

They'd made a small campsite inside the forest's edge, and Bree poured each man a large mug of drass. Kit sat beside Rafe, her arm tucked into his, but he was as stone-faced as Gato.

"Are either of you seriously hurt?" Kit said.

"We are not," Rafe said.

"Then what's the problem?" Bree said.

Their faces were grim.

"We took out the caravan," Rafe said.

"And...?" Kit said.

Gato spat. "There *was* no power station. The caravan we destroyed was a decoy."

"You're certain?" Bree took Gato's hand.

He nodded. "We did a thorough job of surveying the wreckage. All we found was an empty shell weighted with rocks. We failed."

Sybi paced their aerie's great room, Kes having gone to the command center, where he and others would finalize the movements for an array of avian and ground troops.

Bree, Kit, and their mates had arrived at the CastOut village hours ago. Alive, thank Father Sky. But they had fought long and hard to merely destroy a dummy. Rafe and Gato, battle experienced, were top generals in the coming war, with Kit and Bree acting as their Seconds, while Arina and Maximus were their First Commanders.

Rafe and Kit would direct Compass True's mistral legion, while Gato and Bree led the Felidae cohort, which included human, symbiont, and non-symbiont pumas, tigers, lions, and other cats. Still other Alphas commanded the Bears, the Wolves, and other Clan troops, while battalions from other continents were on their way to the Northern Quadrant, their travel was slow and ponderous.

All of their assemblage might be moot, as Alchemic City could move wherever and whenever it wanted to on the planet, not to mention their missiles and speedy hovercars. But Asher had explained their small window of time to attack, from the power station's arrival to when it had ramped up enough to fly the city. He wished they knew how long the process took.

A scratch at the door, and Sybi opened it to greet Terras with a smile. "What? I can't believe you left Kes and all the action to visit me."

Do you need me? He crept up her pant leg, her shirt, and onto her shoulder, perching with his usual temerity. The peregrine never injured her, though most of her clothes now bore holes from his claws.

Restless, yet worn out after their escape from the city, she was a tsunami of emotions. The idea of losing this new life with Kes, her sisters, and the CastOuts ground on her like a pestle to mortar. They might all die or she might fail.

That was the crux of her anxiety. Mother Tree said *she* was supposed to defeat those bastards. Sybi didn't have a clue how.

"With Mother gone," Sybi said to Terras. "I don't know what to do or how to help."

You will.

"You sound like Mother, Terras. Her avatar or not, mystical pronouncements don't help." The hollow within her shouted Mother's absence, her wisdom, power, and humor erased. Mother's many voices had gone silent, and though the trees still sang and would do Sybi's bidding, their presence felt disordered without their shepherd, their unity beginning to fragment.

Terras tucked his head into the crook of her shoulder.

"Sweet Terras."

How did Mother wish her to proceed? Perhaps Ohtli knew, or the key was locked inside Kes.

Or maybe she would never understand.

Thoughts of Gareth and Cragon and the dead mermaid increased her anger and frustration. The Alchemics must never again conduct their evil experiments, and the idea of Earth in their grasp chilled her.

She stared at her friend. Somehow, Terras always showed up when she needed him.

Look inside yourself. His head bobbed toward hers.

She nodded. On the sofa, she sank into Sukhasana, or easy pose, entering a deep meditative state that felt both familiar and fresh.

When she opened her eyes, Terras was gone, the clock on the mantle saying an hour had passed. A long breath later, she entered her studio. Her answers must be in her drawings and her notes from her conversations with Mother.

Sybi had jotted down everything, including what she'd heard or imagined in the glass pod. An hour of review later, she called Bree and Kit and arranged a meeting, their destination the scorched earth where Mother had died.

Fluffy clouds scudded across the blue-blue sky, a sharp breeze lifting Sybi's cloak and ruffling Terras' feathers as he rode atop her shoulder. When she arrived at the grassy hillock ringed by redwoods, Kit and Bree were there before her, their mistrals grazing.

"You both look exhausted." Sybi fluffed a blanket onto the ground.

Kit hugged her. "A squadron's lead mistral came up lame. Given Rafe and I command those squadrons, I need to find a replacement. I can't stay long."

"I can't, either," Bree said. "The Cats' refrigeration hover stalled, its food supplies spoiled. Everything. One of the healers came up sick, too. Both fixable, but I've got to get back."

"This won't take long," Sybi said, passing around mugs of troff.

When Luciana stepped into the clearing, she froze, a flush dusting her cheeks.

Sybi hugged her and offered her some troff, though her flush only deepened. She was fangirling on Kit and her stunning victory at the Challenge, the Eleutian Olympics but with more blood.

Luce sat, and Bree squeezed her stepdaughter's hand and whispered. "Kit pees just like we do."

Luciana laughed as she laid her bundle on the blanket. "Careful no one sits on the muffins."

"I think I've figured out what Mother Tree wants me, us, to do," Sybi said.

Bree waved a hand. "Give."

"During the battle for Alchemic City, we must unite. I think it relates to Father Tree."

"There's a Father Tree?" Kit said.

"I saw him," Sybi said. "That first day in the forest, a spectral creature approached me. He *floated* toward me dressed in a ragbag cloak of different fabrics. In my head, he said 'come to me.'"

"Did you?" Luciana asked.

"No." Sybi shook her head. "I was terrified. Father Tree looked like the Nazgûl from *Lord of the Rings*. Very weird. I only saw his hand, but his flesh was a mishmash of multi-colored skin as if sewn together."

Bree snorted. "And that's not creepy. At all."

"It was." Sybi opened her folder with her sketches and notes, flipping pages until she found a particular drawing. "See this sketch?"

Sybi held up the one of the patchwork tree.

"I have never seen its like," Luciana said.

"I asked around," Sybi said. "Nobody else recognized it, either. I'd done it in a frenzy of sketching. It *has* to mean something. Earlier, with all my sketches laid out on the table, I saw the one I'd drawn of the specter ages ago." Sybi drew a loose page from her folder and held it beside the one of the tree. "See?"

"The hand," Kit said. "Father Tree's hand is a patchwork like the tree."

"Yes!" Sybi said.

"The way you sketched that bony hand." Luciana pointed to Sybi's tree drawing. "It reminds me of this tree."

"I believe Father Tree, the specter, and my patchwork tree are the same being." Sybi sat back.

"Suppose they are," Bree said. "What's that mean?"

Sybi rifled through her loose pages until she found what she was looking for. "Mother's words. I've distilled them. She talked about, 'the rule of threes.'"

"I'll assume that meant the three of us," Kit said.

Luciana's smile appeared. "You fit together like puzzle pieces, complementing each other."

"This is our purpose," Sybi said. "Why they pulled us to Eleutia."

"They?" Bree said.

"The Fates," Luciana said. "And other entities like Mother and Father Tree influence our world. They engineered these events to rid Eleutia of the Alchemic blight."

"Rafe said the Fates can't intervene," Kit said.

"They cannot," Luciana said. "But they can influence. Mother and Father Tree and the other... What did you call them, Sybi?"

"Demigods."

"Those entities can act," Luciana said.

"Mother said 'Your call will be answered.' So that means I have to call for some one or some thing. She also said, 'That will help at the end.'"

"The end. The coming battle?" Kit's fingers curled into a fist. "It will either end Alchemic rule or they will end us."

"Yes." Sybi lifted a muffin and chewed. "To quote Mother: 'Your call will be answered. Only you can call, and when you do, you must be bound to the three.' So I have to call while you two are there."

"You're going to call Father Tree?" Luciana's voice held skepticism.

"I think that's what Mother was trying to tell me," Sybi said. "Mother is gone, but—"

Terras pecked her cheek.

"Ow!" Sybi said.

"Why did he do that?" Kit said.

"A reminder." Luciana chuckled. "Terras is Mother's avatar. Many say since Terras lives, so does Mother Tree. I believe that."

Sybi closed her eyes, squeezing them tight, her heart full. She wanted to believe. "Mother repeatedly reminded me that Father Tree lived."

"Our tales say Father Trees lives mostly in the Southern Continent," Luciana said.

Kit bit into her muffin, chewed, and let out a loud gulp, her complexion green. "Banana nut."

"Your favorite," Sybi said.

Kit winced and put the muffin aside. "Not anymore. Sorry, Luciana."

Bree gave Kit a long, assessing stare. "When we fought those monsters, Rafe said... You've gained weight, too. You're pregnant!"

Kit placed a hand on her belly, her smile shy.

Amidst fist pumps and happy tears, each woman gave Kit a fierce hug.

"Rafe's gone all twitchy about it," Kit said, leaning back against a redwood's trunk. "He doesn't want me to ride into battle, and I'm worried he'll do something radical."

"He'd better not." Bree squeezed Kit's arm, then turned to stare at Sybi. "*You're* not pregnant, are you?"

Heat burned Sybi's cheeks, and she shook her head. The idea of having a child terrified her. But it thrilled her, too. Mother Tree had shown her the image of the red-haired little girl. Or she could have a boy, and pictured a little Kestrel toddling around their aerie. *Would their child phoenix?*

"I'm not pregnant," Sybi said. "The last time Kes and I made love, I had my period."

Luciana stiffened, and Kit wore her game face, her Elder Sister one.

"On Eleutia," Kit said, placing her hand over Sybi's. "Human reproductive cycles are more like horses and other animals. We menstruated on Earth, but here we have an estrous cycle, like when horses bleed."

"That means..." Sybi said, voice faint.

"Yup." Kit grimaced. "When we bleed is the *ideal* time to get pregnant."

"We'll see whether your preggers or not," Bree said.

Sybi took in their words, shocked. A huge thing to ponder at another time. "All that matters now is figuring out a plan of action. From Mother's words, we three must be at the same place at the same time during the battle."

"I don't see how," Bree said. "During the battle, if Rafe lets Kit fly, she and I will be all over the place."

Luciana's eyes sparked. "While the Fates cannot directly intervene, they will guide and aid. Have faith."

CHAPTER

TWENTY-FOUR

Late that afternoon, Sybi found Marcos bent over a screen and a board of dials, deploying some battalion or other.

Marcos straightened. He was such an arresting man, though he was isolated, too. No, that wasn't right. Not isolated but contained within himself, like his own individual planet. His sable skin glowed in the light and he was as fit as any warrior. He was, in fact, a renowned one and a great strategist, and yet his battle prowess was eclipsed by his legendary healing powers.

Either way, Marcos intimidated her, and yet she respected and liked him very much.

"How can I help, Made One," Marcos said, his James Earl Jones voice vibrating inside her. "You appear stressed."

Urged on by her conversation with her sisters and Luciana, she stood on tiptoe and whispered. "I'd like you to check me out. Nita saw a gray spot in my belly with her X-ray eyes. I'm concerned."

His eyes widened. "Come." His large calloused hand took her elbow and ushered her down a corridor and into what looked to be a break room, complete with a desk, couch, coolfreeze, and a table and chairs. All pretty normal except for the constellation of photographs across an entire wall. Many included smiling people, while others were of exotic landscapes, and still others depicted the Snow Leopard Clan. Examining them, Sybi saw parts of Eleutia she had only heard or read about.

"You decorated," she said.

"I do not like purely clinical spaces."

"Your Clan is Snow Leopard?"

He gave her a white-toothed grin. "How could you tell?"

"What a handsome group." No one knew what made Marcos a CastOut. Not for her to ask.

"Come," he said. "Lie on the couch face up, and I will examine you.

As she began to remove her pants, he shook his head. "You need not undress."

She lay on her back, her arms at her sides. "Like this?"

"Perfect." Rather than pulling the chair over, he retrieved a rolled-up pad from a closet, unrolled it beside the sofa, and kneeled. Hands spread wide, he began to move them from her feet lightly up her body.

A calming warmth infused her and a renewed sense of well-being.

Marcos' furrowed brow relaxed when he reached her lower abdomen. He tilted his head, took a deep breath, and resumed. Sweat beaded his temples, but his expressive face never changed.

Whatever he was doing felt like an inner massage that awakened all her nerves, sending her blood zooming through her body. Fizzy and wonderful.

A bead of sweat dripped onto Sybi's arm. "Are you all right?"

He drew in a long breath and continued upward, ending with his large hands clasping her skull. He remained silent for long moments.

"So?" She chuckled, all nerves. "What is it?"

"Strange." Marcos leaned back on his heels. "I do not know. But I can say this—I do not believe the mass is cancerous. I cannot see inside it."

"That's unusual?"

"Yes," he said. "But I would not be concerned. You were reborn by the phoenix. A singular occurrence."

Surprised at his knowledge of her rebirth, she would try not to worry. "Thank you for taking the time, Marcos. I know how busy you are."

He pursed his lips. "Are you in pain?"

"No." She sat up.

"Good. My readings say you are exceptionally healthy. But let us check again in a week, Made One, to confirm all is as it should be. Once we are done with the Alchemics, I will arrange an appointment with Kicks, the Wolves' medical doctor. At present, she is with the troops preparing for battle."

Sybi thanked Marcos and left the command station, trying not to obsess. Just one more thing to add to the shitstorm.

Dammit, she would not be cowed by what *might* happen. She had lived with the death sentence of Huntington's, hadn't she? On Earth, she'd learned tomorrow only *might* come. She bit her lip, squared her shoulders, and headed for the market to purchase a new blade sharpener and oil for Kes.

The market, really a general store, was one of the small wooden buildings facing the village green and backing onto the massive redwood forest. Sybi loved the place and shopped there often, all due to the Made Ones' fund.

She opened the red-painted door. From the outside, the store appeared small, with the same feel upon entry. A tiny place that suited the CastOut village. The grocer waved from behind his counter stocked with goods and sundries, and she waved back.

The place was classic, with scuffed wooden floors and dim lighting, as if magic waited within. The ambience's true purpose was to disguise the store's size. In actuality, the place was huge, continuing many yards into the redwood forest.

Sybi walked down the narrow aisle to a near-invisible door and into the space beyond, which contained the bulk of the store's goods.

The entire village was a study in camouflage, from the clothing the CastOuts wore to the stores they shopped to the homespun buildings hiding all manner of sophisticated equipment. The CastOuts' true reality was far more expansive and state-of-the-art than outsiders knew.

Sybi headed for the weapons counter when a group of children snagged her attention—three boys, ages six to perhaps fourteen—and in their center stood Ohtli. The child wore a pretty green blouse, brown leggings, and lace-up boots, with a jaunty flat cap on her head. Adorable. As she neared the children, their rapid chatter disappeared. She smiled, but the male trio's wary expression said "stay away." Only sweet Ohtli grinned, her eyes eager, and she launched herself at Sybi and gave her a full-body hug.

Sybi's arms fluttered around, wanting to hug Ohtli, but knowing how dangerous that could be for the girl. "Ohtli, won't this bring on one of your visions?"

The child hugged her tighter. "No." She sighed, her pleasure obvious. "I have been working with Marcos."

Hugging the girl for the first time nearly brought her to tears. "How's the new infirmary docent?"

Ohtli released her and shrugged. "He's all right, I guess. I cannot go home yet, though."

"No?"

The child tapped her fingers together, a nervous gesture almost like prayer hands. "The docent, um, my sensitivity, my burns, and...well, I..."

Sybi clasped Ohtli's hands in hers, stilling them. "You're wise to wait, hon." What a bunch of horse-hockey. Ohtli's burns were healed, and she was surprisingly comfortable around others. The reason was simple—Ohtli's foster parents didn't want her.

"Who are your friends?" Sybi pointed to the trio watching their exchange.

"Want to meet them?" Ohtli said.

"I would love to."

Sybi chatted with the boys, enjoying their banter once they relaxed as Ohtli introduced them. Excusing herself, she purchased a fine whetstone and sharpening oil for Kes and herself. Pleased with her purchases, she left for home, but her thoughts fixated on Ohtli and her parents, not that they deserved that title.

Mother said Ohtli was a world walker, like herself and Marie. That made them almost sisters, right? She smiled imagining the perfect solution—she would bring Ohtli into *their* home.

But first she would talk to Kes, and most important, ask Ohtli what *she* wanted. Kes would agree. How could he not?

Sybi was so pumped, she ran and in minutes spotted smoke curling from their chimney. Kes was home. A thrill hit her, and not just because of Ohtli. When Kes walked into a room or when she was about to see him, she always felt joy. She took the stairs slowly as she crafted a strategy to get Kes to see things her way. Her radical idea about Ohtli must be properly presented.

Most CastOuts considered their fosters as their own, and the children were showered with warmth and love. Her conversation with Tifu and Nita made it clear Ohtli was not. True, Ohtli attended school with No Land's other children and had nice clothes, books to read, and screens to watch. But her home was an emotional desert. Sybi shivered.

Ohtli deserved more—someone to pet her and to be caring and open with her.

Sybi squeezed the stair rail. She loved Ohtli. How could she not? There was so much about the girl to love, plus she reminded her of Marie—all warmth and quirkiness encased in a warm heart.

Her excitement grew as she flew into the aerie. Kes would consider Ohtli living with them, wouldn't he? He would come to love her, though he probably already did, his heart as huge as all Eleutia. Plus, the man was wise and would lavish the girl with affection and care.

Entering their aerie, Kes was nowhere to be seen. Betting she knew just where he had holed up, Sybi entered the weapons room to see him cataloging a variety of them while laying them on the scarred table at the room's center.

He startled, and reeked of guilt. The man was planning a mission. A secret one without her.

"Where's *my* sword?" she said walking up to him, standing on tiptoe, and kissing his cheek.

"This situation will not require you, sweet syr."

Ah. She'd been right. Not on her watch, buster. Not after Mother's words and their recent "jaunt" to Alchemic City.

She set the whetstone and oil on the table. "These are for you."

He smiled. "Thank you." He slid an arm around her waist, hugged her to him, kissing the top of her head, then moved her purchases beside a mean-looking katana. The "take" pile, she assumed.

"I'm going with you, Kes." Sybi laid a hand on his bicep.

He straightened, peering at her with intensity. "No."

"Yes," she said. "This is when I fulfill Mother Tree's prophecy. My sisters see it that way, too. All three of us will be together, and it will take place in Alchemic City."

His nostrils flared, face rigid. "I struggle with this."

She wound her arms around him and squeezed. "I know. You want to keep me safe. I want you safe, too. In the village, I can't act on Mother's words."

"Your work in the infirmary will be essential."

"Agreed, but there are plenty of villagers helping out there. I am going with *you*."

Kes blew out a ragged breath. "You must understand, Sybelle. I will strike when our troops surround Alchemic City. I will end Fukkes." He lifted the katana and laid it on a stained corner table. "As the Alchemics' leader, he must fall."

"I don't understand my path, not exactly, but The Fates—"

"Curse The Fates."

"Kes!"

"The danger is exponentially increased," he said. "The city can still lift off."

She got it, his real mission. "You're going to blow up the power station, aren't you?" And Fukkes with it, she suspected.

"Yes."

She didn't need to see him grind his teeth or clench his jaw to know he was doing both.

"The city must not fly." Kes plucked a cloth from the clean stack beside the table and began to wipe the blade of old oil. "The survival percentage is low for the mission. Very low."

She placed her palm above his heart. "Then my presence will raise that percentage. I can't lose you, Kes. You are my heart."

"Romantic hyperbole." Still avoiding her gaze, he tossed the used cloth into its bin.

"No, it's not," she said. "Mother said that together we will defeat them. *Together.*"

One hand fisted. "Even Mother Tree will not dictate my decisions."

He stomped out, slamming the door.

Kes stormed to his study and paced, trying to gather his fractured thoughts.

His sweet syr had been excited when she had bounced into the room, eyes alight, face aglow, a woman who added profound meaning to his life. He had doused that flame with swift efficiency.

He poured a beaker of kevitt and stood by the window in search of certitude. Accusing Sybelle of hyperbole had been unfair, for she was his heart, too. He sighed, failing to picture life without her.

Were Sybelle to die, he would phoenix and not be reborn. He could do that, for rebirth took great strength of will. Without his sweet syr, there would be no point.

She was the only creature on Eleutia he cherished.

If he refused her request to accompany him, she would follow and end up in the thick of it. For all he knew, Mother Phoenix would reappear and carry her.

His heart pain was so severe he slumped onto the old hassock, its leather worn smooth after years of use.

Kes could devise a ruse and leave undetected. But like tree roots, their mate bonds now resembled crisscrossed threads, their sacred union steel strong. To dupe his sweet syr... He could not.

Back at the window, he smiled. Sybelle was leaning over the deck rail refilling the bird feeders, her passion for his brother and sister finches and sparrows immense. Task complete, she had begun watering her beloved plants who reached out their leaves to touch her.

The woman awed him. His busy mate was always thinking up solutions, even if some gave him nightmares. She was much like himself, one of a kind, a unique shining star in the black firmament.

Though neither of them would likely survive the mission, she would accompany him, and he would do all in his power to protect her.

Kes downed the remainder of the kevitt and went to find his mate.

Sybi was still out of sorts when Kes found her in her studio watering the white jasmine, queen of the night, and purple and pink violets. She smiled, putting on her game face—he would not go without her to the city. *Finis.*

Her love's black eyes burned, and she set down the watering can. "Kes?"

He prowled toward her.

Oh, ho! Her flesh tingled with want—to touch him, to hold him, to love him.

When his lips grazed hers, so soft, Sybi opened for him in all ways, their bond aflame.

Like the barbarian he pretended to be, he swooped her into his arms, and she expected a trip to their bedroom.

But his impatience got the better of him, and he took her down to the rug, covering her and peppering her with gentle kisses. Naked in seconds, he entered her with a fierce thrust.

Each time, *each time*, his entry sent a wave of delight from her toes upward.

Kes said little, but his eyes, his hands, and his lips spoke of love and care, a harmony of sense and song, as if he poured all of his Essence into hers combining their spirits into one.

The love she felt for him unnerved her, it always did, and she told him its story with murmured words, loving touches, and a fierce passion only he had unlocked.

They crested together, a rare, welcome occurrence, and she saw all of him down to his fears, his courage, and his loving heart.

Moments later, he carried her to their bed for a delightful encore.

Bliss.

Much, much later, Sybi lay in Kestrel's arms, complete. He strengthened her, empowered her, and she *was* strong, far stronger than in her Earthly life. He filled the crevices in her soul in ways beautiful and strange, a feeling so intense she'd swear she saw the world from *his* eyes, a world of unimagined detail and color.

Yet Kes made her feel special, too, her own person whose thoughts and feelings mattered.

She breathed him in, nuzzling her cheek against his damp chest, and he tightened his arms further around her.

In the wide world, only they existed.

"Sleep, sweet syr. We will both journey to Alchemic City."

"Thank you, Kes." A drowsy fog weighted her lids. "This is the calm before the storm, isn't it?"

"It is." He stroked her hair.

"Mother believed we would survive."

After long moments he said, "For all her wisdom and power, Mother Tree was not god."

"A demigod, then," she said in a drowsy voice. "Good enough for me."

"Sleep."

Sybi dozed, warm and safe in Kes' arms until a horn's blare jerked her awake. "What was that?"

Kes' eyes hardened, his gaze distant.

"Kes?"

His eyes devoured her, his face a combination of elation and sorrow. "The Horns of Eleutia calling us to war."

We begin.

Terras mind-spoke to Kes about the troops' assemblage. The Clans would surround the city with thousands of men, women, and animals, even knowing Alchemic City could take flight. Their attack would distract the Alchemics long enough for Kestrel to enter the city, destroy the power station within, and kill Fukkes.

On their previous mission, he had scouted the station's bunker. Once in the city, he would blow up the station, which would not take long.

The horns had fired his blood, as intended, and though Eleutia had other, swifter methods of communication, the tradition of the war horns always inspired.

Kes and Sybelle rose and showered, and minutes later they were gathering their arms, including the carry bag he used in his bird form. The harness he had made for Sybelle enabled her to ride him with ease, and Terras would be held by jesses clipped to a harness ring.

He stepped across the hall and through the connecting passage into the command center, closing the door behind him to block out the burble of voices and machines. Marcos, Asher, and Luciana were all speaking into their comms, while half-a-dozen other CastOuts worked beside them as they amassed thousands of troops.

Asher was armed to the teeth and must be about to fly Pedro. Together, they would gather the avian Clans' flyers and the vast flocks of birds.

Marcos spared him a fleeting glance as he pressed buttons while speaking into his comm. The healer would oversee all troop movement, while Luciana coordinated communication.

Kes scanned Marcos' three screens. Masses of troops assembled —Cats and Wolves, Tigers and Bears, Ferrets and Badgers, and dozens of other Clans. They would pour down the hills and up the valley to surround Alchemic City— jaws clamping the city in their tight grip.

Emotions swirled, flowing across him like slipstreams—excitement, fear, fury, and others too subtle for him to grasp. The screen on Marcos' left showed Rafe and his father, Ulfr, galloping their mistrals across the earth as they led the Wolves, and though he looked for Kitlyn, he did not see her.

On his right, Gato and Breena flew their mistrals above Gato's sister, Arina. The Cats' First Commander rode a fiery stallion, the panther Bartholomew running beside her as they led the mass of Cat troops, both two-legged and four.

Thousands of horse and foot soldiers filled the landscape on the center screen, a singular company of women in battle gear. Their presence shocked him, given female scarcity on Eleutia. Of mixed Clans, they must have overruled their Alphas in their determination to fight.

"We go," he said to Marcos.

Marcos wrinkled his brow. "We?"

"Terras and Sybelle accompany me."

Marcos nodded. "As ordained by Mother Tree?"

Kes nodded.

"This troubles you," Marcos said.

Few but Sybelle and the healer saw that deep within him, and he needed no words.

They grasped each other's forearms. "May the Fates guide you, and may Father Sky and Mother Terra protect you all."

"If we fail," Kes said. "You know what to do."

"Yes." Marcos grumbled. "I still do not like it."

"I know." Kes quirked a lip.

Sybi was calm as she donned her leathers, strapped on her sword and knives, and holstered her laseblaster. She had packed Kes' carry bag with clothes and weapons, along with power bars, water, a small medkit, glowlights, and other necessities. Now, they stood on a promontory where Kes would change to hawk.

This was it, the culmination of Mother's prophecy. It no longer mattered if the enemy spotted his flight with so many avians, mistrals, and machines in the air. They would blacken the skies. Sybi hoped.

"What's wrong?" Kestrel strode into the aerie, Terras riding his shoulder.

The bird cooed, and she scratched his head, forcing a smile. "Nothing out of the ordinary."

"Ah, my sweet syr," he said. "Today is a good day to live."

"Yes, it is!" She stormed over and kissed him hard. "Hell, I'm all nerves."

"Good. That will keep you sharp." He swept up the carry bag and they left the aerie, walking to a meadow within a thick grove of trees. Kes doffed his shirt and vest, stowing them in a pack, strapped on his weaponed baldric, and changed to his avian form. As always, his transformation awed her. Looming over her on his human legs, his feathers shining in the sun, Kes dipped his kestrel head, and she stroked it, breathing in his scent.

"I love you, Kes." Sybi strapped on his harness, fastening it in place and double-checking the leather and clips. Next, she affixed Terras' leather jesses and lifted him to Kestrel's back, locking the jesses onto the harness with a carabiner. After she hooked on the carry bag, she hopped onto Kes's shoulder and attached her belt's carabiner to its harness ring.

She checked their gear one last time. All secure, she nodded to Terras, who curled his talons into the leather harness, while Sybi grabbed the wooden handles beside her knees.

"We're ready, Kes," she said, her mouth dry.

Kestrel nodded his massive head, and beneath her thighs, she felt the bunch of powerful muscles. In one swift thrust, he rocketed into the sky. A shocking feat.

Her nerves quieted, her stomach relaxing. No more waiting. They would do or they would die.

Kes leveled off just above the trees, flying so low their tops nearly brushed his chest. The flight was like nothing she had ever experienced, her braid whipping behind her as they flew toward the city.

The wind teased her loose strands of hair, and she raised her face to the sun. Terras gloried in the flight he could never achieve on his own, his single wing flapping along with the thunderous beat of Kestrel's massive ones, his joy incandescent.

Their mission might be filled with terror and uncertainty, but what a thrill.

They landed in the same meadow as on her ride with Mother Phoenix, and though Bear sentries must be near, they remained invisible. Sybi unhooked Terras and sat him on her shoulder, then undid the carry bag. It thumped to the ground as she swung off Kes. She began undoing his harness, after she unlatched the final buckle, he changed.

Kes was glorious, breathing harsh, hair a wild thing with feathers sprouting from his head, the sun pouring over him. She handed him his clothes from the carry bag and pulled hers out as well.

Above their leathers, they donned the loose linen pants, tunics, and cloaks worn by most traders.

Kes plucked out his head feathers, while she knelt to unfasten Terras' jesses, then stowed their gear beside a tree. A large, calloused hand reached down, and she gripped it, allowing Kes to pull her close.

"You are my sweet syr," he said. "The woman who has opened my soul, my eyes, and the world to me. I love you, my Sybelle. If we do not succeed, I want you to know this."

Her eyes burned, but she held on amidst the storm of emotion.

He'd never said that he loved her, and she thought she didn't need the words. Perhaps not, but it seemed she had wanted them very much. Now, they were hers to keep forever.

"We'll win the day," she said. "All Eleutia will. I love you too, to the moon and back."

Eyes brimming with love, he bent closer, his whisper rusty. "I do not think I could fly that far."

The laughter in his voice was everything.

Their walk to Alchemic City was swift and quiet, though she suspected several Bear warriors paced them for protection. Trees swayed and bent as they passed, many touching her face or brushing her arms. Sybi returned each touch with her own, acknowledging their blessings.

They reached a high point of land, well shielded by the trees, and Kes halted. The huge city sprawled before them amidst a vast green meadow that extended far into the distance until banded by another border of trees, the wide swath of meadow grasses undulating downward to the valley floor below.

As they crossed the meadow to enter the city, they would lose the trees' protection.

Kes pressed his earpiece and spoke low.

The earth began to rumble.

"The armies come," he said. "A diversion."

Horns blared, feet stomped, and hooves thundered, and though the trees obscured the troops at first, soon Sybi saw thousands of men, women, and animals marching up the mountain from the valley below.

Sybi gasped—the army's size and precision awed her, their banners snapping in the wind. High above, Asher lay prone on Pedro, who directed the mass of avians. Flying below Asher and Pedro, Rafe led the troops of mistrals in wedge formations. Without Kit.

Damn. Rafe must have insisted Kit stay at WolfHome, and her sister had complied. Sybi's plan fractured. How would the sisters unite to call Father Tree?

No choice but to trust the Fates and Mother that all three sisters would come together.

On the ground, Ulfr commanded the Wolves, as did the Tiger, Bear, and other Alphas coordinating their horse and infantry contingents. Seconds later, she spotted Breena and Gato flying above a huge cohort of Cats.

Clans brandished their colors, and while all wore swords and knives or bows and arrows or other analog weapons, many also carried laseblasters, lasecannons, and enough tech to garner the Alchemics' attention.

Music filled her ears. The chirp of pipes, the bellow of horns, and the thunder of drums rent the air, calling Eleutians to war against a Clan bent on devouring their world with deception and oppression.

"We go," Kestrel said. "We will use the uncharted door revealed in your recent sketch."

Sybi hoped she had been dead-on. Terras hopped from her shoulder to Kes's, and they crouched to zigzag toward the city while the troops distracted the Alchemics. They aimed for a specific location on the city's circular outer wall. Veering left, Kes led and Sybi followed, her breath harsh in her ears. Reaching the wall, they hugged it as they ran for long minutes.

With each step, her heartbeat sped up, and she reached for her sensei's mantra to calm herself. Not a resounding success.

Kes raised a hand, and Sybi jammed to a stop, her throat a squeezing noose. Much as she wanted to speak, she clamped her teeth tight.

Up ahead, floating around the city's curve, a huge bronze cube bobbed toward them.

Rather than exploding as the others cubes had done, this cube opened with a soft whoosh, its sides parting like angular flower petals. Inside bobbed a creature, a yellow spherical thing, shiny like Silly Putty, its surface crawling with dozens of eyes and half-a-dozen, plump-lipped mouths.

Dearest goddess!

The mouths widened to smiles. Toothless black gums grinned back at them. Then the creature pursed its lips, a sibilant breath hissing, to mist the air purple and the smell of a moldering corpse.

Sybi ran backward as it neared, holding her breath as long as possible until she gasped to gulp in a dose of the miasma.

Beside her, Kes slid his sword from its scabbard and thrust it into the yellow blob.

Then he was gone, the cube gone, too.

Her father stood before her, a man who had died many years ago.

His quirky smile bloomed. "Hel-lo, daughter."

A tremor shook her. This was not real. *He* was not real.

Father touched her hand. His was warm and firm and large enough to encompass hers.

"Go away, Dad," she said. "You're not real." Though she wished he were.

His startled look transformed into rage.

She recoiled, having seen that expression often. Sybi knew the consequences of his fury.

"You never measured up to your sisters, did you, Sybelle?"

"Fuck you." Her own words shocked her, words she would never have voiced when her father was alive. But now Sybi was a woman with skills and purpose, no longer the meek mouse.

This is not real, she repeated. He *is not real*.

As her "father" reached for her, Sybi feinted backward and went over the top with her fisted right hand, knocking him off his feet with a solid right cross.

Staring down at him, a fierce triumph welled.

Before her eyes, his body morphed.

Sybi jumped back, blinking furiously to clear her eyes. The vision remained.

Marie. Not the beloved ten-year-old child, but a woman grown to a young-adult's full beauty.

In a fluid move, Marie stood and shook out her frilly green dress studded with snowflakes, her cornflower-blue eyes sad. "Why did you hit me, Sybi?"

That voice. Sybi shook her head. No. Marie was *not* real. Yet a terrible compulsion urged her to hug her long-lost sibling, to hold her close and stroke her luxuriant hair.

Sybi's fury erupted. Marie had been denied this—growing into womanhood, having a full life. This simulacrum was *not* Marie. Could not *be* Marie. She backed away, though everything inside urged her forward.

Marie walked toward her, arms outstretched. "Hold me, sister."

A brush of Marie's hand across her cheek. Sybi froze.

That hand was soft and loving.

Her fingers ached, wanting to touch Marie, but she squeezed her eyes tight, her voice a wet mess of pain. "You're dead, Marie. An illusion."

A finger bopped her nose, and Sybi's eyes flew open.

Marie was smiling, the shy one that always melted Sybi's heart. "I am real. Remember the time we stole Papa's fishing rod and..."

A spell of remembrance spun Sybi to another time as Marie told tales from their childhood, her will beginning to crumble. Maybe this *was* her sister? Working with DNA, perhaps the Alchemics had brought Marie back, too. Sure. It was possible.

One foot moved forward, then another toward her sister, the dearest girl in the world.

But she was not real.

"I'm as real as you are, Sybs." Marie tilted her head. "How can you not see that?"

Oh, stars above she wanted her sister. Another step forward.

Marie's eyes bloomed with hope. "Sister?" Marie flung her arms wide, calling Sybi to them.

This close, she noticed the dimple in Marie's chin, the small scar on her forehead, the heart necklace dangling from its gold chain. All real and true.

A breeze rippled Marie's dress. Funny, from a distance she'd seen the white dots as snowflakes, yet they were pale blue forget-me-not flowers. Mother had given Marie the dress on her seventh birthday, a pretty dress but... Sybi struggled. Something about the dress.

Sybi sucked in a breath. When her sister was four, she'd gotten lost in the forested hills by their Maine home and ended up in a field of forget-me-knots, a sea of them. Surrounded by those flowers, Marie had felt trapped, and she remained frozen in place for hours. Forever after, Marie associated forget-me-nots with terror.

Marie loathed the dress and refused to wear it.

Sybi lept backward, tears streaming from her eyes as she drew her laseblaster. *I must.* She took a knee and fired, collapsing, unable to look at what she had done.

Hands lifted her from the ground, and Kes crushed her to him, drawing them back against the city's wall.

"Hallucinations," Kes said, holding her fast.

She hooked an arm around his nape, her breath hitching. "I saw my father. And Marie as a young woman. She talked to me, and it was wonderful, Kes. My head *knew* it wasn't real, but my heart... It sounded like Marie, looked like Marie." She lay her cheek on his chest and shattered.

"You did not kill your sister," he said.

Sybi looked down at the shriveled blob of a thing, eyes wide, mouths open. She sobbed. How she wished her sister lived. But Marie was well and truly gone.

"Come," Kes said. "We must go."

She evened her breathing, exhaling her sorrow and fears. "I'll be all right. I *am* all right."

Terras chirped a cheerful sound as Kes released her and took her hand.

Marie is gone as Mother Tree is gone. I miss them, too.

"Thank you, Terras." Leave it to the peregrine to comfort her.

Still shaky, she found her footing and followed Kes around the city's walls.

As they walked, her hand in Kes', Sybi settled, which was when

Luciana's words pounced into her brain: *Many say since Terras lives, so does Mother Tree.* Luciana believed that.

Could Marie live, too? Impossible. And yet... Speculation was for later.

Kes paused to run his hand down the seamless wall, his hawk's eyes seeing things she couldn't. She inched closer, noting faint horizontal and vertical lines scoring the wall. Kes pressed his earpiece and spoke. They waited.

Dust rose from the distant Eleutian troops march up the hill, their pace measured like those old Roman legions—thud, thud, thud, the sound one of thunder.

Kes listened to his com, nodded, and pressed a spot on the wall's right corner, then stepped back. A crack about six feet wide and high in the wall, then a door swung inward.

Blackness yawned before them. Kes ducked as he entered, pulling her inside, then reached behind her to push the door closed.

His grip wrapped her hand like steel, and they moved forward, his raptor's eyes seeing what hers could not. In an instant, an Alchemic might spring at them, kill them. Jittery, she forced one foot in front of the other down a long, desert-dry passageway stinking of grease and oil. Far in the distance, a pinprick of light expanded as they neared.

Kes drew her around a corner and plunged them back into darkness.

Terras stared at her, his eyes glowing an unearthly blue in the pitch black. Her half-winged friend, so amazing and strange, was Mother's avatar, and with those implications he'd muttered about Mother Tree and Marie, she would learn in detail what that meant when they finished their mission.

A beam of light made Kes halt so swiftly she smashed into his back. Peeking around his shoulder, she recognized their location— the prisoner's courtyard lay beyond the arch. She could no longer see the Eleutian troops, marching ever closer, but their reverberations quivered through her legs.

"Be ready," Kes said over his shoulder. "We must traverse the courtyard on our way to the power station."

It is about time. Typical Terras, full of snark.

"I'm ready," she said.

A lone soldier crossed the stone pavers, slow as dirt. They waited. When the soldier vanished through a door at the courtyard's far left, three more heartbeats passed before Kes said, "Go."

CHAPTER

TWENTY-FIVE

Fukkes smiled. He could not help it as he watched the ridiculous display by the Eleutian animals. They were all animals, whether they walked on four legs or two.

The Cabal had tried. *He* had tried, researching the Clans and their animal symbionts in hopes of improving the pathetic race. He had hoped to bring them into the light of knowledge and truth. His race was so far beyond them, they were near gods, the Eleutians mere ants crawling across their planet.

On occasion, and this was one, the Cabal failed in their world mission. Unfortunate, but not a tragedy. Thousands of worlds existed to be explored and improved upon, most especially the Earthian one the Cabal would next inhabit. He was eager.

Darva took her position at the console to his left. He trusted her implicitly and had raised her to near Cabal status. But born and bred on Eleutia as she was, she was not their kind, and thus would not accompany them to Earth. Thankfully, Darva did not know that.

Ah, well. He glanced at the screens before him, and while other Cabal members did the same, three of his screens were unique to him as Comstat. The one on the right was of particular interest.

"Why are you smiling?" Darva said.

"Come see."

She moved close to his station and gasped. "They dare?"

"Of course they do. The multi-eyed cube almost ended the Made One."

"The Made One?"

Fukkes nodded, then sighed. "It was delicious, but she managed to defeat it."

Darva squeezed his shoulder, an unusually intimate gesture he found shocking.

"I admit, the woman's grit impressed me," he said. "But the sound sensors will get them. *All* of them."

An anticipatory thrill surged through him. He would finally have The Kestrel in his hands and soon, Mari and Xenon would live once again. So close.

Almost there, beloveds. On the morrow, we leave for Earth.

"When will you ping the sensors, Comstat?" Darva said.

"Soon."

"Why wait?"

"The sensors will drop all in their tracks, but there will be that moment, that infinitesimal flicker where they realize they are doomed. I wish to see their eyes at that moment."

"Ah," Darva said, and returned to her station.

Placating him. The woman did not *see* at all. "Why so impatient, Darva? These points in time are to be savored as we gain under-standing from them." As well as pleasure.

"You are correct, Comstat." She pressed a button on her console, and pulled a small lever, precisely maneuvering a sensor for the greatest effect. "As always."

Sybi and Kes crossed the courtyard in quick strides, Kes' sword unsheathed, Terras' head swiveling right and left. No one stopped their progress, and they made it to an archway where Kestrel paused and sheathed his sword, Sybi replacing her knife in its holder.

"Until we reach the power station, we act as if we are visiting traders."

Sybi nodded as they walked with purpose, and though they passed others, some walking, others running, no one paid them any mind.

The city itself whooshed and wheezed.

"They prepare to take to the skies," Kes said.

"Will we be in time?"

He nodded, and they continued through courtyards large and small, some empty, others bustling with people, while above them, transparent raised skyways connected building to building, and low-flying hovercraft dotted the sky.

They traipsed through yet another arched hall and spilled onto an immense open plaza where soldiers and Alchemics, tradespeople, and visitors bustled about. Fountains played, oblivious to the unfolding drama, their sounds dampened by the approaching army's din. Bushes and flowers flourished throughout the stone-paved plaza, while sculptures and benches were sprinkled about, but the stumps of large and small trees marred the courtyard's intended tranquility, their destruction either a paranoid gesture or a cruel one. She touched a small rose bush, feeling its fierce sorrow over the trees' demise.

"They killed all the trees, Kes," she said. "The remaining plants are sad. They might be small, but they will help us."

He nodded, pointing beyond a parapet. The mass of Eleutian troops neared the city.

The sun blazed, and a strong scent of pine wafted on the air. Several dozen Alchemic soldiers prowled the courtyard, and six robed Alchemics lined the parapet, observing the army's progress.

The cacophony of drums and pipes and horns from the Eleutian army grew to a near-deafening volume.

Kes paused, nostrils flared to scent the air. He released her hand, his shoulder naked.

"Kes, where's Terras?"

"Gone."

She loved Kes madly, but he could be the most literal man on Eleutia. "I meant, where did he go?"

Kes shrugged and pulled out a tablet, an unusual one. "Walk beside me, and keep your eyes on the tablet. It is of Alchemic making and will not arouse suspicion."

They strode across the plaza at a healthy pace, but not too fast, nor too slow. From the corner of her eye, an Alchemic in purple robes turned to speak with a soldier.

Fukkes!

Sybi's heart sped, and she clenched Kes' hand, not that she meant to, but due to her frustrating, knee-jerk fear. She wanted out of there now.

Absurd.

Though seeing Fukkes was scarier than fighting that horrible miasma by the wall, she grabbed her fear by the throat and throttled it.

Sweet Christmas, would they never finish crossing the damned plaza? The place was the size of a football field.

The army's noise increased, and she spotted Rafe in the skies atop his immense golden mistral.

To her left, the air rippled, and she snapped around to see... *Ohtli!*

Dammit, another illusion cube had burst. The group of Alchemics nearby failed to notice, their attention fixed on the army's approach. Kes had, for he was staring at the girl with narrowed eyes.

"Ohtli" held up a finger, shushing them. The child wore bright blue linen pants, her tunic a vivid red, making it obvious she was an illusion. CastOuts always wore colors that blended with their environment.

"Be on your guard," Kes said to Sybi. "She will come at us."

The child walked toward them.

Kes dissolved into the shadow of a large sculpture and drew his sword. Sybi's knife was in her hand, arm pressed against her thigh as she prepared for battle with another disturbing illusion, one which replicated Ohtli down to the way she walked.

So had her vision of Marie.

Sybi had ended *that* illusion, and she would do the same to this one.

"Ohtli" smiled standing not six feet away, though she remained silent.

"Fark!" Kes said, and he raised his sword.

She followed his gaze.

Fukkes stared back at them, a smile on his face, eyes alight with joy, and then he vanished into the crowd.

Kes blurred as he rushed "Ohtli," sword swinging in a downward arc.

Sybi jerked to a stop.

Ohtli had vanished then reappeared on Kestrel's left.

"I am real," Ohtli said, her smile oddly peaceful.

Of course she was. Not. Sybi ran towards her as Kes swung again.

Ohtli popped into the space between them, the red bow in her hair coming undone. "I told you I have been practicing my teleportation. Feel me, Ma'am Sybelle."

Could she do it, lift her dagger and stab "Ohtli" in the heart?

Sybi blinked.

Terras sat on Ohtli's shoulder, and damn the bird for looking at Sybi with reproach.

Ohtli *must* be real. Then why the hell was she here?

Kestrel might have been carved in marble, his eyes haunted.

Ohtli rested her hand on his forearm. "It is all right, Kes."

"Security is approaching," Kes said. "On my word, run."

"No," Ohtli said. "We have work to do."

"Work?" Sybi said.

Sword drawn, Kes tugged them into the shadows beneath a balcony's overhang.

"Your drawing." Ohtli looked at Sybi with sweet eyes. "The one you left with me. You drew Father Tree. I saw him in a vision."

As Sybi had concluded. "I think you're right."

"You must call him," Ohtli said.

Now?

Fukkes was out there, somewhere, and the courtyard bristled with soldiers carrying laseblasters.

"Do not worry," Ohtli said, laughter in her voice. "We have this in hand. Please cover your ears and press hard." She scrunched her face, squeezing with all her might against her ears.

Kes raised a brow, as if wondering what the hell Ohtli was talking about.

Do it, Sybi mouthed.

Kes covered his ears, as did she.

"Really tight," the ten-year-old yelled. "Really, really tight."

Tall, thin metal stalks grew upward from the pavement, dozens of them. A long pulse buffeted Sybi, and she stumbled and stared.

Seconds before the plaza had bustled. Now, only the security forces and the robed figures at the balustrade remained standing. Everyone else lay slumped on the ground. Which was when she noticed the army's rumble no longer rippled through her.

"No." Sybi swallowed hard.

Like those in the courtyard, the Eleutian army had collapsed. Foot soldiers sprawled on the ground, and while most on horseback remained atop their steeds, they lay slumped in their saddles.

The avians! Asher remained alert atop Pedro, the avians' and mistrals' flight unaffected. Thank Father Sky.

She would bet those damned Alchemics failed to anticipate *that*.

Ohtli dropped her hands from her ears and grinned. "We are safe now. I will return momentarily."

The air trembled, and both Ohtli and Terras were gone.

"I have no idea what Ohtli's doing, Kes," Sybi said.

Alchemic soldiers drifted around them in twos and threes.

"Fates alive, I almost took the child's head off," he said.

"But you didn't." She peered at the soldiers now ringing them. "Why are they just standing there and not coming after us?"

"Fukkatsu is fond of games."

Ohtli and Terras reappeared, with Kit hugging Ohtli like a monkey. On firm ground, her sister released the girl. "What the hell?"

The Alchemic soldiers leapt back, some making motions with their hands as if to ward off evil, while others barked their surprise.

"I have no clue," Sybi said to Kit. "But I assume Ohtli's going for—"

Ohtli reappeared, Bree wound around her, and Terras hopped from Ohtli's shoulder as Bree staggered to stand. "What a fucking ride!"

"It is time to call," Ohtli said in a calm voice.

"You teleported them," Sybi said with awe.

The child nodded. "Like I told you, Ma'am Sybelle, I have been *practicing.*"

Sybi could see that. Holy shit. Now she was supposed to call Father Tree. Sybi hadn't a clue how, but as the words had exited Ohtli's mouth, the Eleutian avians began dive-bombing the sound amplifiers. Raptors' beaks snapped sensors in half, while in a coordinated effort, smaller birds gripped them with their talons and flapped their wings, knocking the tubes over. The Eleutian troops began to stir as more and more amplifiers fell to the avian assault. The mistrals and their riders who had escaped the sound blast had begun firing lasepipes at the Alchemic stronghold, sending shards of the city flying into the air like so much shrapnel.

The courtyard security forces, still surrounding them, inched closer, though several peeled off to help unconscious or injured Alchemics. Most kept their eyes on Kes, and those eyes gleamed with fear. Fukkes reappeared beside an Alchemic officer, and his Cheshire smile said they were a buffet he was about to devour.

Fukkes spoke to an officer, clasping the man's arm. The officer paled.

"Call Father now, please," Ohtli said.

"I'll do my best." Sybi crouched down. "I've never spoken to Father Tree."

Ohtli pulled a piece of paper from her tunic pocket and unfolded Sybi's tree drawing. She held it up. "This. Picture him."

Looking to Kes, laseblaster in one hand and sword in another, he shrugged.

Big help he was.

Call Father. Terras, chiming in.

Her call must be powerful, for if the tree was as mercurial as Mother, he would insist on it. Her summons must hold urgency and passion.

"Come on girls." Sybi grabbed her sisters, and stood them on a patch of grass, then she stood tall, flowing into mountain pose, *Tadasana.*

"Yoga?" Bree said. "What the hell, Sybs?"

"You've studied this," she said. "Just follow along. I'll call out the poses."

She moved into child's pose, knees folded, hands on Mother Terra, then straightened her spine and sat up. She tapped her fingers above her heart once, twice, three times.

Kit and Bree copied her. Their trio had done this all their lives, moved as one in beautiful synchronicity.

"We're calling Father Tree." Sybi sat in what her teacher called "normal pose," legs comfortably crossed, the backs of her forearms resting on her thighs, hands forming Prithvi mudra. Of the earth. Her sisters mirrored her.

Fear rose, for Kes, for Ohtli, for her sisters, for all Eleutia. She shook, grasping, groping for her center.

A flutter on her back, then Terras curled his talons into her shirt, digging into the leathers beneath the linen. All fear dropped away as she found her center again.

An Alchemic command. "Raise arms!"

The ring of soldiers stepped forward, pointing their weapons at their small group, and even with her thoughts directed inward, she caught the rippling hem of purple fluttering toward them. Fukkes.

Now. Terras, of course.

She grasped each sister's hand, their circle complete, and held on tight. "Mūla Bandha."

The trio's breathing soon synchronized.

"Father Tree, you don't know me, but I was Mother Tree's friend. Please help us rid Eleutia of the Alchemic scourge."

Bree and Kit echoed her words.

Nothing.

Beneath her, the city began to rumble, the sound of generators coming online. Shit. If the city lifted off, she didn't think Father Tree could help.

"Mother called me a world-walker. She said the power of three would triumph."

Too much? Too little? "Father Tree, help us. Help us rid Eleutia of the Alchemic scourge."

Nothing.

The city wobbled, a loud whooshing of air like a jet plane.

Princess Leia's words to Obi-Wan were as good as any. Why not? "Father Tree, you are our only hope. Please, *please* help us save our Eleutia."

Bree and Kit said the words simultaneously with Sybi. They had become a chorus.

Again and again, they chorused the words, and inside her, a million leaves rustled, while beneath, the earth rumbled, the *earth*, not the city.

Pure silence enveloped Sybi as if she inhabited a different realm, and from the crown of her head, a sense of release poured downward to weave through her.

A deep breath later, Sybi rose with the deliberate movements of an old woman to stand beside her sisters, all looking gobsmacked. With Terras on her shoulder, Kes and Ohtli took positions on her right.

"Well done, sweet syr." Though Kes' eyes remained on the Alchemic soldiers, his smile was bright.

"That was really neat," Ohtli said.

Was it? The earth might have rumbled, but no Father Tree had poofed into the plaza.

The city vibrated, as if readying for lift-off.

"What was that?" Bree said.

"The city preparing to fly," Kes said, though his eyes remained calm.

Fukkes stepped before them, eyes hungry, crystal teeth flashing a grin.

Father Tree, help us, she repeated.

Fukkes nodded to the soldiers surrounding their little group, and they closed in. Sybi ignored them, her focus on Fukkes.

The triumphant grin Kes shot her made her toes tingle. "What?"

"He comes."

Power whirled from the soul of Mother Terra, and the earth moved.

Cries from the plaza, people stumbling, falling, a soldier in front of her collapsed to his knees.

Kes grounded her, rock steady, as she swayed like a surfer above Mother Terra's waves.

Kes sheathed his sword.

"Surrender?" Fukkes took a step closer. "How disappointing. I wondered how many of my men it would take to subdue you. It seems none."

A gash tore the earth, a deafening rip.

Leaves, a vast crown of them, burst upward sending paver stones, lampposts, benches, and amplifiers flying.

Father Tree had answered.

Chaos as Father rose and rose, growing taller, thicker, a Godzilla-sized being of differing barks and leaves.

Above the courtyard's din, the Eleutian army roared as they neared the city's walls.

A stone grazed her head and she skittered backward.

"We go." Kes slung Ohtli over his shoulder and raised his sword. She and her sisters clasped hands, her free one in Kes'. They ran.

Fukkes had vanished, the soldiers' ring broken, a sea of people dashing helter-skelter, as screams and shouts pierced the thunder of Father Tree's emergence.

Their group was jostled this way and that, but Kes' grip on her was iron, and they managed to stay together, battle raging around them.

An officer careened into them, laseblaster drawn.

Kes' flattened him with a quick fist.

People prodded and pushed, an Alchemic blade carving the air above her. Someone shoved her hard before she was sliced in two.

But Sybi no longer held Kes' hand. She steadied herself against a jagged wall, her eyes sweeping the plaza.

Kes, her sisters, and Ohtli were nowhere in sight. Sybi slammed down her panic.

Father Tree rose and rose, his massive trunk eating the plaza alive.

COME TO ME.

Father, his thousand-fold bass bearing a galaxy of voices. She was shoved and jostled, but Sybi pushed toward Father Tree as he grew ever higher.

The tree dwarfed any real or imagined living thing, his arresting silver and gold bark woven of disparate trees that blended one into another, a radiant patchwork that glowed in the twilight.

A collective battle cry boomed as the Eleutian forces reached the city, the winged mistrals and avians firing lasecannons and blasters and dive-bombing the opposing troops, the noise cacophonous. The ramparts crawled as creatures both four-legged and two roiled over the wall in an epic wave. A smashed gold cube lay beside the remains of an alien creature, seemingly trampled in the crush.

Battle raged, foot soldiers and archers, mistrals and horses, birds and cats, and bears and wolves. And CastOuts—a boy shooting flame, a woman exhaling death, and more. Many more.

Sybi's heart soared as she neared Father Tree, too close to see the whole of him. Father compelled her as he grew ever higher, his trunk increasing in girth. Buildings crumbled, parapets tumbled, metal shrieked, and balconies flew from their moorings to crush those who fled, and beneath the remnants of a courtyard arch a cube lay crushed.

"Father." Sybi placed her palms and forehead on his trunk, the coolness of his bark surprising. Joy spun through her, an indescribable whirling bliss.

YOU HAVE FULFILLED YOUR PURPOSE, CHILD. GO.

She needed Kes and began to push and shove her way toward an exit, skirting debris and bodies, sure in the knowledge that Alchemic City would never fly again. She laughed. Father Tree had anchored the city to Eleutian soil.

Even now, as Father continued his upward trajectory, she could barely see his leafy top above the dust-filled air.

"Sybelle!" Kes, calling for her.

"Kes!" She ran toward his voice.

Father kept growing.

A creature crashed into her, hairy, simian-like with a huge nose and long claws. A goddart, its curved canines razor-sharp. She stumbled backward, onto her ass, terrified the thing would attack or she would be crushed in the scramble of people and pounding feet.

As if by magic, a space cleared.

The goddart leaned closer, clacking its teeth.

A pair of green sequined shoes booted the goddart aside. Fukkes stood before her and she stared into his eyes.

The Alchemic fisted a hand in her shirt and lifted her upright. His curved obsidian blade rose, his crystal teeth forming a feral howl. "You! You have destroyed all of it."

"I'd get out of here if I were you." She swallowed hard, bravado steadying her voice.

"Sybelle!" Kes ran toward her.

But Fukkes' blade would fall long before he reached her.

"Leave or die, Fukkes!" She slipped her knife from its sheath, wishing her bluster matched her reality.

"Bitch!" Spittle flew from Fukkes' mouth as his arm began to descend.

Never again would she go quietly into the night. Knife at the ready, she bunched her muscles and leaped.

Expecting the pain of Fukkes' blade, she felt none.

YOU TOOK MOTHER TREE'S LIFE. I TAKE YOURS.

Fukkes had vanished.

Overbalanced by her leap, she twisted into a flip, but Kes caught her before she landed.

"Look, my Sybelle." Kes pointed to Father Tree.

A huge branch curled around Fukkes raised him high, massive twig fingers holding the Alchemic in its grip. Fukkes struggled, slashing his knife into those "fingers." Father Tree held firm.

Father paused, skyscraper tall, Fukkes dangling, as dozens of Father's branches continued to swing with destructive force.

Fukkes stabbed Father, again and again, screaming for his troops, calling the Cabal.

Not a one answered.

And Father Tree drew Fukkes slowly toward his trunk and swallowed him, shrieks and screams coming from within until one was cut off. Father stilled.

Sybi gripped Kes tight. "Where are Ohtli, my sisters?"

The plaza began to quiet as Eleutian troops filled the courtyard, surrounding the remaining Alchemics, while dozens of Eleutian soldiers ringed Father Tree in a protective stance. The incongruity was not lost on her—Father was the last being to need their protection.

Amidst the cries and moans of the injured, a few more desultory shots rang out, but those soon quieted as well with the Eleutian troops far outnumbering the Alchemics. Once Father Tree rose, the battle had been short-lived.

Kes set her on her feet and blew an exasperated breath. "Ohtli teleported away, and I do not know where she or your sisters have gone."

"We've got to find them."

"We will. You seem to have lost Terras as well."

And so she had. Lately, he had been popping in and out like a magic bean.

More dust bloomed in the air, along with the scents of smoke, char, and death. Blood painted the pavers red and bodies littered the courtyard, thankfully far fewer than she had feared. Most of the injured and dead were Alchemic soldiers, but Alchemic robed figures and Eleutian human and animal warriors also lay on the ground. A bloody tiger and two broken hawks sprawled by a bench, with other Eleutian animals, men, and women scattered around, most injured, a few dead. A lone capuchin monkey lay crumpled in a flower bed, an Eleutian warrior weeping beside it.

As Sybi watched, order gradually returned to the plaza and what remained of the city. She spotted Kit and Bree with their mates and waved.

"I will return." Kes walked to Rafe and Gato, who stood with other Compass True leaders, all bruised, some bloody.

Sybi felt safe enough to search for Ohtli and Terras, her gut saying she would find the two together.

Her sisters trotted toward her, and they all hugged and laughed and hugged some more.

"We did it!" Bree fist-pumped as they broke apart.

"Isn't it grand?" Sybi said.

"I'm in trouble with Rafe." Kit grinned. "But I'll survive."

"What's wrong, Sybs?" Bree said.

Kit laid a hand on her arm. "You keep looking around."

"I can't find Ohtli or Terras."

Kit shook her head. "The child amazes me. She plucked me from

Moonrise's saddle, I was headed to the battle, and told me to 'hold on.' Then I was on the ground facing you."

Sybi was so proud of Ohtli and her accomplishment. "She's a prognosticator, a real one, *and* a teleporter. She must have seen what to do. She's a world walker like me."

"Impressive," Bree said. "I was scared out of my tree, but teleporting was cool."

"Pretty cool from my end, too," Sybi said.

They agreed to go in three different directions, Bree toward the inner courtyards, Kit to the dining hall, while Sybi took the area encompassing the prisoner compound and labs.

As Sybi searched, she passed the three remaining Cabal members in separate cells. Good. During the battle, hovercraft had left the city, according to Kes. And though they contained Alchemics, the Eleutians let them pass. Away from their city and most of their tech, Compass True would easily ferret those Alchemics out.

Most Alchemics remaining in the city had been born of animal Clans and were given the option to return to their birth clan. Those born into the Alchemic Clan itself were more problematic, and Sybi was glad the problem was not hers.

Sybi checked the cells, shuddering as she relived what she and Kes had found, then headed for the labs. Minutes later, she spotted Bree heading down a side corridor.

"Breena!" Sybi ran after her, dodging fallen stone and crumpled walls, and slipped into a well-lit corridor. Maybe Bree had seen Ohtli or Terras.

Soft lighting lit the white walls, making the dust motes sparkle, and Sybi paused. The corridor was empty.

Where had Breena gone?

She ran, turned a corner, and crashed into someone wearing an Alchemic cloak.

"Oof!"

Both women jumped back, with Sybi drawing her knives. A tall, slim woman with long blonde braids stood before her, the woman's eyes widening.

"Excuse me." The woman brushed past her.

"I'll walk with you," Sybi said, pacing the blonde.

"No need." The woman sped up.

"I don't mind." The blonde had not attacked her. Should Sybi arrest her? Question her? Let her pass? She sheathed her weapons, except for one knife, and matched the blonde's pace, suspicious. If the Alchemic thought she would escape, the idea was laughable. The city was overrun with Eleutian humans and animals.

"Are you headed to the judiciary?" Sybi said.

The blonde rounded on Sybi, her blaster raised.

"Bad idea," Sybi said.

The Alchemic smiled. "It will be satisfying to end you, Made One."

CHAPTER

TWENTY-SIX

A steely calm descended on Kestrel in the battle's aftermath. He stood high atop the remains of a massive sculpture and surveyed the plaza as troops continued to pour over the city's walls. Plumes of smoke drifted skyward while a swatch of Fukkes' purple robe trembled in the air to float down to the statue's handless arm.

He reached for it, noting the stains and lifting it to his nose. Blood. Fukkes' blood. A sense of rightness spun through him. Father Tree had ended the despot's rule.

Terras appeared on his shoulder.

Hello, friend.

A day I have longed for, Terras replied.

As have I.

Where is Ohtli?

Safe.

Rafe and Gato crossed the plaza, accompanied by Gato's bonded panther, Bartholomew, and Rafe's coywolf friend, Paulo.

Kes hopped down and met them, and they slapped backs and gripped forearms, earlier unable to be so convivial surrounded by other Compass True leaders. The Wolf's arm had a bloody cut, and Gato's face was blessed with a fist-sized black bruise. Naturally, both men were smiling.

As he did, the sense of triumph expanding. "It is done."

"With thankfully few Eleutian deaths." Rafe scanned the city. "The Alchemics will rise again, and Compass True will help while keeping a close watch until the putrefaction has been thoroughly expunged."

"That will take years," Gato said. "Ahanu has expressed a willingness to lead the reconstruction."

"Your brother would suit," Kes said. "He is a fair and just man."

"Also an angry one," Gato said. "Father Tree denied him his revenge on Fukkes."

Rafe chuckled. "One does not argue with Father."

"One cannot," Gato said. "Have you seen Breena?"

Rafe raised a brow. "You have lost her again?"

Gato snorted. "Constantly. She is like a bee refusing to land."

"Where is your Kitlyn?" Kestrel asked.

"With her sisters, I suspect." Rafe grinned. "She texted the three were searching for the child."

"I nearly toppled off Bellerophon when my *poosha* vanished into thin air."

"You are not alone in that," Rafe said.

Kes explained what had happened to the sisters and how the trio had called Father Tree."

"Amazing," Rafe said, clearly awed.

"To make up for my near death, Breena has promised more adventure when we return home."

"Ohh, la, la." Rafe, usually the more serious of his two friends, waggled his brows.

"Your Sybelle must be on the hunt, too," Gato said.

Kes' skin itched, a bad sign. "I suspect she is." He understood why she searched, but he wished she would stay close. To him. Always.

"We begin anew today." Rafe rested a hand on Kestrel's shoulder, the other on Gato's. "We have begun a challenging journey, but one that will be infinitely rewarding."

"To Eleutia," Gato said. "Sad we have nothing to drink."

Kes grinned. "True. I would raise my cup to the land and her creatures. And to The Fates, Father Sky, and Mother Terra, who will guide us in all things."

The men pounded backs again and peeled away, Kes determined to find his Sybelle.

After many steps and several wrong turns, he scented her, trotting down a corridor with cracks in the walls and debris everywhere. He saw no injured, nor any bodies, and he thanked Mother Terra.

An urgent squawk from Terras, his agitation palpable. Kes ran.

Flying around corners, he leapt over debris and ran until he spotted two women, his Sybelle and an Alchemic with a laseblaster aimed at his sweet syr's heart. Too distant for his sword, his blaster empty, he drew his knife in what Sybelle would call a "hail Mary play."

"No?" the woman said to Sybi, the blaster steady in the Alchemic's hands. "It will be satisfying to end you, Made One. We created you—Fukkes chose me, Darva, to assist. I do see it as fitting. Don't you?"

Sybi smiled with a shrug.

"My liege is gone, my city destroyed." Darva's eyes lit with fury and pain.

"You are Eleutian born," Sybi said, as she inched her arm forward, the better to aim her knife. "You can have a life with the renewed Alchemic Clan."

"I *had* a life, and you stole it." Her lips compressed, eyes taking on a crazed shine. "We were to leave, to journey to Earth and assume roles of incredible prominence." She gestured wildly. "I would have been Fukkes' consort as we ruled the planet."

Imagining Earth ruled by the Cabal gave Sybi the creeps. "You're nuts. You think no one on Earth would notice the changes?"

"We have studied these Earthian leaders intensively. We will thrive!"

"Perhaps you *would* have thrived," Sybi said. "But that's impossible now. You're going nowhere."

In a heartbeat, the woman's eyes changed from lunacy to lethal.

Stuttering a breath, Sybi saw death and felt its irony. Eleutia was finally free of Alchemic rule. She and Kes could live without fear of oppression or attack. They were to begin the life Mother said would be theirs.

Though she didn't stand a chance, she nonetheless plunged her knife forward.

Darva's head exploded.

Brains and blood rained down on her, the body collapsing to the ground. Sybi reeled, gasping. She wasn't dead. Not even a little.

"Tsk, tsk. You should have lowered the blaster, Darva."

Hip thrust, smirked lips, Bree stood there in all her snarky glory. So beautiful.

Bree ran over waving a cloth that has seen better days. "Sorry for the mess, sis."

"Thanks, to say the least." Hand shaky, Sybi wiped as much glop off her face as possible, unwilling to look down at the decapitated body.

Bree took Sybi's hand, holding it tight, and pointed to the corpse. "She was the bitch who betrayed Compass True's Calix. Who got Neela killed. Rafe suspects she had more victims to her credit. What the hell were you doing?"

"*Sweet Christmas*, Bree, I was looking for you."

"Leave it to you to find trouble instead."

"That's unfair."

"You're a Balážová, aren't you?"

Sybi sighed. "Ain't it the truth?"

"I'll go tell Gato about Darva," Bree said. "He's in charge of clean up."

Kes pressed a hand to the wall, his reaction soul-shattering. His love had almost died. Again. That was it. She was never leaving their nest. Never.

The women had not seen him, and in the aftermath of the shooting, the women's love for each other crashed through him. A power.

He had seen that power in Father Tree's emergence.

Decision made. He and Sybelle would have at least two hatchlings, for he wished their children to know that sibling bond. But first, he would corral his wild emotions before approaching them, or he would steal Sybelle away and lock her up.

Another glance reassured him she was alive and hale. Many deep breaths later, muscles tight, with Terras nuzzling his cheek, he strode to the women.

When Sybelle spotted him, her face became the joyful one he so loved. She crashed into him, her arms around him, and he held her tight, closing his eyes against the powerful emotions roiling over him.

"It seems like I am *de trop*," Breena said. "I'm going to find my own mate and kiss him senseless."

Kes' eyes held Sybelle's. "You are well? I would see you leave the city and be safe."

Her jaw tightened, her eyes narrowed, and his stubborn woman stared back at him. "No. It's safe now, and I can help."

"Though I find it challenging when we are apart, I wish you to be secure, my Sybelle." He left off, unable to voice more words.

Her hands framed his face. "I'm pretty much done with this separation business. I'm not leaving your side again. And I am most certainly not going home."

Home. On this day of all days, the word played a melody of the land he loved, of its people and creatures, and of this woman whom he treasured above all else. "Yes. You will stay by my side."

Her shy smile rose. "Always."

Six months later, much had changed on Eleutia.

The aftermath of the battle had been ugly. Corpses were burned, including the emaks the army had destroyed, and clean-up was endless.

All Eleutia mourned the dead who had sacrificed their lives, and the world wept at the discovery of a hoard of mistral bones, hundreds of them neatly sorted by type, their senseless deaths devastating.

They also discovered the Cabal's tech for their Essence transport to Earth. Not a single machine remained whole. But the Eleutians disassembled and destroyed what was left.

One sun-drenched day, a presence called the Overseers announced themselves. Invisible, they literally rippled the air of Eleutia with their voices, reaching all corners of the planet when they spoke.

The Overseers were a cool chorus, mirthless and mysterious. "We apologize for the chaos our kind has caused," they said, their words comprehensible to all Eleutians, no matter their language. "We will retrieve those who remain. They will be punished for violating our covenants."

Not a request, but a pronouncement.

The three living Cabal members imprisoned at WolfHome vanished from their cells, as had the nine remaining Earthly Essence balls stored at CatHome.

Sybi hoped the Overseers would infuse them back into their rightful bodies.

Those vanishings were the last sign the Overseers had visited Eleutia, so swift, they could have been a fevered dream.

Father Tree remained in the soil beneath Alchemic City, yet when Sybi visited him, he never spoke to her again. At least, he hadn't yet.

At Sybi's request, she and Kes had walked to the site of Mother Tree's demise and buried the diamond from Mother deep in the earth, her faint hope the planting would prompt Mother to rise again.

"It could be," she said to Kes. "Mother said 'We always endure.' Maybe the diamond is some sort of key or something."

His eyes bored into the soil as if he were willing Mother to grow. "Perhaps."

Today, the Northwest Quadrant celebrated the birth of Kitlyn and Rafe's daughter at WolfHome, the party in full swing. Men and women performed incredible dances and many symbiont animals sang. The Cats, the Wolves, the Bears, and the CastOuts—all the local clans had joined in the occasion, giving it a carnival atmosphere.

Rafe and Kit's infant was one month old, which was when Eleutians celebrated a child's arrival. They had named her Nadja or Hope, a perfect name. Each day, more girl children were being born on Eleutia, but it would take many years for the male-to-female birth ratio to equalize.

Sybi tapped her toes watching, not feeling up to the dance.

"Do you see that?" Bree said, handing her a mug of kamla.

"Marcos and Arina?"

"They're like two spitting cats."

"Because they like each other," Sybi said.

Bree shook her head. "I swear, they'll be mated by the new year." She waved as Fudge and Ax twirled by them. "I wish it was Makena and Ahanu."

Kit joined them. "Lucky stars, are they still not speaking?"

"Only formally," Bree said. "It's driving the den crazy."

"What about Max and Tilde?" Sybi said.

Across the room, Tilde stood deep in conversation with Yuan, who waved Kit over.

"Where's Max?" Bree said.

Sybi peered around, but didn't see him. She rubbed her belly, the din overwhelming, her pregnancy having turned her senses acute.

Months earlier, Marcos had seen the "shadow" as a child, much to Sybi's relief and Kes' delight. He said the baby's abilities were seeping into Sybi, amplifying them. All well and good, but along with morning sickness and a clichéd desire for pickles, her sensory acuteness was driving her nuts.

Breena, never one to be bested by either sister, was also in the family way. With twins. A boy and a girl, their birth expected in four months. Though Bree complained about the weather, the food, and her increased poundage, in truth she was over-the-moon happy with her mate and the impending births. So were Barth, Audi, and Fortis, usually glued to her like velcro.

"Let's get out of here," Sybi said to Bree. "I feel a little woozy." At seven months, her bump was oddly small, and she worried, yet she felt the child's warmth through her entire being, like a comforting massage. Marcos scanned her weekly, and though he saw a faint outline of the embryo, he could not determine their child's sex—she or he remained cloaked by that gray amorphous shadow. The healer wasn't concerned, but their baby's sex would be a surprise.

They found a small lounge off WolfHome's enormous central Hall. A banked stone fireplace, couch, and two plump chairs beckoned, and Sybi made a beeline for the sofa.

"I don't understand why I'm so tired, Bree." She slumped on the couch, unable to get comfortable. "Or why I want to eat pickles all the time. Marcos says it's normal."

Bree smiled. "It is, Sybs. Look at me. I'm already tank-sized, and I have months to go. Pegasa will soon refuse to carry me."

Sybi stared downward. "My bump is so small, and I'm due in two months, Bree."

"Given Kes' epic size, that sounds like a good thing." Bree plopped beside Sybi and wrapped an arm around her waist. "You said Marcos told you that the babe is healthy and so are you, Sybs. It will be all right."

"I know. And I'm excited," Sybi said. "But I wish I didn't feel so lousy. And strange. One minute, I'm floating on air, the next, I want to puke my brains out. Maybe you should get Kes."

Bree started to rise.

Sybi put a hand on Bree's arm. "No, I'm being selfish. He deserves to enjoy himself with Rafe and Gato, a thing he could rarely do before the war. Did you see the three of them dance? Incredible. He's going to play his luteon in a bit, and we're going to sing."

"You? In public?"

"Yup."

"Well, hooray! A first. Your voice is incredible."

A cramp hit Sybi, doubling her over.

"What is it?" Bree said.

"Just another cramp," Sybi said on a forced breath. "I have to work through them. I've been having them for a couple of days now."

"What did Marcos say?"

"That I needn't worry. The cramps are false labor, and not unexpected. He and Kes hover like vampire bats, and I sometimes feel smothered. Let's change the subject. I'm still trying to reach Father Tree. I have to alter my tactics, I'm thinking."

"Father hasn't moved since he burst through the city."

"I have a feeling he'll remain there for a long time. I have to get him to speak again. I want to know about Mother."

"Good luck with that." Bree snorted.

"One of these days, he'll answer. You'll see." Another pain clamped her mouth tight.

"Shit!" Bree shouted.

Ohtli stood in front of them wearing a broad grin—Little Miss Teleportation—and leaned forward to hug Sybi. "I wanted to be here and I wanted to tell you a secret."

Sybi hugged Ohtli back. "Sweetheart, we've talked about your popping in uninvited. It's fine with me, I've gotten used to it. But you surprised Bree. Please be more careful. It's not polite to just appear. Makes sense?"

"All right," Ohtli said with a faux-somber nod of the head. Her teenage years... Heavens' light, Sybi didn't want to think about that. "What secret, sweetheart?"

"I'm bleeding."

Sybi startled. "Where? What happened?"

Ohtli grinned and leaned close to Sybi's ear. "You know. My girl parts. I am eleven now, after all."

Terror clamped a fist to Sybi's heart. Ohtli would see her death...and die.

A shadow passed across Ohtli's eyes, then vanished. "I saw 'the movie,' like we've been practicing. I was really old and wrinkly. But I did not see the ending."

"You..." Sybi couldn't mouth the words.

"Marcos' hypnosis, it was so neat, it worked, and there was no end, just a recycling of the movie. He said it worked because I do not want to die. And because you and Kestrel and Terras love me. But it was scary."

"Oh, Ohtli." Sybi drew her daughter onto her lap, her fierce hug making the child squirm.

"Ow!" Ohtli said.

Sybi pulled back. "You are amazing, dear one."

"I am. You're crying happy tears, right?"

That playful grin made Sybi want to hug her all over again. "I sure am."

"I want to be here for the arrival," Ohtli said. "Is that okay?"

"Arrival?" Bree said.

"Mama's baby." The child stood, gathered a throw from a chair, and drew it over Sybi.

"I'm not due for two months, hon." Sybi smiled at her girl, now legally adopted.

Ohtli shook her head. "You will see."

The child spoke in her own definitive way. Once she and Kes talked to Ohtli's parents, they'd released her, eagerly, without even a token fight for their child. That still bugged Sybi.

She, Kes, Terras, and Ohtli had become a family, no foster anything. Now Ohtli knew she was secure and cherished and loved, and she had bloomed, her confidence soaring. The girl was so bright and willing, and Sybi was convinced their family's security and love bolstered the hypnosis process. Ohtli would live to become a full-blown prognosticator.

Ohtli tilted her head. "Our baby is coming now. I'm excited, Mama!"

That couldn't be. It was too early, her bump too small. "We've talked about this, hon. Human babies take nine months to gestate."

Ohtli said nothing, but Sybi worried at her smug smile.

The peregrine materialized on her shoulder.

"Dammit, Terras," Sybi said. "You and Ohtli keep popping in and out like jumping beans."

"Nope." Bree laughed. "They're more like jack-in-the-boxes."

Another cramp, a harder one. What if she was losing the baby? What if Ohtli saw that? She rose to fetch Marcos... And sat back down, pain leveling her.

"Get Marcos," she said to Breena with a gasp.

"I'm not leaving you with a bird and a child," Bree said.

"What if Ohtli is right?" Sybi said. "What if the baby's coming early?"

Breena flashed a concerned look and ran for the door, colliding with Kestrel, who nearly flattened her.

"Terras says you're having our baby," Kes said.

Sybi's eyes burned, and she couldn't stop the tears, not this time. "The baby is only seven months. I'm so small. We need Marcos. We need to stop this."

"On it!" Bree raced out the door.

Kes lifted her from the sofa and laid her across his lap. His face was fierce, but his eyes were filled with worry. "Sweet syr, I do not know what to do. I have studied all the breathing techniques, the books on children and babies and birth, as you asked. Yet I do not feel prepared."

"You're not the only one, my love." She would *not* lose this baby. Kes would be devastated and blame himself. She would be crushed, too, as would Ohtli. The girl might panic, which could damage her. Heavens knew what Terras would do.

The cramps came and went, Kestrel pouring comfort and love through their bond. Forever seemed to pass even as her cramps worsened. She looked around the room, sweat dampening her temples.

Kes, Ohtli, and Terras were all here. Her family. Even if Marcos didn't arrive in time, even if her babe... No. She would survive surrounded by so much love. *They* would survive.

Marcos and Dr. Kicks bustled in along with Breena and Kitlyn, their spouses not far behind, while Sybi's cramps pounded her with greater intensity. Dr. Kicks' medical degree reassured her. Along with Marcos, Sybi had visited her clinic at WolfHome several times. All had been well. Like her sisters, she was a Made One, and exceptionally fit and healthy.

Another cramp. Something was very wrong. The small room was crowded with people, the air thick, the murmurs deafening.

Goddess save me, it hurt so much.

If she miscarried, she didn't want anyone near but Kes. Knowing Terras, he would stay, too. But Ohtli had to leave before any tragedy unfolded.

Sybi looked at Kes, who continued to cradle her. He smiled, going for confidence, except his confusion and concern were obvious. Fear had grown thick, the air loud with worry.

"Kes, please ask everyone to leave but you and the doctors."

He nodded wearing his battle face. "Get out. All but Marcos and Kicks."

Her mate would never be a diplomat. She sighed through a cramp.

"What?" he said, peering down at her.

Sybi kissed his cheek. "Nothing, sweetheart."

"We're not leaving," Bree said, arms crossed.

"Sybi needs us," Kit said.

Kes leveled his gaze on her sisters. "Leave."

Rafe and Gato took hold of their respective partners and steered them from the room, her sisters' displeasure loud.

Excepting the doctors, only Ohtli and Terras remained.

"Hon," she said to Ohtli. "You are our daughter, but you need to go. This won't be pretty."

"It will so be pretty." The girl's obstinate expression was a now-familiar one.

"I doubt that," Sybi said. "And I would rather you not see and hear, sweetie."

Ohtli stamped her foot. "No."

Sybi took the girl's hands in hers. "Please."

Ohtli beamed a smile. "Do you trust me, sweet syr?"

She started at Ohtli's use of Kes' term for her. "Of course."

The child's serious blue eyes stared into Sybi's. "Then trust me and let me stay."

"I agree with our daughter." Kes nodded.

What a traitor. A cramp stole her breath and she gritted her teeth, managing at the end to smile. A somewhat twisted smile, true, but a smile nonetheless. "All right. But please sit in a chair out of the doctors' way. Can you do that?"

With a solemn nod, Ohtli pushed a chair near the head of the couch and slipped onto it. The girl flounced her skirt and crossed her ankles, and in a serious voice said, "I am ready."

Sybi was not, but she would have chuckled if it weren't for another hideous cramp. She growled, puffing out breath.

Marcos spoke to Kes. "It will be best if you lay Ma'am Sybelle down on the sofa."

"No." Kestrel's nostrils flared white.

"Fine," Marcos said.

Sybi didn't miss the healer's eye roll. *Why was everyone being so contrary?* She wanted peace and quiet. And for the pain to go away.

Marcos thundered a frown. "Kestrel, sit with your legs stretched out, your back supporting hers. Understood?"

They rearranged themselves, with Kes unfolding his legs so

Sybelle's were between them and lifting her back against his chest. He laid his hands lightly on her shoulders.

"Good!" Dr. Kicks said with a chirp, and she moved to Sybi's feet and began to remove her shoes, then pulled off her leggings and panties, leaving Sybi's long tunic in place.

Sybi raised her legs as she would for a gynecological exam, and her pain had increased to where she didn't care she was naked and exposed. Dr. Kicks continued to reassure, saying to call her "just Kicks," though the doctor could not hide the concerned glance she shot Marcos.

The healer had begun moving his large hands down Sybi's body, calming her and easing the pain.

"Heavenly," she said.

Kicks caught Sybi's eye. "You are ten centimeters dilated. The baby is about to come, and given that you are a Made One and The Kestrel is, well, The Kestrel—"

"But the baby can't come yet," Sybi said.

"Even at seven months, babies can thrive," Kicks said.

Kes whispered in her ear. "All will be well, sweet syr. Whatever comes, whatever happens, we will be fine."

His scent wound around her, and she drank in a soothing breath.

A jagged pain.

A scream.

"Push!" Kicks shouted.

She pushed as tears bathed her face. *No.* She would not cave to negativity, dammit. Babies were born early all the time.

A searing pain lashed her, and she pushed again on a scream.

"Yes!" Kicks caught the tiny babe, so small Sybi couldn't see it. So quiet, too.

Sybi's tears dried. Now was not the time. It was over. It was all over.

"Holy shote!" Kicks' shocked eyes stared at Marcos.

The healer grinned.

Kes kissed her cheeks and the top of her head, his arms wrapping her tight.

A few after-birth pains rippled through her, and then her belly stilled. Sybi quieted, too.

The room's silence was deafening.

"Why are you smiling, Marcos?" Sybi pushed up, trying to see her babe.

"Wait, Sybelle." Kicks held up her hands.

In her hands rested an egg, a huge one, colored reddish-brown and mottled with steel blue.

Sybi felt drunk. An egg?

Kes laughed softly, an occurrence so rare and precious it made her smile.

"Kes?"

His laughter boomed around the room, and it went on and on.

"I can feel her," Kes said. "She is well and eager to meet us."

"But..."

He stared down at her with eyes the color of love. "She will emerge from her shell in two months."

And so, she did.

EPILOGUE

A year later four young children and a twelve-year-old played in Sybi and Kes' aerie, their three fathers about to collect them all for the opening of the new Alchemic gathering hall. All the Northern Quadrant would be there, and according to Bree, the party would be another epic one.

Within the great room lounged an adult panther, his two teen cubs, a coywolf, a one-winged falcon, and a prognosticating girl, while an eight-month-old child with bright red hair poked at the bobbing leaf of the tailung plant floating in a bowl of water. Her black-haired twin brother beside her giggled and pushed her. The red-haired girl pushed back. Like Bree and Gato, their twins were precocious. All the sisters' children were, to no one's surprise.

The second girl child, auburn-haired and thirteen months, slapped her legs and leaned forward as if riding her pony. Kit's ever-curious Nadja was already horse obsessed. The fourth child, a year and also a girl, watched in silence, her chubby legs poking in front and her blue-and-bronze hair sprouting baby kestrel feathers at its crown.

When Rowan Avalyn emerged from her egg, a comet of joy blazed through Sybi. Avi's gray eyes missed nothing, and she and Kes had named their firstborn for the Celtic rowan tree of mythology, the Tree of Life, to honor Mother Tree. Sybi had picked Avalyn to celebrate Kes, for it meant beautiful bird. And Avi was beautiful in all ways.

After what looked like serious deliberation, Avi plucked the leaf from atop the water and flipped it over.

"Very good, Avalyn!" Breena clapped, then took in all the children. "You all did very well, very well indeed." Seeing her twins about to wail, Bree bent and picked them up like sacks of beans. "Grace and Rodrigo, you will succeed one of these days. It's a challenge that you will ultimately win."

Grace nodded, her bottom lip thrust out, while Rodrigo grinned, the devilish glimmer in his eyes matching Gato's own. Sybi hoped Bree survived the pair.

The auburn-haired Nadja looked to her mother, arms outstretched, and Kitlyn scooped her up.

"Moon!" The child demanded. "Want Moon!"

"Moonrise will be here soon, sweetheart. Papa, too. All right?"

Nadja beamed.

Sybi left the children sitting in a circle playing a game of Peekles overseen by Kit and Bree. If the men didn't arrive soon, their group would be late.

"You good?" she said to her sisters. "I have to go change."

Ohtli, holding Avi on her lap, winked.

"We've got this, Sybs," Kit said.

She smiled, worried Avalyn might win the game of Peekles against the other children. Again. Sybi and Kes' child was preternaturally advanced.

Minutes later, having changed to her formal silk tunic and flowing pants, bronze and steel blue, Sybi reentered the great room. "What did I miss?"

They had enlarged the room to accommodate not only their growing family but their relatives and guests. Somehow, with four children, pre-teen Ohtli, three lounging panthers, a busy Terras and Paulo, not to mention her sisters, the room still didn't seem large enough.

A look out the window. "Holy shit." Sybi's throat tightened.

A giant head peeked through the windows.

Terras landed on Sybi's shoulder. *Grandmother is here.*

"I can see that!"

Grandmother Phoenix was a hoverer who crowded the children and whose feathers bristled over the slightest misstep by anyone not of their family circle. The phoenix had taken helicopter grand-parenting to epic heights.

"You can't poof us to the party," Sybi said, walking onto the deck to greet her semi-mother. "No conflagration. Period."

The phoenix glared back, then began to sulk.

Can we get rid of her? she asked Terras.

Why?

Because if we don't, Grandmother Phoenix may fly the children away to play.

She heard Terras' sigh in her head. *I cannot make her leave. Nor can you.*

Squawks and hisses from the phoenix as Rafe, Gato, and her beloved Kestrel climbed the stairs, all dressed in formal Eleutian garb. The three, working with Gato's brother, had led Compass True's efforts to rehabilitate and re-establish the Alchemics, now known as the Seeker Clan. A choice approved by all the clans.

The men piled into the great room. Much kissing and hugging ensued, and Sybi's heart squeezed when Kes embraced Ohtli and Avalyn and lifted them into his arms. He was an incredibly loving parent to both girls.

Life was good, though challenges remained. They still hunted rogue Alchemics, helped rehabilitate those who had surrendered, and continued the difficult, but rewarding work of helping the creatures transformed by Alchemic experimentation.

In the time that had passed since the war, the CastOuts had changed, too, with some leaving the village for their native animal Clans. She and Kes discussed moving to the Falcon Clan, but never seriously, preferring to stay right where they were. To everyone's surprise, some "normals" from various Clans had joined their group, and most of the Alchemic's manipulated subjects had become CastOuts as well. Once again, the village was growing.

Sybi stared across the trees to the Titanus sea beyond, missing Mother Tree, and imagining Marie was here. Her sister would have embraced their life on Eleutia and brought them all great joy.

"What is it, sweet syr?" Kes wrapped his arms around her waist, pulling her close.

"Nothing," she said.

"Something," he said.

She shrugged.

"Tell."

"I was thinking of Mother and Marie."

"Ah." He tightened his hold, resting his chin atop her head.

Terras landed on her shoulder and nuzzled her neck.

"We have so much," she said, taken by a strange melancholy. "We are blessed. I shouldn't be sad."

"Our lives are full," he said. "But missing those you love is a testament to them."

"Mother and Marie should be here."

"That they should."

"Time to go, guys!" Breena said.

Sybi turned in Kes' arms and kissed him, long and hard and with all the huge love she felt for her mate. "By the way, Grandmother Phoenix is coming, too."

His stoic face collapsed into chuckles. "This will be interesting."

"That's one way to put it."

They collected Avalyn and Ohtli, along with the baby's bag and other necessities. Everyone else was doing the same, contributing to the chaos of leaving the nest.

She scanned the room, checking that all animals, humans, and baby paraphernalia were out of the aerie, and began closing the door.

MOTHER WILL RETURN. SHE GROWS.

What. The. Hell. Sybi gripped the doorknob. No one else had reacted to the booming voice. Father Tree. At last.

Sybi whirled on Kes, brow raised, head tilted.

He hadn't heard, either.

For all her attempts, Father Tree had never spoken to her after the battle, though she had tried to reach him many times. That booming voice was definitely Father and a great gladness lifted her —Mother was growing again.

Sybi smiled, her tears mingling with giddy laughter.

MARIE GROWS AS WELL.

"Father?"

No answer.

Her whole body shook.

"Sweet syr?" Kes said winding an arm around her waist.

"Father Tree just spoke to me," Sybi said with a whisper. "He said Mother grows, that she'll return."

His eyes warmed. "As we hoped."

"Yes." Sybi stood on tiptoe, unwilling to have anyone else hear. "He also said 'Marie grows as well.' I'm shaken. I don't know what he means."

Avalyn toddled over, beaming a smile, arms raised. Sybi lifted their daughter onto her hip.

The child leaned close. "Mama?"

"Yes, hon?"

"Marie who?" Avi said.

Sybi's eyes flashed to Kes, then back to her daughter. "How do you know that name, sweeting?"

"Father said."

Kes was Papa. *Dear heavens.*

The Kestrel chuckled softly and took her lips with his.

~Finis~

THANK YOU! AND NEWSLETTER

Thank you for reading *Ascendant*!

Reviews mean everything—they're an author's lifeblood as readers find us through your reviews. If you enjoyed *Ascendant*, leaving an honest review would be a kindness.

Would you like a free book? Do sign up for my newsletter and receive my bonus novel, *Body Parts*. My monthly newsletter contains info on The Made Ones Saga, the Afterworld Chronicles, life in L.A., and lots more yummy stuff.

Come visit with me... VickiStiefel.net
Facebook • Instagram • Twitter • BookBub

SECRET PROJECT
AKA WORKING TITLE: THE REGENCY

CHAPTER 1

Rosamund was worried. Scared, really.

She checked her clothes, the boy's riding breeches and shirt from Milo and the felt hat from Seth. The boots were Robert's, and she hoped to return them before he missed them.

Before the mirror, Rosamund twirled. She made a fine boy, if she did say so herself.

Her deception was part of her plan to save Tessa.

Last night, when she had snuck into the drawing room after bedtime, she had hidden in her usual spot behind the curtains to watch and listen while the grown-ups chattered. That way, she could learn important things, like about the horses or herself or Maman[Maman in French], things that Papa did not like to share because he said she was too young.

Maman knew she was there, for it was Amalie who had made a fun game out of teaching Rose wariness and stealth. Rosamund knew why, but neither she nor Maman spoke of it.

What she heard last night was worse than anything she had ever heard before. Papa was going to drown Tessa and her puppies.

Maman had said to Papa that it was time to build the whelping box for Tessa's pups, and how they could put it in the barn where it was warm and safe. Papa had chuffed and made that mean smile he had. He said there was no point. And then he said he planned to get rid of Tessa's pups! To drown them!

Maman had been as horrified as Rose was and had asked Papa why. "The Earl of Chatsworth does not permit half-breed anything, no less his daughter's dog's whelps to live on the estate."

"Killing Tessa's whelps will destroy your daughter," Maman said.

Papa had gotten that tight look on his face. "She needs toughening up. Indeed, she will never know."

"And what about Tessa?" Maman said.

Papa had laughed. "The dog has become a nuisance. She goes, as well. We will get her a new pet, one less prone to stray."

He would kill her beloved Tessa, too, and like a cloud of swarming midges, worry ate at Rosamund.

Her parents went on talking, but Rose stole back to her bedroom. She had much to think about. Tessa was there, in her poof bed, though she had grown too fat for it and her back legs dripped over the side. Rosamund sprawled on the floor and hugged Tessa tight, snuggling as close as she could.

"I won't let you die."

Tessa licked her chin, then went back to sleep.

The pups would come soon, Maman had said, and Rose had to do something fast. Today.

Though Maman sometimes wanted to, she would never thwart Papa. Maman called Papa a "stern" man. He was not bendy like Maman. Rosamund thought she was bendy, too, though she was not sure.

In the times Maman had spoken up, she had remained in her rooms for a day or two, and then returned looking bruised and sick. Papa liked hitting Maman, but he never hit Rose, though she expected he would someday.

So she could not ask Maman for help because Maman would get in trouble. It was on Rose's shoulders to take care of Tessa, and she would.

Maman had given her the English setter puppy when Rosamund was three, and Tessa was five now and her best friend. Tessa could not go away and she could not die.

A stray mongrel had gotten Tess pregnant, that was what Maman said, and each day Tessa's belly had grown bigger and bigger. Rose didn't see how it could get any bigger, and yet it had. Rose was excited about the puppies, her focus on the impending birth and being surrounded by little Tessas. Her mother had even shown her a painting of puppies nursing at their mama's belly and explained that would happen once the puppies came. Foals nursed standing up at their mother's belly, she'd seen that plenty of times, but Tessa would lie down to give her puppies milk. Different, but similar enough, she guessed.

At eight years old she did not fully understand how an animal got puppies or foals or kittens in their bellies, but she had seen enough mares birth foals to know the messy and exciting process of birth.

Dressed in her boy clothes, Rosamund and Tessa left long their home before dawn broke and before her governess Lucy was awake. But Lucy was a good secret keeper. Unlike Nellie, her maid who reported everything Rose did to her father. Nellie was his spy, and so Rose must be back before Nellie brought her morning chocolate.

She walked Tessa across the hills and dales of the manor's property holding the rope leash she had fashioned, Tessa waddling behind her. If she had taken Tessa's leash, people would know, and those people would tell Papa that she and Tessa were gone.

Tessa was good on a leash and so the rope was efficient. Rose liked efficiency. They went slow because by now Tessa could not walk fast now, and Rose didn't want anything to happen before they reached their destination—Ravenscroft. The Marquis of Ravenscroft's estate marched beside theirs, larger and even more splendid. And she had heard rumors about the marquis. Good rumors.

The day was glum, the sky full of dark mean clouds like fists. An angry sky. It would rain soon, and by the time she reached Ravenscroft, she would be drenched. Her horse, Lightning Bug, or Bug for short, loved the rain, though most of their horses didn't. Bug would prance, and if she was unsaddled, be sure to roll in the mud, her white coat turning to brown mush. Papa got angry when she did that. Rose sighed. So many things got Papa angry.

If he found out what she was doing, Papa would be angry at her. Later, when she was home without her sweet Tessa, Maman would protect her.

Rose bit her lip. She worried about too many things. Maman always said that, but how could she not worry when Maman kept getting skinnier and skinnier. Each time she went to Maman for help, and mama always helped after a session with her father, Maman seemed more and more...broken. Her cheeks, once puffy and soft, now reminded her of a skeleton she had once seen, the bones of a tramp discovered on the estate.

Tessa spotted a rabbit and ran. Anna flew into the air holding on hard to Tessa's rope, and she landed okay even if her hands burned. She was glad she had held on.

They walked and walked, crossed two streams, and came to the Afrodis river that frothed like dozens of horses scampering on the water's surface. They neared the big bridge that crossed the river, the one dividing their property from that of Ravenscroft. If she and Tessa crossed that bride, Papa's watchmen would see her, her mission a failure.

Rose veered south, and after a few minutes, Tessa whined. Her belly had gotten all tight. The puppies would come out soon.

"Not yet, Tess," she said with desperation. "Please, not yet."

Downriver where they were headed, someone had placed a fat log across the river. Years ago, the stable master's son had shown it to her, and she often used it to practice her balance for riding. She didn't know who put it there, but it was plenty easy for her to cross. She hoped Tessa would find it easy, too.

When they arrived at the crossing, the log wasn't quite as fat as Rose remembered, though the big drop to the river churning below was. It wasn't that far. Really, it wasn't. They could do this.

Rose waited until Tessa's belly relaxed after another squeeze, stepped on the log first, and moved forward. Tessa dug all four paws into the dirt and sat. Rose pulled and tugged, but Tessa would not step onto the log. Down below—far, far below—the river raged, like it wanted to eat her alive, the same mean gray as the sky. Tessa was too heavy to carry. She weighed more than five stone. Bleak though it might be, dawn was beginning to break. Maybe they should go back to the big bridge.

They could not. They would be seen.

She walked off the log and went to Tessa's rear end. Tessa must cross. She had to. Rose swung a leg over Tessa and straddled her like she did Bug, but she didn't put any weight on her pup.

Her bones melted. She'd stayed up too late worrying, got up too early for this adventure. Rose was tired. She thought about how she really wanted to turn around and go home, crawl back into her warm bed, and wait for her morning chocolate to be delivered.

But if she did that, Tess would die.

So she wrestled Tessa's left front paw up and placed it onto the log.

"Walk, Tessa! Come on. We need to get across."

Tessa stood stock still, her entire body frozen. Oh, no. Her belly was moving again, another stiffening. Tessa whined. It hurt, but that was how the puppies would come out. Horses foaling cried out, too.

"Come on, Tess. You can do this."

She pushed her shoulder to Tessa's rear and tried to pull, which wasn't easy. Tessa put one paw in front of the other on the log.

Good.

From years of riding her pony and then Lightning Bug, Rose had great balance. Soon, she and Tessa were inching across the log, Rose putting pressure on Tessa's rear end, Tessa taking a step forward, and Rose following one slow step at a time.

The skies opened and the rain poured down, drenching Rose and making her shiver. Tessa did, too. Maman always said to bring a jacket, and she should have worn her barn coat. Should've. Would've. Could've.

A tremble hit her, and she paused before taking her next step. Except a patch of moss grabbed the sole of her boot, her foot slick with rain, and she slipped, teetered...

She would tumble into the river and there was only one thing to do. Releasing Tessa, Rose scissored her legs out, hoping. She crashed onto the log—boy, that hurt—and wrapped her legs around it. But she was halfway off, her weight insisting she plunge into the river below. Rose clung to the log gripping it as if it were Bug and he was bucking. Her legs tightened as her arms pinwheeled, searching for the balance that suddenly eluded her.

Oh, no.

She slid all the way around, her head aimed at the raging river below. She reached for the log to pull herself up, but couldn't quite manage the stretch.

Her hat tumbled to the waters below, swirling and whirling, then gone. Seth's favorite. He would murder her.

Muscles screaming with fatigue, rain pounding her face, she began to swing her torso and arms backward and forward, like she was flying.

Her legs slipped, but she hung on, and she swung again and again as the rain pounded, coating her from head to toe and running in rivulets down her back. Once more. And again. Almost there.

Yes. Her fingernails dug into the bark and for a minute she hung there like some demented monkey. Panting, and with a mighty heave, she twisted herself around to the log. Across the river, Tessa stared at her from the opposite shore, the rope dangling from her neck.

For a moment, Rose hugged the log tight. With a heave, she got her feet under her in a crouch but paused. Rain pounded her back and got under her clothes. She might slip again, fall into the river.

Tessa whined, her belly expanding and tight. Another birth pain.

With a mighty push, Rose leapt to a stand, arms spread. She almost cried because once again she had found her footing.

One step. Then another. And she was across and down on her knees hugging Tessa, uncaring of the mud and rain and simply thankful she had made it to the other side.

Rose swiped a hand across her face, rose, and took the end of Tessa's rope, and they continued on.

The rain paused, and Rose swiped a wet sleeve across her even wetter face. Tessa has started to pant and every time one of those birth pains hit, they would stop. The contractions hurt her sweet Tess and made Rose want to cry. Why did it hurt Tessa so? Was something wrong? They had to make it to the Ravenscroft stable. She knew horses and she knew horse people. The Ravenscrofts were like that, or so she had been told. Most often, horse people were animal people, too, and Ravenscroft was her best bet to save Tess and the pups.

The wood was thick with brambles and dead leaves, and their passing silenced the small woodland creatures. On and on, up and down, over rocks and branches until they reached the wood's edge. Down the hill, a meadow spread before them where long grasses waved in the cruel breeze.

The sun might be up, but the roiling clouds remained angry and thick, and she knew, she just knew, they would soon be drenched all over again. But she couldn't make Tess walk faster. It hurt too much. And she prayed they made it to the stables before the downpour began again or Tessa had her puppies.

She worried about her disguise, especially with her hat gone, but she took the bandana from her neck and wound it over her head with her long hair tucked inside. That would work. It had to work.

If the Ravenscroft people told Papa or Maman, she would be in terrible trouble. But Tessa would be safe.

As they walked on, the rain poured down again.

Rose was stupid. In the midst of the downpour, she sat on a rock and retied her boots. She had taken Robert's because her boots were too dainty and would give her away. But Robert was bigger than she, by a lot, and every step sloshed and raised blisters on her feet. They hurt a lot.

Tessa was panting hard now, all the time. And they were both hungry, tired, and dirty, but they continued on through a small copse of trees.

Dawn was full-on, though it made little difference in the rain. She and Tessa stood on a soft hill before a rolling swath of grass. Perched on the opposite hill stood the Ravenscroft manor, its bricks painted darkest red from the rain. Rose swiped her face. Almost there.

Now to find the stable.

The winding road before the manor curved outward like a branched tree. At the end of one of those branches, Rose identified the outbuilding, where three crouched low at the road's branching ends. The fourth building, taller and buttoned up tight, had to be the stable.

The snap of a shotgun's being cocked. Fear shot down her spine.

A man stood by the copse. He was smaller than papa but large enough to have a good five inches on her. And he had cocked his shotgun, though he hadn't aimed it at her. But any minute he could lift the barrel in her direction. He wore a huge, wide-brimmed leather hat on his head, so she couldn't see his face. He might be a stable hand, with those thick boots and a barn jacket that nearly came to his knees. He un-cocked the gun and walked toward her with confident strides, hefting his shotgun to his shoulder.

She was here because everyone said the Marquis of Ravenscroft loved animals, from conversations overheard in the drawing room. So did their stablemaster, according to Maman, who had claimed the Ravenscroft mare Dulce was not a good fit for the Earl of Chatworth's stable.

Papa had been so angry, his voice thick with scorn when he spoke about what he called the marquis' "animal weakness." Maman blurted out Ravenscroft had been an army general, which was when Papa squeezed Maman's arm. She had cried out, but then Papa had kissed her.

That had been enough for Rose to flee. It was horrible when Papa hurt Maman and embarrassing when they did kissy face.

The man was almost upon her when he spoke in a husky voice. "What are you doing on our land?"

When she began this mission, Rose knew she would have to speak to the Ravenscroft people, and she had practiced lowering her voice and being gruff, so the man would think she was a boy. "I am here to see your stable master."

"Where are you from?" he said.

One of Tessa's contractions came on, and looking at the dog, he tilted his head as if not understanding.

What? Had he never seen any creature have a baby? Rose pointed in the vague direction of their estate.

"Chatsworth, then," he said. "How did you get here?"

Boys could be so dumb. "We walked." Obviously.

He said nothing for a long time. What was his problem? She should just start down the hill towards the stables and ignore him. He wouldn't shoot her. Probably.

"I will give you a ride home in our wagon," he said.

No. She would not turn back now. "Thank you, but I need to see your stable master."

The rain had eased up, but a chill wind blew from the west and her shivering began again. Oh, how she wanted to be in her bed, cozy beside Tessa who would lick her face. No. "I won't go home until I see the stable master." She crossed her arms like Papa did when he was angry to show that he was in charge. It was a little awkward with the rope, but she managed.

Again, the man didn't say anything, which was really annoying. Then he swung the shotgun from his shoulder.

Rose leapt back, and the villain chuckled. "Come with me, then."

Rhys could not believe that the scrawny girl with her pregnant dog had walked from the Chatsworth estate to theirs. Her thinking was not sound, not at all. The odds she would be injured were high. Or the dog could have gone into labor. Crossing the log bridge, the girl might have slipped and fallen, and she was a tiny thing. Ridiculous.

He would get her and her dog to the barn and drive them home in the trap. Not as elegant as a carriage for the daughter of an earl, but he suspected she would not wish to announce their arrival at Chatsworth Manor.

When they reached the barn, Fergus stepped from the stable, skepticism writ large on his face. Their stable master was a canny one, and shot Rhys a look that said the girl's disguise had failed to fool him, as well.

The child ran up to Fergus and held out her fisted hand holding the rope. "Please take Tessa. Please."

Fergus' dark gray eyes bored down onto the child. "And why would I do that, young sir?"

Odd. For some reason, Fergus was going along with the ruse. Rhys shrugged, then shrugged. It didn't matter to him.

The child inched closer to Fergus, bent down, and petted her dog's head. "Tessa is a purebred English setter. She got herself in the family way." A flush brushed the child's cheeks, but she didn't seem to care. "You must take her. You must." The girl notched her chin as she stared at the six-foot-tall, grizzled stable master who brooked no nonsense. Many a time that steel-gray gaze had sliced Rhys to ribbons. The girl did not flinch, determination taut in every fiber of her being.

"And what am I to do with the pups?" The stable master said. "We would have to feed and house a litter of whelping pups. That costs quite a bit of pennies."

The child smiled. "I can help with that. I get a monthly gift of pence from my papa, and each month I will give it all to you if you will take Tessa and raise her puppies. You could give some away if you wanted to. Only to good homes, though."

Rhys almost laughed aloud but managed to bite it back. "You have an awful lot of demands."

"My Lord," The stable master interrupted. "I would suggest returning to the house before your father notices you are in possession of the shotgun and prowling around the home wood on your own. You may be tall for your age, but you are only half-grown."

Rhys puffed up. At twelve, he was nearly a man. Boys of fourteen went off to war and that was but two years away. But Fergus cut him down like a hatchet against a sapling.

The girl twirled to stare at him. "You are only a boy, too, but you were acting like a grown-up, like someone in charge."

Rhys gave her teeth, but Fergus's eyes warned him not to over-step. He almost had said he was a viscount, for her information, as his sarcastic younger brother would do. But he hadn't because he admired her pluck. Hard not to. She was something special, and nothing like he imagined an Earl's daughter to be.

The girl thrust the dog's rope toward him. "Take her. Please, take her."

Her desperation and those big green eyes gave him pause. She was terrified of something, and it obviously had to do with the dog. Rumors filtered through his mind, ones about the Earl of Chatsworth. Unpleasant ones.

He had met the Earl and his countess last year when they had attended a soirée held by his father, the marquis. The Countess' eyes had held that same sincerity and desperation, though a dark smudge of fear had lurked within, as well.

He held out his hand for the rope, and the girl's eyes morphed to a mixture of joy and sorrow.

With tight lips she handed him the rope, got down on her knees, and hugged the soggy setter, burying her face in the dog's fur. She inhaled deeply, then whispered in the pup's ear. He could imagine what she said when parting from a beloved animal.

The girl rose, her mobile face struck of emotion. Nor did she weep. But those eyes, those damned eyes, drew him in with a look of tragedy he would never forget.

"Thank you," she said. She turned and thanked Fergus, as well, then strode back toward the hill.

"Wait," he said. He handed Fergus the dog's rope and ran after her. "Hold up." She patiently waited with her soggy clothes and sad eyes. "I will give you a ride home."

She shook her head. "No thank you, my lord."

Gurr. Stubborn, too. "I will take you in the trap and pretend I'm delivering an order to the stables' kitchen. That way, no one at the house will know you were gone."

She assessed him as if he were worthy or not. She must have seen something acceptable because she nodded. "All right. Thank you."

He readied the trap. "Climb onto the seat. What is your name? And I already know you're a girl, so don't bother giving me something fake."

"Rosamund."

"Rosamund. Rose. But you're not a Rose, though you are prickly enough for one. No, with that shade of hair—"

She scrunched up her little face like a bulldog. "Do not say carrot. Don't you dare."

He grinned. "I was about to say poppy."

"Poppy? Why?"

Such a fierce little girl, determined and curious. "That's for you to figure out. My name is Rhys."

"What is your full name?" she said, getting in front of his legs and lying down. "I need to know, my lord."

He placed a basket of vegetables beside her head and flung a blanket atop the pile of girl and produce. He had already learned people saw what they expected or wished to see. "My name is George, but—"

"Your full name."

He groaned. "George Rhys James Alistair Lansdowne. Friends call me Rhys."

"I will call you Raven. If you are giving me a nickname, then I can give you one, too."

He laughed. "Understood. I expect we will become friends after this."

She remained silent, but he knew the truth of what he had said. Rhys flicked the reins, and off they went.

TO BE CONTINUED...

ACKNOWLEDGMENTS

Thank you, my readers, for giving me daily inspiration! You're the best.

Many thanks to those who helped shepherd *ASCENDANT* through to the finish line. Once again, my incomparable editor, Aria Jones, worked her magic. Thank you!

To the extraordinary Camille Cotton—this book wouldn't exist without you. To the amazing Rosemary Hill, whose friendship, aid, and insights are both invaluable and inspirational. To Monica—for your fantastic blurb help.

To my much-loved Betas: Ro, Camille, Joanie, Wayne, Pilar, Meri, and Vivi. for their invaluable critiques and friendship. To Lorelai—who keeps me smiling through the sweat and tears. To my exceptional cover artist, Mirela Barbu—you turn dreams into reality, including mine. Thank you! And to Blake, my brilliant graphics sounding board.

To Award-winning Master Karen Darabedyan of KD Mixed Martial Arts Academy. You are one of the kindest gentlemen I've ever met. Once again, your martial arts help was incomparable.

To the Illuterati and my Facebook pals who inspire me with warmth, humor, and truth-telling. To the Warrioresses, who soothe my heart, and to Parris Afton Bonds, who soothes my soul.

To Let's Ride, and all its denizens both two- and four-hooved. To Andrea Urban, Suzanne Hendrich, Pat Murphy, Donna Cautilli, CJ Williams, Linda Windels—love you. To Cindy's Knitters for the many stitches we wove together. To Betsy Bair, Georgi Mueller, and

Karen Waxman for your love and friendship. To Cynthia Michaels, for your friendship and giving Cranberry love.

To Peter, Kathleen, and Summer—your love and profound support mean the world. Love you! Finally, to my beloved boys, Blake and Ben—for all that you are, for all that you have gifted me, and for your abiding love. I'm the luckiest mom in the world.

Any errors or screw-ups are mine alone.

About the Author

Award-winning author Vicki Stiefel's romantic science-fantasy series, The Made Ones Saga, launched with *Altered*. Vicki continues work on her Afterworld Chronicles, a five-book series begun with *Chest of Bone*. Her mystery/thrillers feature homicide counselor Tally Whyte, and Vicki's knitting love produced *Chest of Bone The Knit Collection* and *10 Secrets of the LaidBack Knitters*.

Having grown up in professional theater, Vicki planned to become an actress. Instead, she slung hamburgers, managed a scuba shop, and taught at Clark U. She's a mom to two wonderful humans and is currently playing with her pups, Penny and Sebastian, staying safe, and pounding the keys on a "Secret Project."

Come visit with me...
vickistiefel.net

ALSO BY VICKI STIEFEL

The Made Ones Saga

Altered

Changed

Ascendant

The Afterworld Chronicles

Chest of Bone— Also on Audible

Chest of Stone

Chest of Time

Chest of Fire (to come)

Tally Whyte/Homicide Counselor Series

Body Parts • *The Dead Stone* • *The Grief Shop* (DAPHNE DUMAURIER AWARD WINNER) • *The Bone Man* (DAPHNE DUMAURIER AWARD FINALIST)

Nonfiction

10 Secrets of the LaidBack Knitters

Chest of Bone The Knit Collection

Visit with Vicki:

Website • Facebook • Instagram • BookBub

www.ingramcontent.com/pod-product-compliance
Lightning Source LLC
Chambersburg PA
CBHW021241200726
48288CB00014B/150